# SHE HAD NO WARNING

A mailed hand from nowhere jerked her reins down, bloodying Godluc's mouth. The gelding screamed. A sword-slash cut one stirrup leather: she jerked in the high-backed saddle, grabbing with her free hand for the pommel and balance.

Sixty Visigoth knights in mail and coat-of-plates rode past and over and through her escort, streaming out across the hill.

A spear thrust home from behind into Godluc's quarters. His hind hooves lifted, his head dipped, and she went straight over his head.

The mud was soft, or she would have died with a broken neck.

The impact was too hard to feel. Ash felt nothing but an absence, realized that she lay, staring up at the black sky, stunned, hurt, chest an acid void; that her hand gripped her sword and the blade had snapped off six inches from the hilt, that something was wrong with her left leg and her left arm.

She felt herself lifted, thought that it might be Burgundians or her own men; recognized, at last, that the language they spoke was Visigothic and that it was dark, the sun nowhere in the sky, and that what rocked and shook unsteadily beneath her was not a field or road or hay-cart, but the deck of a ship.

Her first clear thought came perhaps a day later. *This is a ship and it is sailing for North Africa.*

# MARY GENTLE

# CARTHAGE ASCENDANT
## THE BOOK OF ASH, #2

AVON • EOS

This is a work of fiction. Names, characters, places, and incidents either are the product of the author's imagination or are used fictitiously. Any resemblance to actual events, locales, organizations, or persons, living or dead, is entirely coincidental and beyond the intent of either the author or the publisher.

AVON BOOKS, INC.
*An Imprint of* HarperCollins*Publishers*
10 East 53rd Street
New York, New York 10022-5299

First Avon Eos Printing: February 2000

AVON EOS TRADEMARK REG. U.S. PAT. OFF. AND IN OTHER COUNTRIES, MARCA REGISTRADA, HECHO EN U.S.A.

Printed in the U.S.A.

WCD 10 9 8 7 6 5 4 3 2 1

# Note to the Reader

Since both political and historical considerations have led to separate publication of the four Books of ASH, this note is intended to bring the reader up to date with previous volumes.

The first volume, *A Secret History,* covered the career of Ash, a fifteenth century mercenary commander, through the early summer of 1476; her involvement with the Holy Roman Emperor's brief war with Burgundy; and her own later engagement with the Visigoth invasion force from North Africa landing at Genoa.

Between June and August of that year, Ash had discovered that the "saint's voice" that she hears in battle is, in fact, the voice of the Visigoth *machina rei militaris* (the best translation, perhaps, is "tactical computer"). Ash has also discovered that her exact physical resemblance to the Visigoth general, the Faris, is a result of their both being part of the long-term project to breed a Visigoth slave who can "hear" the machine over long distances. Ash appears to have been abandoned as an infant in Carthage.

The Faris, guided by the *machina,* currently leads a massive invasion force that has conquered all Europe up to the southern borders of Burgundy. Ash and her company have taken refuge in Burgundy, in Dijon, and are planning a strike force to go overseas to North Africa and destroy the *machina rei militaris* in the enemy capital, Carthage.

In this volume, the translation begins with material from the Del Guiz *Life* and the Angelotti manuscript, as in *A Secret History,* but by far the greater part is a direct translation of the previously-undiscovered "Fraxinus" manuscript, unknown until briefly published—and suppressed—in *Ash: The Lost History of Burgundy* (2001).

Anna—here's my rough aerial sketch of the ruins of present-day Carthage, and a proposed geography of 15c Visigoth Carthage.

I've included a possible new Visigoth harbour (which, like

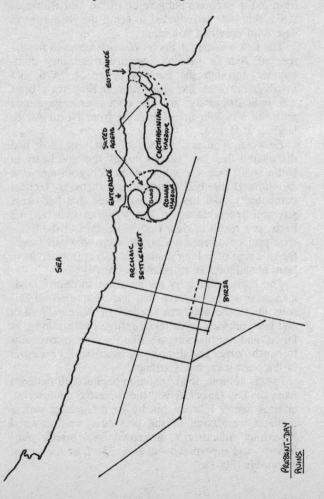

areas of the Roman/Carthaginian ones here, and the one at Leptis Magna, may have silted up in the interim).

The exact site of the Byrsa or walled hiss during the 15c is conjectural, based on textual evidence.

—Pierce                                                November 2000

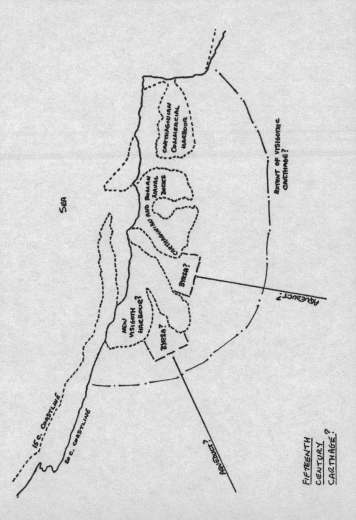

# PART ONE

17 August AD 1476–21 August AD 1476

*THE FIELD OF BATTLE*

I

DIJON RESOUNDS TO the thundering of watermills.

Afternoon's white sunlight blazed on distant yellow mustard-flowers. Rows of trimmed green grapevines hugged the ground between brown strips of earth. Peasants thronged the strip-fields. The town clock struck a quarter to five as Ash eased Godluc between a tailback of ox-wains and onto the main bridge into Dijon.

Bertrand stuffed her German fingered gauntlets into her hand, and fell back breathless beside Rickard, in the dust lifted up by the horses. Ash rode away from members of the company who had gone off scouting and now clutched at her stirrups, breathlessly reporting back, to take her place between John de Vere and her own escort.

"My lord Oxford." Ash raised her voice, and lifted up her head as they came in over the bridge to the town gate. Scents raised the hairs on the back of her neck: chaff, overheated stone, algae, horse-dung. She shoved her visor up, and bevor plate down, to get the benefit of the cool air over the river that served as a moat.

"I have the latest estimate of the Visigoth forces outside Auxonne," the Earl said; "they number nearly twelve thousand."

Ash nodded a confirmation. "They were twelve thousand when I was outside Basle. I don't know the exact number of their two other main forces. The same size, or larger. One's in Venetian territory, scaring the Turks from moving; the other one's in Navarre. Neither can get here within a month, even with a forced march."

A burning smell of hard-spinning mill-wheels filled the air, together with a faint golden haze. The mail shirts

3

of the guards on the gate, and the linen pourpoints, hose, and kirtles of the men and women bustling through it, were tinted with the finest chaff. The taste of it settled on her tongue. *Dijon is golden!* she thought; and tried to let the heat and smells relax the cold, hard fear in her gut.

"Here is our escort." John de Vere reined in, letting his brother George go ahead to speak with the nine or ten fully armored Burgundian knights waiting to take them to the palace.

De Vere's weathered, pale-eyed face turned to her. "Has it occurred to you, madam Captain, that his Grace the Duke of Burgundy may offer you a contract with him, now? I cannot finance this raid on Carthage."

"But we have a contract." Ash spoke quietly, her voice just audible under the grinding of mill-wheels. "Are you telling me to find some pretext for breaking my word—which *I* didn't give—to an exiled, attainted English Earl, because the reigning, extremely rich, Duke of Burgundy wants my company . . . ?"

John de Vere looked down from his saddle. What she could see of his face, with his close-helm's visor pinned up, was a mouth set in a firm line.

"Burgundy is wealthy," he said flatly. "I *am* Lancaster. Or Lancaster's only chance. But, madam, I am at the moment the leader of three brothers and forty-seven men, with enough money to feed them for six weeks. This, weighed against the employment of the Burgundian Duke, who could buy England if he chose . . ."

Ash, deadpan, said, "You're right, my lord, I won't consider Burgundy for a minute."

"Madam Captain, as a captain of mercenaries, the most precious goods you have to sell are your reputation, and your word."

Ash snorted. "Just don't tell my lads. I've got to sell *them* on the idea of Carthage . . ."

Ahead, George de Vere and the Burgundian knights seemed to be exchanging deferential greetings and arguments about precedence of riding order, in about equal measure. Dijon's cobbles felt heat-slick under Godluc's hooves. She reached forward and put a reassuring hand on his neck, where his iron-gray dapples faded to silver. He threw up his head, whickering with what, Ash realized, was a desire to show off in front of the people of Dijon. Around her, the city's whitewashed walls and blue slate roofs glittered.

Ash spoke over the louder noise of grinding mills. "This place looks like something out of a Book of Hours, my lord."

"Would that you and I did, madam!"

"Damn. I knew I was going to miss my armor . . ."

George de Vere turned in his saddle, beckoning the party forward. Ash rode beside the now smiling Earl of Oxford, into the center of the group of Burgundian knights. They moved off, their horses making slow time through the cobbled streets despite the escort in Charles's red-crossed livery; winding between throngs of apprentices outside workshops, women in tall headdresses buying from stalls in the market square, and oxcarts grinding their continual way to the mills. Ash pushed her visor up, grinning back at the cheerful waves and the comments called by the subjects of Duke Charles.

"Thomas!" she hissed.

Thomas Rochester dug his heel into his bay gelding and rapidly rejoined the party. A young woman with bright eyes watched him go from where she leaned out of an overhanging second-story window.

"Put her down, boy."

"Yes, boss!" A pause. "Any time off for R&R?"

"Not for you . . ." A touch to Godluc brought her back to the Earl of Oxford's left flank.

"I think you would never break a *condotta*, madam. And yet you consider it, now."

"No, I—"

"You do. Why?"

It was not the tone, or the man, to let her get away

without an answer. Ash snarled in a whisper, glancing covertly at the Burgundian knights:

"Yes, I say we should raid Carthage, but that doesn't mean I'm not afraid of it! If I remember right from Neuss, Charles of Burgundy could have upwards of twenty thousand trained men here; and supplies, and weapons, and guns, and, if I had a choice, I'd like *all* twenty thousand of them between me and the King-Caliph! Not just forty-seven men and your brothers! Is that a surprise?"

"Only a fool is not afraid, madam."

The rhythmic pounding of mill-wheels drowned speech for a minute. Dijon sits between two rivers, the Suzon and the Ouche, in the arrow-head spit of land where they join. Ash rode along the river path. The walls here enclosed the river within the town. She watched the slats of watermill-wheels rise up into the sun, dripping diamonds. The water under the wheels was black, thick as glass, and she could feel the pull of it from where she rode among the knights of the Duke's court.

They rode past the nearer mill.

Speech impossible, Ash did nothing for a moment but study the streets they rode through. A cluster of men in shirts and rolled-down hose, fixing an ox-wain's wheel, moved aside. They removed their straw hats, Ash saw, but neither rapidly nor fearfully; and one of the Burgundian riders reined in and spoke to their foreman.

Ash glimpsed an open space ahead, between diamond-paned-windowed buildings. The street opened out into a square—which she saw, as she rode into it, was a triangle. Rivers flowed past on the two sides, this land being at the very confluence of both. The high city walls gleamed, and the men on guard there leaned on their weapons and looked down with interest. They were well-armed, clean, with the kind of faces that have not suffered famine in the near past.

"You understand, your Grace," Ash said, "that rumors are getting out—that I hear voices, that I *don't* hear voices, that the Lion Azure are really still paid by the

Visigoths, because I'm the Faris's sister. That sort of thing."

De Vere looked at her. "You have no wish to be abandoned as a bad risk?"

"Exactly."

"Madam, the responsibilities of a contract work both ways."

De Vere's battle-hardened voice gave his words no particular emphasis, but Ash found herself painfully and fearfully abandoning a habitual cynicism. The sun dazzled her eyes. Ash felt her voice catch.

As steadily as she could, she said, "Their general, their Faris, she's slave-born. She doesn't make any secret of it. And I . . . look like her. Like two pups in a litter. What does that make me?"

"Courageous," the Earl of Oxford said gently.

When he met her gaze, she looked straight ahead, with hard eyes.

He said, "Because your method of hiding from this is to put a plan to me, to attack the enemy in their strongest city. I could have reason to doubt your impartial judgment over that, if I chose to take it as such—but I do not doubt it. Your thoughts chime with mine. Let us hope the Duke agrees."

"If he doesn't," Ash said, gazing at the richly apparelled knights in the escort, "there's damn-all we can do about it. We're broke. This is a very rich, very powerful man, with an army outside this city. Let's face it, your Grace, two orders and I'm his mercenary, not yours."

Oxford's voice snapped, "I have responsibility for my brothers and my affinity![1] And for someone I have taken under my protection!"

"That isn't quite the way most people regard a *condotta* . . ." Ash reined back to where she could look at him. "But you do, don't you?"

---

[1] "Affinity"—For a feudal magnate, this would include his dependent lords, maintained in his livery; his political allies among other feudal lords; and any commercial interests dependent on him for grace and favor.

Watching him, she was confirmed in her opinion that people would follow John de Vere well beyond the bounds of reason. And only wonder why afterwards, when it would be far too late.

Ash took a deep breath, feeling unusually constricted by the plate brigandine she was wearing. Godluc snorted breath from wide nostrils. Ash automatically shifted her weight back, halting him, and looked for what had worried her mount.

Two yards ahead, a line of ducklings fluttered up from the river's edge, and pattered across the cobbled space. Preceded by a mother duck, they fluttered, squawking, toward the mill on the far side of the triangle, and the other, swift-flowing river.

Twelve Burgundian knights, an English Earl, his noble brothers, a viscount, a female mercenary captain and her escort all reined in and waited until nine ducklings passed.

Ash shifted up from leaning over in the saddle, about to speak to John de Vere. She found herself looking up at the Ducal Palace of Dijon. Soaring white Gothic walls, buttresses, peaked towers, blue slate roofs; flying a hundred banners.

"Well, madam." The Earl of Oxford smiled, slightly. "The court of Burgundy is like no other court in Christendom. Let's see what the Duke makes of my *pucelle* and her voices."

Dismounting, she was met by a sweating Godfrey Maximillian, on foot; who fell in with the rest of Thomas Rochester's men, behind her banner.

Inside the palace, the size of the space enclosed by stone stunned her. Soaring thin pillars jutted up, between long thin pointed windows; all the stonework fresh, white, biscuit-colored; and with the late afternoon sun on it, looking, she thought, like fretworked honey.

She shut her gaping mouth and stumbled in John de Vere's wake, a clarion call ringing out and a herald shouting their names and degrees, loud enough to shake the banners hanging down each side of the hall; and a hundred faces turned, men of wealth and powe[r] at her.

They were all dressed in blue.

She gazed rapidly at sapphire, aquamarine and royal blue silk, at indigo and powder-blue velvet, at the rolled chaperon hats as deep as the midnight sky, and the long robe of Margaret of York, the color of the Mediterranean sea. Her feet took her in the Earl of Oxford's wake, quite independently; and Godfrey bent his bearded head close, whispering rapidly in her ear:

"There are Visigoths here."

*"What?"*

"A deputation. An embassy. No one is sure of their status."

"Here? In *Dijon?*"

"Since noon, I hear."

"Who?"

Godfrey's amber eyes moved away to survey the crowd. "I could not buy names."

Ash scowled. She ignored the dazzling profusion of jewelled badges on chaperon hats, gold and silver linked collars around noble necks, brass folly-belly sewn to younger knights' doublets, tissue-thin linen veiling the noble women.

*All, all in blue*, she suddenly realized. With a blue velvet brigandine she was moderately in the fashion, or at least, enough in it not to offend. She spared a glance for the four de Vere brothers and Beaumont, all of the noble English in full harness, a blaze of steel against the velvet and silk robes of the Burgundian court.

"Godfrey, *who's* here? Don't tell me you don't know. You've got a damn network of informers out there! Who's here?"

He deliberately dropped back a pace on the checkered tiles. Without causing confusion, and drawing attention to herself, there was no way she could continue to question him. She clenched her fist, for a second wanting nothing more than to hit him.

"Your Grace," she said, without looking at the Englishman's face, "did you know there's a Visigoth delegation here?"

"God's bollocks!"

"I'll take that as a 'no,' shall I?"

They were escorted on down the great hall. There was more: paintings set in niches, tapestries of great hunting expeditions hung from the walls, but Ash couldn't take it in. Above it all that noble architecture soared up, ogee window and clustered columns, to the clear glass windows that disclosed the other roofs of the Ducal palace of Dijon, and the fine, white-gold finials of stone piercing up toward the afternoon sky.

A flutter of doves flurried past the glass. Ash dropped her gaze, halting, her heels trodden on painfully by Dickon de Vere. Both escorts—hers, and de Vere's—parted, letting the other brothers come through to stand beside the Earl of Oxford. Godfrey kept to the back, his face calm, his eyes giving away nothing of what he might feel, confronted by so many churchmen, as well as so many nobles and their ladies.

Ash stared around, could see no Visigoth robes or mail anywhere.

John de Vere knelt, and his party also, Ash scraping down onto one knee and dragging her hat off in haste.

A youngish man in white puff-sleeved doublet and hose sat on the Ducal throne, his head bent, conferring with another man at his elbow. Ash saw his somewhat lugubrious face, and black shoulder-length hair cut straight across the forehead, and realized this must be him: Charles, Duke of Burgundy, nominal vassal of Louis XI, more splendid than most kings.[2]

"An inauspicious day, then?" the Duke said, quite clearly, as if unconcerned that his private conversations might be overheard.

"No, Sire." The man at his elbow bowed. He wore a long, azure demigown, his arms out of the hanging

[2] Born in Dijon in 1433, Duke Charles was in fact forty-three at this time.

sleeves, and his hands busy with papers marked with diagrams of wheels and boxes. "Say, rather, an opportunity to avenge an old wrong."

The Duke signaled him to move away, and leaned back, looking down from the dais at the kneeling Englishmen. The sole man in white, he stood out among his court for simplicity. Ash thought, *Signifies a Virtue— probably his day for representing Nobility or Chivalry or Chastity. I wonder what the rest of us are?*

His voice, when he spoke, was pleasant. "My lord of Oxenford."

"Sire." De Vere stood up. "I have the honor to introduce to you my mercenary captain, whom your Grace wished to see. Ash."

"Sire." Ash stood up. Behind her, Thomas Rochester and Euen Huw wore the Lion Azure livery; Godfrey gripped a Psalter. She smoothed her hair on the left side, assuring herself that it covered the healing injury there.

The rather dour young man on the Ducal throne, who could not yet have been thirty, leaned forward with one hand on the arm of it, and stared at Ash with eyes so dark as to be black. A faint color touched his pale cheeks. "You tried to kill me!"

This was not an occasion to smile, Ash guessed, the Valois Duke of Burgundy not looking particularly susceptible to being charmed. She schooled her face and her bearing to modesty and respect, and remained silent.

"You have a notable warrior there, de Vere," the Duke remarked, and turning his head away from her, spoke briefly to the woman at his side. The Duke's wife, Ash noted, did not take her eyes off John de Vere, Earl of Oxford.

"Perhaps," Margaret of York spoke up in a clear voice, "it's time this man told us why he takes advantage of your hospitality, Sire."

"In time, lady." The Duke beckoned two of his advisors, spoke to them, and then returned his gaze to the group in front of him.

Ash weighed up the cost of the Duke's simplicity: his

demigown was buttoned, and with diamond buttons, and the seams of the shoulders looked to be sewn with gold thread. And all the rest of the seams of his garments, sewn with the finest gold thread . . . In the blue sea of his court, he gleamed like snow with the faintest tinge of winter sun gilding it; and the grip of his bollock dagger was decorated also with gold, and with pearls.

"It is our intention," the Duke said, "to discover what you know of this Faris, maîtresse Ash."

Ash swallowed, and managed to speak in a voice that could be heard. "By now, everybody knows what I know, Sire. She has three major armies, of which one lies just beyond your southern border. She fights inspired by a voice, which she claims comes from a Brazen Head or Stone Golem device, across the seas in Carthage, and," Ash said, holding to her line of thought with difficulty under Charles's stare, "I have myself seen her appear to speak to it. As to the rest of it: the Goths have burned Venice and Florence and Milan because they don't *need* them—there's an endless supply of men and materials being shipped across the Med, and when I left, it was still coming."

"Is this Faris a knight of honor, a Bradamante?"[3] Duke Charles asked.

Ash judged it time to make herself both less spectacular and more human in his eyes. Rather bitterly, she replied, "A Bradamante wouldn't have stolen and kept my best armor, Sire!"

A subdued merriment made itself felt in the court, dying out as soon as it became apparent that Duke Charles was not smiling. Ash held his gaze, the bright black eyes and almost ugly face—certainly a Valois!—and added, "As for knights, heavy cavalry doesn't seem to be their strong point, Sire. No tournaments. They have medium cavalry, huge numbers of foot-soldiers, and golem."

---

[3] A legendary female knight, notably popularized in Ariosto's *Orlando Furioso* (1516).

Duke Charles glanced at Olivier de la Marche, and the big man, with a nod for Ash, loped up the dais steps in a very uncourtly manner. The Duke whispered in his ear. He nodded, dropped to one knee to kiss the Duke's hand, and strode off. Ash didn't turn her head to watch, but guessed he was actually leaving the hall.

"These dishonorable men of the south," Charles said, more publicly, "dare to put out the sun above Christian men, and shroud us in the same penance as their own Eternal Twilight. They have not expiated the sin of the Empty Chair. We—under God, we are not sinless! But we do not deserve to have the sun which is the Son taken from us."

Ash untangled that one after a glance at Godfrey. She nodded hastily.

"Therefore—" the Duke of Burgundy broke off at an insistent mutter from Margaret; seated beside him on a smaller throne. A short and, Ash thought, rather sharp exchange ended with the Valois Duke leaning back magnanimously. "If it eases your mind, we will consent to your asking him. De Vere! The Lady Margaret wishes a word with you."

Slightly above Ash's head, George de Vere whispered, "That'll be the first time!" and Dickon snickered.

The English noblewoman gazed down at de Vere, his brothers and Beaumont, ignoring Ash and her priest and banner. "Oxford, why have you come here? You know you cannot be welcome. My brother, King Edward, hates you. Why do you follow me here?"

"Not you, madam." John de Vere, equally blunt, gave her no noble title. "Your husband. I have a question to ask him, but since you have an army on your borders, my question will wait for a better time."

"No! Now. You will ask it now!"

Ash, aware that so many currents ran deep under this particular river, thought that Margaret of York might not ordinarily be a shrill woman, or an impetuous one. *But something's biting her. Biting her hard.*

"It is not the time," the Earl of Oxford said.

Charles of Burgundy leaned forward, frowning. "If my Duchess asks, it is certainly time for you to answer, de Vere. Courtesy is a knightly virtue."

Ash shot a glance at de Vere. The Englishman's lips were pressed tightly together. As she watched, his face relaxed, and he gave a chuckle.

"Since your husband wishes it, madam Margaret, I will tell you. His Grace King Henry, sixth of that name, being dead and leaving no close heir of his body,[4] I have come to ask the next Lancastrian claimant to the English throne to raise an army, so that I may put a legitimate and honest man there, instead of your brother."

*And I thought I could be tactless . . .*

Under cover of the outrage and shocked comments, Ash glanced back down the mirror-stone tiled floor, judging the distance to the great doors and the Ducal Guard.

Great. The Visigoth Faris puts me in prison. I get here. I get hired by de Vere. De Vere gets us all put in prison. This is not how I wanted things to be!

A tiny ripping noise sounded: the edge of Margaret of York's veil knotted and torn between her clenched fingers. "My brother Edward is a great king!"

Oxford's voice cracked out loud and hard enough to make Ash jump.

"Your brother Edward had my brother Aubrey's bowels torn from his body, while he lived, and his cock cut off and burned in front of his eyes. A Yorkist execution. Your brother Edward had my father's head cut off, with no ounce of English law behind him, since he has no claim to the throne!"

Margaret got to her feet. "Our claim is better than yours!"

---

[4] Henry VI and Margaret of Anjou had only one son, Edward, killed at the battle of Tewkesbury. Any claim of the Lancastrians to the English throne thus devolved to more tenuously related men (ultimately to Henry Tudor, whose Welsh grandfather had married the widow of King Henry V). The Yorkist Edward IV, meanwhile, held the throne.

"But your claim, madam, is not as good as your husband's!"

Silence dropped, like a blade coming down. Ash became aware she was holding her breath. All the de Vere brothers stood upright, hands to scabbards; and the Earl of Oxford himself glared, like a war-weathered bird of prey, at the woman on the throne. His pale gaze moved to Charles, and he inclined his head stiffly.

"You must know, Sire, that being as you are the great-grandson of John of Gaunt and Blanche of Lancaster, then the nearest living Lancastrian heir to the English throne is now—yourself."[5]

*We're dead.*

Ash clasped her hands behind her back, keeping her fingers away from the hilt of her second-favorite sword with an effort powered by sheer fear.

We're dead, we're done for, our ass is grass; sweet Christ, Oxford, couldn't you just for once keep your mouth *shut* when someone asks you for the truth?

She was astonished to open her mouth and hear herself say, quite loudly, "And if that doesn't work, I suppose we can always invade Cornwall . . ."

An instant of appalled silence, so short it was only long enough to stop the breath in her throat, broke with a shout of laughter from a hundred voices; this a fraction of a second after Duke Charles of Burgundy smiled. A very wintry, tiny smile; but nonetheless, he smiled.

"Noble Duke," Ash said quickly, "the French Dauphin had his *Pucelle*. I'm sorry I can't manage one of those for you—I'm a married woman, after all. But I pray that I also have the favor of God, as Joan did; and if you give me, not troops, but some of the wealth of your army, then I'll try and do for you what she did for France. Kill your enemies, Sire."

---

[5] In fact, Charles had registered his formal claim to the English crown in 1471, five years previous to this, but took no further action over it before his death.

"And what will your seventy-one lances do for Burgundy, maîtresse?" the Duke asked.

Ash flicked up an eyebrow, having not had the exact numbers from Anselm's muster that long herself. She kept her head raised, aware that her face and hair were to some degree speaking for her, and that she would have been far more impressive in full harness. "It would be better not in open court, Sire."

The Duke of Burgundy clapped his hands. Ash had barely got to her feet before clarions sounded, the choirs at the sides of the great hall burst into song, ladies rose, men in rich pleated short gowns made their exits, and she—and Godfrey, and the de Veres—were ushered into a chapel or side room.

Quite some time later, Charles of Burgundy came in, a handful of attendants with him.

"You've upset the Queen of Bruges," he remarked to Oxford, waving his staff away.

Ash, bewildered, glanced at Oxford and the Duke.

"My wife, being governor of that city, is sometimes called its queen," the Valois Duke said, lowering himself into a chair. His demigown, unbuttoned, showed a gold-embroidered pourpoint beneath, and a drawstring-neck shirt of linen so fine it was hardly visible. "She has no love for you, my lord Earl of Oxford."

"I never thought she did," Oxford said. "You forced me to that one, Sire."

"Yes." The Duke switched his prim gaze to Ash. "You have an interesting fool. She is young," he added.

"I can command my men, Sire." Ash, uncertain whether to cover her head, which marks respect in a woman, or uncover it, as a man does, settled for standing bare-headed, her hat in her hand. "You already have the best army in Christendom. Send me to do what your armies won't—take out the heart of the Visigoth attack."

"And where does that heart lie?"

"In Carthage," Ash said.

Oxford said, "It's not lunatic, Sire. Only audacious."

The walls of this chamber were set about with tapestries in which the Burgundian Heraldic Beast, the Hart, shone white and gold through the wild wood; pursued by hunters and worshippers. Ash shifted, hot in the late afternoon sun through the windows, and met the flat, gold-embroidered stare of the Hart, the Green Cross worked finely between its many-tined antlers.

"You are an honest man, and a good soldier," the Duke of Burgundy observed, as a page served him, and then Oxford, with wine. "Otherwise I would suspect this for some Lancastrian device."

"I am only devious on the field of battle," the Englishman said. Ash heard amusement in his tone; could see it pass Charles of Burgundy by.

"Then, do we have here the proof? That this 'Stone Golem' is where they claim—over the sea, far from us, and yet speaking to this Faris?"

"I believe that we do, Sire."

"That would be much."

So much depends on this man, Ash suddenly thought. This ugly, black-browed boy, with twenty thousand men and more guns than the Visigoths: so much depends on his decisions.

"I have the Faris's blood, Sire," she said.

"So my advisors tell me. They tell me," Charles added, "that the likeness is remarkable. God send you are good, mademoiselle, and not some device of the devil."

"My priest can answer you best, Sire."

Waved forward by her hand, Godfrey Maximillian said, "Your Grace, this woman hears mass and takes communion, and has made confession to me these past eight years."

The Duke of Burgundy said, "Prince as I am, I cannot silence rumor's tongues. It begins to be said that the Visigoth general's voice is a devilish engine, and that we have no defense against it. I do not know, lord Oxford, how long your condottiere's name will be kept out of this."

"The Faris herself may not know that she is . . ." de

Vere hesitated, searching for a word. "That she is over-heard. We cannot rely on that state of affairs continuing. She already seeks the girl, here, for interrogation. We have a short time in which we can act. Sire, a matter of weeks—days, if we are unlucky."

"You are willing to let this matter of the Lancastrian succession drop?"

"I am willing to put it into abeyance, Sire, until we have faced this danger that comes on us from the south."

Without looking around, the Duke said, "Clear the room."

Within thirty seconds, pages, squires, falconers, Thomas Rochester, and the men-at-arms were ushered out of the chamber; leaving only Ash, Godfrey Maximillian, Oxford, and his brothers.

Charles of Burgundy said, "We are not what we were, de Vere."

The wind through an open window brought the scent of chaff, and roses.

"I have had the armorers of Milan make me a harness of finest quality," he said, "and if I could, sirs, I would be armed in it as a man should, and ride out to this despoiling army, and myself best in battle their champion, and that would decide the matter. But this is a fallen world, such honor and chivalry are no longer for us."

"It would save a lot of people getting killed," Ash said flatly, adding, "Sire," as an afterthought.

"As will a raid on Carthage," de Vere said. "Cut off the head, and the body is useless."

"But you do not know where—if it is in Carthage—where, exactly, this Stone Golem is kept."

Godfrey Maximillian, stroking his Briar Cross, remarked, "We can discover that, Sire. Given two hundred gold crowns, I undertake to bring you the news, within a very short time."

"Mmm." Charles of Burgundy switched his gaze to de Vere. "Tell me."

Oxford set it out for the Burgundian Duke in brief,

military sentences. Ash did not interrupt, knowing that for the plan to be accepted, it would have to be put forward by a man; and having it put forward by one of the better battle-commanders of Europe wouldn't hurt a bit.

She glimpsed Godfrey's shoulders relax, briefly, at her silence.

*What* Visigoths? What won't you tell me?

The priest gazed at the hangings of the little chamber in awe. There was no way she could speak confidentially to him. Ash stared at the tiny lattice-paned window and the later afternoon sky, and wanted to be outdoors.

"No," the Duke of Burgundy said.

"Do as you think best," John de Vere rumbled. "God's teeth, man!—your Grace. What use is a battle, whether we win it or not, if the main enemy is untouched?"

The Duke sat back, waving John de Vere away. "I am determined to fight a battle against the Visigoths, and soon. My diviner advises me that it should be before the sun passes out of Leo, to be auspicious. The twenty-first of the month of Augustus is the feast of Saint Sidonius."

Ash saw Godfrey frown, be caught with the expression by the Duke, and steel his face to unctuousness as he rumbled an explanation. "Very fitting, Sire. Since Sidonius Apollinaris was martyred by early Visigoths, this should be a day for avenging him."

"So I think." Satisfied, the Duke said, "My preparations have been in hand since I returned from Neuss."

"But—" Ash bit her lip.

"Captain?"

She spoke with reluctance. "I was about to say, Sire, that I don't think even the armies of Burgundy can defeat the numbers they have here, let alone the numbers they have coming in by galley every day from North Africa. Even if you and the Emperor Frederick and King Louis united—"

Ash was familiar with catching the expression which tells you that, upon this one subject, a man is not rational. Having mentioned Louis XI, she was seeing it now on the face of Charles of Burgundy. She shut up.

"You won't put up gold for an attack on Carthage?" the Earl of Oxford demanded.

"No. I think it unwise. It cannot succeed, and the battle that I shall fight, that can." He looked at Ash. Disquiet stirred her stomach. He said, "Maîtresse Ash, there are Visigoths already present in my court, being ushered in under a flag of parley this morning. They have many demands—or humble requests, as they prefer to say. One of which is, their seeing the standard of your camp outside the walls of Dijon, that you yourself should be given up to them."

His black eyes watched her. By the quiet consternation among the younger de Veres, this seemed as though it must be that rare thing, a genuinely secret delegation.

*But not for long*, Ash thought, and said aloud, "The Visigoths broke their *condotta* when they imprisoned me, but I don't seriously suppose I can resist you handing me over if that's what you're going to do, Sire. Not with the whole Burgundian army at your disposal."

The Duke of Burgundy gravely turned his rings upon his fingers, and made no answer.

Dizzy with news of the Visigoths so close, Ash said bluntly, "What do you intend to do with me, Sire? And—please—will you reconsider funding this raid against Carthage?"

"I will consider both these matters," the Duke said. "I must talk to de la Marche, and to my advisors. You will know . . . by tomorrow."

Twenty-four hours on hold. God damn it.

The Duke rose, ending the audience.

"I am a prince," he said. "If you meet, here in my court, with these men from Carthage and their renegade allies, be assured that no man will harm you."

Ash let none of her skepticism show on her face. "Thank you, Sire."

*But I shall be in the Lion Azure camp, just as fast as I can ride.*

The Duke's intense, lugubrious expression darkened.

"Mademoiselle Ash. As a bastard slave of a Visigoth House, you are legally a bondswoman. They claim you, not as their paid captain, or their prisoner, but as their property. That claim may well be valid and lawful."

ii

ASH, HER MEN at her heels, finally halted at the bottom of a flight of stairs. She realized she had left the Earl of Oxford and his brothers way behind, had ignored court officials, got through ceremonial farewells purely mechanically, in the shock of that realization:

*I can be bought and sold.*

The Duke will hand me over for political advantage. Or, if not because of that, then because he can't be seen to ignore the law. Not when law keeps anarchy away from his kingdom . . .

Vespers rang through the chambers of the Ducal palace.

*Maybe I need prayers!*

Wondering where the nearest chapel was, about to ask Godfrey, she did not see a party of men approaching. Thomas Rochester coughed. "Boss . . ."

"What? Shit." Ash folded her arms, which the sleeves of her mailshirt under her brigandine did not make particularly easy.

Light shone down into the antechamber in front of her, falling from tall thin windows onto flagstones, bouncing back from the whitewashed walls and high barrel-vaulting, making the whole place airy and light and entirely not a place where one might stay unnoticed.

Ahead, a group of men in Visigoth robes began to slow their steps, seeing her.

"Wish they'd let us bring the dogs in," Ash murmured. "A leash full of mastiffs would come in very handy right now . . ."

Thomas Rochester grunted. "So let's see if the Duke's peace holds, or if we have to kick ass, boss."

Ash took a glance at the Ducal guards lining the walls of the antechamber. She began to smile. "Hey. We're the ones on home ground here. Not the fucking Goths."

"That's right, boss." Euen Huw grinned.

"Banjo 'em with a fucking poleaxe," one of Rochester's lance rumbled.

"Do nothing unless I say so. Got me?"

"Yes, boss."

The mutual reply was reluctant. She was aware of Euen and Thomas at her shoulders. The first man in the group of Visigoths speeded his pace, walking up to her.

Sancho Lebrija.

*"Qa'id,"* Ash acknowledged the Visigoth, steadily.

"Mistress *jund.*"

A tall man in Lebrija's wake, in Milanese armor, proved to be Agnus Dei. The Lamb grinned at her, teeth yellow in his black beard.

"Madonna," he greeted. "That's a nasty cut you have there."

She still carried her hat in her hand, from being in the Duke's presence. Her hand went up to the side of her head automatically, fingers brushing a patch of shaven scalp.

Godfrey Maximillian said warningly, at her ear, "Ash—"

Soldiers in mail and white robes, four or five of them, accompanied the Visigoth delegates. As they halted, Ash saw a young man among them. He carried his helmet under his arm; was instantly recognizable.

"—of course!" Godfrey whispered vindictively. "It had to be! He can bribe some court chamberlain to find out when Charles is having audiences, and who with. Of course he can."

Fernando del Guiz.

"Well, look who it isn't," Ash remarked loudly. "That's the little shit who told the Faris where to find me in Basle. Euen, Thomas: you want to remember that face. Some day soon, you'll be spoiling it!"

Fernando seemed to ignore her. Agnus Dei said a word in Lebrija's ear that made the Visigoth *qa'id* bark out a short laugh.

Lamb continued to smile.

"*Cara.* You had a pleasant journey here from Basle, I trust?"

"A *fast* one." Ash did not take her gaze from Fernando. "You want to watch it, Agnus. One of these days they'll steal your best armor, too, if you don't look out!"

"The Faris wishes more speech with you," Sancho Lebrija said stiffly.

Meeting the Visigoth's pale eyes—none of the charm of his dead brother there—Ash thought, What would you say if I told you how badly *I* want to talk to *her* again?

*Sister, half-sister, twin.*

"Then let's hope for a truce," she said, making her voice carry clearly enough to be overheard by any court intriguers. "War's always better when you're not fighting. Any old soldier knows that—right, Agnus?"

The mercenary grinned sardonically. Behind him, the Visigoth soldiers carrying swords made no aggressive move on the Duke's premises. Ash recognized an *'uqda* lance-pennon[6] with the escort, looked for the *nazir* who had taken her from the gardens of Basle, and saw his brown face scowling at her from behind the nasal bar of his helm.

There was an uncomfortable silence.

Sancho Lebrija half-turned, glared at Fernando del Guiz, and then turned back to say, "Madam *jund*, your husband wishes to speak with you."

"He does?" Ash said skeptically. "He doesn't look like he does."

The Visigoth *qa'id* put his hand firmly behind the

---

[6] The *'uqda* was carried by a *nazir*'s troop of eight men.

German knight's back, pushing him forward. "Yes. He does!"

Fernando del Guiz still wore white robes and Visigoth mail. It cannot be much more than a week, ten days, since she saw him in Basle—the thought is a shock; so much has happened—but his face seems leaner, his golden hair untidily shaggy as it grows out of its crop. Not, as it was at Neuss, long enough to fall down over his young, broad, muscled shoulders.

Ash dropped her gaze, fixed her eyes on his strong hands—bare; his gloves tucked into his belt.

The smell of him in her nostrils hit her below any guard she might have made; a smell that jolted her back into warm linen sheets, the silk-smooth skin of his chest, belly and thighs, the thrust of his velvet-hard cock in her body. A flush rose up from her breasts, up the column of her throat, and reddened her cheeks. Her fingers moved of their own accord: she would, if she had not stopped herself, have reached out and touched his cheek. She made a fist, her pulse dry in her mouth.

"We'd better talk," Fernando del Guiz mumbled, not looking at her.

"Asshole!" Thomas Rochester said.

Godfrey Maximillian pulled at Ash's arm. "Let's leave."

She resisted the priest's force without effort, without looking at him. Studying the closed expression of Sancho Lebrija, and Lamb's malice, she murmured, "No. I *am* going to talk to del Guiz. I've got things to say to this man!"

"Child, *no*."

She removed her arm from Godfrey's grip, casually, and indicated an area of the antechamber a few paces away. "Step into my office, *husband*. Thomas, Euen, you know what to do."

She crossed the flagstones, and waited in an area where red and blue light from the stained glass windows dappled the floor, under hanging battle standards from old Burgundian wars against France. It took her far enough away to put her out of earshot of the Visigoth delegation, and of Duke Charles's guard.

*And it's public enough that any harm he tries to do me will be instantly seen—but, sadly, that works both ways.*

She busied herself removing her gloves, rested the palm of her left hand on the pommel of her sword, and waited.

He left Lebrija and approached, alone, boots clicking on the worn, checkered tiles. The echo hissed back from the walls. The early evening heat might have accounted for the sweat on his face.

"So," Ash prodded. "What do you want to say to me?"

"Me?" Fernando del Guiz gazed down at her. "I don't think this was my idea at all!"

"Stop wasting my time."

All her authority was in her tone, although she was quite unconscious of it. She was only aware that he blinked, startled; glanced back over his shoulder at Lebrija; and finally spoke:

"This is awkward . . ."

" 'Awkward'!"

Unexpectedly, Fernando reached out and put his hand on her arm. Ash looked down at his blunt, square-cut nails; the texture of his skin; the faint blond hairs at his wrist.

"Let's talk this over somewhere else. Alone." Fernando's hand came up, brushing her cheek.

"And do what?" Ash reached up and put her hand over his. Meaning to move it away, she found herself holding his hand, wrapping his strong fingers around hers. The warmth of it was so welcome, she did not immediately let go. "What, Fernando?"

He lowered his voice, uncomfortably watching her priest and her men-at-arms. "We'll just talk. I won't do anything you don't want me to do."

"Yes, I think I've heard that one before."

Looking into his face, she thought she could see the

young man still there—the young noble, riding to hawk and to hounds, golden and glorious among his wide affinity of friends, never needing to work out whether he could afford this wine or that horse, not ever needing to choose between shoeing his horse and shoes for his own feet. A little road-worn, now, but still the golden boy.

Her fingers still clasped his. The warmth of them made her hands shake. She opened her hand and drew it away, feeling cold. Absently, she put her hand to her face, breathing in the particular scent of him.

"Oh, come *on*." Ash's lips pressed together, in extreme skepticism. A quiver went through her belly. She was genuinely unsure whether it was lust, or plain nausea. "Fernando—I don't believe this. Are you trying to *seduce* me?"

"Yes."

"Why?"

"Because it's easier."

Ash opened her mouth, found she had no words, and stood for a count of ten staring at his face. Outrage hit. "Are you—what do you *mean*, 'because it's easier'? Easier than *what*?"

"Refusing the Faris and her officers." All the humor faded from his expression; perhaps it had been no more than momentary. "Even when they say a good fuck might get you into their hands again, so why don't I go give it to you?"

" 'A good fuck'—!" Ash bellowed.

Across the floor, Agnus Dei put a restraining hand on Sancho Lebrija's arm, both men scowling; this shouted row obviously reaching them, obviously not what either of them expected to hear. Ash glimpsed Godfrey take a few steps forward, staring at her, his face drained and pale.

"*Seduce* me?" she repeated. "Fernando . . . That's *ridiculous*!"

"Okay. So it is. So what do you suggest I do, with half a dozen sword-happy maniacs watching every word I say to you?" He stood half a head taller than she did, looking down at her, a young man in foreign armor. "At the moment, thanks to you, I'm the Faris's pimp. The least you can do is not laugh at me."

"Wh—" Ash ran out of breath and the impetus to speak. Something in his appalling honesty touched her, despite herself. "The Faris's *pimp*?"

"I don't want to be here!" Fernando shouted. "All I want is to go back to Guizburg, stay there, stay in the castle, and not come out until this fucking lunatic war is *over*. But they married me to you, didn't they? And you turn out to be some relative of the Faris. So who do they think knows all about the mercenary commander Ash? Me. Who do they think is an influence on you? Me." He drew a gasping breath. "I don't care about politics. I don't want to be in the Faris's affinity. I don't want to be at the Visigoth court. *I don't want to be here.* But because they think I'm a source of information on you, here I am! And all I want is to fucking go back to Bavaria!"

He finished, panting; little white dots of spittle at the corners of his mouth. Ash realized he had spoken in German, that both Lebrija and Lamb were looking puzzled now at the rapid, slurred, foreign speech.

"Jesus Christ," she said. "I'm impressed."

"I'm only here because of you!"

The contempt and fury in his tone made Euen Huw and Thomas Rochester both reach for their sword hilts, watching Ash out of the corners of their eyes, to see if she would let him get away with it. She noted Godfrey's hands, almost hidden in his robes, whitening into fists.

"I thought you *wanted* to be well in with the Faris," she said mildly. "Making a place for yourself in the Visigoth court. I thought that was why you got me knocked on the head at Basle."

Ignoring that, he spluttered, "I don't want a place at court!"

Ash's tone became acid-edged with sarcasm. "Yeah, that's why you're in Guizburg now, not standing in front of me! Like you're not here with Lebrija for political advantage, or reward, or promotion."

Catching his breath, Fernando glared down at her. "I'll tell you exactly why I'm here. The Faris would happily have stuck my head on a spear, as an encouragement to any other minor German nobles. She didn't because I took one look at her, and told her that she had a double."

"You told her."

"I suppose having a bastard Visigoth wife is mildly better than having a French soldier-bitch."

"*You* told her?"

"You think I'm some knight out of the chronicles. I'm not. I've had men pointing spears at me, and I know it: I'm just another man with legal title to a few acres of land, and a few men wearing eagles on their clothes, and that's *it*. Nothing remarkable. Nothing valuable. No different from any other man they've butchered in Genoa or Marseilles or wherever."

She looked at him, seeing in his face some echo of that split-second of trauma. "Roberto said you were some damned stupid young knight with ideas of death-or-glory. He was wrong, though, wasn't he? You took one look at glory and decided you'd save your own skin!"

Fernando del Guiz stared. "Sweet Jesu. You're *ashamed* of me."

It was a distinct glint of humor. His tone was self-mocking.

"You wouldn't say this to your friend Lamb. Or did you? Did you say to him, why didn't you fight off the Visigoths at Genoa, there were two hundred of you and only thirty thousand of them?"

Her mind squirrelled away the figure of thirty thousand men without conscious thought. Her face reddened. She said, "Lamb negotiated a *condotta*. That's what he does. That's what I do. You just shat yourself and threw yourself on their mercy—"

He put his hand on the shoulder of her brigandine.

Her hand clenched, to knock him away. She felt herself shake with the restraint of not doing it.

"*You* sent me off. Right into them."

"You're trying to blame *me* for this? Hey. I wanted my command back. I didn't want you ordering my lances into a field they couldn't win." Ash snorted. "Bit ironic, really. I should have let you give them an order. It would have been 'run like fuck!' "

He flushed, the pale freckled skin going pink from his throat to his brow.

Ash yelled, "And you could have! It wouldn't even have been *difficult*. Up into the foothills, lose yourself in the mountains. They'd barely got a grip on the coast, they weren't going to go off chasing twelve horsemen!"

Anger is translatable into any language. As he startled back, a green-robed shoulder appeared in front of her, between her and Fernando—Ash grabbed Godfrey Maximillian and pushed him away. For all the priest was twice her bulk, she used balance and momentum to put him straight past her.

"STOP!" she bellowed.

Thomas and Euen Huw instantly appeared one either side of her, hands on hilts. She threw out her hands, palms open, as Lebrija's men began to stride forward.

"Okay! Enough! *Back off*."

One of the Burgundians—a captain?—thundered, "You are under truce! In God's name, no weapons here!"

The Visigoths halted, uncertain. A Burgundian knight near the door shifted to combat stance. Ash jerked a thumb, saw out of peripheral vision Thomas, Euen, and (reluctantly) Godfrey backing off again. She kept her gaze on Fernando.

His voice not quite controlled, Fernando del Guiz said, "Ash . . . when you're cautious, it's caution; when you change sides to the stronger force, it's business. Don't you understand fear?" He hesitated, then: "I thought you understood this—I did what I did because I was afraid of being killed."

He said it plainly, with quiet emphasis. Ash opened her mouth to say something, and shut it again. She looked at him. Both his hands, holding his upturned helmet now, were white-knuckled.

He said, "I saw her face—the Faris. And now I'm alive. For telling some Carthaginian bitch she's got a bastard cousin in the Frankish armies. I was too afraid *not* to tell her."

"You could have run," Ash insisted. "Hell, you could at least have tried!"

"No. I couldn't."

The whiteness of his skin made her think, suddenly, *he's still in shock, he's in combat-shock without having been in combat*, and she said, automatically gently, as she would to one of her own: "Don't feel too bad about it."

His gaze snapped to her face. "I don't."

"What?"

"I don't feel bad about it."

"But—"

"If I did," Fernando said, "I'd have to believe that the people like you are right. I saw it all, in that second. You're crazy. You're all stark, staring *mad*. You go around killing other people, and getting killed, and *you don't see there's anything wrong with it.*"

"Did you do anything when they killed Otto and Matthias and the rest of your guys? Did you even *say* anything?"

"No."

She looked him in the eye.

"No," Fernando said. "I didn't say a word."

To another man, she might have said *that's war, it's shit but it happens, there wasn't anything you could have said that would have made a difference*.

"What's the matter?" she needled. "Pissing on twelve-year-old girls more your style?"

"Perhaps I wouldn't have done that, if I'd realized how dangerous you are." His expression changed. "You're a bad woman. A butcher, a psychopath."

"Don't be bloody ridiculous. I'm a soldier."

"That," he echoed her, "is what soldiers are."

"Maybe so." Ash's voice sounded hard. "That's war."

"Well, I don't want to make war anymore." Fernando del Guiz fixed her with a bright, rueful smile. "You want the honest truth? I want no part of this. If I had any choice, I'd go back to Guizburg, pull up the drawbridge, and not come out until this war's over and done with. Leave it to blood-thirsty bitches like you."

I have been to bed with this man, Ash thought, marveling at the distance between them. And if he asked me, now—

"Is that my cue to walk out?" Ash hooked her hands into her belt. The blue leather was decorated with brass rivets in the shape of lions' heads; it was not, she thought, something that would ever be worn by a woman. "As seductions go, this is pretty crap."

"Yes. Well." Fernando glanced over his shoulder at Sancho Lebrija, looking painfully embarrassed to be overheard failing to persuade an errant wife. "My track record isn't brilliant, recently."

*He looks tired,* Ash thought. A pulse of sympathy for him ruined her carefully hoarded anger.

No. *No.* I'm fine, hating him. That's what I need to do.

"Your track record's fine. The last thing you did to me was betray me. Why didn't you come to me at Basle?" she demanded. "When they'd locked me up, why didn't you come?"

Fernando del Guiz looked blank. "But why should I have?"

Ash hit him.

The movement was not under her control, all she could choose was not to draw her sword. Not wanting a guard's blade struck through her midriff had something to do with it—but, more than that, the picture flashing in front of her eyes stopped her: Fernando del Guiz's face spidered red with blood running from a cleft skull.

That mental image brought a jolt of nausea. Not for

the killing, that being her business, but the simple
thought of harm to this body, a body caressed with her
own hands—

She hit him in the face with the fist clenched, and her
leather gauntlets off; swore; wrung her hand and tucked
her throbbing knuckles under her armpit, and stared at
Fernando del Guiz who rocked back on his heels, eyes
flown wide with shock. Not with anger, she saw, but
with sheer shock that a woman had dared to hit him.

Behind her: shifting feet, the ching of mail, polearm
butts going down on the tiles, men about to plunge forward again—

Fernando del Guiz did not move.

A small red mark swelled below his lip. He breathed
heavily, his face scarlet.

Ash stood watching, flexing her throbbing fingers.

Finally, someone—not one of her own men, one of
the Visigoths—laughed coarsely.

Fernando del Guiz stood in front of her, still not moving.

She looked at his face. Something almost like pity—if
pity can sear and burn, the way that hatred does; if it
can bring an absolute inability to bear another person's
shame and pain—something went through her like
edged steel.

Ash winced, put her fingers to her hair again, feeling
again the sun-warmed heat of it and the spiky gut
stitches still jutting from her skin, and caught the smell
of him on her skin.

"Oh, Christ." Her stomach jolted. Tears pushed under
the lids of her eyes, and she blinked, ferociously, threw
her head back and said, "Euen! Thomas! Godfrey!
We're leaving!"

Her heels rang on the flagstones. The men-at-arms fell
in, either side, matching her step; and she strode straight
past the face of Sancho Lebrija, past his men, ignored
Lamb; strode out through the iron-bound oaken doors,
not looking back, not looking to see what expression
Fernando del Guiz might have on his face now.

*     *     *

Walking without direction took her out of the Ducal palace, into Dijon. She passed and ignored men from the company, striding out blindly through the crowds. A voice called after her. She ignored it, turning away, climbing stone steps. They brought her up into the open, high above the alleys, on the massive stone walls of Dijon.

She paused, breathless, above the man- and horse-crowded streets; surveying the city defenses through absent-minded habit. The men-at-arms, outdistanced, clattered up the steps behind her.

*"Shit!"*

Ash sat herself down on the crenellations, in the late afternoon sunlight. She stared out between blocks of granite. A long way below, beyond the dusty white road leading into the city, diminutive figures worked in the fields. Men in shirts, their split-hose rolled down below their knees, binding up sheaves of the dusty white-gold wheat and lifting them onto ox-wains, working more quickly now that the deadly heat of afternoon was waning . . .

"Child?" A panting Godfrey Maximillian came to stand beside her. "Are you all right?"

"Christ on the Tree, that cowardly son of a bitch!" Her heart still shook her body, made her hands tingle. "Fucking Visigoths—and I'm going to be handed over to *them*? No way!"

Thomas Rochester, scarlet in the heat, said, "Christ, boss, calm down!"

"Too hot for running around like this," Euen Huw added, unbuckling his helmet, and standing up on the crenellations to catch any breeze, and to survey the apparently endless tents of the Burgundian army outside the city walls. "More to worry about than that boy, haven't we?"

Ash flashed a look at them, at Godfrey; calming down. "So I have twenty-four hours to decide whether

I should wait for the Duke's verdict, or pack up my stuff in a spotted hanky and start walking . . ."

The men laughed. Noise came up from the foot of the wall, outside the city. Sixty feet below, a number of her men were swimming in the moat, white limbs flashing as they ducked each other, the camp's dogs yelping and barking at their bare heels. As she watched, a cocky-tailed white bitch bounded into the air and pushed Euen Huw's second, Gwillim, off-balance and off the narrow bridge that formed Dijon's gateway. The sound of the distant splash came up through the hot air.

"There goes Duke Charles." Ash pointed at a caval-cade of riders moving out of the city gates, riding toward the woods; their brilliant clothes bright against the dust, hawks poised on wrists, musicians walking behind them and playing an air which came distantly up to the walls. Ash leaned her back against the cool stone. "You'd think he's got nothing to worry about! Well, maybe he hasn't. Compared to wondering whether he's going to be handed over to the damn Visigoths in the morning!"

Godfrey Maximillian said, "May I speak with you alone, Captain?"

"Oh, sure, why not?" Ash looked over her shoulder at Euen Huw and Thomas Rochester. "Guys, take five. There was an inn at the bottom of these steps, I saw the bush. I'll meet you in there."

Thomas Rochester frowned darkly. "With Visigoths in the city, boss?"

"With half of Charles's army in the streets."

The English knight shrugged, exchanged a look with Euen Huw, and strode lightly down the steps from the wall, the Welshman and the others following. Ash had a shrewd idea they would go no further than the foot of the stone steps.

"Well?" she leaned her face up to the slightest of breezes, bringing a dust of chaff golden from the fields. She hooked one knee up and leaned her elbow on it. Her fingers still faintly trembled, and she looked down at her sword-hand in some puzzlement. "What's bothering you, Godfrey?"

"More news." The big priest gazed out from the walls, not looking at her. "This 'father' of the Faris, Leofric. All I can hear is that this Lord-*Amir* Leofric is one of their least-known nobles, and supposedly resides in Carthage itself, in the Citadel. The rest is just rumors, from unreliable sources. I have no idea what this 'Stone Golem' even looks like. Do you?"

Something in his tone bothered her. Ash glanced up. She patted the flat stone between the crenellations invitingly.

Godfrey Maximillian remained standing on the inner wall walkway.

"Sit down," she said, aloud. "Godfrey, what's bothering you?"

"I can't get you better information without a great deal of money. When does Lord Oxford intend to pay us?"

"No, that isn't it. What, Godfrey?"

"Why is that man still alive!"

His voice boomed, loud enough to momentarily stop the bathers below shouting. Ash startled. She swung around and dangled her legs over the inside of the wall, staring up at him. "Godfrey? Which? Who?"

Godfrey Maximillian repeated, in an intense whisper, *"Why is that man still alive?"*

"Oh, sweet Christ." Ash blinked. She rubbed the heel of her hand across one eye-socket. "You mean *Fernando*, don't you?"

The big, bearded man wiped his sweating face. There were rings of white skin under his eyes.

"Godfrey, what is all this? It was a joke. Or something. I'm not going to murder a man in cold blood, am I?"

He took no notice of this appeal. He began to stride up and down, in short agitated paces, not looking at her. "You are *quite* capable of having him killed!"

"Yes. I am. But why should I? Once they leave, I'll probably never see him again." Ash put out a hand to stop Godfrey. He ignored it. The coarse linen of his robe flicked her fingers as he passed. She scented, still, Fernando del Guiz on her skin; and as she breathed in, suddenly looked up at the big bearded man. He's not old, she thought. I never think of Godfrey as young, but he's not an old man.

Godfrey Maximillian stopped in front of her. The descending sun put gold light on his face, reddening his beard, showing her something like pain in his creased eyes, but she was not sure if it were merely the brightness.

"One of these days there'll be a battle," Ash said, "and I'll hear I'm a widow. Godfrey, what does it matter?"

"It matters if the Duke hands you over to your husband tomorrow!"

"Lebrija doesn't have enough men with him to force me to leave here. As for Duke Charles . . ." Ash gripped her hands over the edge of the stone wall, and pushed herself down onto her feet on the walkway. "Scaring myself shitless tonight won't tell me what the Duke's going to decide to do tomorrow! So what does it matter?"

"It matters!"

Ash, studying him with the sunlight on his face, thought *I haven't looked at you properly since we ran from Basle*, and made a grimace of apology. She noticed now that he had a gaunt look. Just to either side of his mouth, his beard had white hairs among the wiry brown.

"Hey," she said quietly. "This is me, remember? Tell me about it. Godfrey, what is it?"

"Little one . . ."

She closed her hand over his. "You're too good a friend to worry about telling me something bad." Her eyes flicked up to his face, and her grip froze. "Okay, I wasn't born of freemen. Technically, I guess somebody in Carthage owns me."

That made her grin, wryly, but there was no answering smile from Godfrey Maximillian. He stood and stared at her, as if her face was new to him.

"I see." Ash's heart thumped, once, and then beat hard and rapid. "It makes a difference to you. Fucking hell, Godfrey! I thought we were all equal in the eyes of God?"

"What would you know about it?" Godfrey sprayed spit across her, suddenly shouting, his eyes wide and bright. "Ash, what would *you* know? You don't believe in our Lord! You believe in your sword, and your horse, and your men that you pay money to, and your husband that you can get to shove his cock into you! You don't believe in God or grace and you never have!"

"Wh—" Breath taken away, Ash could only stare.

"I watched you with him! He touched you—you touched him, you *let* him touch you—you *wanted* to—"

"What does it matter to you?" Ash sprang to her feet. "In fact, what business is it of yours? You're a damn *priest,* what would you know about fucking?"

Godfrey bellowed, "Whore!"

*"Virgin!"*

"Yes!" he snapped. *"Yes.* What other choice have I got?"

Breathing hard, silenced, Ash stood on the flagstone walkway facing Godfrey Maximillian. The big man's face twisted. He made a noise. Appalled, she watched the tears well out of his eyes; Godfrey crying hard, as a man cries, wrenched deep out of him, deep from the inside. She reached up to touch his wet cheek.

Almost in a whisper, he said monotonously, "I left everything for you. I followed you halfway across Christendom. I've loved you since I first saw you. In my soul's eye I still see you, that first time—in a novice's robe, with your head shaved, and that *Soeur* beating your back bloody. A little white-haired scarred brat."

"Oh, shit, I love you, Godfrey. You know I do." Ash grabbed both his hands and held them. "You're my oldest friend. You're with me every day. I rely on you. You know I love you."

She held him as if she held a drowning man, gripping

him painfully hard, as if the tighter the grip, the more chance she stood of rescuing him from his anguish. Her hands whitened. She shook him, gently, trying to catch his eye.

Godfrey Maximillian reversed the grip and closed his hands around hers.

"I can't stand to watch you with him." His voice broke. "I can't stand having to see you, know that you're married, you're one flesh—flesh—"

Ash tugged her hands. They did not come free, trapped in Godfrey's broad fingers.

"I can bear your casual fornications," he said. "You confess to me, you're absolved, it means nothing. And there have been few of them. But the marriage bed— and the way you look at him—"

Ash winced at his grip. "But Fernando—"

"*Fuck* Fernando del Guiz!" Godfrey roared.

Silenced, Ash stared at him.

"I don't love you as a priest ought." Godfrey's bright wet eyes met hers. "I made my vows before I met you. If I could wipe out my ordination, I would. If I could be anything other than celibate, I would."

Fear thumped in her gut. Ash wrenched her hands free. "I've been stupid."

"I love you as a man does. Oh, Ash."

"Godfrey—" She stopped, not sure what she would have protested, only that the walls of the world were falling down around her. "Christ, this isn't a decision I want to take! It's not like you're just another priest, I can kick you out, hire another one. You've been with me from the beginning—before Roberto, even. Sweet saints. What a time to tell me."

"I'm not in a state of grace! I say mass every day, when I know that I wish him dead!" Godfrey began to twist his rope belt between his fingers, in agitation.

"You're my friend, my brother, my father. Godfrey . . . You know I don't—" Ash sought for a word.

Godfrey's face went crooked. "Don't want me."

"No! I mean—I don't want to—I don't *desire*—oh,

shit, Godfrey!" She reached out as he spun around and strode toward the steps. She barked out, "Godfrey! *Godfrey!*"

He was too quick, outpacing her, a big man moving with reckless speed, almost running down the stone steps that clung to the inside of Dijon's city walls. Ash stopped, staring down at him, a broad-shouldered man in a priest's robe, pushing his way into the cobbled street, between women with baskets, men-at-arms, dogs running underfoot, children playing at ball.

"Godfrey . . ."

She noted that Rochester and Huw were indeed not far from the foot of the steps. The small Welshman had a mug of something, and as she watched, Thomas Rochester gave a tavern boy a small coin in exchange for beer and bread.

"Oh, *shit*. Oh, Godfrey . . ."

Still in two minds whether to go after him, try and find him in the crowd, Ash saw a golden head at the foot of the wall below her.

Her heart stopped. Rochester lifted his head, said something, and waved the man through—a man who, as he began to climb the steps, was not a man at all: was Floria del Guiz, and not her brother.

### iii

ASH MUTTERED AN obscenity under her breath, and stalked back to the crenellations, pulse thumping.

A white ghost of a crescent moon had begun to show against the blue daytime sky, low down toward the west. A wain creaked over the bridge, into Dijon, below Ash: she leaned out to watch it. Golden heads of grain drooped, heavy in their sheaves, and she thought of the watermills on the far side of the city, and the harvest, and the winter conditions of the land not forty miles away.

Floria loped up the last steps to where Ash stood. "Damn fool priest nearly knocked me off the steps! Where's Godfrey going?"

"I don't know!"

Seeing the woman's surprise, Ash bit back the anguish in her tone, and repeated, more calmly, "I don't know."

"He's missed Vespers."

"Do you want something?" Without stopping to think, Ash added, "Now that you've bothered to appear again. What bloody relative are you avoiding *this* time? I had enough of that in Cologne! What the fuck use is a surgeon if she—if *he's* never here!"

Floria's elegant brows went up. "I suppose I did think I might approach my Aunt Jeanne cautiously. Since she hasn't seen me in five years, it might come as something of a shock, even though she knows I dress as a man for traveling."

The tall, dirty woman shook her head, putting precise sardonic verbal quotation marks around the last words.

"I don't believe in rubbing people's noses in things they find difficult."

Ash glanced deliberately down at herself, and her brigandine, and man's hose. "And I do rub people's noses in it, is that what you're saying?"

"Whoa!" Floria held up her hands. "Okay, I give in, start weapons practice again. For God's sake go and hit something, it'll make you feel better!"

Ash laughed shakily. A tension in her relaxed. A breeze ruffled against her face, welcome after the stifling streets. She hitched her sword-belt around, the scabbard having begun to rub against the sides of her leg-armour. "You're happy to be back here, aren't you? In Burgundy."

Floria smiled crookedly, and Ash could not make out what lay behind her expression.

"Not exactly," the surgeon said. "I think your Faris-General is mad as a rabid dog. Being behind one of the world's best armies seems a good idea to me, if it keeps me away from her. I'm happy enough here."

"Hey, you've got family here." Ash looked out, away from the walls, at the moon in the western sky; gold now beginning to shade pink on the clouds. She fisted her hands and stretched her arms, the brigandine's enclosing weight hot and familiar and reassuring on her body. "Not that family are an unmixed blessing . . . Christ, Florian! So far I've had Fernando telling me he wants my beautiful body, Godfrey throwing ructions, and Duke Charles not able to make up his mind if he's going to hand me back to the Visigoths!"

"If he's going to *what*?"

"You didn't hear?" Ash shrugged, turning toward the woman, who leaned, slender in stained doublet and hose, against the gray masonry, her insouciant face alive with questions. "The Faris has sent a delegation here. And, among the minor matters like declaring war and invading us or France, she wants to know if she can please have her bondswoman mercenary commander back."

"Rubbish," Floria said with abrupt, complete confidence.

"She might have a case in law."

"Not once my family lawyers see the documentation. Give me a copy of the *condotta*. I'll take it to Tante Jeanne's attorneys."

Noting how her surgeon avoided the word *bondswoman*, Ash said, "Would it matter to you if I weren't legitimate?"

"It would startle me considerably if you were."

Ash almost laughed. She choked it back, shot a glance at Floria del Guiz, and licked her lips. "And if I'm not freeborn either?"

A silence.

"You see. It *matters*," Ash said. "Proper bastards are

okay, so long as they're the bastards of noblemen, or gentlemen-at-arms at the very least. Being born a serf, or a slave—that's something else. Property. Your family probably buys and sells women like me, Florian."

The tall woman looked blank. "They probably do. Is there *proof* of your been born from a slave mother?"

"No, there's no proof, as such." Ash dropped her gaze. She rubbed at her sword's steel pommel with her thumb, picking at nicks with her nail. "Except that by now, a lot of people are hearing what someone's been using serfs for, in Carthage. Breeding soldiers. Breeding a general. And, as Fernando was happy to remind me, throwing out the ones they don't think will grow up to standard."

With a spurious air of unshockability, Florian snapped, "That's stock-breeding, that's what you do."

"To give them credit," Ash said, her voice altered, her throat constricting, "I don't suppose my company are going to give a fuck. If they'll wear me being female, they won't care if my mother was a slave. So long as I can get them through a battle, I could be Beelzebub's great scarlet whore for all they care!"

And when they know that I don't hear a saint, I don't hear the Lion, I just—just *over*hear someone else's voice? Someone else's machine. That I'm just a mistake, on the way to breeding *her*. What then? Does that make a difference? Their confidence in me is always a thin thread—

She felt a pressure, a weight, and lifted her head to find Floria del Guiz's arm around her shoulders, the surgeon trying to force her touch through the armor.

"There's no way you're going anywhere near Visigoths again," Floria said briskly. "Look, you've only got that woman's word for it—"

"Fuck it, Florian, she's my twin. She knows she's slave-born. What else *can* I be?"

The tall woman lifted a hand, touching grimy fingers to Ash's cheek. "It doesn't matter. Stay here. Tante Jeanne used to have friends at court. She probably still does; she's that kind of woman. I'll make sure you're not sent anywhere."

Ash moved her shoulders uncomfortably. The breeze, dropping, left the upper walls of Dijon as hot as anywhere else. A noise of singing and drunken shouts came up from the tavern at the foot of the steps; and the clash of polearm-butts, as the guards on the bridge changed to evening shift. Above, in the airy emptiness, color drained slowly from the sky.

"*It doesn't matter.*" Floria's hand insistently turned Ash's head, forcing Ash to look at her. "It doesn't matter to me!"

The warm pressure of her fingertips dug into Ash's jaw. Ash stared up, close enough to Floria's face to smell the woman's sweet breath, close enough to see the dirt in the crow's feet at the corners of her eyes, and the glimmer of light in her brown-green irises.

Making eye-contact, Floria grinned lopsidedly, released Ash's jaw, and trailed a fingertip along the scar on her cheek.

"Don't *worry*, boss."

Ash gave a great sigh, relaxing back against Florian. She slapped the woman's back. "You're right. Fuck it, you're right. Come on."

"Where to?"

Ash stood. "I've taken a command decision. Let's go back to camp and get completely rat-arsed!"

"Good idea!"

At the foot of the steps, they picked up the escort, and strode back through the streets toward the south gate.

Arm-in-arm with the surgeon, Ash came to a stumbling halt as Florian suddenly stopped. Thomas and Euen's men instantly faced outward, hands on weapons.

An elderly woman's voice said coldly, "I might have known that where Constanza's brat is, you would also be. Where is your half-brother?"

The woman was fat, in brown kirtle and white wimple, and clasped a purse against her belly in both her hands. Her clothes were rich silk, embroidered; and the visible gathered neck of her shift made from the finest lawn. All that was visible of her lined, sweating white face was a double chin, round cheeks, and a snub button nose.

Her eyes were still young, and a beautiful green.

She demanded, "Why have you come back to shame your family? Do you *hear* me? Where's my nephew Fernando?"

Ash sighed. She murmured to herself, "Not *now* . . ."

Florian backed up a step.

"Who's the old bat?" a billman at the back of the escort demanded.

"Fernando del Guiz is in the Duke's palace, Madame," Ash cut in, before Florian could speak. "I think you'll find him with the Visigoths!"

"Did I ask you, abomination?"

It was said quite casually.

There was a shifting among the men in Lion tabards; assessing that there were no Burgundian soldiers in this street, that the woman—although nobly dressed—was out with no escort. Someone sniggered. One of the archers drew his dagger. Someone else muttered, "Cunt!"

"Boss, you want us to do the old bitch over?" Euen Huw asked loudly. "She's an ugly old shite, but Thomas here will fuck everything on two legs, isn't that right?"

"Better than you, you Welsh bastard. At least I don't fuck everything with *four* legs."

They were moving as they spoke, broad men in armor, hands going to bollock daggers. Ash barked, "Hold it!" and put her hand on Florian's shoulder.

The elderly woman screwed up her eyes, squinting at Ash against the bright sun that slanted down into the street, between the gabled roofs. "I am not afraid of your armed thugs."

Ash spoke with no asperity. "Then you're downright stupid, because they won't think twice about killing you."

The woman bristled. "The Duke's peace holds here! The church forbids murder!"

Seeing this woman, in her neat chaff-flecked gown, with the folds of her white headdress neat under her chin—knowing just how quickly it could all be changed, to cloth ripped off to show gray hair, kirtle slashed, shift bloodied, skinny legs sprawled naked on the cobbles—all this made Ash speak quite gently.

"We kill for a living. It gets to be a habit. They'd kill you for your shoes, never mind your purse, and they're even more likely to do it for the fun of it. Thomas, Euen, I think this woman's name is—Jeanne?—and she's some relative of our surgeon. Hands off. Got me?"

"Yes, boss . . ."

"And don't sound so damn disappointed!"

"Shit, boss," Thomas Rochester remarked, "you must think I'm *desperate*!"

They seemed to fill the street: the bulk of men who have padded doublets under mail, steel plates strapped to legs, long-hilted swords swinging from their hips. Their voices were loud, and under cover of Euen Huw's beery "Couldn't get laid in a whorehouse with a bag of gold louis!" Ash said, "Florian, this is your aunt?"

Florian stared ahead, her face set. She said, "My father Phillipe's sister. Captain Ash, may I present Mademoiselle Jeanne Châlon . . ."

"No," Ash said feelingly. "You may not. Not today. Today, I've had just about enough!"

The elderly woman stepped straight into the group of soldiers, oblivious to their only brief amusement. She seized the shoulder of Florian's doublet and shook her, twice, with little jerky movements.

Ash saw it momentarily as Thomas and Euen did: a small, fat old woman catching hold of their surgeon, and the tall, strong, dirty young man staring down with an appalled helplessness.

"If you don't want her hurt," Thomas Rochester offered to Florian, "we'll just take her away for you. Where's the family live?"

"Teach her a few manners, on the way." Wiry, black-haired Euen Huw thumbed his dagger back into its sheath, and took hold of both the woman's elbows from behind. As his hands tightened, Jeanne Châlon's face turned white under its summer flush and she gasped, and went limp against him.

"Leave her alone." Ash stared the Welshman down until he relaxed.

"Let me look, Tante Jeanne!" Floria del Guiz reached out, with long-fingered hands, taking the woman's fat arm, and moving it gently at the elbow. "Damn it! Next time I have you in the surgeon's tent, Euen Huw——"

The Welsh lance-leader shifted his grip, uncomfortably aware that he was still supporting the woman against his chest. Half-fainting, Jeanne Châlon flapped her free hand, slapping at him. He attempted to support her without gripping her wide waist and hips, grabbed her as she slid downwards, finally lowered Jeanne del Guiz to the cobbles, and grunted, "Fuck, Florian, boy; get rid of the old cow! We all got families back home, don't we? That's why we're out here!"

"Sweet Christ on a stick!" Ash shoved the men bodily back, breaking up the sweat-soaked, airless crush. "She's a *noblewoman*, for Christ's sake! Get it through your thick heads, the Duke can throw us out of Dijon! She's my fucking *husband's* aunt, as well!"

"She is?" Euen sounded doubtful.

"Yeah. She is."

"Shit. And him with all those Visigoth friends, now. Not that he doesn't need them—skid-marks in his hose, that boy's got."

"Quiet," Ash snapped, her eyes on Jeanne Châlon.

Ruthlessly, Florian stripped the white linen headdress away. The woman's eyelids fluttered. Wisps of gray-white hair plastered themselves to her forehead. Her red, sweating complexion became more normal.

"Water!" Florian snapped, holding her hand up without looking. Thomas Rochester lifted the strap of his water bottle hastily over his head and stuffed it into her hand.

"Is she all right?"

"Nobody saw us."

"Shit, I think there's Burgundians coming!"

Ash gestured, cutting off the comments. "You two, Ricau, Michael, get down to the end of the street, make sure it stays private up here. Florian, is she dead, or what?"

The crêpe skin, under Florian's fingers, fluttered with a pulse.

"It's too hot, she's overdressed, you scared her shitless, she fainted," the surgeon rattled off. "Is there any *more* trouble you can get me into?"

Under the sharp bravado, Ash heard the woman's voice shaking.

"Don't worry, I'll fix it," Ash said confidently, and with absolutely no idea of how anything might be salvaged from this disaster. She saw her confident tone steady Florian, for all that the surgeon might be very well aware Ash had no answers.

"Get her up on her feet," Ash added. "You, Simon, get wine. *Run.*"

It took minutes for the page of Euen's lance to run back to the inn, for the men-at-arms to begin to shuffle, remember they were in a city, become awed by the sheer number of streets and people, and remember the Burgundian army encamped outside. Ash saw their faces and heard their comments, while she knelt down beside Florian, staring at the old woman.

"I raised you!" the woman slurred. Her eyes opened, fixing on Florian's face. "What was I, to you? No more than a nursemaid? With you always whimpering for your dead mother! What thanks did you ever give me?"

"Sit up, Aunt." Florian's voice was firm. She put a wiry arm behind the woman's back, shifting her upright. "Drink this."

The fat woman sat on the cobbles, unaware of her sprawling legs. She blinked against the bright light, the legs of the men surrounding them; and opened her mouth, dribbling the wine that Florian poured between her lips.

"If she's well enough to slag you off, she'll live," Ash said grimly. "Come on, Florian. We're out of here."

She got a hand under the surgeon's arm, hoisting. Florian shook her off.

"Aunt, let me help you up—"

"Take your hands off me!"

"I *said*, we're leaving," Ash repeated urgently.

Jeanne Châlon gave a subdued shriek, and grabbed her ruined headdress up from the road. She clutched the linen over her gray hair. "Vile—!"

The men-at-arms laughed. She ignored them, glaring at Florian.

"You are a vile abomination! I always knew it! Even at thirteen, you seduced that girl—"

Her next words were inaudible, drowned in raucous comments. Thomas Rochester reached down and thumped the surgeon on the back. "Thirteen? Randy little sod!"

Florian's mouth curved, unwillingly. Bright-eyed, reckless, she said, "Lizette. Yes. Her father kept our hounds. Black curly hair . . . pretty girl."

One of the crossbow-women, at the back of the escort group, chuckled. "He's a ladies' man, our surgeon!"

"—*Enough!*" Jeanne Châlon shrieked.

Ash bent down and hauled Florian bodily to her feet. "Don't argue, just *go*."

Before the surgeon could move, the fat woman sitting on the cobbles shrieked again, loudly and urgently enough that the men fell silent around her:

"*Enough of this vile pretense.* God will never forgive you, little whore, little bitch, little abomination!" Panting, Jeanne Châlon heaved in a breath, staring up, wet-eyed. "Why do you tolerate her? Don't you know that she damns you, pollutes you, just by being with you? Why else is she forbidden her home? Are you blind? *Look at her!*"

Faces—Euen, Thomas, the billmen—turned to Ash, and then to Florian. And from Florian back to Ash.

"Okay, that's enough," Ash said quickly, hoping to take advantage of their confusion. "We're leaving."

Thomas gazed at Florian. "What's she on about, man?"

Ash filled her lungs. "Form up—"

Jeanne Châlon shuddered, rose, scrambling unaided to her feet in a flurry of skirts and shift. She was panting. One hand went out, grabbing Euen Huw's livery tabard.

"You *are* blind!"

She faced Florian.

"Look at her! Can't you see what she is? She's a whore, an abomination, she dresses in man's clothes, *she is a woman*—"

Ash, under her breath and without realizing it, said, "Oh fuck."

"God be my witness," Mademoiselle Châlon shouted, "she is my niece, and my shame."

Floria del Guiz smiled, tautly. In an absent-minded voice, she said, "I remember that, after Lizette, you threatened to lock me up in a nunnery. I always thought that had a certain lack of logic about it. Thank you, Aunt. Where would I be without you?"

There was already a rumble of comment from the men-at-arms. Ash swore, violently, under her breath, spitting out the obscenity. "Okay, form up, we're out of here. Come *on*."

The men clustered in a group around Florian and Jeanne Châlon, who stood face to face, as if no one else in the world existed. The shadows of doves from a nearby cote flickered over them. The rumble of mills was the only sound in the quiet.

"Where *would* I be?" Florian repeated. She still held the flask of wine that Simon had brought, and she lifted it and drank, absently, gulping the liquid down and wiping her sleeve across her mouth. "You drove me out. It's hard trying to pass as a man, train with men. I would have come home from Salerno in the first week, if I'd

had a home to come back to. But I didn't, and so I'm a
surgeon. You made me what I am, *Tante*."

"The Devil made you." Very coldly, into the silence,
Jeanne Châlon said, "You lay with that girl Lizette as if
you were a man."

Ash saw identical expressions of shock on the faces
of the men-at-arms; and on Thomas Rochester's face, an
awed, superstitious disgust.

"I could have had you burned," the old woman said.
"I held you in my arms when you were a baby. I prayed
I would never see you again. Why have you come back?
Why couldn't you stay away!"

"Something—" Florian's voice thinned, losing its
husky depth, "—something I have always needed to ask
you, Aunt. You paid to have me freed by the Abbot of
Rome, when he would have burned me because I had a
Jewish lover. Tante, could you have bought her, too?
Could you have paid him for Esther's life?"

The men's faces turned to Jeanne Châlon.

"I could have, but I would not! She was a Jewess!"
The fat woman sweltered, dragging her kirtle and shift
around her, treading her purse unnoticed under her feet.
She shifted her gaze away from Florian del Guiz, as if
for the first time aware that she had an audience.

"She was a Jewess!" Jeanne Châlon repeated, in high-
voiced protest.

"Well . . . I've been to Paris, and Constantinople, and
Bokkara, and Iberia, and Alexandria." Florian's voice
held a hopeless, vitiated contempt: Ash suddenly realized, seeing the surgeon's face, that she had held long
hopes of this occasion, and of it being different to this.
"I've met nobody I despise as I despise you, *Aunt*."

The Burgundian woman shrieked, "And *she* dressed
as a man, too!"

"So does boss," Thomas Rochester growled, "and nobody's fucking burning her."

Ash felt the balance in the air, the moment which can
be crystalized. They don't know *what* to think: Florian's
a woman—but this Châlon bitch isn't one of us—

She caught Ricau signaling. A number of Dijonaise turned into the narrow street: millworkers, on their way home.

The woman shrieked, "Phillipe should never have fathered you! My brother suffers in Purgatory for that sin!"

Floria del Guiz pivoted on her foot, brought her fist through, and punched Jeanne Châlon in the face.

Rochester, Euen Huw, Katherine, and young Simon spontaneously cheered.

Mademoiselle Châlon fell down, shrieking, *"Au secours!"*

"Okay," Ash called deliberately, her eyes on the approaching citizens of Dijon, "time to go: let's get our surgeon out of here."

There was no hesitation: all the men-at-arms closed in around Florian, hands on sword-hilts or gripping bill-shafts, and began a fast walk toward the end of the street and the city gate that had the citizens of Dijon leaping back out of their way.

"If anybody asks," Ash bent down to Jeanne Châlon, "my surgeon's under arrest, by my provosts, and I'm dealing with her discipline myself."

Oblivious, the old woman sobbed, bloody hands over her mouth.

Running in the wake of her men-at-arms, Ash glanced up at the early evening sun over the roofs of Dijon, and had time to think *Why did we ever come to Burgundy?*

And what is the Duke going to say to me now?

## iV

"WHY IS IT," Ash said under her breath, "that when the brown and sticky hits the fan, I'm always standing real close by?"[7]

Thomas Rochester shrugged. "Just lucky, boss, I guess . . ."

Among subdued laughter, Ash strode on across the common ground beside the silent Florian del Guiz. Behind them, the gable roofs of Dijon lay limned with gold, the white dots of Orion and Cassiopeia beginning to pattern the milk-blue sky.

Crows and rooks squabbled on the camp middens as they approached the wagon-perimeter; the carrion-eaters flapping up, black pinions outspread.

"Don't leave the camp, master surgeon," Ash ordered calmly, "under any circumstances."

The lowering sun colored Florian's blue doublet and hose with warmth, turned her hair red-gold. The woman raised her dirty face as she walked, staring up, her arms folded around her body. Her eyes reflected the empty sky.

"Don't sweat." Ash slapped the surgeon's shoulder. "If the town militia turn up, *I'll* deal with it. Stay in the surgeon's tent tonight."

The woman's head lowered. Now she watched her bare feet, treading down the sharp-edged dry grass. She didn't look at the men-at-arms.

The men and women of the escort walked, talking quietly among themselves, weapons slung over shoulders, left hands going down to steady scabbards. Ash

---

[7] The original text has "fortuna imperatrix mundi."

heard comments about the vast encampment that was the Burgundian army, arrangements for off-duty drinking with acquaintances from other campaigns now with the Burgundian mercenaries—nothing at all about their surgeon.

She made her decision.

*No. I'm not going to say anything. Give it a few hours—tomorrow—and depending on what Charles of Burgundy says, we may have bigger problems than our surgeon being a woman ...*

The city walls lay in shadow now, only the topmost roofs gilded with sharp-edged red light. Dew dampened that masonry, and dampened the straw here, underfoot, spread outside the camp. An ox still out in the fields lowed, and a pack of dogs ran yelping and barking. Welcome coolness came into the air with sunset.

At the gates, where the straw was trodden down flat by hundreds of passing feet, a hubbub of voices and a crowd of men in Lion livery drew her attention. They stood red-faced and grinning, and parted to let her through with a suppressed excitement: a scowl for the provosts, and several grins for her.

With a resigned sigh, she said, "What is it this time?"

Two young men of about fifteen, all legs, and baby-fat burning down to muscle and youthful energy, were shuffled to the front of the crowd. Both were fair-haired, brothers by their faces; and she recognized them as men of Euen Huw's lance.

"Tydder," she said, bringing the name to mind.

One of the boys muttered, "Boss—"

His brother slammed an elbow into the other's bare ribs. "Shut up, you!"

Both of them had their shirts and pourpoints rolled down to the waist, chests bare and burning red, and everything more or less held up with their dagger-belts. Ash was about to snarl something when she noticed that the bundle of cloth around one of the waists was thicker. She pointed silently.

The young soldier unwrapped the cloth and shook it out.

A quartered rectangular flag of blue and red, about two yards across, flopped down from his big hands. Ash found herself looking at two ravens and two crosses.

There was a rise in the noise around her, someone laughed; the anticipation all but tangible.

"That," Ash said, with no intention of disappointing them, "wouldn't happen to be a personal banner, would it?"

The brother holding the flag nodded rapidly. The other brother grinned, ferociously.

"Cola de Monforte's personal banner?" she queried.

"You got it, boss!" the younger brother squeaked, flushing at his voice.

Ash began to grin.

Behind her, Floria suddenly broke her silence. "Christ on a stick! How are you going to explain this one?"

Her appalled expression made Ash burst out laughing.

"Oh, I'm not going to explain it," she said cheerfully. "I don't have to. In fact . . . you two—Mark and Thomas, isn't it? And Euen Huw . . . Carracci, Thomas Rochester . . . and Huw's lance—" Ash pointed at a dozen or more men. "I suggest you wrap this banner up very neatly, and you take it over to the gate of the Monforte camp, and you present it to Master Cola—in person—with our compliments."

"They do *what*?" Floria exclaimed.

"It can be really embarrassing to lose your personal banner. If we just *happened* to find it lying around," Ash emphasized, "and took it back to them, in case they were worried about it—"

Laughter drowned her out.

Under cover of the lances sorting themselves out, finding armor to wear up to the Monforte mercenary camp, and girding on their most impressive weapons, Floria del Guiz asked, "And just how did we come by that banner?"

"No point me asking." Ash shook her head, still grinning. "Remind me to tell Geraint to double the perimeter guard. And double the guard on the Lion standard. I feel there's going to be a lot of this—"

"—this crap!" Floria snarled. "Complete waste of time! Boys' games!"

Ash watched Ludmilla Rostovnaya and her lance-mate Katherine shouldering arquebuses to form part of the impromptu honor guard, some two dozen strong, moving off across the river meadows in the direction of the Burgundian mercenary camps.

"If they want to play at flag-stealing, I'm going to let them. Either Duke Charles will fund the raid, or he'll call for war. Either way, in a few days' time, they could be in your surgeon's tent. Or buried. And they know it." She twinkled at Florian. "Hell, you think this is bad, you've seen what they're like *after* they've won a fight . . . !"

The woman looked as though she might have said something; but a hail from the surgeon's tent—one of her assistants, a deacon—took her attention, and she nodded abruptly at Ash and walked off.

Ash let her go.

"If the town militia turn up here," she said to the captain on the gate, "you send for me at once. And you don't let them in, got that?"

"Sure, boss. We in trouble again?"

"You'll hear about it. In this camp, everybody hears everything . . ."

The captain of the gate-guard, a big Breton man with plowman's shoulders, said, "Yeah, we might as well live in a fucking village."

I wonder which you'll find most scandalous—that the Duke's lawyers think the Visigoths own me, or that your pox-doctor is a woman?

" 'Night, Jean."

" 'Night, boss."

Ash strode off toward the command tent, her bodyguard-escort dispersing now they were inside the camp, half a dozen mastiffs jumping and yelping around her. Geraint ab Morgan came for passwords for the night guards, Angelotti notifying repairs ongoing with guns (the organ-gun *Barbara's Revenge* having cracked her shaft), Henri Brant needing money from the war-chest; all this within a few yards, so that it was a full half-hour before she got to the tent, took one look at the busy confusion inside her pavilion—Bertrand sulkily rolling her leg-armour in a barrel of sand to clean it, under Rickard's impatient direction—and sniffed at her armpits as they removed her brigandine, turned command over to Anselm, whistled up the dogs, and went down to the river to swim in the last of the light, Rickard accompanying her.

"It's not like I have to *worry* about Florian." She buried both hands in the scruffs of mastiff-necks, feeling their warmth, smelling the dog-smell. "Anyone who objects to serving with women—doesn't sign up with me. Do they?"

Rickard looked confused. The powerful dog Bonniau snuffled.

Reaching the river bank, she stripped off hose and doublet as one (still pointed together at the waist) and her yellowing linen shirt, wringing wet with sweat. The mastiffs settled on the banks, heavy heads resting on their paws, one brindled bitch—Brifault—curling up on Ash's discarded, sweat-soaked shirt, doublet and hose, and shoes.

"Got my sling," Rickard offered.

Neither fox, polecat nor rat was safe near company refuse, Ash was well aware; her own lance's foxtail came from one of Rickard's kills.

"I want you here with the dogs. Even if we are inside the camp."

Ash waded out, and threw herself in. The cold water grabbed her, shocked her skin, pulled her downstream. Gasping, grinning, she stood up and plodded back to the shallow eddy, thick with flag-irises, where the river cut a bow in the bank.

"Boss?" Rickard's voice said, among the mastiffs.

"Yeah?" She ducked her head under the surface. The weight of her wet hair swirled with the current. Standing up, the wet mass of it clung to her from head to knees, glinting palely in the sunset light. She scratched at sunburn and skin-rash. "You know, if I didn't take the time out to eat, wash, or sleep, this camp would function perfectly . . . what is it?"

His features could not be seen in the fading light. His boy's voice was abrupt. "I can hear a noise."

Ash frowned. "Leash the dogs."

She walked up to the bank, legs lead-heavy, and put her wet hair back from her ears. The usual noise from the campfires, and the sound of men drinking, echoed across the river valley.

"What did you hear?" She reached out for her shirt and began to scrub her skin dry.

"That!"

"Shit!" Ash swore, as a shout went up, from in the camp. Not men getting drunk, and fighting: too raw for that. She struggled into her clothes without drying herself off, the cloth sticking to her skin, and grabbed her sword and buckled it around her waist while she walked, and took the mastiffs' leashes from Rickard as he sprinted after her.

"It's the doctor!" the boy shouted.

In the growing dark, men massed, shouting.

The surgeon's tent went over as Ash came striding up unnoticed into the crowd of off-duty men. The pennant and pole tipped as knives hacked away the guy-ropes; the canvas suddenly sagged.

A rose of yellow flame blossomed out of the canvas, brown-edged, brilliant in what was by contrast almost the darkness of the late sunset.

"FIRE!" Rickard shrieked.

"Pack it in!" Ash roared. She went forward without thinking about it, into the middle of them, dog-leashes clutched in both hands. "Anhelt, what the fuck do you think you're doing! Pieter, Jean, Henri—" picking out faces from the surging mass "—back off! Get the fire-watch! Get buckets, get sand on that thing!"

She was briefly aware of Rickard at her back, the boy struggling to draw his worn, munitions-issue sword. Someone cannoned into both of them. The dogs snarled, a frenzy of hound-bodies throwing themselves forward; and she bawled, "Bonniau! Brifault!" and let the leashes out to her arm's length.

The men went back from the dogs, clearing a space around her and the collapsing tent. A figure fell down into the folds of canvas—Floria?

Ash yelled, "*Hold!*"

"WHORE!" a billman bellowed at the wreckage of the surgeon's tent.

"Kill the cunt!"

"Woman-fucker!"

"Fucking filthy pervert, fucking bitch, fucking dyke—"

"Fuck him and kill him!"

"Fuck her and kill her!"

Between their shoving bodies, she glimpsed other men running from other parts of the camp, some with torches, some with fire-buckets. The heat of the burning blew against her back. Charred fragments of canvas drifted past her.

Ash pitched her voice to carry. "*Get that fire out before it spreads!*"

"Drag her out of there and fuck her," a man's voice shouted: Josse. His face contorted as he spat. "Fucking *surgeon*! Cut her cunt up!"

Ash said quietly to the boy, "Get Florian out of the tent: *move*," and stepped forward, still with the mastiffs' leashes around her gloved hands, glaring around at the men.

In that moment she realized that most of the faces she could see were from Flemish lances. Some surprises— Wat Rodway, from the cook's tent, with a filleting knife; Pieter Tyrrell—but mostly it was red-faced men rawly shouting, hoarse, the stink of beer on the air, and more than that: an edge of real violence.

They're not just going to stand and shout, and destroy a few things.

Shit.

I shouldn't stand in front of them because they're going to come right over me. There's my authority gone.

The man Josse came forward, stomping over the slippery dry straw, regardless of her; reaching out to shove her aside with one hand, this woman with wet hair hanging to her thighs; his other hand going to his scabbard.

One of the Flemish lances' crossbowmen: she has a second to recognize him as one of the men taken with her at Basle, one of the first to greet her on her return to camp.

Ash released the mastiffs' leashes.

"*Shit!*" Josse screamed.

The six dogs bounded forward, silent now, and leaped; one man wrenching himself backwards with his arm clamped between heavy jaws, screeching; two men going down with dogs at their throats; a pennant and torches visible over the heads of the mob—

Over the noise of men screaming and swearing, and the howl as someone cut at one of the mastiffs, Ash pitched her voice to battlefield volume:

"BACK OFF! DOWN WEAPONS!"

She caught a sound of voices behind her: Florian and Rickard, some of the surgeon's-tent assistants. She didn't take her eyes off the billmen and archers massing in the firebreak between tents. Bashas opposite were being trodden down as the crowd grew: men inside them yelling protests. The crackle of flame grew behind her.

"Brifault!"

The mastiffs, hallooed back, came to heel. She felt the switch of attention: the crowd no longer a mass of men who might just push past her, not even seeing one more person in the confusion of the camp, but men in mailshirts, with daggers in their hands, and torches—one, Josse, with a drawn sword—facing her.

Ash, aware that reality is what consensus says it is, feels it begin to slip: from mutual agreement that she is commander of the company, to being just a young woman, in a field, at night, surrounded by men who are bigger, older, armed, drunk.

Entirely automatically, she started to mutter, "Armed revolt, in camp, thirty men—"

*"Re-establish command and control by—"*

"Who do you think you fucking are!" Josse sprayed spit from his mouth as he bellowed. The sheer volume of voice from that big a man blasted the air. He glared, said, "You're fucking dead," and lifted his falchion.

The movement of a live blade triggered every combat reflex.

Ash grabbed the neck of her scabbard with her left hand and her hilt with her right hand, ripping the sword out of the sheath. In the space of that second, Josse's arm went up, torchlight flashed off his falchion's edge, and the heavy curved blade chopped down. She whacked her sword in behind it, parrying, accelerating it down; slammed his blade down so hard into the dirt between them that her feet came off the ground. Landing, balanced, she slammed one foot onto his blade and held it; and lifted up her sword pommel-first and rammed it straight into his unprotected throat.

A voice among the gathered men whispered, "Shit . . ."

Ash felt wetness on her hands. She pulled the weapon back. Josse put both hands to his crushed trachea and fell, wheezing whitely, onto the smouldering straw at her feet. Simultaneously, sudden and final: one foot kicked; his bowels relaxed; the breath made a loud, harsh noise in his throat.

Men at the back still pushed to get forward, the shouting still went on there; but here, at the edge of the crowd around the surgeon's tent, shock and silence.

"Shit," Pieter Tyrrell repeated. He raised bright, drunken eyes to Ash. "Oh, shit, man."

A billman said, "He should've known better than to draw sword."

A sudden influx of men, in plate, and under Anselm's

pennant, thrust in from one side; and Ash lowered her sword, seeing the provosts going in, breaking up what she now estimated in the darkness to be a crowd of fifty or sixty men.

"Well done." She nodded acknowledgment to Anselm. "All right, get this man . . . buried."

Deliberately, she turned her back on the men, letting Anselm sort it. She rubbed her glove over the stained pommel of her sword, wiping off blood, and sheathed the weapon. The mastiffs closed in around her legs.

Rickard and Florian del Guiz, in the wet smoking wreckage of the surgeon's tent, stared at her: the boy and the woman with identical expressions.

"He was going to *kill* you !" Rickard protested shrilly. He stood with his feet planted apart and his head down, much the way that Anselm habitually stood; watching the departing men with awkward bravado and fear. "How can they do that! You're the boss!"

"They're hard men. If they're drunk, nobody's boss."

"But you stopped it!"

Ash shrugged, gathering up the mastiffs' leashes. She rubbed Bonniau's muzzle, the dog's wet drool sliding over her hands. Her fingers shook.

Florian stepped out of the wreckage of the pavilion: over burned canvas, wooden chests smashed open, spoiled surgical instruments and scattered, trodden bunches of herbs. Someone had started on smacking the disguised woman around, Ash saw: her lips bled, and her doublet-sleeve was ripped out of its point-holes.

"You okay?"

"Motherfuckers!" Florian stared at the squad pulling Josse's body away in a blanket. "I've had them under my knife! How could they come here and do this!"

"Are you badly hurt?" Ash persisted.

Florian spread pale, dirty long fingers in front of her, and looked down at the tremors shaking her hands. "Did you have to *kill* him?"

"Yes. I did have to. They follow me because I can do that without thinking about it, and I sleep nights afterwards." Ash reached out and lifted the surgeon's chin, studying the bruises.

Dark fingermarks stood out on the woman's flesh, where she had been grabbed and held.

"Get one of the deacons here, Rickard. Florian, killing doesn't matter to me. If it mattered, I'd've gone down the first time thirty armed thugs marched up to my tent and said, 'That's our war-chest, piss off, little girl.' Wouldn't I?"

"You're mad." Florian shifted her head away, staring down at the wreckage. One wet streak marked her cheek. "You're all fucking mad! Bloody maniacs, bloody soldiers! You're no different!"

Ash said dryly, "Yes, I am. I'm on your side."

To the deacon who trotted up with a lantern, she said, "Get the doctor bedded down in the field chapel. Is Father Godfrey back yet?"

The man gasped, "No, Captain."

"Okay. Feed her, keep an eye on her, I don't think she's hurt too bad, there'll be a guard along later," and as Robert Anselm returned, his armor rattling as he strode up to her, Ash continued, "I want Florian in the chapel tent, and a guard on it, nothing too obvious."

"It's done." Anselm gave orders to his subordinates. Turning back to Ash, he said, "Girl, what the fuck was that?"

"That was a mistake."

Ash looked down at the trodden straw. There was dark blood on it, not very much, but visible in the lantern's light. The stink of burned canvas and spilled herbs rose up in the night air.

Thomas Rochester, at Anselm's back, said, "You couldn't disarm him. He was twice your weight. I reckon you only had one chance, and you took it."

Robert Anselm stared after the departing surgeon. "He's—she's a woman, and she fucks women?"

"Yeah."

"You knew about this?" At her hesitation, he spat on

the straw, swore softly, and fixed her with expressionless eyes. "You fucked up here."

"Yeah. Josse was good in a fight. I fucking needed him." Ash scowled. "I need all the good men I've got! If I'd seen this coming, I wouldn't have had to do that."

"Shit," Robert Anselm said.

"Yeah."

"Get that cleared up," Anselm directed his returning men. Ash walked aside with him, down the path between pavilions, as the physic-tent was sifted, shifted, and cleared.

"Do I call a meeting and talk to them?" Ash mused, aloud. "Or do I let it sink in what they've done, and let their heads clear in the morning? Have I still *got* a surgeon? One they'll trust?"

The big man sniffed, thoughtfully, and prodded with his sabaton at a wisp of extinguished straw, grinding it into the dew-wet dirt. "He's been with us five years, half of them have been put back together in—her—tent. Give 'em a chance to work out it's still the doc. First time somebody hits 'em, most'll come running."

"And those that don't?"

The pennant that had been lurking about at the back of the crowd became clear as it moved forward. Ash's face took on a grim expression.

"Master van Mander," she called. "I want a word with you."

Joscelyn van Mander, Paul di Conti, and five or six more of the Flemish lance-leaders picked their way through the confusion; van Mander's face white under his helmet.

"What the *hell* were you doing, letting your men do this?"

"I couldn't stop them, Captain." Joscelyn van Mander reached up and took off his helmet. His face was flushed, his eyes bright; she smelled wine on him, and on the others.

"You couldn't stop them? You're their lance-leader!"

"I command only by their consent," the Flemish commander said, unsteadily. "I lead by their wishes. It's the same for all us officers. We're a mercenary company, Captain Ash. It's the men who matter. How *could* I stop them? We're told the surgeon is a devil, a demon; a lustful, perverted vile thing; an offense to mankind—"

Ash raised a brow. "So she's a woman: so what?"

"She's a woman who has lain with other women, who knows them carnally!" His voice pitched high with outrage. "Even if I could bring myself to tolerate it, because he's, she's, your surgeon, and you're commander—"

"That's enough." Ash cut him short. "Your duty is to control these men. You failed."

"How could I control them, their disgust at this?" His breath blasted, warm and beer-laded, across the space between them. "Don't blame *me*, Captain. She's *your* surgeon."

"Get back to your tent. I'll tell you your penalties in the morning."

Ash stared the Flemish lance-leader down, ignoring for the moment the other lance-leaders with him; noting, as he turned and stalked away, who followed his pennant, and who stayed to undertake the clear-up of the area.

"God*dammit*!" Ash said.

"We've got trouble," Anselm said phlegmatically.

"Yeah, like I really need *more* trouble." Ash smoothed her still-wet shirt sleeves down. "Maybe I should look forward to Charles handing me over to the Visigoths . . . it can only be an improvement!"

Robert Anselm ignored her temper, which she was used to him doing.

"I'll hold some kind of enquiry tomorrow. Fines, beatings; stop this before it gets out of hand." When she glanced up at him, Anselm was watching her. "And I'll be interested to know if van Mander's lances overheard any 'chance remarks' from Joscelyn before this riot."

"Wouldn't surprise me."

"I'd better go check on Florian."

"About Josse." Robert Anselm halted her as she was

about to walk off into the camp. "Stop by my tent later. I've got wine."

Ash shook her head. "No."

"We can have a drink. To Josse."

"Yeah." Ash sighed, in gratitude for Anselm's particular understanding. She grinned. "I'll be along. Don't worry about me, Roberto. I don't need the wine. I'll sleep."

A hot, muggy mist came up with the next day's dawn. Granules of water hung suspended in the air inside the palace. The misty whiteness of the presence chamber tinged with gold as the sun rose over the horizon.

Ash stood beside the Earl of Oxford, welcoming the coolness of the early morning. De Vere and his brothers being awarded a place not far from the Ducal throne, she was able to look about her, see the Burgundian nobles assembled, the foreign dignitaries—but not, so far, the Visigoths.

The clarions rang and the choirs began to sing a morning hymn. Ash took off her chaperon hat and bowed her knee to the white marble floor.

"I have no idea what the Duke will do," John de Vere said, as the hymn finished. "I'm an outsider here, too, madam."

"I could have had a contract with that man," she whispered, voice barely a breath.

"Yes," the Earl of Oxford said.

"Yes."

They mutually looked at each other, and as mutually shrugged, each with a quiet smile on their faces as they got to their feet, Duke Charles of Burgundy seating himself on his throne.

Her satisfaction vanished with the automatic glance she gave to find Godfrey, and listen to Godfrey's prompting voice at her ear. The place beside her was taken by Robert Anselm, Godfrey Maximillian not being present.

Robert might believe Godfrey would stay overnight

in Dijon, last night, but he's wondering where our clerk
is right now. I can see it on his face. And I don't have
anything I can tell him. Godfrey, where the fuck have
you gone?

Are you coming back?

"Hell!" she added, under her breath, and realized at
de Vere's curious glance that she had spoken aloud.

Under the cover of the Duke's chamberlain and chan-
cellor speaking, the Earl of Oxford said, "Don't worry,
madam. If it comes to it, I'll think of something to keep
you here, out of Visigoth hands."

"Like what?"

The Englishman smiled confidently, seemingly
amused by her caustic tone. "I'll think of something. I
often do."

"Too much thinking's bad for you . . . my lord." Ash
tagged his title onto the end. She raised her head, trying
to look across the heads of the crowd.

Complicated heraldries of Burgundy and France
blazed silver and blue, red and gold, scarlet and white.
Her eye travelled over the various groups, some standing
in corners, others seated by the great open fireplaces full
of sweet rushes. Nobles and their affinities, merchants
in silk, because of the growing heat; dozens of pages in
Charles's white puff-sleeved livery jackets, priests in
their somber browns and greens; and servants moving
rapidly from one group of people to another. The fresh-
ness of the early morning made voices lively—but with
a particular tone, she noted: solemn, grave and reverent.

Where's Godfrey when I need him?

Listening for intelligence, she overheard a tall man
discuss the virtues of bratchet bitches for hunting; two
knights speaking of a tournament combat over barriers;
and a large woman in an Italian silk robe talking about
honey glazes for pork.

The only political conversation Ash could hear was
between the French ambassador and Phillipe de Com-

mines:[8] it mostly involved the names of French Dukes with which she was not overly familiar.

So where's this court's factionalism and politics? Maybe I don't need Godfrey to feed me details, not here.

But I need Godfrey.

An automatic check behind assured her that Joscelyn van Mander was not only present, but sober and with his ego reasonably subdued, that her men-at-arms wore clean livery jackets over polished armor—or as polished as it was reasonable to expect, a week after fleeing two hundred leagues across winter country—and that Antonio Angelotti as well as Robert Anselm stood at her elbow. Robert, in respectful conversation with one of the de Vere brothers, didn't notice her glance. Angelotti grinned out at her from between a mass of tangled, golden curls. She beckoned him to the front of the group, reflecting, We might as well *look* good.

A stir at the far end of the presence hall drew attention.

Ash straightened, resisting an urge to stand on tiptoe. She saw a pennant at the great oak doors, and heard the liquid accents of Carthaginian Latin. Her hand dropped to her sword hilt for reassurance. She rested it there, standing with her weight casually back on one heel, as the chamberlain and his servants announced and brought in Sancho Lebrija, Agnus Dei and Fernando del Guiz.

The solemn grandeur of the Duke's court looked as though it were having some effect on Fernando del Guiz. He shifted uncomfortably in the open space before the dais, his eyes flicking around from face to face. Ash clasped her shaking hands behind her back. That his physical presence dried up her mouth and confused her thoughts was something she had almost grown used to.

---

[8] Phillipe de Commines or Commynes (1447–1511), historian and politician who first served the Burgundians, then betrayed them for the French. He became advisor to Louis XI four years previously, in AD 1472.

What confused her still further was her immediate pang at seeing him now, beleaguered, turn-coat, isolated from his own.

Beside her, the Earl of Oxford stood more erect. Ash came out of her reverie. It took her several seconds to pay attention to the Duke's voice. The early fog, still drifting in the high stone hall, cast a cool haziness over the gathered noblemen and rich merchants. The slanting eastern gold of the light fell in now through the rose windows of the palace, as the sun rose higher: warming Oxford's face, where he stood next to her, his head bowed to catch some comment of Robert Anselm's; bringing fire from Angelotti's Italian beauty; coloring the armor of Jan-Jacob Clovet and Paul di Conti with an antique sheen, so that to her eyes they seemed briefly all of a piece with Mynheer van Eyk's angels, dreaming through eternity in the presence of God.

Something tore at her heart. That feeling of their permanence, over and above earthly affairs, vanished. A feeling of fragility overtook her, as if her companions might be utterly valuable and at the same time utterly endangered.

The sun, rising higher, altered the angle of light in from the windows, and with that change the feeling was gone. Almost bereft, Ash turned her head to hear Duke Charles of Burgundy saying, "Master Lebrija, I have considered your request with my advisors. You ask us for a truce."

Sancho Lebrija made a stiff, formal bow. "Yes, lord Prince of Burgundy, we do."

The lugubrious face of the Duke was all but lost in the finery of rolled hat, dagged tail, puffed doublet sleeves, and golden neck-chains: a heirophantic image of courtliness. Abruptly he leaned forward on his throne, and Ash glimpsed the rich and powerful man with a keen affection for guns, who spent as many months of the year in the field as he could spare.

"Your 'truce' is a lie," Duke Charles said clearly.

A burst of noise: Ash's men around her speaking

loudly enough that she signaled them to silence, and leaned forward to hear the Duke.

"Your halt at Auxonne is not for a truce, it is to spy out my lands, and receive your reinforcements. You stand at our borders in darkness, armed for war, the atrocities of this summer behind you, and you ask us to sue for peace—to surrender, in all but name. No," Charles of Burgundy said. "If there were but one man of my people left to defend us, he would say, as I say, that right is with us, and where right is, there God must be also. For He will stand at our side in battle, and cast you down."

Ash bit back what would have been an automatically cynical mutter to Robert Anselm. The shaven-headed man had dragged his hat off, and stood gazing open-eyed at the richness of the Duke, surrounded by bishops, cardinals and priests.

The Duke's voice echoed back from the vaulted roof. "Right may sleep, but it does not rot in the earth as men's bodies do, or rust as the treasures of this world, but remains unchangeable. Your war is unjust. Rather than sue for peace, I will die here on the land that my father ruled, and his fathers before him. There is not a man of Burgundy, be he never so poor a peasant, nor a man who has asked sanctuary of Burgundy, who shall not be defended with all might, all main, and all the prayers that we may raise to God."

The hush was broken by the French ambassador stepping forward into the open space on the black-and-white tiled floor. Ash saw his left palm close around his sword-grip.

"My lord Duke," he glanced back at Phillipe de Commines in the mass of people, and went on, "cousin of our Valois King, this is sophistry and treachery."

No one spoke. Ash's mouth felt dry. Her stomach twisted.

The French noble's face went taut. "You hope, by this one threat, to make Burgundy seem a dangerous land to attack, and thus turn these invaders into my lands, and into the lands of King Louis! That is all your strategy! You wish this bitch Faris and her armies to weary themselves for the next few months fighting *us*. And then you'll defeat them, and pick up what lands you can from us—Charles of Burgundy, where is your liege loyalty to your King?"

Where, indeed? Ash thought ironically.

"Your King," Charles of Burgundy said, "will remember that I myself have bombarded Paris.[9] If I desired his kingdom, I would come and take it. You will be silent now."

Ash was aware of chamberlains and other court officials closing in around the ambassador as the Duke turned his attention back to Sancho Lebrija.

"I will not accede to your request," Charles added, with finality.

The Visigoth *qa'id* observed, "This is a declaration for war, then."

Ash, aware of her own escort's low-voiced comments, caught sight of the face of Olivier de la Marche. The big Burgundian captain began to smile with a whole-hearted, infectious joy.

"*Said* we needed a fight," Anselm growled, at her ear.

"Yeah, well, you might get one sooner than you expect." Ash looked at Sancho Lebrija; kept her gaze from Fernando del Guiz. "I'm not going to be handed over."

Anselm's quick look said, plainer than words, *Be real, girl! You don't have any choice.*

"No," Ash said gently, "you don't understand. I don't care if I have to take on the whole of this court, and Charles's army, and Oxford into the bargain: I am not going with them. The only way we're going across the middle sea is fully armed and eight hundred strong."

Anselm shifted his stance, with the air of a man settling himself into some decision. Abruptly, he muttered, "We'll get you out. If it comes to it."

Aware of shifting feet behind her, Ash thought *You*

---

[9] 1465.

*might but I'm not sure about van Mander* and moved to one side as the Earl of Oxford, summoned by the Duke's chamberlain, moved to the front of their group.

"Sire?" he said mildly.

"I am not your liege lord," Charles of Burgundy said, leaning back on his throne and ignoring the Visigoths, "but I pray that it will please you, my lord Oxford, to bring your company of men to the field, under my banner, when we ride to Auxonne?"

*Shit. So much for the raid.*

"Do it ourselves?" she murmured to Anselm.

"If you can fucking pay for it!"

"We can't *pay* for anything. We're only getting credit with our suppliers in Dijon because of Oxford's name."

Angelotti said something blunt in Italian, on the other side of Robert Anselm, that made Agnus Dei raise his black brows where he stood with the Visigoths.

"Honored," the Earl of Oxford agreed curtly. "Sire."

Sancho Lebrija moved forward, mail hauberk chinging. "Lord Prince of Burgundy, before there is war, there is the law. Our general has asked that you return to her her property, the bondswoman there." His gloved finger flicked out, indicating Ash. "The legal title of the House Leofric to this woman is clear. She is born of a slave mother, and a slave father." He repeated, "She is the property of House Leofric."

In the silence, Ash breathed deeply of the meadow-sweet smell of the flowers and rushes strewing the floor of the presence chamber. A tingle of apprehension dizzied her. She put it away from herself. Clear-headed, she lifted her scarred face and stared at the Burgundian Duke.

"He'll do it," she murmured to Anselm and Angelotti.

For only the second time since she had met him, Ash saw a wintry small smile on Charles of Burgundy's face.

"Ash," he said.

She stepped forward, beside Oxford, surprised to find that her legs were weak.

Gravely, the Duke said, "It has always pleased me to

hire mercenaries. For whatever reason, I would decline to let any experienced mercenary commander leave my forces. In this case, however, I do not hold your contract. That is held by an English lord. Over him, the laws of Burgundy have no jurisdiction."

Rapidly, solemnly, the Earl of Oxford rapped out, "I couldn't go against the wishes of the premier prince of Europe, Sire, and you *have* requested our presence on the field of battle . . ."

"I hear the sound of bucks being passed," Ash murmured. She kept a smile off her face with difficulty.

"You claimed *right*." Sancho Lebrija's harsh, battle-field voice cut through the courtliness. "You claimed right, lord Prince of Burgundy. 'Right may sleep, but it does not rot.' "

Oxford's stance warned Ash, changing from benevolent courtesy to alertness. She made herself look confident, aware that her men-at-arms were looking from her, to the Duke, to the Visigoths, and back to her.

"What is your point?" the Burgundian Duke asked.

"Right does not sleep. We have the right, the law, with us." Sancho Lebrija's pale eyes slitted, as the morning sun found the place where he and his white-robed men stood in the chamber. Light struck fire from mail, from belt-buckles, from the hilts of worn swords.

"Will you stand convicted of mere expediency, lord Prince of Burgundy? This is defying the law, for no more reason than you wish a few more hundred men for your forces. It is greed, not right. It is despotism, not the law."

He hesitated, breathless; then nodded curtly, as Fernando del Guiz said something at his ear.

"No one could fault you, lord Prince, for saying you fight a just war against us. But where is your justice, if you set the law aside as it pleases you? She belongs to the House Leofric. You know—it is known to all, by now—she has my general's face. She is her living image. Lord Fernando here will stand witness to it. You cannot deny her to be born of the same parentage. You cannot deny that she is a slave."

Lebrija halted, his eyes on the Duke, who did not speak. The Visigoth finished:

"As a slave, she has no legal right to sign a *condotta*, so it does not matter who she has signed one with."

Oxford's mouth made a bitter twist. He scowled, said nothing, looked to be furiously thinking.

"He's going to do it," Ash whispered to the two men beside her: Anselm sweating, his head aggressively down; Angelotti's hand on his dagger with deadly grace. "Maybe he won't do it for political advantage—maybe he's different from Frederick—but he's going to listen to Lebrija. He's going to hand me over because they *are* legally right."

Behind her, the small group of her officers, men-at-arms, and archers began to shift, spread out a little; some men checking how far they were standing from the doors of the presence chamber, and where the guards were.

"You got any ideas?" she added, to Oxford.

The Earl scowled blackly, his pale eyes puzzled. "Give me a minute!"

The noise of a clarion cut through the Ducal presence chamber: fine and high and clear. More knights in full harness, with axes, entered by the ornate doors, taking up their stations around the walls. Ash saw de la Marche give a satisfied nod of approval.

Charles of Burgundy spoke from his throne.

"What will your Faris-General do with the woman, Ash, when she has her?"

"*Do* with her?" Lebrija looked blank.

"Yes, do with her." The Duke folded his hands in his lap, neatly. Young and grave, a little pompous, he said, "You see, it is my belief you will hurt her."

"Harm her? Lord Prince, no." Lebrija had the face of a man realizing he sounded unconvincing. He shrugged. "Lord Prince, it is not your concern. The woman Ash is a House slave. You may as well ask if I mean harm to my horse when I ride it onto the field of battle."

Some of the Visigoth soldiers with Lebrija laughed. "What will you do with her?"

"My lord Prince, it is not your concern. It is for you to uphold the law. By law, she is ours."

Charles of Burgundy said, "That, I think, is certainly true."

The frustration that emanated from the men with her was all but tangible: they glared around at the armed Burgundians, swore; all internal dissent momentarily united. Anselm said something restraining to Angelotti.

"No!" Antonio Angelotti snapped. "I have *been* a slave in one of their *amirs'* houses. Madonna, I will do anything to keep you out of that!"

Robert Anselm snarled, "Master gunner, be silent!"

Ash stared across the chamber at Agnus Dei as Lamb slapped Sancho Lebrija congratulatorily on the back. Behind the Italian mercenary, Fernando del Guiz listened to some comment from his escort and smiled, throwing his head back, gold in the sunlight.

Her decision crystalized.

"I'm happy to kill all of the Visigoths here." Ash spoke steadily, loudly enough to be heard by Anselm, Angelotti, van Mander, Oxford and his brothers. "There are nine men. Take them out, now, fast; throw down our weapons—then let the Duke declare us outlaw. If they're dead, we'll just be thrown out of Burgundy, not handed over—"

"Let's do it." Anselm stepped forward; the men-at-arms in Lion livery moving as he did; Ash with them. She heard van Mander mutter something panicky about the guards—thought, in a acceptance, *yes, we'll take casualties*—and Carracci swear excitedly, saw Euen Huw and Rochester simultaneously grin, hard men reaching for their swords with reckless aggression.

"Wait!" the Earl of Oxford commanded.

The clarion rang out again. Charles, Duke of Burgundy, stood. As if there were no armed mercenaries ten yards from his throne, as if the armed guards were not moving to obey de la Marche's abrupt signal, he spoke.

"No. I will not order the woman Ash turned over to you."

Utterly affronted, Lebrija said, "But she is ours by *law*."

"That is true. Nonetheless, I will not give her to you."

Ash dimly felt Anselm's hand grip her arm, with painful force.

*"What?"* she whispered. "What did he just say?"

The Duke looked around, at his counselors, advisors, lawyers and subjects; a slight expression of satisfaction crossing his features as Olivier de la Marche bowed heavily, and indicated the armed men in the chamber.

"Furthermore, if you attempt to remove her by force, you will be prevented."

"Lord Prince, you are an insane man!"

"Fuck me, he's right," Ash said under her breath.

De Vere laughed out loud, and cuffed Ash's shoulder at much the same strength as he might one of his brothers. She had cause to be glad that she was wearing a brigandine: even so, she heard the riveted steel plates crunch.

Over what was an undoubted cheer from Ash's men, Charles of Burgundy addressed the Visigoth delegation:

"It is my will that the woman Ash stays here. So be it."

As if the Burgundian Duke, at least ten years his junior, was no more than a recalcitrant page, Sancho Lebrija exclaimed, "But you're *breaking the law*!"

"Yes. I am. Take this message to your masters—your Faris: I will continue to break the law, at all times, if the law is wrong." Stilted, and still a little pompous, Charles of Burgundy said, "Honor is above Law. Honor and chivalry demand we protect the weak. It would be morally wrong to give the woman to you, when every man listening here knows that you will butcher her."

Sancho Lebrija gazed up at him, utterly bemused.

"I don't get it." Ash shook her head, bewildered. "Where's the advantage? What's Charles getting out of this?"

"Nothing," the Earl of Oxford said, beside her, clasping his hands behind his back as if he had not just been drawing sword. He glanced keenly at her. "Absolutely nothing, madam. No political advantage. His action will be thought indefensible."

Ignoring the raucous pleasure of the Lion contingent, Ash gazed across the presence chamber at the Visigoth delegation, marching out flanked by Burgundian troops; and then at the throne, and at the Burgundian Duke.

"I don't *get* it," Ash said.

V

ASH CAME BACK to her command tent by a circuitous route. She spoke, on her way from fire-pit to fire-pit, to a hundred or more of the teenage males[10] who sat around drinking, talking inaccurately about their success with women, and even more inaccurately about the capabilities of their longbows or bills.

"It's war," she said, outwardly cheerful. And listened, both to what they said and didn't say; squatting by the flames that flickered invisibly in sunlight, drinking beer here, and eating a bowl of pottage there; listening to excited voices. Listening to what they had to say about war. About their surgeon. About the drumhead court's penalties after Josse's death.

She paid particular attention to that side of the camp that was made up of the thirteen or fourteen Flemish lances that had signed on with Joscelyn van Mander.

Arriving at her tent, she surveyed her officers' meeting. A tiny frown dinted her silver brows. She stepped

---

[10] The text gives us "iuventus," referring to young men between, say, sixteen and twenty; in our terms, these are teenagers.

outside again, picked up her escort of six men from (this time) an English knight's lance, and their dogs, and walked back down the straw-trodden paths between the tents and bashas.

"Di Conti," she called. Paul di Conti loped up, a broad grin on his sun-reddened face, and dropped to one knee in front of her. "I don't see you or the Flemish lance-leaders in my tent. Get your asses in gear; there's a meeting."

The Savoyard man-at-arms beamed up at her. In his soft accent, he said, "Sieur Joscelyn said he would attend in our places. Willem and I don't mind, nor the others. Sieur Joscelyn will pass on all we need to know."

*And di Conti's not even Flemish.* Ash made herself smile.

Di Conti, his grin fading slightly, added, "It saves us crowding in, boss!"

"Well, I guess it saves half of you sitting on my lap! Right." Ash abruptly about-faced, striding back to the center of camp.

Walking, thinking furiously, she did not at first notice herself being shadowed by a very large, dark-haired man. His skin was pale despite the south Burgundian sun, and his sparse beard black, and he stood—she continued to look up, and up—something above six foot high. One of the dogs yelped at him and he skipped, surprisingly lightly, to one side.

"You're . . . Faversham," she recalled.

"Richard Faversham," he confirmed, in English.

"You're Godfrey's assistant priest." She could not, for some reason, find the English term in her mind.

"Deacon. Do you wish me to hold Mass until Master Godfrey returns?" Richard Faversham asked, solemnly.

The Englishman was not much above her own age; sweating as he walked in the dark green robes of a priest, the sharp edges of cut straw spiking in vain against the hardened soles of his feet. One cheek had a small cross tattooed on it in blue ink. A clanking mass of saints' medals hung suspended around his neck. Ash, identi-

fying several prominent St. Barbaras,[11] thought he might
have the right idea.

"Yes. Has he notified you of when he's coming back
from," she crossed her fingers behind her back, "Dijon?"

Deacon Faversham smiled benevolently. "No, boss. I
make allowances for Master Godfrey's unworldliness. If
there is a poor man, or a sick man, and he's met them,
he'll stay until he's remedied their trouble."

Ash nearly choked, coming to a dead stop amid men-
at-arms, leashed hounds, tent guy-ropes, and the round
balls of sweet-smelling horse droppings. " 'Unworldly'?
*Godfrey?*"

Richard Faversham's small black eyes narrowed uncertainly against the sunlight. His voice, however, remained sure. "Master Godfrey will be a saint one day.
There's no billman so low, or whore so dirty, that he
won't bring them God's Bread and Wine. I've known
him minister to a sick child forty hours at a stretch—
and do the same with a sick hound. He'll be one of the
Community of Saints, when he dies."

Ash, her breath returning, managed to say, "Well, at
the moment, I could do with him on earth! If you see
him, tell him boss needs him *now*; meanwhile, go prepare for a Mass."

She moved on, back to the command tent, diverting
only once—to speak briefly to John de Vere; and the
visiting Olivier de la Marche, conveniently in conversation with the English Earl—and then stood under the
Lion Azure standard, in front of her tent, and called all
her officers out onto the open piece of ground.

They stumbled out into the bright Burgundian sun:
Geraint with his points undone and his split hose rolled
down to his calves, Robert Anselm in a breast and backplate; Angelotti in a white silk doublet—Ash muttered

---

[11] St. Barbara, a Roman saint previously appealed to for protection
against being struck by lightning, was adopted as the patron saint of
gunners, presumably on the grounds that one explosion is very like
another.

*"white!"* and *"silk!"* under her breath in equal amazement, noting her master gunner to be clean—and Joscelyn van Mander, blinking hooded eyes against the glare.

She lifted her arm. Euen Huw put a clarion to his mouth and blew for general assembly. She was not too surprised at the speed with which the men made their way to the empty ground at the center of camp, crowding it, pushing back into the open fire-break paths between the tents. Sometimes, she mused, the rumors of what I'm going to do get around before *I've* thought of it . . .

"Okay!" Ash pushed a squawking hen off an upturned barrel, at the foot of the Lion Azure standard, and sprang neatly up on top of it. She put her hands on her hips. The blue and gold standard hung, stiffened, above her, no breeze to ripple it on the air, but you couldn't have everything, she thought, and let her gaze travel across the crowd, picking out faces here and there, smiling as she did so.

"Gentlemen," she said, projecting only enough that they had to be quiet to hear her. "Gentlemen—and I use the term loosely—you will be pleased to hear that we're going to war again."

A muted rumble greeted this, part pleasure, part groans of dismay (some of them genuine).

Ash did not know what her grin did to her face as she stood there facing them, did not quite realize how it made her face blaze with brightness, with a sincere content. It broadcast, in the anticipation of a battle, her absolute (if unconscious) certainty that all was right with the world.

"We're going to fight a battle against the Visigoths," she called. "Partly because we like the sun here in Burgundy! Mostly because my lord the Earl of Oxford is *paying* us to do this. But mainly," she added emphasis, "mainly we're fighting the Visigoth bitch because *I want my fucking armor back!*"

What had been raucous, deep male laughter and

cheers came together as a shout of laughter, and a loud yell of triumph that almost jarred the earth under the upturned barrel. Ash held up both arms over her head. There was a silence.

"What about Carthage?" Blanche called from one of the wagons.

*What did I say about rumor?*

"That can wait!" Ash made herself grin. "Three or four days and we fight a field against the rag-heads. I've got you an advance on your pay. Your duties for the rest of today are to go out and get rat-arsed, and fuck every whore in Dijon twice! I don't—" The loudest roar of noise overwhelmed her, she tried to make herself heard, gave up, grinning so hard it hurt; and at the first drop in the sound level, completed what she had been going to say: "I don't want to see a sober man wearing the Lion Azure tonight!"

A Welsh voice shouted, "No danger of that, boss!"

Ash raised a silver brow at Geraint ab Morgan. "Did I say that included officers? I don't *think* so."

The noise at this was, if anything, louder than before; eight hundred male voices baying with pure pleasure. Ash felt herself lifted up on the adrenalin.

"Okay—whoa! I said, whoa! Shut *up*!" Ash took a breath. "That's better. Go get pissed. Go get laid. Those of you that *do* come back are going to fight a battle, and give the rag-heads fucking *hell*." She slammed a hand against the standard-pole, shaking the folds of the silk above her. "Remember, I don't want you guys to die for your flag—I want you to make the Visigoths die for theirs!"

There was a cheer for that, and men at the back of the crowd began to drift away. Ash nodded once to herself, and turned around precariously on the barrel. "Mynheer van Mander!"

That stopped most of them moving. Joscelyn van Mander stepped forward from the officers' group, his movements uncertain. He glanced around. Ash saw him make eye-contact with Paul di Conti and half a dozen Flemish lance-leaders.

"Come here." She beckoned, insistently. As soon as he came within reach, she bent down and seized his hand, shook it firmly, and turned to the men crowding in close, and held the Flemish knight's arm up with hers. "This man! I am going to do something I haven't done before—" she leaned forward and embraced the startled van Mander, her cheek against his rough cheek.

Deep voices whooped, in startlement and glee. Those men-at-arms and knights who had begun to drift off pushed back into the central ground. A thunder of questions arose.

"Okay!" Ash spun around, holding both hands up again, and getting silence. "I want to publicly acknowledge my debt to this man. Here and now! He's done great things for the Lion Azure. The only thing is— there's nothing else I can teach him!"

Flemish men-at-arms, deliriously proud, banged fists against breastplates, their faces alight. Van Mander's broad features were caught halfway between pride and apprehension. Ash kept herself from grim laughter. *Get out of this one, sonny . . .*

Waiting while the noise died down again, she watched Paul di Conti's face, the other lance-leaders. And Joscelyn van Mander's expression.

*Your officers don't take orders from me now, they take orders from you. Therefore they are not my officers . . .*

*Therefore, they have no reason to be in my camp.*

"Sir Joscelyn," she said, strongly and formally, "there is a time for the apprentice and the journeyman to leave the master. I have taught you everything I know. It is no longer for me to command you. It is time now for you to lead your own company."

She gauged the quality of the hush that followed; judged it satisfactory.

She swung her arm around, indicating the assembled troops. "Joscelyn, there are twenty lances, two hundred

Flemish men here, who will follow you. I myself began
the Lion Azure with no smaller number of men."

"But I don't want to leave the Lion Azure," van Mander blurted.

Ash kept a smile on her face.

*Of course you don't. You'd rather stay as a significant
number of men and officers in my company, and try and
sway the way I run it. That's why you want a weak
leader—you get all the power and none of the responsibility.*

*Put you on your own and you're a very small number
of men, with no influence whatsoever, and the buck
stops with you. Well, tough. I've had enough of this
company-within-a-company. I've had enough of things
I can't trust—Stone Golem included. I certainly won't
take a split company into a battle in four days' time . . .*

Joscelyn van Mander began frowning. "I won't
leave."

"I have—" Ash spoke loudly over him, getting their
attention again. "I have spoken to my lord of Oxford,
and my lord Olivier de la Marche, Duke's Champion of
Burgundy."

A pause to let that sink in.

"If you wish, Sir Joscelyn, my lord Oxford will give
you a contract with him. Or, if you want to be employed
on the same terms as Cola de Monforte and his sons,"—
she saw the famous names of these mercenaries hit home
among the Flemish lances, and moreover, saw van Mander see it—"*then Charles, Duke of Burgundy, will employ you direct.*"

The Flemish knights roared. Looking around, Ash
could already judge which of the Flemish men-at-arms
would be sneaking back into the Lion Azure camp tonight under assumed names; and which English billmen
would be speaking fluent Walloon under Olivier de la
Marche's direct command.

Ash shifted her weight back onto one heel. The upturned barrel was solid beneath her. She let the warm
air blow over her face, and, with one finger to the mail

standard at her neck, let a little air into the sweaty warmth of her neck. Joscelyn van Mander looked up, his lips pressed together into a thin line. She could make a guess at the words he was holding back—would have to hold back, now, or precipitate a public quarrel.

*Which will have the same effect: he and his lances will have to leave.* Ash let her gaze travel over the heads of the men-at-arms, and the crowding support staff from the wagons; reckoning up with a practiced eye how clean a split it might be.

*Better five hundred men I can trust than eight hundred I'm doubtful about.*

A hand tugged the skirt of her doublet. Ash looked down.

Richard Faversham, deacon, said in his high English voice, "Might we hold a celebratory Mass, to pray for God's good fortune on this newly made company of the Flemish knights?"

Ash surveyed Faversham's face, boyish despite the black beard. "Yes. Good idea."

She lifted a fist for attention, got it, and projected her voice out to the edges of the crowd to make this known. Her own attention remained on Joscelyn van Mander, huddled in a knot with his officers. She checked by line of sight where her escort was, where her dogs were, and the impassive expressions of Robert Anselm and Geraint and Angelotti. Nowhere in the packed mass of people could she pick out Florian de Lacey, or Godfrey Maximillian.

*Fuck*, she thought, and turned back to find Paul di Conti raising, on a billshaft, a hastily tied livery coat—one of van Mander's original ones: the Ship and Crescent Moon. This makeshift standard lifted into the air, the better part of the two hundred men that Ash had earmarked for this began to move toward it.

"Before you leave the camp," she said, "we will hear Mass, and pray for your souls, and for ours. And pray that we meet again, Mynheer van Mander, in four days, with the army of the Visigoths lying dead on the earth between us."

As Deacon Faversham raised his voice to order things, Ash got down from the barrel, and found herself standing beside John de Vere, Earl of Oxford.

The Earl turned from a conversation with Olivier de la Marche. "More news, madam Captain. The Duke's intelligence brings him word that the Visigoth lines are overstretched—their supplies liable to be cut off. There are Turkish troops a scant ten miles from here."

*"Turks?"* Ash stared at the Englishman. He, composed, and with a glint of excitement in his faded blue eyes, murmured, "Yes, madam. Six hundred of the Sultan's cavalry."

"Turks. Fuck me." Ash took two steps on the rough turf and straw, ignoring the crowd of men; swung around, her gaze elsewhere, calculating. "No, it makes sense! It's exactly what I'd do, if I were the Sultan. Wait for the Carthaginian army to commit itself, take out their supply lines, get them cut up by us, and pick up the pieces . . . Does Duke Charles *really* think he won't have a Turkish army on his doorstep, the morning after we beat the Visigoths?"

"He is anxious," the Earl said gravely, "to have an army left, to take the field against them. He is calling his priests to him, now."

Ash absently crossed herself.

"For the rest," de Vere added, "the bulk of his army will march south, detachments moving today and tomorrow: we move with the rest of the mercenaries, the morning after next. Leave a base camp here. Get your men ready for a forced march. We will see, madam, how much of a commander you are without your saints."

Forty-eight hours passed in chaos, herded into order by the Lion's officers: neither Ash nor any man in the command group slept more than two hours.

Yellow clouds massed on the western horizon, flickering with summer lightning. Humid heat increased.

Men scratched under constricting armor, swore; fights broke out over loading kit onto packhorses. Ash was everywhere. She listened to three, four, five different voices at a time, gave orders, responded, checked supplies, checked weapons; dealt with the provosts and gate-guards.

She held her final command meeting in the armory tent, in the stink of charcoal, fires, soot, and the banging of munition harness being hammered out rough and ready.

"Green Christ!" Robert Anselm yelled, wiping his streaming forehead. "Why can't it fucking rain?"

"You want to march this lot in bad weather? We're *lucky*!"

The oppressiveness of the storm nonetheless made Ash's head throb. She shifted, uncomfortably, as Dickon Stour strapped a new greave to her shins, the metal rough and black from the forge. She flexed her knee to the ninety-degree angle that that armor allowed.

"No, it's cutting into the back of my knee." She watched him undo roughly riveted straps. "Leave it: I've got boots, I'll just wear upper leg harness and poleyns."

"I got you a breastplate." Dickon Stour turned, picked it up, held it out in black hands. "I've cut the arm-holes back?"

There is not time to forge a new harness. She turned, let him hold it against her, brought her arms together in front of her as if she gripped a sword. The breastplate's edges rammed into her inner arms. "Too wide. Cut it back again. I don't care about rolled edges on the metal, I just want something I can wear for four hours, that'll deflect arrows."

The armorer grunted discontentedly.

"Have the Great Duke's men gone?"

"Moved out at dawn," Geraint ab Morgan shouted, over the noise of arrow-heads being hammered out, at production-line speed.

In these forty-eight hours, nearly twenty thousand men and supplies have gone south: it will take them until

the feast-day of the saint to cover the forty miles between here and Auxonne, here and the Faris's army.
Empty dust, mud, and trodden common ground surrounds Dijon. The town and the country for miles
around are stripped of supplies.

Summer thunder rumbled, all but inaudible under the
sharp clangs of the armorers hammering out arrow-heads
by the hundred. Ash thinks briefly of the road south. A
few miles down the river-valley and Dijon will be behind them: there is nothing but a few farms, villages in
clearings in the forest, and great swathes of empty pasture, common land, and wilderness. An empty world.

"Okay—two hours and we ride."

Traveling south, the land grows colder.

By evening, ten miles south of Dijon, Ash rode aside
from the long column of men and packhorses, spurring
her riding horse up onto a rise. Smudges of black rose
from fields ahead.

"What's that?" She leaned down to Rickard as the boy
ran up.

"They're trying to save the vines!"

"*Vines?*"

"I asked this old guy? They had frost here last night.
They're making smoky fires in the vineyard, trying to
keep the frost from forming tonight. Otherwise there'll
be no harvest."

Two or three men-at-arms were riding out from the
column: further orders needed. Ash spared one more
glance for the hillsides and the vineyards, row upon long
row of cropped vines clinging to the earth; and the distant figures of peasants moving between the smudge-
fires.

"Damn; no wine," she said. Turning her horse, she
noted Rickard had four or five fresh coney-carcasses
slung off his belt.

"This will be a bad year," the Earl of Oxford remarked, bringing his barrel-chested gelding up with her.

"I'll tell the lads we're fighting for the wine harvest. *That'll* make them kick Visigoth ass!"

The English Earl narrowed his gaze, staring at the countryside to the south. One church's double spire marked an isolated village. For the rest, there was nothing but forests, uncultivated land; the road to Auxonne clearly marked by deep ruts, horse-droppings, trodden grass and the debris of an army passing.

"At least we shan't ride astray," Ash ventured.

"Twenty thousand is an unwieldy number of men, madam."

"It's more than she's got."

The evening sky darkened in the east. And now, perceptibly, darkened in the south as well: a shadow that did not fade with any day's dawn, the closer they drew to Auxonne.

"So that is the Eternal Twilight," the Earl of Oxford said. "It grows, the closer we come."

On the eve of the twenty-first of August, the Lion encampment stretched under the overhang of the wildwood three miles west of Auxonne. Ash picked her way between makeshift shelters, and men queuing for the evening rations, being careful to seem cheerful whenever she spoke to anyone.

Henri Brant, the chief groom with him, walked up to ask, "Will we fight before tomorrow morning? Shall we start feeding the war-horses up in preparation?"

Even trained war-horses are still herbivores who need to constantly graze for strength. More than an hour's fight, and they will lose stamina.

A thunder-purple sky was just visible through the oak leaves above her head; humid air moved against her skin. Ash wiped her face. "Assume the horses will need to be fit to fight any hour between dawn and nine, tomorrow. Start giving them the enriched feed."

"Yes, boss."

Thomas Rochester and the rest of her escort had fallen into conversation, under the trees, with Blanche and some of the other women. Ash breathed in, realized *No one is asking me questions! Amazing!* and then let out a sigh.

Shit. I preferred it when I didn't have time to think.

And there's still something to do.

"I'm not going far," she said to the nearest man-at-arms. "Tell Rochester I'm in the physic-tent."

Floria's tent stood a few yards away. Ash stumbled over guy-ropes tethering it to tree-trunks, in the root-knotted soil, as the sky yellowed and the first big drops of cold rain dropped onto the leaves above.

"Boss?" Deacon Faversham said, emerging from the tent.

Concealing apprehension, Ash said, "Is the master surgeon there?"

"She's inside." The Englishman did not seem at all uncomfortable.

Ash nodded an acknowledgment, and ducked under the tent-flap he held up. Inside, by the light of a number of lanterns, she saw not an empty tent, as she had feared, but half a dozen men on pallets. Their conversation stopped abruptly, then picked up in undertones.

"We're moving too fast." Floria del Guiz, bandaging an arm fracture, didn't look up. "In my office, boss."

Ash, with a word to the injured men—two crushed foot injuries, from loading sword-boxes onto pack-horses; one burn; one self-inflicted injury with a dagger, falling over when drunk—went through the inner, empty chamber of the pavilion, to the small curtained-off area at the far end.

Rain rattled on the tent-roof. She used flint and tinder to light a candle, lit the remaining lanterns with that, and was just done when Floria pulled the curtain aside, entering and sitting down with a curt grunt.

Going directly to it, Ash said, "Men with injuries are still coming to the company surgeon, then?"

Floria raised her head, hair falling back from her face. "I've had nineteen hurt men in here, the last two days. You'd think no one ever hit me—!"

She broke off, and put her dirty fingers together, fingertip to fingertip.

"Ash, you know what? They've decided not to think about it. Not for now. Maybe, when they've been hacked up, they won't care who's sewing them back together. But maybe they will."

Floria looked up sharply at Ash.

"They don't treat me as a man now. Nor as a woman. A eunuch, maybe. A neuter."

Ash pulled up a back-stool and sat down, silent while one of the lay assistants came to pour wine, and bring Floria a light cloak against the summer night's chill.

Ash said carefully, "We'll be fighting tomorrow. Everybody's too busy, right now, preparing. Most of the troublemakers went with van Mander. The rest can either lynch you—or have their lives saved when they're injured. In a lot of ways, we need this fight."

The woman surgeon snorted. She reached out for wine, in an ash-wood cup. "Do we, Ash? Do we need to see those young men chopped and stabbed and stuck with arrows?"

"That's war," Ash said levelly.

"I know. I could always work elsewhere. Plague towns. Lazar-houses. Jewish children, that Christian physicians won't touch." Shadows from the swinging lamps made the woman's features merciless. "Maybe tomorrow will be worth it."

"This isn't Arthur's last battle," Ash said cynically. "This isn't Camlann. We don't beat them here and then they pack up and go home. Winning the field doesn't give us the war, even if we wipe them out."

"So what does happen?"

"We've got nearly a two-to-one advantage. I'd prefer three, but we'll beat them. Charles's army is probably the best, most-advanced left in Christendom."

Unspoken, Ash's thought is *But the Faris beat the Swiss.*

"Maybe we kill the Faris, maybe we don't. Either way, if she's defeated here, she doesn't have much of an army left, and her momentum's gone. It's one of those things: once they've *been* beaten, then they can be beaten."

"And then?"

"And then there's two more Carthaginian armies out there." Ash grinned. "Either they do pick a soft target—maybe France—or they dig in over winter, or they fall out with the Sultan. The last one's ideal. Then it isn't Burgundy's problem anymore. Or Oxford's. He goes back to the *goddams'* wars."

"And we go and get paid by the Sultan?"

"By any side but hers," Ash confirmed.

Acute, and unwelcome, Florian said, "You want to speak to her again. Don't you?"

"I can get by without a machine's voice in my head. I've been fighting since I was twelve." Ash sounded harsh. "What does it matter, in practical terms? What can she tell me, Florian? What can she tell me that I don't already know?"

"How and why you came to be born?"

"What does that matter? I grew up in camps," Ash said, "like an animal. You don't know about that. I feed my baggage train, I don't let them sink or swim on what they can plunder when the soldiers have had the best of it. The only time someone will starve is when we *all* starve."

"But the Faris is your . . ." Floria paused, questioningly. "Sister."

"Several times over, possibly," Ash said, ironically. "She's quite mad, Florian. She sat there and told me, her father breeds sire to dam, and daughter to son—she means he breeds slave-children back to their parents. Generations of the sin of incest. Christ, I wish Godfrey was here."

"Every village has *that*."

"But not so—" Ash groped in vain for the word *systematically*.

"Their scientist-magi have given Christendom most of the medical skills I learned," Floria said, "Angelotti learned his gunnery from an *amir*."

"And so?"

"And so, your *machina rei militaris* isn't evil." Floria shook her head. "Godfrey never said it was a sin, did he? If you haven't got the use of it, that's sad; but never mind, you can do your butchery quite well on your own, we all know that."

"Mmm."

Floria said bluntly, "Is it true Godfrey's left the company?"

"I—don't know. I haven't seen him in days. Not since we left Dijon."

"Faversham told me he'd seen him with the Visigoths."

"*With* the Visigoths? The delegation?"

"Talking to Sancho Lebrija." When Ash said nothing, the woman added, "I can't see Godfrey going over to them. What is this, Ash? What's going on with you and him?"

"If I could tell you, I would." Ash got up and walked restlessly around. Deliberately changing the subject, she said, "The town militia never came out to the camp. Mistress Châlon must have kept quiet."

Staccato, Floria snapped, "She would. She'd have to admit I'm her niece. She won't do that. I'm safe enough if I stay away from Dijon. If I claim nothing from her."

"You still think of yourself as Burgundian," Ash realized.

"Oh yes."

Floria's dark gaze felt oddly foreign, Ash thought, bearing in mind that none of them had what might be termed a nationality. She smiled. "I don't think of myself as Carthaginian. Not after all this time. I always assumed I was Christendom's bastard."

Floria chuckled, deeply, and poured more wine.

"War doesn't have a kingdom," she said. "War belongs to the whole world. Come on, my little scarlet Horseman. Have a drink."

She stood, unsteadily, and walked behind Ash, a hand on her shoulder, to put the cup down in front of her.

"I didn't thank you for seeing those guys off," she said.

Ash gave a modest shrug, leaning back against Florian.

"Well, thanks anyway." Florian dipped her head. Her lips pressed, very lightly and quickly, against Ash's mouth.

"Christ!" Ash sprang up and pushed her way out of what seemed to be encircling female arms. "Christ!"

"What?"

Ash wiped the back of her hand across her mouth. "Christ!"

*"What?"*

An expression came to Ash's face that she was entirely unaware of: flat, cynical, tense. Her eyes, blank, seemed to be seeing something quite different from her surgeon.

"I'm not your little Margaret Schmidt! What is this? You think you can seduce me like your brother?"

Floria del Guiz stood up slowly. She went to say something, stopped, and spoke with restraint. "You're talking complete nonsense, Ash. This is—nonsense. And leave my brother out of this!"

"Everybody wants something." Ash, standing with her arms limp by her sides, shook her head. Above, the canvas cone of the tent roof shifted, under the drumming of chill rain.

Floria del Guiz made as if to reach out and thought better of it. She sat back.

"Ah." Floria stared at her toes. She paused, then, looking up, said, "I don't seduce my friends."

Ash stared at her in silence.

"One day," Floria added, "I'll tell you about being kicked out of my home at thirteen, and going to Salerno, dressed as a man, because I'd heard they let women study there. Well, I was wrong. Things have changed since Trotula's day.[12] And I'll tell you why Jeanne

---

[12] The 11th century Dame Trotula of Salerno was a clinician, and the

Châlon, who is my mother in all but name, commands no 'loyalty' from me whatsoever. Boss, you're all to pieces. Come on." Floria gave a lopsided grin. "Ash, *honestly*!"

The scorn in that brought color to Ash's face, partly from shame, partly from relief; and she shrugged with an attempt at carelessness. "It's been a rough few days, I'll give you that. Floria, I'm sorry. It was a genuinely stupid thing for me to say."

"Mmm-hmm." Floria flirted an eyebrow at her, over-doing the naturalness somewhat. "C'mon."

Ash turned, moving toward the tent-flap, and standing looking out. From this point, under the edge of the trees, it was possible to see the fires of the main Burgundian army, further south, and the growing silver of the moon.

*About two days before first quarter*, she thought, au-tomatically estimating its swelling curve.

It *is* only a few weeks. Christ, so much has happened! What is it, about the middle of August now? And the skirmish at Neuss was the middle of June. Two months. Hell, I've only been *married* for six weeks—

"Hey." Floria's voice came from behind her, in the tent. "Have more wine."

The moon rising over the eastern hills blurred silver in Ash's field of vision.

"Boss?"

She turned around, everything suddenly sharp and clear: the painted anatomy charts hanging on the tent walls; Floria's face with the casual laughter falling from it. The kind of clarity that comes with shock or combat, she thought, and said, "Florian, did I pass blood when I was ill?"

Floria del Guiz shook her head, frowning. "No, I

author of *Passionibus Mulierum Curandorum (The Diseases of Women)*, among other medical works. She was regarded as one of the foremost medical authorities of the medieval period. Other "mulieres Salernitanae" or woman physicians were also trained in Salerno, but this practice may have ceased by the 15th century.

watched. There was no flux of blood at all. It wasn't that kind of injury."

Ash shook her head dumbly.

"Christ," she said at last. "Not that kind of blood. Woman's blood. I've missed twice, this month and last month. I'm pregnant."

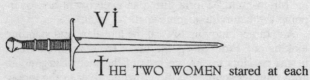

## VĮ

THE TWO WOMEN stared at each other.

"Didn't you use something?" Floria demanded.

"Of course I did! Do you think I'm stupid? Baldina gave me a charm to wear. As a wedding present. I had it in a little bag around my neck, both times we—every time." Ash felt the close evening air bring sweat out on her forehead. Her injury throbbed dully.

She saw Floria del Guiz survey her: did not know that the woman was seeing a young girl in hose and a big doublet; sword belted at her side, and gloves tucked under the belt; nothing female about her except her cascade of hair, and her face, momentarily looking all of twelve years old.

"You used a charm." Floria's voice sounded flat. She spoke quietly, as if afraid they could be heard outside the command pavilion. "You didn't use a sponge, or a pig's bladder, or herbs. You used a charm."

"It's always worked before!"

"Thank *Christ* I don't have to worry about any of this! I wouldn't touch a man if—" Floria took two or three quick steps, back and forth on the boards laid down against mud, her arms tucked tightly about her body. She stopped in front of Ash. "You feel sick at all?"

"I thought that was the head injury."

"Tits tender?"

Ash considered. "I guess."

"And you bleed what time of the moon?"

"It's been the last quarter, most of this year."

"When did you last bleed?"

Ash frowned, thinking back. "Just before Neuss. Sun was still in Gemini."

"I'll have to look at you. But you're pregnant." Floria spoke with conclusive abruptness.

"You're going to have to give me something!"

"What?"

Ash reached behind herself with one hand, touching the back-stool, and slid down to a sitting position, adjusting her scabbard. She brought her hands around in front of her, clasping them first across her belly, and then around the grip of her sword. "You're going to have to give me something to get rid of it!"

The blond woman dropped her arms to her sides. The lantern swung, as the tent creaked in the night wind. She squinted uncertainly into the light at Ash's face. "You haven't thought about this."

"I've thought!" Cold inside, flooded by terror, Ash gripped the leather-bound wood of her sword-hilt and stared down at the faceted, wheel-shaped pommel. She had a sudden urge to draw the blade, and cut. An urge to proclaim that her self is still her self. She tried to feel any sensation inside her body, to feel a difference, and felt nothing. No sense that she might be carrying a fetus.

"I can give you herbs in wine, to calm you down," Floria said. "Let me send Rickard for my kit."

With that note of caution, of professional calming of an overwrought patient, Ash's rage flared. She stood up. "I'm not going to be treated like some whore off the street! I will not have this baby."

"You'll have it." Floria del Guiz took hold of her arm.

"I will not. You'll have to cut it out of me." Ash shook herself free. "Don't tell me there's no surgery for that. When I was growing up in the wagons, any woman

who would have died from another baby got rid of it by
the company surgeon."

"No. I've sworn an oath." Floria's voice became flat,
angry, tired. "You remember your *condotta*? This is
mine. 'Never to procure an abortion.' For anybody!"

"And now they know you're a woman, they say you
haven't got the wit to take an oath. *That*'s what your
fraternity of doctors think of you!" Ash shifted her blade
an inch out of the scabbard, and banged it home. "I will
not have that man's child!"

"You're sure it's his, then?"

The slap was deliberate, a solid whack across the face
that left Floria's cheek bright red, and her eyes running
water. Ash yelled, "*Yes*, it's his!"

Floria's dirty face shone, some emotion twisting her
features that Ash couldn't identify. "It's a legitimate
baby. Christ, Ash. It could be my nephew! My niece!
You can't ask me to kill it."

"It's not quickened, it hasn't kicked, it's *nothing*."
Ash glared. "You didn't understand me, did you? Listen
to me: I will not have this baby. If you won't abort it,
I'll find someone who can, *I will not have this baby*."

"No? You'll come round. Trust me." Floria shook her
head. Snot ran clear from her nostril, and she wiped her
sleeve across her face, leaving a smear of clean skin.
She laughed, a break in her voice: "You won't have it?
Not when it's his, and you can't keep your hands off
him?"

Ash's mouth remained a little open; she said nothing.
Her mind struggled, racing for a reply. A sudden picture
came into her mind of a small child, about three years
of age, with solemn green eyes and flaxen hair. A child
to run about the camp, fall off horses, cut itself on the
edges of weapons, be sick of a fever, die maybe in a
famine some lean year; a child that would have the same
features as Fernando del Guiz, and maybe the same humor as Floria—

She met the eyes of Floria del Guiz and said with
utter certainty, "You're jealous."

"You think I want a baby."

"Yes! And you never will have." Conscious of saying the unforgivable, powered more by fear than rage, Ash plunged on in razor-edged sarcasm: "What are you going to do, get Margaret Schmidt pregnant? A niece or nephew is as close as you'll get."

"That's true."

"Uh." Ash, expecting her rage, was confused. "I'm sorry I said it, but it's true, isn't it?"

"Jealous." Floria looked at Ash with an expression that might have been sardonic humor, or relief, or betrayal; or all three. "Because I won't cut a baby out of your belly. Woman, I don't want to see you bleed to death or die of childbed fever; but for Christ's sake *have* the thing! You won't die. You're strong as a bloody peasant, you can probably drop it one day and get back on your war-horse the next. Don't you understand that getting rid of it is *dangerous*?"

"A battlefield isn't *safe*!" Ash remarked with asperity. "Look, I'd as soon not go to a city doctor, I don't trust them, money-grubbing bastards, and besides, there isn't time to get one now. I don't want to use the remedies they use on the wagons unless I have to. And I trust you because you've patched me up every time someone's hacked a chunk out of me!"

"Holy Saint Magdalen! Are you completely stupid? You—might—die."

"Am I supposed to be impressed? I train for that every day. I'm fighting tomorrow!"

Floria del Guiz opened her mouth and shut it again.

Unhappy, Ash said, "I don't want to give you an order."

"An order?" Floria's face, in profile, dripped a clear drop from her eye, that still ran from Ash's blow. She didn't look at Ash. "And what are you going to do if I *don't* perform an abortion? Throw me out of the company? But you'll have to do that anyway."

"Christ, Florian, no!"

Her hand came up and grabbed Ash's arm. "It isn't

'Florian,' it's 'Floria,' I'm a *woman*. I love other women!"

"I know that," Ash said, hastily. "Look, I—"

"You don't know it!" Floria let go of Ash's arm. She stood for a moment with her head lowered, and then turned her face to Ash. "You don't have the slightest idea, don't tell me you do. What am I supposed to do when people go mad around me, because I've lain with a woman? What? I can't *fight* them. I couldn't hurt them even if I did! I *have* to pretend I'm something I'm not. What if someone decides to burn me because I'm a woman-lover and I practice medicine?"

Ash shifted uncomfortably.

Floria del Guiz held out her hands, palm up.

In the cool air and lantern light, Ash saw familiar white marks on the surgeon's fingers.

Floria said, "These are burn scars. Old burns. I got them trying to drag—trying to drag something out of a fire, after it was much too late, because I wanted just something, a relic, a memory, if I couldn't have her alive, with me, with me." Floria pushed her hands across her face, sweat and tears dampening her hair. "Some man *pissed* on you once and you think you know about this? Don't you tell me you know what it's like, you thug, because you *don't* know! You've never been defenseless in your life!"

The empty air echoed to her shout. Outside the tent, the guards stirred. Ash walked to the tent-flap, to give quiet orders.

Floria del Guiz spat, "So now you've having a baby. So welcome to being a woman!"

"Christ, Floria," Ash protested.

She didn't let Ash finish. "Maybe you shouldn't have been so damn eager to fuck my brother!"

Ash could only look at her. Between amazement and the shock of feeling kicked in the gut, she couldn't put her thoughts in order to find an answer, couldn't say anything at all.

"I'd do anything for you! I always have. But I won't

do this!" Floria's voice scaled up an octave. "Don't just sit there! *Say something!*"

Ash stared in panicked silence; tried to speak; then dropped her gaze from the woman's fierce face and stared down at the rush-strewn forest-earth.

Clear and decisive, the thought came into her head: *I should tell Fernando.*

But if it's a son, he'll take it away from me.

And I can't have it, anyway.

More than one woman's ridden into battle with a belly on her.

Yes, and more than one woman's got a fever after the birth and died, and the surgeons no use to her at all.

Equally clearly, a realization came to her: I won't have it *because* it's his.

Floria's voice snarled, *"Ash!"*

Ash ignored her.

Very cautiously, she began to consider the thought of carrying the baby to term.

*It isn't that long out of my life. Months. Bad timing, though, if we're facing war . . . well, women have fought wars like this before. They'd still follow me. I'd make damn sure of it.*

The strength of her fear of her body changing out of her control, the sheer enormity of that physical reality, left her amazed. *But when it's done? Born?* Conscious that she was, to some degree, indulging herself in a pretty dream, Ash imagined a son or a daughter.

At least then I'll have blood kin. Someone who looks like me.

With that, a chill quite literally moved the hairs on the back of her neck.

You've already got someone who looks like you. *Exactly* like you.

And who knows what I'd give birth to? Some deformed village idiot? Christ and all the saints, no! I can't give birth to a monster.

It could already be almost forty days. I've got to get rid of it now, before it quickens.

Before it gets a soul.

The woman's voice abruptly broke her concentration:

"I'm off. What am I supposed to do? Wait for you forever? Sit around here until those assholes out there make up their minds whether a dyke doctor is just fine and dandy? *Keep* your damn company."

Floria turned and walked away, to the tent flap; not slowing as she went out.

"*And* your baby! It's your problem, Ash. Solve it. You don't need me. Ash doesn't need anybody! I'll be with the Duke's Surgeon-General on the field tomorrow—where I can do what I trained for."

Before dawn, with the woods scarcely light enough to move without stumbling, Ash went out with the other commanders to walk the ground for the battle.

Air moved against her face. Condensation gathered on the inside of her helmet's visor, smelling of rust and armories. Her boots skidded on the wet leaves. She almost barged into the Earl of Oxford, standing back a little from the main group of the Duke of Burgundy and his officers on the main Dijon–Auxonne road. A growing paleness on her left showed her John de Vere's silhouette.

Ash asked quietly, "Is the Visigoth army still in position? What's the Duke planning?"

"They are. The Duke will fight this field outside Auxonne," Oxford murmured succinctly. He added, "Their campfires are where the scouts reported, near enough. A half-mile south, on the main road. You and I, madam, are to take the left of the line, with his other mercenaries."

"He doesn't trust us, does he? Or he'd put us on the right, where the fighting's heaviest."[13] Ash slid her hand down to adjust the buckle of her cuisse: even with an extra hole bored in the strap, the borrowed leg-armor did

---

[13] Since most combatants are right-handed, close combat battles tend to rotate counterclockwise.

not fit her very well. "Will he at least let us try a flying wedge attack? We could take out the Faris."

"The Duke says not: she will have battle doubles[14] on the field."

The silhouettes of shoulders moved against the light. Here the road and river swung suddenly away east, on her left hand, away from the shallow slope blocking the river valley to the south. Men moved off the road, onto rough pasture, striding up the hill in front of them. The sky was barely brighter than the earth. Ash realized de Vere's brothers were with him; peered over her shoulder for Anselm—present—and a bleary-eyed Angelotti.

"Okay," Ash said steadily to Oxford, as they stumbled into the cold morning, "so we might have to take her out several times! Let me put a snatch-squad together, my lord. Go around the flanks with about a hundred of us, we could be in and out and away. It's been done."

"The Duke requests that I bring your company to the field, under his banner," Oxford said, voice bleak. "We do as we're commanded. And hope that by this evening it is no longer necessary to think about raiding Carthage."

The ground lifted under her feet. Dew blackened the leather of her boots, and the lower part of her scabbard. The air remained chill, but clear: no more rain.

"My lord, my sources—" Godfrey's contacts now reporting direct to her "—say they're still bringing up supplies, in the dark. We might have caught them on the hop," Ash said. "Some of their wagons are being pulled by their messenger-golems. Maybe they're desperate!"

"God send they are overstretched," de Vere said, grimly for a man with a force that outnumbers his enemy.

Boots skidding in mud, Ash topped the hill, breathing harsh in her own ears; and peered out across the dimness.

A spur of hill here jutted into the river valley. They

---

[14] Wearing duplicate armor and livery.

stood on its shallow western knoll, with the ancient wild-wood hard up on her right hand. No way to move troops through it. Scouts reported not walking the ground so much as scrambling ten feet above it on clotted dead-falls.

This should bring us north of their camp—wonder if the heralds have gone down yet? Well, at least we found each other . . . ! Could have wandered around this wil-derness for *days*.

The temptation to murmur, to that interior part of her-self that hears a voice, *Battle commander, Visigoth army, probable location?* is almost irresistible.

Could the *machina rei militaris* answer that one? Would it lie? Would she know I've asked—?

No point wondering. Act as if she would. It's the only safe thing to do.

They set off down the slope in front. She clattered in the Duke of Burgundy's wake, aware that most other commanders would ride the ground, but that Duke Charles wants to know what this hill is like for men on foot, and men with gun-carriages. She was mildly im-pressed; cheered. Rapid, low-voiced conferences went on ahead of her. She squinted into the weak light of dawn.

Her strides ate up ground, going downhill, and her calves ached. At the foot of the long slope, she noted that the ground was squashy—thickets and reeds blocked the dawn, that side: marshes, maybe? On this edge of the river?

The pre-dawn grayness did not grow any brighter.

A skyline of hills and thick forest, ahead. A faint bell split the darkness, maybe from the abbey in Auxonne. She had the thought, *Are the other side out walking the territory, right now? If we met—!*

The officers and Duke's men moved off, Cola de Monforte saying something quietly. She heard only *per-fect choke-point*. Walking back around the eastern end of the spur, they met the road beside the river. Move-ment became easier with the ground sure underfoot. Ash glanced up at the steeper eastern end of the spur, overhanging the Dijon road.

If we set up on the ridge, that's going to be the left of the line; that's where we'll be. If they try to move past on the road, we'll hit their unprotected backs. If they try and flank us up that cliff—well, I don't know about the rest of the Burgundian army, but we're going to be fine!

Except that what they'll do is prep for combat, and come straight up that southern slope at us . . .

The voice of Duke Charles of Burgundy said, "My lords, we shall return to camp. It is clear in my mind. We will fight as soon this saint's-day morning as we may. Sidonius favor us!"

*A decision!* Ash applauded wryly, in her own mind.

"Guys," she said.

"Boss?" Robert Anselm came instantly to her side in the morning darkness; Antonio Angelotti and Geraint ab Morgan treading on his heels.

The Earl of Oxford gave a stream of rapid orders; Dickon, George and Tom de Vere moved off about his business; he turned and said something to Viscount Beaumont, who laughed. An electricity spread throughout the group of men: knowing, now, that today will see a chance of being killed or of winning honor, money, survival.

"God pardon me if I have ever offended thee," Ash said formally, and reached up and embraced Robert Anselm. He gripped her, stepped back in the dew-soaked turf at the edge of the road, and said:

"As I hope to be forgiven, so I forgive thee, in God's name. We're going in, aren't we?"

Ash gripped Angelotti's forearm, whacked Geraint across the shoulders. Her eyes were bright.

"We're going in. Okay. This is where the Lion Azure does what it's paid to. Get them into battle array."

She speeded up, finishing the circuit, walking back toward the northern treeline and the camp faster than was safe in the dim dawn, and caught up with the Earl of Oxford. She pointed to the Duke of Burgundy:

"If he won't let us take out the Faris . . . My lord Earl, I want to consult with you about the tactics of this battle. I have an idea."

George de Vere, behind her now, sardonic, said, "The four most terrifying words in the language, a woman saying *I have an idea*."

"Oh, no." Ash smiled sweetly at him, in the dim light. "There are two words much more frightening—boss saying, *I'm bored*. You ask Fl—ask my surgeon."

John de Vere seemed to be smiling, under his raised visor.

"We've got numbers," she said. "I don't think the Turks will come in on our side: they're observers. We've got guns. We ought to win it—but the Visigoths beat the Swiss and no one survived the field to tell us how they did it. Just rumors: 'they fight like Devils from the sulphurous Pits' . . ."

"And?" The Earl of Oxford prompted.

"My lord," she said steadily, "look at that sky. There'll be little or no sun today. When we fight this field, we'll be fighting under the shadow of their darkness. Cold, dim—a winter battle."

Unseen, she made a fist, dug her nails into her palms, and showed nothing of what she felt.

"We should talk to our priests." Ash pointed at the Briar Cross that hung around the Earl's neck, dark against his surcoat. "I've got an idea. Time for God to give us a miracle, your Grace."


Within two hours of walking the ground, Ash stood beside Godluc's warm flank, Bertrand holding the warhorse's reins, and Rickard carrying her helmet and lance. Her thigh-armor was borrowed, from a short stocky English knight in de Vere's train. It did not fit.

Half the sky above her was black.

The east, where the sun should have risen on the massive army, was a towering darkness. Only behind them did an odd half-light stir cocks in the baggage wagons to crow late news of dawn.

Glancing downhill, south, she could no longer see the enemy campfires.

Behind her, that part of the sky that was not black had been covered with a back-shadow of morning light. Now it was becoming rapidly overcast, dark as the east and south. Clouds came together, chalk-yellow and fat-bellied, as tall as castle walls or cathedral spires.

Jesu Christ. Five hundred people *organized*. In place. Where they should be.

"I'm too knackered to fight!" she murmured.

Rickard grinned, palely. Her war-horse's breath steamed. Ash looked up the slope to the skyline and the multiple forces of the Burgundian army.

She thought, in the idle moment that follows extreme exertion: *The main view of a field of battle is legs.*

Dismounted, she has the impression of the field consisting of nothing but legs—horses' legs, by the hundred, some masked by livery caparisons hanging limp in the cold wet air, but most bare roan or bay or black: milling as the knights move over the crest of the slope into position. And men's legs, made slender by silver armor, all of the knights and most of the men-at-arms having steel on their lower limbs, even the archers' bright hose having steel cops strapped on over vulnerable knees. Hundreds of legs: feet treading down what had been some lord's wheat and was now churned mud and horse-shit.

Minutes ticking by: past the third hour of the morning, surely? A flurry of cold, wet air blew into her face. Trumpets shrilled. She had barely time to glance back at Anselm, Angelotti, Geraint ab Morgan; all three of them with their clusters of sergeants, gun-captains and lance-leaders thronging around them, orders urgently, furiously being given.

"Mounting up," she murmured, and took her sallet from Rickard, maneuvring it carefully over her braided hair, settling it down on her head. She let the buckle strap swing free for the moment. One foot finding the stirrup, she sprang lightly up into the saddle.

From here, high above ground, her view changed; the field becoming instead all helmets and standards. Silver against black thunderheads, a mass of steel shoulders blocked her view: knights wearing their articulated pauldrons. Riders crowded in knots, shouting to each other, wearing a throng of duck-tailed Italian sallets, and German sallets with long pointed tails, surmounted by heraldic Beasts; dim colors echoed by the sagging wet silk of their banners and standards above.

Robert Anselm slapped his hands together. "Fuck me, it's *cold*!"

"Everybody clear about what they're doing?"

"Yeah." Anselm had his sallet tipped back on his head. He looked out from under it at her. "Sure. All twenty thousand of us . . ."

"Yeah, right. Never mind. No plan ever survived ten minutes after the fighting started . . . we'll wing it."

Up on the backside of the hill here, Ash could look to left and right and see the Burgundian army riding and walking into place: twenty thousand strong.

"I think that's Olivier de la Marche's banner on the right wing," she pointed out to Rickard. The boy nodded jerkily. "And the mercenaries over on the left, and Charles's own banner there—the heavy armored center. You should study heraldry. We could do with a better herald in the Lion Azure."

His flaring black eyebrows dipped. "How many of them can fight, boss?"

"Hmm. Yes. That *may* be a better question than who's a Raven and Lion Couchant . . ." Ash felt her bowels rumble. "About two-thirds of them, I'd say. The rest are peasant levy and town militia."

She shifted Godluc a few steps, leaning sideways, not able to see Angelotti now with the other master gunners, the Duke having decided to mass his serpentines[15] in the center.

---

[15] Small field cannon.

"It's dysentery," she said firmly. "That's why I keep wanting to shit myself. It's dysentery."

Geraint ab Morgan, moving to stand by her other stirrup, nodded. "That's right, boss. Lot of it about this morning."

With a gesture to her officers, Ash rode at a gentle pace up the slope of the hill and over the crest, her personal banner born behind her by Robert Anselm; to where Euen Huw and his lance guarded the Lion Azure standard, in the center of five hundred fighting men. The pommel of her sword tapped arhythmically against her plackart as she rode. A faint moisture began to sting her bare face and uncovered hands.

Where's the fucking enemy—*ah*. There.

Down at the foot of the deceptively gentle slope—*be a bitch to run up*, her mind commented—groups of darkness moved in darkness. Moving units of men. The glint of a banner-spike. A randy mare whinnying to the Frankish war-horses.

"How many men?" Robert Anselm murmured.

"Haven't a clue . . . *Too* many."

"It's always 'too many,' " the older man observed. "Two peasants with a stick is 'too many'!"

Godfrey's deacon sprinted out from the mass of armed men. Ash automatically looked for Godfrey Maximillian to be with Richard Faversham—after four days, was still looking. She had stopped asking.

"What did the bishop say?" she demanded.

"He consents!" Richard Faversham spoke softly enough that she had to bend down from the saddle to hear him, awkward in a brigandine which is not designed to do that.

"How many priests have we?"

"With the army, upwards of four hundred. With the company, but two; myself and young Digorie here."

He's not mentioning Godfrey either. Are we both assuming he's left the company? Without a word?

Ash's bare fist hit the saddle's pommel. She stared down at her cold skin, and reached out for her gauntlets.

Rickard, on toe-tip, put them into her hands. As she buckled the left one on, she continued to look down at Richard Faversham, and the intense, bony, dark young man he had introduced as Digorie.

"Are you ordained?" she asked him.

Digorie reached up a hand that appeared to be all knuckles, and gripped her remaining ungauntleted hand in an extremely powerful clasp. "Digorie Paston,[16] madam," he said, in English, "ordained back in Dijon by Charles's bishop. I won't let you or God down, ma'am."

Hearing the order in which he said it, Ash raised an eyebrow but managed to restrain herself from any comment.

"You're going to win this battle for us, Digorie, Richard," she said. "Well, you and the other three hundred and ninety-eight . . ."

Godluc responded to a touch of the spurs, bringing her around to where she could look down the hill, over the heads of her own men, toward the Visigoth army.

"Oh, *shit*," Ash remarked. "That's all we needed."

In the half-light, she could see dozens of Visigoth command flags, spanning the eastern road from Dijon toward Auxonne, and the thousands of marching and mounted men with them. Narrowing her eyes against the keen wet wind, she recognized positions: they have anchored their right flank hard up against the marsh down *there*, in the north; and got the southern valley *there* sat on with four companies of troops, and—

And.

"Well," Ash's voice sounded thin to her own ears, "that's us fucked. That's us well and *truly* fucked."

Robert Anselm grabbed her stirrup and heaved himself briefly up, high enough to look down across the slope, and see what she was seeing. "Son of a *bitch*!"

He fell back, heels jolting on the mud.

Ash shifted her gaze, slitting her eyes to be sure of what she was seeing in the dimness. There was no mis-

---

[16] No relation.

take. Over the troops who anchored themselves on the Visigoth right—about a thousand archers and light horsemen—white pennants flew.

The wind unrolled the silk on the air, letting her clearly see the red crescents.

"Those are Turkish troops," she confirmed.

Robert Anselm, below her, muttered, "So much for them cutting the Visigoths' supply lines . . ."

"Yeah. Not only are they not cutting their supply lines, there's a detachment of the Sultan's troops in the mainward. Oh, *fuck*," Ash exclaimed. "There's been some kind of treaty, alliance, something—the fucking Sultan's in bed with the fucking Caliph now!"

"I doubt quite that," John de Vere said, riding up beside them.

"Did you know about this, my lord?"

De Vere's face, under his armet's pinned up visor, showed white with anger: "What would Duke Charles tell an indigent English Earl? His intelligence is too good for him not to know—he must think he can beat them," the Earl of Oxford said abruptly. "God's teeth! but he thinks he can defeat the Visigoths *and* the Turks! The greater the enemy, the greater the glory."

"We're dead," Ash murmured, sing-song. "We're dead . . . okay, my lord. If you want my advice, stick with the plan. Let the priests pray."

"If I wanted your advice, madam, I should have demanded it."

Ash grinned at him. "Well, hey, you got it for free. Not everybody can say that. I'm a mercenary, you know."

The constriction of humor at his eyes gave him crow's-feet. The laughter faded, as he and Ash sat their restless horses. In the twilight, it seemed the Visigoth and Turkish battles[17] might be drawing up in what local

---

[17] In medieval military terms, a "battle" is a unit of men, rather than a specific combat. Medieval armies were often divided into three battles or large units, for fighting.

intelligence had suggested would be their optimum position.

"Will your men follow you in this?"

Ash said absently, "They're a damn sight more frightened of me than of the enemy—and besides, the Visigoths might not get them, but my battle police certainly will."

"Madam, much depends on this."

A feeling of great relaxation spread through her body. She reached down to adjust the strap of the plackart that protected her belly, and thought longingly of the protection afforded by full armor. Her hand came to rest on the leather-bound grip of her sword, checking the lanyard chain fastened around it below the pommel, and attached to her belt.

"I've got rid of the liabilities," Ash said, looking back at him. "Most of the rest of these men have been fighting for me for three years now. They don't give a fuck about Duke Charles. They don't give a fuck about—beg pardon—the Earl of Oxford. They give a fuck about their lance-mates, and about me, because I've got them out of fields worse than this in one piece. So yes, they'll do it. Maybe. All other things being equal."

The Earl of Oxford looked curiously at her.

Ash avoided the Englishman's gaze. "Okay—we're facing people who beat the Swiss: morale isn't *that* good. You ask Cola de Monforte!"

A clarion rang out across the field. Momentarily, men's voices stilled. The sounds of horses, their tack, the clatter of barding and the snorts of breath gave way to the distant shout of Sergeants of Archers, and an unholy noise of singing from the gunners' position. Ash stood upright in her stirrups.

"Meanwhile," she said, "it isn't quite hopeless, and I've got a contract with you."

The Earl of Oxford saw his brothers approaching, and Ash saw the rest of her officers coming up; all with questions, needing orders and direction, and the time ticking away now to nothing.

John de Vere formally offered his hand, and Ash gripped it.

"If we survive the field," he said, "I shall have questions to ask you, madam."

"Good thing they don't do guns," Ash murmured to Robert Anselm. "They'd do what Richard Gloucester did to your Lancastrians at Tewkesbury, and blow us right off the top of this hill!"

Anselm nodded approvingly. "The Duke's got it well thought out."

"Bugger Charles of Burgundy!" Ash remarked. "Why do I have to fight a fucking hopeless battle before we can do anything useful? It isn't that lot we need to take out—it's her fucking Stone Golem, that's telling her how to win! This is a sheer waste of time."

"Particularly if we get killed," Anselm grunted.

Both of them sat in their saddles, gazing down the long muddy slope at banners galloping, as the Visigoth light cavalry got themselves into position. The Faris's banner held their center—as Ash's scouts had informed her, it was a Brazen Head, on a black field. Ash absently rested her hand on the skirt of her brigandine, over her belly.

She missed, suddenly and painfully, whatever Florian might be saying at this moment, if she were here—something caustic about the stupidity of military life, and battles, and getting cut up for no good reason.

"Florian would say I have to fight harder because I'm a woman," Ash said inconsequentially, watching her officers moving along the back of lines of men. "She means, a male commander could get taken prisoner, but I'd get gang-raped."

Anselm grunted. "Yeah? It was me that found Ricardo Valzacchi after Molinella, remember? Tied across a wagon with a poleaxe shaft up his arse. I think he's—*she's* getting war confused with something else . . ."

What little she could see of Anselm's face in the vee between bevor and raised visor was hidden, now, by the dark sweep of clouds across the sky; a sweep of dank shadow that took the brightness out of blue and red and yellow banners, dulled the hooks and points of bills, and caused a muttered swearing among the archers and crossbowmen.

A blast of cold air brought rain into her face; stingingly cold, almost sleet.

Ash stirred, tapped stirrups to the big gelding's flanks and rode down in among the company lines. Godluc's big feathery feet picked a way between men and women bundled into jacks and helms and standing on the wet trampled crops.

Ludmilla Rostovnaya shouted up, "It's dampening our strings, boss."

"All bows unspanned and unstrung!" Ash ordered. "You'll get your chance, guys. Keep your bowstrings under your helmets. It's going to get bloody nasty, around about—now."

With that, the church bells of distant Auxonne rang out across the hills. A great noise of voices went up from behind the Burgundian battle line. A choir, singing Mass. Ash raised her head. A whiff of incense caught in her nostrils. A little further up the crowded slope, Richard Faversham and Digorie Paston knelt in the mud, crucifixes in hand, young Bertrand holding up a stinking tallow candle. Around Ash, voices muttered, "Miserere, miserere!" She caught a flash of black and white as a magpie flew swooping down across the field, and automatically crossed herself and spat.

A bolt of blue color, about as big as her fist, shot across the wet crops, under Godluc's nose. His red-rimmed nostrils flared.

Ash watched the kingfisher dart away.

She tapped spurs into Godluc's flanks again, rode up and took axe and lance from Rickard, and as she reached to close her bevor up and visor down, the first flakes of white dusted across Godluc's blue and gold caparisons.

She raised her head, the duck-curled metal tail of her sallet allowing her to look up. Above, in a dark sky, white dots floated down.

In an instant, a howl of whiteness swirled out of the clouds, snowflakes turning from a powdery dust to thick, wet flakes; plastering her plackart, whitening Godluc's silk caparisons, cutting her off from everyone except the three or four closest: Anselm, Rickard, Ludmilla, Geraint ab Morgan.

"Hold them!" she ordered the Welshman sharply.

Wind drove into her back. Snow flew. The wet mud under Godluc's hooves went from black-and-brown to white in a matter of seconds. She rode a few yards, collecting her officers, halting close to Richard Faversham's high-voiced Latin.

Lance holstered, hands going up, she wrenched off her sallet and listened, standing upright in her saddle.

Far off, on the left and right wings of the Burgundian army, hoarse loud voices cried orders. A second's pause, then the unmistakable *thunk* and *whirr!* of arrows being launched. One flight—and no other orders: an inhuman silence, all along the line.

"Shit, they're good," she whispered.

Somewhere below, a Visigoth man screamed.

Digorie Paston reached out and closed his bony hands over the English deacon's, his face screwed up, prayer spilling out of his mouth.

Ash turned her head. Wind lashed her plates-covered shoulders and back. A hard wind, rising—and a blast took the breath from her mouth, her face blinded with snow, and she scraped a gauntlet across her features, grazing skin, and leaned down:

"Ludmilla, go forward!"

The Rus woman slid out of her company and went forward into the driving snow. Ash cocked her head, listening. The shrill snarl of an arrowstorm went up, all in one second, and her bladder pulsed, a trickle of hot urine soaking her hose. It is the sound. Nerve-shredding to hear coming: worse when it stops.

Her clumsy hands got her helmet back on her head; all around her, her men were shoving their visors down and leaning forward, as if into a wind, to present the deflecting surfaces of steel helmets to the arrows' barbs and bodkin points.

"Shit, shit, shit," Geraint ab Morgan swore monotonously.

The abrupt cessation of the whistling sound told her the arrows had hit—something. She rode forward. No one screamed, or fell.

A white-plastered figure, stumbling, caught at her stirrup.

Ludmilla Rostovnaya shouted, "They're hitting earth! Thirty feet in front of the line!"

"*Yes!*" Ash tried to look behind her, into the wind, coughed out a mouthful of sleet, and shouted, "Rickard!"

The boy ran up, an archer's sallet crammed over his head, and a falchion at his belt. "Boss?"

"Get runners down here! I can't see the Blue Boar flag, we're going to have to rely on runners and riders. Go!"

"Yes, boss!"

"Ludmilla, ride to the Earl of Oxford, *tell him it's working!* I want to know if it's working on the rest of the field!"

The woman lifted a hand, and plunged on up the slope, slipping and sliding in snow and mud. Ash shivered, steel's cold entering her body even through the padded arming doublet and hose beneath. Her crotch felt chill and wet. She swung Godluc around and rode back and forth in the snow in front of the Lion Azure's five hundred men, leaving Anselm in charge of the infantry and Geraint in charge of the archers; and the knights under the dubious restraint of Euen Huw.

A thrumming whirr burst on the air.

Ash held Godluc in, needing the rein to do it. The big beast under her shivered. She stood in the stirrups, bowels unsettled; and very slowly paced up and down before the ranks. One arrow buried its fletching in the mud fifteen feet in front of her.

The sound of bowstrings cut the air. Arrow shafts shrilled. The noise grew until she thought there could

not be another arrow left in Christendom, flight upon
flight from the recurved Visigoth bows, flight after flight
of German arrows, from the Imperial troops glimpsed
down among the enemy.

The wind from behind the Burgundian lines blew so
hard that the snow flew vertically southwards.

"Keep praying!" she yelled at Digorie and Richard.
The Mass from Charles's mainward came by fits and
starts through the howling wind.

*"Now . . ."* she breathed.

It isn't much of a miracle—given what weather conditions are like anyway, with the sun out—but it *is* a
miracle.

The snow. The snow—and the *wind.*

Whiteness blocked the air, swirling, until she lost all
sense of depth or distance. She held onto Godluc's
warmth, and his steaming breath, and rode in close
among the lines; a word here to a man with a brother-
in-law fighting for Cola de Monforte, a word there to a
woman archer who drank with the whores following a
refugee contingent of German knights, all of it serving
no particular purpose of information, only it brought
them near enough to her to see, hear or touch her.

"This is what we do, this is what we're here for," she
said, again and again. "Let them keep shooting. Wasting
arrows. A few more minutes, and we'll give them the
biggest shock of their lives. The *last* shock!"

The snow thinned.

Digorie Paston and Richard Faversham held each
other up, kneeling in the mud. Bertrand put a wine flask
to the lips of each in turn, his fat white face gaunt with
fear. They prayed in harsh gasps. Christus, she thought,
*Godfrey, we need you!*

Digorie Paston pitched over, flat on his face in two
inches of snow.

"Prepare to shoot!" she yelled to Geraint ab Morgan.

The snow thinned still more. The sky grew brighter.
The wind began to drop. Ash turned and spurred Godluc
across the slope; page, squire, escort and banner-bearer

with her; to Geraint ab Morgan and the archers; one fist
up, sword out and held high. She watched the skyline
as she rode, searching hard among the banners in the
mainward for the Blue Boar.

Up the slope, Richard Faversham fainted.

The fall of snow stopped, abruptly; the air clearing.

The Boar standard dipped.

Ash didn't wait for the runner. As the west grew
lighter, and the snow dropped to powdery drifts, she
jerked her sword down. "Span and string!"

"Nock! Loose!" Geraint ab Morgan's harsh Welsh
bellow echoed flatly across the hillside. Ash heard other
orders roared, in the wings and further along the mainward; and she unconsciously braced herself. The Lion
Azure's archers and crossbowmen readied their weapons, spanned bolts and nocked arrows, and at Geraint's
second shout, loosed.

The better part of two thousand arrows blackened the
cold twilight air. A thousand of which, she reflected in
a moment's irony, undoubtedly came from the bows of
Phillipe de Poitiers and Ferry de Cuisance, whose archers from Picardy and Hainault she had run away from
at Neuss.

*I was right, too . . .*

Ash's whole body quivered with their release, and she
lifted her head as they flew; and the second flight of
shafts was already black in the air, crossbows cranking
furiously, longbow archers loosing at ten or twelve
shafts a minute, snatched up from the porcupines of arrows jammed into the wet wheat and mud—still shooting with the wind behind them—

A distant horse squealed.

Ash stood up in the stirrups.

Three hundred yards away, down a hill littered with
a brushwood barrier of thousands of Visigoth arrows,
the first shafts of the Burgundian army struck home.

She can just see, at this distance: Visigoth men fall,
clutching at their faces, spiked through eye and cheekbone and mouth. Their riders jerk on wheeling mounts.

A great bulk of horses screamed and bolted, crashing back and south, opening holes in the lines of men with pike and swords; a man in white robes sprawling, skull crushed by a hoof, banners dipping in chaos—

Ash looked over her shoulder at the exact moment that Angelotti, and the other gunners with Duke Charles's center, opened fire. A thundering *bang!* shook the ground under Godluc's hooves, and the stallion reared up a good eighteen inches; this in full armor.

*They shot into the wind, and fell short. We shot with the wind and didn't. And they couldn't see that!*

"Deo gratias!" Ash yelled.

The gunfire from the center ran raggedly out to silence—it was always a moot point if the gun-teams could re-load before the enemy charged. Ash reined Godluc in as he thumped one hoof down on the reverberate ground and skittered his haunches around, wanting to charge forward.

"Runners!" she yelled at the scattered escort as they reformed; took a minute to spur Godluc back of the battle line, her personal banner following. Armed men on horseback closed in around her. She wheeled the gelding, seeing a man-at-arms come running down the slope toward the company, toward her banner—

A bone-shaking jolt threw her forward in the saddle.

One man's hand was under her chest, pushing her back up. She shoved Thomas Rochester aside, spat, shook her head dizzily; and found herself staring at a scar in the earth. A giant furrow, a spray of soil and turf and a man's severed hand—

She has time to think *They're not supposed to have guns!* and a second impact thuds into the ground close to the group of horsemen. Mud flies up, splatters her face.

"Captain!" One of the runners, hanging on her stirrup. "The Earl says pull back! Pull the line back! Over the top of the hill!"

"ANSELM!" she yells, prising mud out of her mouth with armored fingers. She spurs to him. "Get them back

over that hill, *now*! You—and you—*run*—orders for
Geraint: *get them back.*"

She can hear trumpets signaling, orders being shouted,
the bark of lance-leaders hauling their men back, up the
snow- and mud-slippery corn toward the skyline; only
then does she turn.

Down at the foot of the slope, in the rain-pale twilight,
the mass of Visigoth men in the center battle have
moved aside. There are wagons there.

As she watches, a figure that is larger than a man
pushes a wagon into place, marble-and-bronze body
wheeling it with no apparent effort. Light glints off the
sides of the wagon. It is iron-slabbed, armored: a Visigoth war-wagon. The sides, released, fall forward and
down—studded with nail-points; you can't run at them,
ride up them—and the great wooden cup of a mangonel
goes back: snaps forward—

A boulder the size of a man's torso arcs through the
air.

Ash shifted her weight sideways, brought Godluc
around, and leaned forward to urge him up the hill.
Men's backs closed around her; the banner jiggled overhead. A thud: a great screaming noise—rock-splinters
whined through the air, plowing into men's bodies.

She lifted her head and looked at a swathe cut through
the battle line. Earth and corn crushed, heads and bodies
crushed; a plowed mass of dark red blood under the pale
sky.

She rode behind the company, the mud under Godluc's hooves red with blood, blue-pink with intestines;
men screaming; women pulling them up the hill toward
the skyline. Rode slow—walking pace—Thomas Rochester at her left flank with tears running down his face,
under his visor.

*Bang!*

"For Christ's pity, ride!" Rochester screamed.

Ash turned, as far as high saddle and brigandine
would allow, staring back down the hill.

Twenty or thirty of the iron-armored wagons stood

at the foot of the hill. Men swarmed around them, hammering chocks under the mangonels, adjusting the elevation of the catapults; and tall above them, on the weapons-platforms, the clay figures of golem bent down, effortlessly lifting rocks into the cups, effortlessly hauling the cup down to cock it, not even bothering to wind the time-consuming winch—everything that a man can do, that *men* can do; but stronger, *faster*.

Five boulders plowed into the slope to her right, impacting with great sprays of mud; another five hit in sequence—*bang! bang! bang! bang! bang!*—and the far end of the line of knights stopped being men riding. She stared at a mass of threshing hooves, rolling bodies, bloody liveries; a few unharmed riders trying to climb to their feet—

Rate of fire's phenomenal, Ash thought dreamily; at the same time that she was shouting, "Rickard, get to Angelotti! Tell him to pull back! I don't care what the rest of the guns are doing, the Lion's pulling back! We've got to get over the hill!"

Ahead, the great three-yard-square Lion standard dipped, recovered, and went steadily back up the slope. She muttered, "Come on, Euen, come *on*!" and put both spurs back into Godluc's sides. The gelding slid, caught himself, and sprang up the slope, bringing her up level with the backs of the great mass of running billmen and archers.

Thomas Rochester yelled, *"Shit!"*

A great curving streak of fire blasted up the hill past Ash's right-hand side. She screamed. Godluc reared. In a clatter of barding barely heard above the screaming men, he thudded down; her teeth clicked painfully together.

The mud steamed and hissed under a jet of blue-white fire.

It suddenly cut off. Black streaks blotched her vision: retinal after-images. Through them, Ash glimpsed large numbers of men sprinting up the hill toward the crest.

Down the hill, below the brushwood barrier of

thousands of Visigoth arrows, uselessly stuck in the earth and burning now—

Ash saw the moving figures of golem, ahead of the Visigoth mainward. Thirty or forty of them; each with huge brass tanks fixed to their backs, nozzles in their hands that spat flame. Carrying the weight of the tanks with no effort, bearing the heat of the flame with no hurt.

"Get Angelotti to me!" she roared at Thomas Rochester.

The jolt of Godluc scrambling up the slope knocked breath out of her; page, escort and riders all with her, all on the heels of the company's archers. She reined in; slowing deliberately; felt the ground flatten as she came up over the crest, and rode down in among the company as they went down into dead ground, out of mangonel-range, and spurred forward to the banner marking the guns.

"Angeli!" She leaned down from the saddle. "Get the hackbutters! Those damn things are made of *stone*, arquebus balls will *crack* them—"

"Got you, madonna!" the master gunner shouted.

"Jesus *Christ*! War-golems! Greek Fire![18] We should have been warned! Can't the scouts get *anything* right?"

Between screaming one order and the next, she realized there must be a battle going on out on the right flank, but that was all a wet confusion of banners streaming, gouts of mud kicked up by frantic riders, and one huge, immense roar of male voices that she guessed to be heavy cavalry going down the hill toward the wagons, the golem, the Greek Fire.

"Fuck, no!" Thomas Rochester gasped, riding to her side. "This is no time to be a hero!"

---

[18] Used by Roman, Byzantine and Arab cultures, in both naval and siege warfare, the exact constituents of "Greek Fire" remain unknown, although naphtha, sulphur, oil, tar, saltpeter, and pitch have been suggested. Its nature as a terror weapon, however, is well recorded in history.

"If Oxford doesn't send orders—" Ash stood in her stirrups, trying to pick out the Blue Boar, or the Burgundian banner, as great throngs of men streamed past her; men-at-arms in Burgundian livery running; and she exclaimed, "Shit, have we routed, and nobody's told us?"

Man after man was carried back past her on hurdles ripped up by the women of the baggage train. She registered heads hanging down, hair matted with blood, mouths open; a man screaming with his leg bloody and the big bone of the thigh stuck up white though the skin; a woman in a kirtle, bloody from chin to hem, staring at her hand, lying a yard away in the mud. All faces she knew. She felt nothing, not even numb. She felt only the intensity, the necessity, of getting them through it as whole as she could.

Anselm appeared at her side on a rangy bay. "What now, boss?"

"Get scouts on the ridge! Tell me if they're advancing. Draw up into battles. We're not running yet!"

It is far easier to be killed running away.

No sun to tell her what hour this might be. She galloped along the front of the Lion Azure lines, partly to show any runners her banner, partly to discourage any man from running away. Two urging strides took Godluc up onto the skyline, even as she thought *This is suicidally dangerous but I have to know what's going on!*

Robert Anselm rode up beside her.

"Roberto, fuck off!"

"There!"

Ash followed the direction of his gauntlet. On the far right, de la Marche's men had galloped down the slope, full charge, lances down, and joined battle. Men-at-arms swarming with them: bills rose and fell like a threshing machine. Among the Visigoth black pennants at the foot of the slope, next to the chevrons of Lebrija, a green and yellow personal banner briefly appeared.

"The Eagle of del Guiz," Robert yelled. His voice

sounded hoarse, electric, excited. "That—*there he goes!*"

Anselm stood in his stirrups and whooped the way a hunt hallows a fox. The nearest billmen in Lion livery took breath to see where he was pointing.

"Boss, your husband's running away!" Carracci bawled.

"Yeah!" Anselm grinned fiercely at Ash. "Petition the Emperor to award him another heraldic beast—the Lying Hound!"

She has a second to think *I am ashamed of Fernando, why am I ashamed of him, why should I care?* and then the bad light and confusion of men slashing away at each other hides banner, standard, the glint of weapons, and men's backs as they run away.

"Captain Ash!" a rider in red X livery bellowed, "The Duke wants you!"

Ash waved acknowledgment, bellowed "You're in command, get off this fucking skyline!" to Anselm, and spurred Godluc—weary, hooves bloody, flanks heaving—across the back of the hill. Back of the lines, and down, into a tiny red streamlet, tributary of the river; splashing across it. She galloped into a paddock between hedges, trampled down by the passing of a thousand men.

A throng of men and riders packed the paddock. Appalled, she thought, *This is the back-of-the-lines HQ, have we been driven back this far, this fast?* She shoved up her visor, stared frantically at colored cloth, and picked out the draggled Blue Boar, with Charles's White Hart. She rode in between the ranks of armed knights. Liveries were useless now, blood and brains and mud soaking their bright colors.

One man made to block her way.

"For the Duke, motherfucker!" Ash shrieked.

He recognized a woman's voice and let her through.

Charles of Burgundy, in full gilded armor, stood as the center of the command group of nobles. Pages held their horses. One roan gelding delicately lipped at the verge of the stream, not willing to drink through mud and body fluids. Ash dismounted. The ground hit her heels, jarring her; she was instantly weary to the bone. She shook it off.

A man, his armet crowned by a blue boar, faceless in steel, turned at her voice. Oxford.

"My lord!" Ash elbowed between four armed knights in bloody yellow and scarlet livery. "We got to regroup. Take out the catapults and the Fire. What does the Duke want me to do?"

He thumbed his visor up, giving her a sight of red-rimmed pale blue eyes, fiercely keen. "The Duke's mercenaries on your left flank are holding back. They won't push an advance. He wants you to go in there."

"He wants *what*?" Ash stared. "Didn't anyone ever tell him, don't reinforce failure?"

She realized she was breathing hard, and shouting too loud, despite the battle fifty yards away.

More quietly and hoarsely, she said, "If we mass the cannon and the hack-buts, we can blast the stone men off the face of this field—"

Her hands move, describing shapes in the air which she knows approximate not to actual men, slicing at each other in this black morning's random confusion, but to their force, their will, their ability to *make* someone else go back: an ability not really dependent on weapons.

"—but we won't do it piecemeal. The Duke's got to give the orders!"

"He won't do it," John de Vere, Earl of Oxford, said. "The Duke is ordering a heavy cavalry charge."

"Oh, fuck chivalry! This is his chance to do something, we're getting chewed up here—" There is no time to argue on the field of battle. "Yes, my lord. What—"

Ash glimpsed something black and whirring and brought up her arm by instinct.

A bodkin arrow-head clicked off her upraised shoulder and glanced into the dirt.

The shock through the brigandine's plates momentarily numbed her right arm. She grabbed left-handed for Godluc's reins—a page in red doublet and white hose knelt before Godluc, slumped forward under her horse's hooves, two shafts protruding from his throat.

Not a red doublet, a white doublet soaked red.

*"Oxford!"* She had her four-foot short axe off the saddle, gripping it between two hands. *When the commanders have to draw weapons, it's trouble.* The scream and shout and sudden battering of hooves broke over the hedge in front of her, new riders piling into the enclosed paddock: ten, fifty, two or three hundred men in robes and mail on desert horses—

A spurt of flame leaped out in front of her.

Ash never saw the hand-gunner, or heard the *bang* and *crack!* of the gun; she was deaf before she knew it.

Another gun spoke. Not a hand-gun but an organ-gun. Between gray smoke, she saw a Burgundian cannon crew sponge, load, ram and fire, in less time than seemed possible. She swung around and the paddock was full of mounted Visigoth knights—and men in white mullet liveries, John de Vere bellowing an attack—and Godluc trampling someone a dangerous two yards from her right hand—and she brought her axe up and over and drove through the impact of flesh, of bone. The axe took off a Visigoth rider's arm, clean, with a spray of blood that reddened her armor from sallet to sabatons.

The impact of horses' hooves pounded up through the soles of her boots. She felt the *bang!* of another gun in the hollow of her chest. She took a grip, braced her feet, yelled as well as she could for Godluc; and turned a lance-shaft aside with a well-timed cut. Coming up on the backswing for the Visigoth knight's leg, she made no connection, almost falling—

"No! I won't ask!" She sobbed it aloud. *"No voices!"*

No riders in front of her.

The paddock was nothing but horses in red and yellow and blue caparisons: galloping Burgundian knights. Ash took three seconds to swing up into the saddle, loop her axe to it, and draw her sword: within that time, there was no longer a man in Visigoth mail and livery alive, wounded horses screamed, butchered; and the great mass of the Burgundian Duke's escort closed up around them—around what had been, she realized, a flying wedge attack.

At her horse's feet, the Visigoth standard-bearer lay face down on his flag, a red rent in his mail shirt, and a broken sword-blade jammed through his eye-socket.

"The Duke!" John de Vere was in the mud, staring up at her. He knelt, cradling a man in gilded armor and Hart livery—Charles, Duke of Burgundy. The gilt articulated steel was leaking thick, red arterial blood. *"Get surgeons! Now!"*

A flying wedge of men from the land of stone and twilight, willing to be chopped apart if it meant one of them could find, under his standard, Duke Charles of Burgundy. She shook her ringing head, trying to make out what the Earl of Oxford was saying.

"SURGEONS!" His voice reached her faintly.

"My lord!" Ash wheeled Godluc. The arch of the sky above her was black, with that lightlessness that she treated now as if it were just another natural phenomenon. North, the morning was distantly bright. Chill wind still blew in her face. She slammed her visor shut, jammed spurs home, and thundered across the slippery slope, her banner-bearer and escort hard put to keep up with her.

The light in the north began to die.

Godluc's gallop slowed instantly to a walk as her attention shifted. His head drooped. His barrel chest shuddered, white with foam. Thomas Rochester's little Welsh mare caught up, with the Lion banner behind him. She pointed, wordless.

Back toward Dijon, over the Burgundian border, the sunlight was beginning to dim.

"Surgeons for the Duke!" Ash ordered. "Ride!"

The slope of the hill rose up in front of her, wet, muddy, slippery with wreckage. The Surgeon-General's tents were fifty yards off, just below the crest. Godluc, doing his best, could not surmount it; she turned and rode with her group hard toward the west, along the contour of the hill, to where the slope would shallow out and allow her to get back, along the crest, to the rear and the surgeons' wagons.

Rochester and the escort outdistanced her, on horses that had done less in the past two hours. She found herself struggling in the rear, behind her banner, behind her escort.

She had no warning.

A crossbow bolt struck the flank of the horse in front: Rochester's mare. Wet meat exploded across her face and body.

Godluc reared.

A mailed hand from nowhere jerked her reins down, bloodying Godluc's mouth. The gelding screamed. A sword-slash cut one stirrup leather: she jerked in the high-backed saddle, grabbing with her free hand for the pommel, and balance.

Sixty Visigoth knights in mail and coat-of-plates rode past and over and through her escort, streaming out across the hill.

A spear thrust home from behind into Godluc's quarters. His hind hooves lifted, his head dipped, and she went straight over his head.

The mud was soft, or she would have died with a broken neck.

The impact was too hard to feel. Ash felt nothing but an absence, realized that she lay, staring up at the black sky, stunned, hurt, chest an acid void; that her hand gripped her sword and the blade had snapped off six inches from the hilt, that something was wrong with her left leg, and her left arm.

A man in the snatch-squad leaned down from his mount. She saw his pale face, behind the helmet bar, satisfying itself about her livery. He hefted a mace in his left hand. He dismounted, and struck twice: once to her left knee, the poleyn locking down, pain blazing through the joint; and once to the side of her head.

She knew nothing clearly after that.

She felt herself lifted, thought for a time that it might

be Burgundians or her own men; recognized, at last, that the language they spoke was Visigothic, and that it was dark, the sun was nowhere in the sky, and that what rocked and shook unsteadily beneath her was not a field or road or hay-cart, but the deck of a ship.

Her first clear thought came perhaps days later. *This is a ship and it is sailing for North Africa.*

*[Original e-mail documents found inserted, folded, in British Library copy of 3rd edition,* Ash: A History of Lost Burgundy, *(2001)—possibly in chronological order of editing original typescript?]*

---

Message: #155 (Anna Longman/misc.)
Subject: Ash, archaeological discoveries
Date: 18/11/00 at 10.00 a.m.
From: Ngrante@ *format address deleted other details encrypted by non-discoverable personal key*

Anna--

I think that you may just have tried to mail me and failed.

To answer points I anticipate you may be asking about the last section: no, I can find no other historical mention of a battle at Auxonne on or around 21 August 1476—although Ash's narrative does bear some resemblance to what we know of a battle fought on 22 August 1485. That date, of course, refers to Bosworth field, which put an end to the Plantagenet Kings in England. And something very like the remarkable occurrence with the arrows is documented earlier, on 29 March 1461, at Towton in England, with the Lancastrians 'not perfectly viewing the distance between them and their enemies' by reason of driving snow and wind; therefore losing that 'Palmsunday field' (and England) to the Yorkists.

Again, Charles Mallory Maximillian footnotes this, in his 1890s edition, as being one more case where the 'Ash' documents have been fleshed out by her contemporaries (especially del Guiz, writing in the early 1500s) with details of their own famous battles.

I feel that this no longer answers the case.

I cannot reconcile what we have here—two opposing sets of evidence. Manuscripts which are apparently (now) fictional; archaeological relics which are evidently, physically, real. I am advising Isobel on 15th century Europe, I am working on my translation, but all I can do, really, is think. How do I explain this? What theory would account for this?

I don't have one. Perhaps when Ash referred to the sun going out as a 'black miracle', I should have listened to her! I am starting to think that only a miracle is going to give me the explanation we need.

--Pierce

- - - - - - - - - - - - - - - - - - - - - - - - - - -

Message: #95 (Pierce Ratcliff/misc.)
Subject:   Ash
Date:      18/11/00 at 11.09 a.m.
From:      Longman@                    *format address deleted*
                                       *other details encrypted and*
Pierce--                               *non-recoverably deleted*

I have no idea why we've got a conflict of evidence, either; and I have to talk to my MD about it. It isn't just my job and your career. We can't publish a book that we know to be academically fraudulent—no, wait, don't panic!—and we can't NOT publish one with something as mind-boggling as a fifteenth century Carthaginian golem backing it up.

Reading your last mailing, I start wondering what your Vaughan Davies would say—maybe not that the resemblance of Auxonne to Bosworth Field is a case of historical Chinese whispers, but that it's an echo of his idealised alternate-history 'Lost Burgundy'. That's poetic, and it got me thinking, because he was a scientist as well as a writer. Maybe it's NOT a poetic thought, maybe it's a scientific one.

A friend of mine, Nadia, said something very interesting to me. I've been reading up on this: we were talking about the theory you mentioned—that there are an infinite number of parallel universes created every second, in which every possible different choice or decision at any given moment gives rise to another different 'branch', etc. (I really only know it from novels, and popular-science books.)

What Nadia says is, it isn't the lost chances she regrets—whether you drove down a different road and avoided an accident, and so on—but the fact that, if this infinite-number-of-universes theory is true, she can never lead a moral existence.

She says, if she chooses not to knock down and rob an old lady in the street, then the very act of refusing to do this gives rise to a parallel universe in which she DOES do it. It is not possible NOT to do things.

I'm not suggesting you've accessed a parallel universe or alternate history—I'm not THAT desperate—but it does make Davies sound less of a mental case if his theory was based in scientific speculation. I was thinking, if we COULD find the rest of his Introduction, maybe it has a perfectly sensible SCIENTIFIC explanation, which would help us now? Even science circa 1939 would be SOMETHING.

--Anna

- - - - - - - - - - - - - - - - - - - - - - - - - - - - -

Message: #156 (Anna Longman/misc.)
Subject: Ash
Date: 18/11/00 at 11.20 a.m.
From: Ngrant@                            format address deleted
                                          other details encrypted by
Anna--                                    non-discoverable personal key

Your Nadia's point is philosophically interesting, but not the case, according to what I understand of our physicists. (Which is purely a layman's understanding, I assure you.)

If what the current evidence seems to point to is correct, then we are not faced with an infinite number of possible universes, but only an infinite number of possible FUTURES, which collapse into one concrete and real present moment: the NOW. Which then becomes one concrete and single PAST.

So your friend chooses not to knock down her old lady, and that state of NOT having done it is what becomes the unchangeable past. It is only in the moment of transition from potential to actual that a choice is made. So it is possible not to do things.

Sorry: raise a philosophical hare with an academic and he will always chase it! To change animals and mix metaphors: let us return to our sheep—

I would take help from ANYONE at the moment, including a

scientific theory of the Thirties about parallel universes! I've tried extensively to find Vaughan Davies's book, though, and failed; and I don't think I can do much about that sitting in a tent outside Tunis.

I want to try these last few weeks out on my colleagues, in detail, and on Isobel's scientist friends, and see if they can come up with any theories. I don't dare do it now. It would bring unwanted attention to the site, here; it would cause Isobel a great deal of distress—and, to be honest, it would finish my chances of being the first man to translate FRAXINUS. I know this is venal, but chances of spectacular success come only rarely; something you will discover as you get older.

Maybe we could do it in a month or so? Start asking around, among experts, getting some REAL answers? That would still be before publication date.


--Pierce


- - - - - - - - - - - - - - - - - - - - - - - - - - - - - -


Message: #96 (Pierce Ratcliff/misc.)
Subject:  Ash
Date:     18/11/00 at 11.37 a.m.
From:     Longman@

*format address deleted*
*other details encrypted and*
*non-recoverably deleted*

Pierce--

But not before copy-editing, and printing! Pierce, what are you trying to do to me!

Suppose we say Christmas? If this problem hasn't resolved itself, or we haven't at least found out what it is, by then—then I'll have to go to Jonathan.

First week of January at the LATEST.


--Anna

---

Message:  #157 (Anna Longman/misc.)
Subject:  Ash, texts
Date:     18/11/00 at 4.18 p.m.
From:     Ngrant@

*format address deleted
other details encrypted by
non-discoverable personal key*

Anna--

Very well. I agree. We raise no alarm before the first week in January. Although, if we haven't arrived at an answer before then— it's all of seven weeks away!—I will most probably have gone mad. But then I'll hardly have to worry about anything if I'm mad, will I!

I have just driven back from seeing John Monkham off at the airport. The photos of the golem are splendid, beyond belief. I'm sorry you won't be able to copy or keep them; Isobel becomes more security-conscious with every hour that passes. I think if John wasn't her son, she wouldn't be letting HIM take them off-site.

I've had a morning to polish my translation. Here it is at last, Anna. 'Fraxinus', as promised. Or at least, the first section of it. Sorry I have only had time to do the bare minimum of footnotes.

--Pierce

---

Message:  #163 (Anna Longman/misc.)
Subject:  Ash
Date:     19/11/00 at 9.51 a.m.
From:     Ngrant@

*format address deleted
other details encrypted by
non-discoverable personal key*

Anna--

I've GOT it.

I've got the ANSWER.

I was right, the simplest explanation is usually the correct one. We've been being too complicated, that's all; complicating things unnecessarily! It's so simple. No need to concern ourselves with Davies's theory, whatever it may have been; no need to worry about what the British Library catalogue says!

What I've only this minute realised is, just because a document is CLASSIFIED as fiction or myth or legend, THAT DOESN'T MEAN IT'S NOT TRUE.

That simple!

It was something Isobel just said to me—I HAD to tell her I was having problems, I was talking about Vaughan Davies's theory: she just said, 'Pierce, what's all this RUBBISH?' And then she reminded me—

The archaeologist Heinrich Schliemann found the site of the city of Troy in 1871, by digging EXACTLY WHERE HOMER SAID IT WAS in the ILIAD. (Although his methods may have left much to be desired.)

And the ILIAD isn't a 'historical document', it's a POEM! With gods and goddesses and all the artistic license of fiction!

It was a thunderstroke!—I still don't know how I came to miss the re-classification of the Ash documents, but in a very real sense, it doesn't matter. What matters is, we have physical evidence here at the site that means—WHATEVER some expert has thought about it—the chronicles of Ash's 15th century actually contain truth. When they mention post-Roman technological 'golem', we FIND them. You can't argue with the evidence.

Truth can be carried down to us through STORY.

It's all right, Anna. What's going to happen is, the libraries and the universities will just have to classify the Ash documents BACK to being Non-Fiction.

And Isobel's expedition and my book will give the incontrovertible evidence of why they must do this.

--Pierce

# PART TWO

6 September–7 September AD 1476

*"FRAXINUS ME FECIT"*

i

SHE MISSED THE weight of her hair.

Never having cut it, she had not been aware before that it *had* a weight: all the hundreds of fine, silver, yard-long strands.

The winds grew colder as they sailed south.

This isn't right. This isn't what Angelotti used to tell me about, when he was under the Eternal Twilight; not this *cold*. It should be getting hotter—

Momentarily, she doesn't see this ship: sees instead Angelotti, sitting with his back up against the carriage of an organ-gun outside Pisa; hears him say *Women in thin, transparent silk robes—not that* I *care!—and roof-gardens where the heat is reflected in by mirrors; the rich grow vines; one long endless night of wine; and always fireflies. Hotter than this!* And she had breathed the sultry, sweating Italian air, watched the blue-green dots of fireflies swell and die, and dreamed of the hot south.

Freezing spray hit her face.

She had not realized, before, how the weight of her hair was with her every day, in every movement, or how it had kept her warm. Now she felt lightheaded, cold about the neck, and bereft. The soldiers of the King-Caliph had left her no more hair than would cover her ears. The whole silver carpet of it had strewn the dock at—where? Genoa? Marseilles?—cut, and trodden into the mud as she was carried aboard, semi-conscious.

Ash flexed her left knee, secretly. A stab of pain went through the joint. She nipped her lip between her teeth, not crying out, and continued the exercise.

The prow of the boat dipped, thudding into the cold

137

waves of the Mediterranean Sea. Salt crusted her lips, stiffened her cropped hair. Ash gripped the stern-rail, rocking with the motion, and stared back, north, away from the lands of the Caliph. A diminishing wake of silver marked their passage on the sea: the reflection of a gibbous moon, cleft by their passing.

Two sailors pushed past her, going to the heads. Ash shifted her body. Her left leg would almost support her full weight now.

*What happened?*

Her nails dug into the wood of the ship's rail.

What's *happened*—to Robert, and Geraint, and Angelotti? What's happened to Florian, and Godfrey in Dijon? Is Dijon even standing? Fuck, fuck, *fuck!*

Frustrated, she slammed her hand down on the grained wood. Wind whucked the sails above her head. Nausea threatened to overcome her again. *I am tired of feeling sick every damn day!*

Stomach empty, light-headed since the wound to her head had been freshly broken open, she still knew from experience that—despite in the past breaking her ribs, her shinbone, and almost all the fingers on her left hand at one time or another—the most dangerous injury she ever had received had been the *nazir*'s tap with a mace to her knee. The most dangerous because the most likely to disable. Knee joints don't move that way.

Better, now, than it had been some days ago?

*Yes*, she concluded tentatively. *Yes . . .*

Ash turned her head, gazing down the well of the ship, past the rowers. The *nazir* who had given the blow, one Theudibert, grinned back at her. A sharp word from the commander of the prisoners' escort squad, *'Arif* Alderic, recalled him to his duties; which as far as she could see only involved Theudibert in seeing that she did not throw herself overboard, or get herself raped and killed by the ship's crew—"raped" is probably permissible, she thought, "killed" will get Theudibert into trouble—and otherwise entertain himself until the ship made landfall.

As well, the Visigoth soldier kept her away from the other prisoners aboard. Ash had barely got a word with one or two of them—four women and sixteen men, most of whom were Auxonne merchants by their dress, except for a man who was obviously a soldier, and two old women who looked like swine-herds or chaff-gatherers; no one who could be worth the cost of bringing across the Mediterranean, even as slave labor.

Carthage. It *has* to be Carthage.[19]

I never heard any voice. I don't know what you mean. *I never heard any voice!*

She glimpsed something ahead, between the lateen sail and the prow, but could not make out enough in the darkness to know if it were land or clouds again. Above, constellations still indicated they sailed southeast.

Ten days? No, fourteen, fifteen, maybe more. Christ, Green Christ, *de profundis*, what's *happened* since they took me? *Who won the field?*

A tread on the deck alerted her. She looked up. '*Arif*-commander Alderic and one of his men approached, the man carrying a bowl of something viscous, white and gruel-like.

"Eat," the bearded dark Visigoth *'arif* ordered. He appeared to be forty or so: a large man.

It had been five days after the battle before her raw, ragged voice came back, and she was able to whisper. Now she could speak normally, apart from her chattering teeth in the cold.

"Not until you tell me where we're bound. And what's happened to my troops."

It was no great effort to decide on a hunger strike, Ash thought, when it was impossible to keep food down. *But I shall have to eat, or I'll be too weak to escape.*

---

[19] Given the date of AD 1476, the text cannot be referring here to the original Phoenician settlement of Carthage, or to Roman, Vandal or Byzantine Carthage. Since the culture is not Islamic, this must be a reference to my presumed Visigoth settlement, possibly at or near the same geographical location, and named "Carthage" for that reason.

Alderic frowned, more in puzzlement than anger. "I was particularly instructed on that point, not to tell you. Come: eat."

She visualized herself though his eyes—a thin lanky woman with the broad shoulders of a swimmer.[20] Cropped silver-fair hair: scalp still clotted bloody where her head had bled ten or fifteen days ago. A woman, but a woman in nothing more than a linen shirt and braies; shivering, dirty, and stinking; and red with lice- and flea-bites. Bandaged at the knee and shoulder. Easy to underestimate?

"Did you serve with the Faris?" Ash asked.

The *'arif* took the bowl that his foot-soldier held, motioning the man away with a jerk of one hand. He remained silent. He held it out, with an expression of determination.

Ash took the wooden bowl and scooped up crushed-barley gruel on her filthy fingers. She took a mouthful, swallowed, and waited. Her stomach lurched, but kept it. She licked her fingers, revolted by the bland lack of taste. "Well?"

"Yes, I served with our Faris." *'Arif* Alderic watched her eat. An expression of amusement crossed his face at the speed of it, now she was able to eat without throwing up. "In your lands, and in Iberia, these past six years, where she fought in the *Reconquista*—taking Iberia back from the Bretons and Navarrese."[21]

"She good?"

"Yes." Alderic's amusement deepened. "Praise God, and praise her Stone Golem, she is very good indeed."

---

[20] The Latin has "upper body strength of a sword-user"; this is the nearest modern comparison.

[21] ???—PR. This is completely baffling! The *Reconquista* involved Spanish Christian forces driving out the remaining Arab cultures from Spain (after the Arab conquest and settlement begun in AD 711), a process completed in AD 1492, some sixteen years after the events supposedly depicted in the "Ash" texts. I can only suppose complete textual corruption here. After five hundred years it is impossible to guess what the "Fraxinus" chronicler actually meant.

"She win, at Auxonne?"

Alderic began to speak. *Got him!* she thought. But within a fraction of a second the commander recalled himself and shook his head.

"My instructions are strict. You are to be told nothing. It was no inconvenience, while you were ill. Now you have recovered, somewhat, I feel it . . ." *'Arif* Alderic appeared to be searching for a word. "Discourteous."

"They want me softened up, before they talk to me. I'd do exactly the same thing."

Ash watched him carefully not ask her who *they* might be.

"Okay." She sighed. "I give up. You're not going to tell me anything. I can wait. How long before we dock at Carthage?"

The man's brows rose up, with perfect timing. The *'arif* Alderic inclined his head, politely, and said nothing.

Her stomach churned. Ash, with deliberation, leaned out over the leeward rail, and threw up what she had just eaten. It was not policy. Dread and pity mixed in her gut, fearful that she might hear of Dijon fallen, Charles dead—but who cares about a bloody Duke of Burgundy?—and worse, the Lion Azure in the front line, rolled up, broken, burned, crushed; all the faces she knows cold and white and dead on the earth in some southern corner of the Duchy. She gagged, threw up nothing but bile, and leaned back, holding onto the rail to keep herself upright.

"Is your general dead?" she asked suddenly.

Alderic started. "The Faris? No."

"Then the Burgundians lost the field. *Didn't* they?" Ash fixed her gaze on him, stating speculation as certainty: "She wouldn't be alive if we'd won. It's two weeks, what can it *matter* if you tell me? *What happened to my people?*"

"I'm sorry." Alderic gripped her arm and lowered her down onto the deck, out of the way of sailors' running feet. The deck heaved up under her: she swallowed. Alderic gazed back at the steersman and the stern, where the ship's captain stood. Ash heard something called, but could not distinguish what.

"I am sorry," Alderic repeated. "I've commanded loyal men, I know how badly you need to hear news of yours. I am forbidden from telling you, on pain of my own death—"

"Well, *fuck* King-Caliph Theodoric!" Ash muttered to herself.

"—and in any case, I do not know." The *'arif* Alderic looked down at her. She saw him note, by a glance, where the *nazir* Theudibert was, and if he was in earshot or not. Not. "I don't know your liveries, nor what part of the field you fought, and in any case I was with my own men, keeping the road to the north clear of the reinforcements from Bruges."

"Reinforcements!"

"A force of some four thousand. My *amir* defeated them; I think in the early hours before you joined battle at Auxonne. Now: enough. Sit there, be silent. *Nazir!*" Alderic straightened. As Corporal Theudibert ran up, Alderic ordered, "Keep your men with you, and guard this woman. Never mind the other prisoners. Don't let *her* escape while we dock."

"No, *'Arif!*" Theudibert touched his hand to his heart.

Ash, hardly listening, found herself sitting on the deck that throbbed to the rowers' change of beat, surrounded by the legs of armed men in mailshirts and white robes.

Reinforcements! What *else* didn't Charles tell us? Hell, we're not mercenaries, we're mushrooms—kept in the dark and fed on horse-shit . . .

It was the kind of remark she could have made to Robert Anselm. Tears pricked at her eyes.

Above, the night sky darkened, familiar stars fading with moon-set. She prayed, by habit and almost without realizing it: *By the Lion—let me see dawn, let the sun come up!*

A settled blackness lay across the world.

The wind bit cold, sieving through her old linen shirt

as if she wore nothing. Her teeth began to chatter. *But Angeli' told me how* hot *it is, under the Eternal Twilight!* Voices shouted, lanterns were lit—a hundred iron lanterns, strung from every rail and all up the mast. Decked out with yellow flames, the ship sailed on; sailed until Ash heard muttering among the soldiers and scrambled to her feet, knee paining sharply, and stood, soldiers' hands gripping her arms, and saw, for the first time that she remembered, the coast of North Africa.

Waning moonlight marked out the lifting swell. A black blob, darker than the sea and sky, must be land. Low. Headlands? The deck jerked under her as they tacked and came around on a different course. Hours? Minutes? She grew cold as ice in their imprisoning hands, and the indistinct land drew closer. She smelled the liminal odor of dying weed, scavenged corpses of fish and bird excrement that is the smell of coasts. The lift and fall of the deck lessened: wood rang and rattled as the sails came down, and more oars dug into the water. Spray hit her numb skin.

A congerie of lanterns shone across the waves—the sea calmer now: she thought *Are we sheltered? Is there an isthmus?*—and became an approaching ship. No—ships.

Something in the first vessel's movement took her eye: a snaking, irregular motion. She clenched her arms across her breasts, against the cold, and stared tear-eyed into the wind. The foreign ship beat up toward them, indistinct; was suddenly twenty yards away, clear in its lanterns and their own—a sharp-prowed, long, thin, *curving* vessel; sides slabbed with wood and some bright substance.

Not metal, too heavy.

It glinted with the exact color of sunlight on the roofs of Dijon, and she thought suddenly *Slate! Thin-split slate, as armor. Christus!*

A single great tiller-oar rose at the poop, shifting left and right. The ship snaked a serpentine course, the whole body of it moving in articulated segments; knifing through the black water, a vision in lamplight: gone into the dark. No sails, no oars: what had stood at the tiller, wrenching it with immense power, had been a golem—

"Messenger ship," Alderic said, behind her. "Fast news."

She made to answer. Her teeth chattered too much; she gave it up.

Behind the articulated wooden vessel, a much larger ship thunked through the waves. Ash had a second to recognize it as one of the troopships she had seen from the hills of Genoa, before it passed on into the wet darkness. She was too low to see its deck; could only guess at the number of soldiers in the shallow-draught hold— five hundred? More? She had a brief glimpse of the curved sides towering above them, shining wet with spray; saw the great blades of the wheel at the stern canted, dipped down into the troughs of the waves; and she saw the clay bodies of golem inside the paddle-wheel, their weight and strength forcing it to turn, to bite into the cold, deep water. It thunked away northeast, into the Mediterranean.[22]

And how many ships like that have gone north?

The thought numbed her as much as the cold. Tranced, in the icy dark, she thought nothing more until the ship's motion altered. An hour past moon-set: it would be dawn. But not in this Twilight—least of all, here.

---

[22] This is obviously either a folk memory of the supreme Carthaginian sea-power in the Mediterranean around the time of the Punic Wars (216–164 BC), or of the Vandals' dominating navy in the 6th century AD.

A very similar passage appears in *Pseudo-Godfrey*; indeed it may have been copied into this. If the author of *Pseudo-Godfrey* was a monk, then he would have access to preserved Classical texts, which he has here conflated with the medieval myth of the Sea-Serpent to depict a mythical segmented "swimming ship," and a "paddle-wheel" powered vessel. Medieval authors are prone to this. We can assume Ash actually saw a double- or triple-oared galley, rowed by Carthaginian slaves.

Still held prisoned by Theudibert's men, she looked up.

The starboard rowers rested.

The ship opened the harbor of Carthage.

Bare masts thicketed the darkness, outlined against the thousand lights of the port buildings.

A thousand ships rocked, moored at rest in the harbor. Triremes and quinquerimes; golem-powered troopships loading men and stores; and European galleys, caravels, cogs, carracks. Deep-hulled merchant ships bringing in bullocks and calves and cows, pomegranates and pigs, goats and grapes and grain: all the things that do not grow or thrive, under the Eternal Twilight.

Oars splashed gently in the black water. Their ship glided on between two stark high promontories covered with buildings, each hairpin street outlined by rows of Greek Fire lights, gaudy and blazing and brilliant. Ash craned her head back, staring up at people on the bastions of the harbor: slaves running, men and women walking in loose, heavy woolen robes; and she heard a bell banging out for Mass from a distant church, and *still* the walls went up—

Nothing was raw rock. All of it was dressed masonry.

She saw the nearer stone dimly in the light from the ship's lanterns as they steered between half a dozen merchant ships, the drumbeat of their rowers echoing across the water and off the heights. Dressed stone: rising up sheer to battlements, bastions, ravelins, the highest walls pockmarked with row upon row of dark holes: arrow-slits, and crenellations, and stations for gunners to fire their cannon.

Her neck ached. She swallowed, lowered her gaze from the sheer immensity. She smelled the salt sea, overlaid by the stench of the harbor: all kinds of rubbish bobbed on the black waters, between skittering tiny craft. Sellers of fruit, sweetmeats, wine and woollen blankets sculled to keep up with their hull. She noted dozens of cargo ships, grain ships, riding high in the water: holds empty. And the black figures of men on the docks stood out against burning bonfires, and braziers full of hot coals. Chill wind blew into her eyes, making them water. The tears froze on her cheeks.

The sweaty fingers on her arm gripped tight. She glanced rapidly at whoever held her, and met the *nazir* Theudibert's bright-eyed, gloating expression. Theudibert slid his other hand up between her thighs. His rough nails snagged her skin and his fingers nipped shut, pinching tender internal flesh.

Ash winced, looked for Alderic, then felt her face burn red with the humiliation of making that appeal. She wanted to reach quickly behind her, grab Theudibert's wrist, bring his elbow cracking down backward over her knee—too many hands dug into the muscles of her arms, holding her: she could not move. His fingers stabbed up between painfully dry skin. She writhed.

*He can't know—my belly's not thick. If anything, I'm thinner; I can't eat for being sick. Maybe if he rapes me that'll shake it loose, and I'll end up grateful to this mother-fucking bastard—*

"This ain't the harbor," Theudibert grated, "*that's* the harbor."

Ash stared ahead. It was all she could do. The rowers were taking them between a multitude of small boats and medium-size cogs and carracks. Now, ahead, four great lanes of black water opened up before them, crowded with shipping.

Stark masonry separated these junctions of the harbor. Surmounting them—she moved her head, dazed—in turn a barracks, a fort, a windowless black building . . . and moored along the quay, great triremes and galleys and black pennanted warships.

Thousands of people swarmed, everywhere she looked: raising sail on ships, bringing donkey-carts steeply down to the quay ahead of them in the first opening, lighting more lanterns along the heights, calling, shouting, loading crates onto carracks. A dozen face-muffled women stared down from pleasure grounds a hundred and fifty feet away up a sheer cliff.

If I scream for help, who'll come?

No one.

The scent of spices, dung, and something odd came to her; something that didn't fit—

Ash wrenched her body. The armed men, taller and stronger, held her tightly; their warm, hard, armored bodies jostling hers. She flinched, her bare feet among their boots. A pang of fear went through her, rising up from her belly to her throat. The muscles of her thighs and knees loosened. She swallowed, dry-mouthed.

It's *real*, now. All the while we were just on a ship, anything could happen, we could have been going somewhere else, I could have escaped, it wasn't real . . .

I would give anything now to have a weapon, and even a dozen men . . .

The sweating soldier who held her, his fingers wet with her body's wetness, wore mail and carried a sword strapped at his belt; more importantly, had eight mates with him, and a commander whose shout would bring a hundred troops from the docks and warehouses.

"Mouthy bitch not so mouthy now?" his voice whispered in her ear. His breath was sweet with rice gruel: her gorge rose.

The knowledge that rape and mutilation are not inconceivable, are possible and even likely, thumped in the pit of her pregnant belly. A cold, cold sensation ran through her. Her hands prickled. She stared at the inexorably approaching dock.

Terror dried her mouth, tautened her body, strung her out to the highest pitch. Almost absently, she identified the odor that jarred her—the wind smelled almost peppery-cold. It stung her nostrils. In the Swiss mountains she would have thought it the scent of approaching snow.

A sudden eddy of wind across the harbor brought dampness.

Cold dots of sleet kissed her scarred face, and her bare legs under her shirt.

Oars backed and withdrawn, the sailors leaped to

prow and stern and slung ropes, and quayside workers hauled them in. Wood grated against stone. The galley docked in a crackle of the ice forming at the foot of the stone quay, and strained hemp cables to a creaking halt.

The *nazir*'s fist hit her in the kidneys, pushing her forward into the gaggle of the ship's other prisoners. Ash stumbled. She pitched forward and fell, unprepared on the gangway, catching herself and grazing her hands on the stone steps that led up to the quay. The first flakes of true snow melted under her palms. A boot caught her in the ribs. She smelled her own vomit.

"Shit!" Her voice came out a dry, high whimper.

No escape from the truth now. I *do* hear a voice. And I did hear *her* voice. The same voice. They don't know it, but they're right. This isn't a mistake. I am the person they want.

And what happens to me, now that they're going to find that out?

ALL THE WAY up the steep, narrow, ruler-straight streets from the dock, marching up steps between iron-shuttered buildings lit by steel-and-glass cages of Greek Fire,[23] the Visigoth soldiers still kept her away from the other prisoners.

She had no time to look at the city. She stumbled, bare feet scraping on cobbles, aware of hands gripping

---

[23] Since this is used for street lighting, this would appear (despite the text's use of the same name) to be a variant of Greek Fire—perhaps using only the ingredient naphtha, which received its name from the Arabic *al-naft*, and has a later history of use for this purpose in industrial England.

her under the armpits. Guards' polearms clashed as they came up to a thick stone arch—a gateway, that pierced an encircling wall stretching away around the hill as far as lights could show her. The wall was too high for anything to be visible beyond it.

The other prisoners from the ship were herded on past, into the body of the city, away from the gate into the citadel.

"What?" Ash turned her head, stumbling. The *'arif* Alderic called something. Two of the soldiers dragged back an old woman, a young fat man, and an older man. Soldiers closed around them.

The arched gateway tunnelled through a defensive wall a good twenty yards thick. She lost her footing in the dark. Theudibert dragged her up with a satisfied obscenity. She flinched back from another wall—no lights, here. A freezing wind blew in her face. She realized she was no longer in the gateway, but in a narrower passage.

None of the buildings to either side had any windows.

Four of Alderic's men lit ordinary pierced-iron lanterns, carrying them high. Shadows now stalked and jerked in the narrow passageway. A street? An alley? Ash squinted up. The last stars, fading into darkness, let her know this was still outdoors. A sharp fist in the back prodded her onward.

They passed a black door, barred with seven thick sections of iron. Thirty yards down the street, another door. None of the buildings were built of wood, or wattle and daub: all were windowless stone. Then they turned a corner, turned again, and again; winding through a maze of dark alleys, a pitiless black day dark above their heads.

Ash hugged her arms around her body as she hobbled on. Clad in thin linen, she would have shivered anyway, but this present cold bit at her hard-soled feet on the cobbles, whitened her fingers, and made her breath steam on the air.

The soldiers of the King-Caliph likewise shivered.

Four of the soldiers ran to unbar a door in a featureless wall. Big enough to be a sally-port, she thought. The *nazir* thrust her through it, into darkness. She banged her injured knee, and screamed aloud. Iron lanterns danced in her dazzled sight, hands shifted her, shoulders and arms banged against her body, hustling her inside, along a long dark passage.

A withered, tiny hand crept into hers.

Ash looked down, and saw that the old woman prisoner had taken her hand. The woman looked up at her. Shifting shadows, and lines and creases, disguised her expression. Her hand felt like cold chicken-bones. Ash tucked the woman's hand under hers, pressing it to her linen-covered body for warmth.

The old woman's hand slid down over her belly. The soft voice wailed in French, "I thought so, on the ship. You don't show, but you're with child, my heart. I could midwife you—*Oh, what will they do to us?*"

"Shut up!"

"What do they want us for?"

Ash felt and heard a mailed fist hit flesh. The woman's hand went limp and slid out of hers. She made a grab; but the soldiers surrounded her, pushing her on, and she stumbled with them out into a great courtyard.

*Back entrance*, she surmised, and *It's a manor house!* The courtyard was much longer than it was wide, surrounded on all sides by stone-barred windows and arched doorways. The building surrounding this interior courtyard on all four sides went up at least three stories. Greek Fire lanterns dazzled: she could not see the sky.

The long courtyard was packed full with people. Some house guards, by their swords. One or two better-dressed. Most of them were men and women of all adult ages, in plain tunics, with iron collars around their necks. Ash gaped at the running slaves, belly cold with familiarity.

Almost all, despite their different faces, had a family resemblance. Almost all had, in the fizzing white light, ash-pale hair.

She looked around for the old woman, missed her in

the crowd, and tripped. She landed, hands and knees, on black and white tiles. She groaned, wrapping both hands around her knee. It felt swollen and hot again. Her eyes teared.

Through water, she saw Alderic step forward with the ship's captain, the two of them speak to a group of house-guards and slaves; and she rolled over and got up. She and the male prisoners were pushed into a huddle. A fountain plashed into its bowl, a few yards away. In the heart of the falling jets, a mechanical phoenix sang.

Ash gripped the hem of her shirt in her two hands, pulling it down over her thighs. Cold sweat ran down between her shoulder-blades. She found herself mouthing, *Oh Christ, help me, help me keep my baby!* and stopped, her face stark. *But I don't want it, don't want to die in childbirth—*

When you think you have reached the end of fear, there is always somewhere to go. She knotted her hands into fists to prevent it being seen that they were shaking. Sentimental pictures of a son or daughter would not stay in her mind, confronted with this too-bright courtyard full of men talking in the Gothic dialect they called Carthaginian, far too fast for her to understand. Only the vulnerability of her hardly noticeable belly remained, and the absolute necessity—and impossibility—of secrecy.

"Poor girl, poor heart." The old peasant woman hung in a soldier's grip, bleeding. The two male prisoners stood with her, their very different faces frozen in identical expectations of fear.

"Come with me." The *'arif* Alderic was at her side, pulling her onward.

Ash shivered, cold deep in her gut. From somewhere she dragged up a grin, showing all her teeth. "What's the matter, you decided I'm the one you don't want? Hey, I could have told you that at Dijon! Or maybe this is where you tell me you want a contract with my company? Consider me softened up, you'll probably get a good deal!"

She could tell she stunk from the expressions of the guards near her, and the more distant glances of the one or two men who might be King-Caliph Theodoric's freeborn subjects, but her own nose was insensible of it. She limped with Alderic on the cold tiles. Her mouth ran on:

"I always thought it was warm enough, in the Eternal Twilight. This is fucking freezing! What's the matter, the Penance getting too heavy for you? Maybe God's pissed off with waiting for the Empty Chair to be filled. Maybe it's a portent."

"Be quiet."

Fear makes one voluble. Ash cut herself off.

Doors opened off the narrow passage. Alderic opened one, bowed, said something, and pushed her though in front of him. Her eyes were dazzled by more light.

Ash heard the door slam to behind her.

A thick voice said, "Is it her?"

"Perhaps." Another, drier voice.

Ash blinked her vision clear of dazzles. The dado of the room was lined with pipes and glass-covered lamps, hissing with Greek Fire. Oil burners stood in the room's corners, and their sweet scent both cleared her head and took her back with startling immediacy to being in a tent, in the field, some year in Italy, with Visigoth mercenaries.

No tent, this. The floor under her feet was tiled red and black, old enough that her bare feet felt every worn dip in it. Mosaic tiles winked back at her in the light of twenty lamps.

The walls glittered, covered in quarter-inch square colors from floor to vaulted ceiling. The images of saints and icons glared down: Catherine, with her wheel, Stephen with his arrows, Mercurius with his surgeon's knife and thief's cut purse, George and dragon. Gold robes and liquid dark eyes stared down at her.

Shadows lost themselves in the ribbed ceiling. Under the pungent controlled jets of Greek Fire she detected a smell of earth. The entire wall at the back of the room was one huge mosaic of the Bull and the Tree, Christ watching her from where he hung, Saint Herlaine at his leaf-pierced feet, Saint Tanitta[24] observing.

It was oppressive enough that she missed what was next said, only managing to concentrate again as the echoes of voices died in the cold, cold room. She looked toward the room's heavy, polished, square-cut settle and tables. Two men confronted her. A thin, white-robed man of about fifty, in the dress of an *amir*, watched her with lined eyes. Crouched by the foot of his chair, a man with the pasty fat face of an idiot watched her and dribbled.

"Go." The *amir* gently touched the retarded man's arm. "Go and eat. You may hear later what we say. Go, Ataulf. Go. Go . . ."

The idiot, who might have been anything between twenty and sixty, passed her with a glance from slant bright eyes, under thick fair brows and thinning hair. His wide-lipped mouth dribbled wetly.

Ash took a step aside as he went out, using it as an excuse to look back. No windows opened into this room. There was only the one double door. The *'arif* Alderic stood in front of it.

"Have you eaten?" the *amir* asked.

Ash looked at the fair-bearded man. She could distinguish some slight physical resemblance to the retard, but his intelligence shone out of his lined face.

Knowing where his kindness came from—that it was an effort to break her by contrast—she nonetheless answered meekly in her best Carthaginian Latin. "No, Lord-*Amir*."

" *'Arif*, have food brought." He pointed to a second carved chair, lower, that stood beside his own; as Alderic leaned back out of the doors to give orders. "I am the *amir* Leofric. You are in my house."

That's right. That's the name. She mentioned you.

---

[24] Possibly a Christianized version of the Carthaginian goddess, Tanit, to whom babies were sacrificed.

You're her not-quite father.

"Sit down."

Her feet became warmer the instant she stepped onto the carpets that covered the brick-red tiles. An ash-blond man entered and moved past her, placing a shallow ceramic dish of hot food on a low table, and retreating out of the room without a word. He was about Ash's own age, she judged; he had a metal collar around his throat, and neither Alderic nor the Lord-*Amir* Leofric took anymore notice of him than they did of the lamps. A slave.

She hid the fear chilling her stomach by walking on across the carpet and sitting herself on a low oak chair. It was padded, with a back that came around under her elbows; she was at a loss, for some moments, as to how you sat in it. *Amir* Leofric appeared to be ignoring any likely infestations from this flea-bitten prisoner: he regarded her with a concerned, inquisitive expression.

The food—two or three objects that were yellow, soft and purse-shaped—steamed in the chill air. Ash scooped up one in her bare dirty fingers, bit into warm brittle pastry, tasted potatoes, fish, and saffron.

"Shit!" She slobbered the better part of a raw egg out of the pastry purse, down her wrists and forearms. In one rapid movement she licked yolk and white off, licked her skin clean. "Now, sir—"

She looked up, intent on taking a verbal initiative, and broke off, springing to her feet, careless of the stained shirt barely covering her legs.

"Oh, Christ, it's a *rat*!" She threw out an arm, pointing at the *amir*'s lap. "It's a plague rat!"[25]

"My dear, nothing of the sort." The Visigoth *amir* had a surprisingly pleasant smile, much younger than his

---

[25] This, and another similar reference, are additions to the original manuscript. Even were they not inscribed marginally in different handwriting, context would prove as much: the role of *Rattus Rattus* in carrying the "plague flea" was not realized until 1896. I suspect a Victorian collector read this document at some point in its existence; a descendant, perhaps, of the man who wrote "Fraxinus me fecit" on the outer sheet in the 1700s.

lined face; teeth gleaming white in his gray-blond beard. He bent his head and chirruped encouragingly.

A pointed furry face emerged from the folds of his white, gold-trimmed velvet robes, pink nose first. Tiny pupil-less black eyes fixed on Ash as the animal froze. Ash stared back, startled at the eye-contact. The animal's fur shone pure white in the softening lamplight.

Encouraged by stillness it glided out onto Leofric's thigh, picking its way carefully over his robe. High haunches were followed by a sleek bald tail. Its body alone was ten inches long. It had (she saw in frozen horror as it emerged) a bare scaly tail. And balls the size of walnuts.

"*That*'s not a rat? Get out of here!"

At her voice the rodent froze, back curving into lordosis. Rats are black, are mice writ large. This, she saw with all the clarity of fear deferred, was broad at the rump, narrow in the fore-quarters. The muzzle seemed blunter than a mouse's. It had small ears, for the size of its broad head.

"A different breed of rat. My family brought them back from a voyage to the Middle Kingdom."[26] The *amir* Leofric murmured quietly. He put one weathered finger down and scratched the rodent behind its ear. The animal stood up on its hind legs, sniffing with a quivering spray of whiskers, and staring into the man's face. "He is a rat, my dear, but a different kind."

"Rats are the Devil's lap-dogs!" Ash moved back two steps on the carpet. "They eat half your stores, all if you don't have a pack of terriers; Jesu, the trouble I've had—! Filthy, dirty—And they give you plague!"[27]

"Perhaps once." Again, the Visigoth *amir* chirruped.

---

[26] Possibly China. By the physical description in the text, this is not *Rattus Rattus*, the Black Rat, but *Rattus Norvegicus*, the Brown Rat, which is Asian in origin.

[27] Ash's concern with the destructive capacity of rodents is original to "Fraxinus," and must have been a similar problem for all army commanders.

It was a surprisingly silly sound to come from an adult man, and Ash thought she heard the *'arif* Alderic snort quietly from the doorway. Leofric's robe moved.

"Who's my sweetheart, then . . . ?" he whispered.

Two more rats came out onto his shoulders. One was yellow, marked with sepia brown at the haunches, toes, and muzzle; the other, Ash would have sworn if the light had been better, was a pale enough slate-gray to appear blue. Two more sets of bead-black eyes fixed on her.

"Perhaps once," Leofric repeated. "A thousand rat-generations ago. They breed much faster than we do. I have records going back through the decades to when these were plain brown—not half so pretty as you, my dear," he added to one of the beasts. "These have known no disease for a century or more. I have many varieties. Rats of every color and size. You must see them."

Ash stared, frozen, as one of the rats reached its furry snake-head up and bit the Visigoth *amir*'s ear. A rat-bite will bring fever, sometimes death; even if not that, then pain like a needle stabbing flesh. She winced in sympathy. Leofric didn't move.

The blue rat, delicate paws holding the unblemished lobe of the man's ear, continued to lick it with a tiny pink tongue. She nuzzled a little in his beard, and then dropped down to all fours and wriggled instantaneously out of sight in his robes.

"They're your familiars!" Ash exclaimed, revolted.

"They are my hobby." The *amir* Leofric switched to talk in French, with a slight accent. "Do you understand me, my dear? I want to be sure that you understand what I say, and that I understand anything you may tell me."

"I don't have anything to say."

They remained staring at each other for a moment, in the lamplit room. The same slave entered and tended to one lamp, pouring in a different oil. A flower scent gradually imposed itself on the room's air. Ash glanced over her shoulder at Alderic's bulk blocking the doorway.

"What do you expect me to say, Lord-*Amir*?" she

asked. "Yes, I'm some relation to your general. Obviously. She says you bred her from slaves. I can see that you did. Too many people here look like me . . . Does it *matter*? I've got five hundred men I can answer for, and despite what she did at Basle, I'm willing to negotiate another contract. What else can I say?"

Ash managed to end with a shrug, despite standing dressed in nothing but filthy shirt and braies, her hair cropped and stinking, itching with bites.

"Sweetheart," Leofric breathed. To the pale blue rat, Ash realized. The Visigoth lord bent his head and the rat on his knee stood up on its hind feet, stretching up slimly. They were briefly nose-to-nose, then it dropped back to all fours. He cupped his hand and stroked the rodent's arched back. It turned its head and licked his fingers with a clean pink tongue. "Touch her, gently. She won't hurt you."

*Anything to put off more questions*, Ash thought grimly, and walked back across the carpet to Leofric's chair, and reached out an extremely reluctant finger. She touched surprisingly soft, surprisingly dry, warm fur.

The beast moved.

She gasped. Tiny claws fixed into her forefinger—she froze, feeling how light the grip was.

The pale blue female rat sniffed delicately at Ash's bitten, dirty nails. She began to lick Ash, sat back, sneezed twice—a tiny, absurd sound in the huge mosaic-walled chamber—and sat up on her haunches, rubbing paws over her muzzle and whiskers, for all the world as if she were cleaning away shipboard filth.

"She's washing her face like a Christian!" Ash exclaimed. She left her hand outstretched, hopeful of the rat investigating it further; and with a sudden jolt of fear to her belly, realized that she was standing so close to the seated *amir* that she smelled his perfume and the underlying odor of male sweat.

Leofric stroked his rat. "My dear, it can take many years to breed a variety. Sometimes the right color will come, and then faults come bound up with it; retardation,

aggressiveness, psychosis, miscarriages, deformed va-
ginas, deformed guts so that they burst of their own
waste products and die."

The blue rat lay down and curled up nose-to-tail on
his lap. He looked back at Ash. "It can take many generations to breed true. To breed sire back to dam, son
to daughter. One culls out the unusable, breeding only
from what is useful—for many, many years. And sometimes success never comes. Or if it does, it is sterile. Do
you begin to understand why you may be important to
me?"

"No." Ash's tongue stuck to the dry roof of her
mouth.

The *amir* Leofric smiled, as if he were simultaneously
recognising her badly hidden fear, and thinking of something quite other. He added, "You will note, these are
most tame, unlike other wild beasts. That is a by-product
of the breeding, and one I did not expect—yes?"

"Sire!" Alderic's deep voice boomed. She turned her
head and witnessed a sudden entry through the double
doorway into the room of collared slaves, Arian priests,
armed foot soldiers, an Abbot, and a man carried waist-
high above the ground in a chair.

"Lord Caliph!" *Amir* Leofric hurriedly stood up, bow-
ing, rats scurrying back inside his clothes. "Sire?"

The back of the room was full of soldiers, Alderic's
men. Between them walked a man in the green robes of
an Arian Abbot—something odd about the cross on his
breast—and an *amir* richly dressed and (seen at close
quarters) rather younger than Leofric.

"I welcome you to my house," Leofric said formally,
in Carthaginian Latin, his voice achieving calmness.

A gesture, and the chair was set down.

"Yes, yes!" An old man sat in the chair, who had
obviously once had red hair, but now it was turned dirty
white, and who had had the warm freckled complexion
that goes with it, which now shone mottled and dark in
the lamplight. Skin hung loose at his arms, and stretched
tight over his nose, brows, and around his mouth. He

wore robes of woven gold tissue. Ash inhaled once and tried to hold her breath: neither of the slaves attending with pomanders could hide the stench of shit and his wasted flesh.

*Theodoric*, she realized, appalled, *it's the Caliph!* and found herself pushed down onto the carpet—trying desperately to favor her left leg—and Alderic's mail-gauntlet forced her down onto hands and knees. She could see nothing but the hems of robes, and richly tooled leather sandals.

"Well?" the Visigoth ruler's voice sounded weak.

*Amir* Leofric's voice said, "My lord Caliph, why are these men with you? This abbot? And the *amir* Gelimer is no friend of my family."

"I must have a priest with me!" The King-Caliph: fretfully.

A full-blown abbot is "a priest"? Ash wondered.

"The *amir* Gelimer has no place here!"

"No? No, perhaps not. Gelimer, get out."

A different, tenor voice protested, "Lord Caliph, it was I who brought this news to you, not *Amir* Leofric, though he must have known it long since!"

"True. True. You will then stay, so that we may hear your wisdom on this subject. Where is the woman?"

Ash's gaze fixated on the plain weave of the carpet. Its fibers felt soft against her palm. She risked turning her head, to see if there was any way to the door; saw nothing but the mailed legs of guards. No friends, no allies, no way to run. She wanted to shit.

"Here," Leofric admitted.

"Get her up," the King-Caliph wheezed.

Ash, dragged to her feet, found herself stared at by two expensively dressed and extremely powerful men.

"This is a boy!"

*Nazir* Theudibert stepped out from the guard and grabbed the front of her linen shirt between his two hands, ripping it from neck to hem. He stepped back. Ash sucked in her belly and stood erect.

"It is a woman," Leofric murmured, respectfully.

The King-Caliph Theodoric nodded, once. "I have come to encourage her. *Nazir* Saris!"

A scuffle at the door, among the King-Caliph's personal guard, made Ash turn her head. A sword slid from its wood-lined sheath. At that sound she jerked instantly back, even in Alderic's grip.

Two of the Caliph's soldiers dragged in the fat male prisoner.

"No! No, I can pay! I can *pay!*" The young man's eyes went wide. He yelled randomly in French, Italian and Schweitzerdeutsch. "My Guild will pay a ransom! Please!"

One of the soldiers tripped him up, the other yanked up his stained blue robes.

Light flashed from the flat of the sword as the soldier lifted it, and chopped precisely down. Blood spurted.

"Oh, *Christ!*" Ash exclaimed.

The room stank suddenly as the fat man's bowels relaxed. His white, bare legs streamed with blood. He lifted himself up onto his elbows, scrabbling forward, screeching and sobbing, face blubbered with tears. His legs dragged after him like two slabs of butcher's meat.

The twin slashes across his ankles that hamstrung him bled freely on the stone tiles.

An asthmatic voice said, "Talk to my counselor Leofric."

Ash forced herself to look away, to look at the man who had spoken—to look at the King-Caliph.

"Talk to my counselor Leofric," Theodoric repeated. In the lamplight, his stretched skin appeared yellow, his eye-sockets two black holes. "Tell him all your heart and all your mind. Now. I don't want you to be in any doubt of what we can and will do to you if you refuse even once."

The man on the floor bled and screamed and thrashed only his upper torso as the soldiers pulled him out of the room. The stone eyes of saints impassively watched him go.

"You did that just to *show* me—?"

Appalled and incredulous, Ash shouted at battlefield volume.

Dizziness sank down through her body; her hands and feet felt hot; she knew she would faint, in a second, and bent over to grip her thighs and inhale deeply.

*I've seen worse, done worse, but to just do it so casually, for no reason—*

It was the speed of it, and the absolute non-existence of any appeal, that appalled her the most. And the irrevocable damage. A flush colored her scarred face. She yelled, in camp patois, "You just ruined that poor fuck's life to *make a point*?"

The King-Caliph did not look at her. His abbot was saying something quietly, into his ear, and he nodded, once. Slaves sluiced down the tiles and retired. The floral scent from the oil-burners did not conceal the copper smell of blood and the stink of feces.

Alderic stepped away from her. Two of the Caliph's soldiers, the same two, took each of her wrists, locking her elbow and shoulder joints to hold her immobile.

"Kill her now," the *amir* Gelimer said. Ash saw Gelimer was a dark man, in his thirties; with a plain, small-eyed face and a braided dark beard. "If she is a danger to our crusade in the north, or even if she is only a very little danger, you should kill her, my lord Caliph."

The *amir* Leofric said hastily, "But no! How will we know what's happened? This must be examined!"

"She is a northern peasant," the King-Caliph wheezed dismissively. "Leofric, why waste your time with this? The best that can come out of it is another general, and I have one of those. Will she tell you why this cold? Why this hellish, devilish *cold* here, since your slave-general went overseas? The further north we conquer in crusade, the harder it bites us here—I truly do wonder, now, what God would have us do! Was this war *not* His will, after all? Leofric, have you damned me?"

The Arian abbot said cheerfully, "Sire, the Penance is a northern heresy. God has always favored us with this darkness that—while it keeps us from tilling soil or growing corn—nevertheless drives us out to conquer lands for Him. It makes us men of war, not farmers or herdsmen, thus it makes us noble. It is His whip, chastising us to do His will."

"It is cold, Abbot Muthari." The King-Caliph cut him off with a motion of his hand. The lantern light showed dark spots mottling his white fingers. Theodoric closed his fragile-lidded eyes.

"Sire," Gelimer murmured, "before you do anything else, Sire, take off her sword hand. A woman familiar with the Devil, as this one is, shouldn't be allowed to continue as a warrior, no matter how short a time you let her live after this."

The voice, and the apprehension of the image in her mind—two white circles of chopped bone in red spurting flesh—came instantaneously. Ash swallowed bile. Nausea and lassitude swept through her like the tide.

A small pointy furry face stared down at Ash from *Amir* Leofric's shoulder. Black eyes surveyed her. A spray of whiskers twitched. As Leofric bent down to speak to her, the rat shifted its pink-toed feet and settled back to groom one pale blue flank—neither wet, nor dirty, nor infested with fleas.

"Give me something, Ash!" the Visigoth *amir* Leofric pleaded in an undertone. "My daughter tells me you're a woman of great value, but I have only hope, not proof. Give me something I can use to keep you alive. Theodoric knows he's dying and he's become very careless of other people's lives these last few weeks."

"Like what?" Ash gulped, tried to see through tear-wet eyes. "The world's over-full of mercenaries, my lord. Even good, valuable ones."

"I cannot disobey the King-Caliph! Give me a reason why you shouldn't be executed! *Hurry!*"

Ash watched in fascination as the blue rat twitched its whiskers and washed behind its ears with delicate pink paws. She shifted her gaze six inches, to Leofric's imploring expression.

Either this will mean I'll be released. Or it'll mean

I'll be killed, probably quickly. Quickly is better; sweet Christ I *know* it's better, I've seen everything you can do to the human body, this is just children playing rose-in-a-ring! I don't want them to start on what professionals do.

She heard her own voice, thin in the cold stone-walled room:

"Okay, okay, I *do* hear a voice, when I'm fighting, I always have had, it's the same as your—daughter—hears, it might be, I'm obviously blood-kin to her, I'm just a discard from your experiment, but I do hear it!"

Leofric thrust his fingers through his hair, spiking up his white curls. His intense eyes narrowed. She realized that the *amir* was regarding her with an expression of skepticism.

*After all this, he doesn't* believe *me?*

She whispered, hard and urgent, *"You have to believe I'm telling you the truth!"*

Sweating, shaking, she remained staring into his blue eyes for a long minute.

The *amir* Leofric turned away.

If a hand had not caught her around her body, she would have fallen: the *nazir* Theudibert supported her across her bare breasts with a wiry, hard-muscled forearm. She felt him laugh.

Leofric said, "She hears the Stone Golem, Sire."

The *amir* Gelimer snorted. "And so would you claim that, now, in her place!"

The King-Caliph's mouth had whitened, and his attention wandered from the conversation to the abbot at his side; Ash saw his eyes snap back to Leofric at Gelimer's comment.

"Of course she says it," the King-Caliph Theodoric remarked, scornfully. "Leofric, you are trying to save yourself with some fable of another slave-general!"

"I hear tactics—I hear the Stone Golem," Ash said aloud, in Carthaginian Latin.

Gelimer protested. "You see? She had no knowledge of what it was called until you named it!"

The *nazir*'s arm pinned her. Ash opened her mouth to speak again, and Theudibert's free hand clamped over it, digging fingers hard into the hinges of her jaw so that she could not bite him.

The *amir* Leofric bowed very low, his rats scurrying for refuge into his robes, and raised himself up again to look at the dying King-Caliph.

"Sire. What the *amir* Gelimer says may be true. She *may* be saying this only for fear of pain or injury."

Leofric's pale faded eyes became bleak.

"There is a way to decide this. With your permission, now, Sire—I shall have her tortured, until it becomes clear whether or not she is speaking the truth."

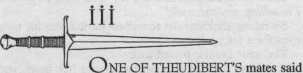

ONE OF THEUDIBERT'S mates said something in Carthaginian which Ash heard as, "Let's have a bit of fun with her. You heard the old boy. It doesn't matter so long as she don't end up dead."

It might have been a blond one, or his comrade; Ash couldn't tell. Eight men—nine, with their *nazir*—all very familiar, despite their light horse mail- and -curved swords kit. They could have been any men in Charles's army, or Frederick's, or the Lion Azure if it came to it and *where am I being taken?* she asked herself, her bare feet bruising on stone steps, staggering, pushed down—down?

Down spiral steps, into rooms below surface-level. Is the whole hill above Carthage harbor riddled with cellars? she wondered. And the obvious thought appeared in her mind: How many go in who never come out again?

Some. It only has to be "some."

What does he mean, torture? He can't mean *torture*. He can't.

The *nazir* Theudibert spoke with a grin in his voice. "Yeah, why not? But you never saw it. Nothing happened to his prize bitch. You never saw nothing, right?"

Eight other excited voices mumbled agreement.

Their sweat stank on the air. Even as they bundled her out of the staircase, into lantern-lit corridors, she smelled their violent high spirits, their growing tension. Men in a group, egging each other on: nothing they would not do.

She thought, as their fists pushed her on: I can fight them, I can gouge out an eye, I can break a finger or an arm, rupture somebody's testicles, and then what? Then they break my thumbs and shins and they rape me forward and backward, cunt and arse—

"Cow!" A fair-haired man grabbed her bare breast and squeezed his fingers closed with all his force. Ash's breasts were already tender, had been every day on ship; she involuntarily screamed and lashed out, catching him in the throat. Six or seven pairs of hands manhandled her, a backhanded blow cracked across her face and spun her around and dashed her against the wall of a cell.

The crack to her head shattered her with pain. She felt baked clay tiles under her knees. A man coughed thickly; spat on her. A soft leather boot, with a man's hard foot in it, kicked her violently three fingers' width below her navel.

Her lungs seized.

She gasped, scrabbling meaninglessly with her hands; found herself scraping a breath down her throat, felt cold clay tiles under left leg, hip, ribs and shoulder. Stinking linen tugged, caught around her neck, and ripped, as someone bending down tore her previously shredded shirt off over her head. She was naked to their gaze.

Ash got half a spare breath, snarled, "Fuck you!" in a voice pitifully high.

Four or five male voices laughed above her. They

kicked teasingly with their boots, laughed each time she
shrank away from the pain.

"Go on, do her. Do her! Barbas, you first."

"Not me, man. I ain't touching her. Bitch got a disease. All them bitches from up north, they got disease."

"Oh, fucking baby, wants his mamma's tit, don't want
a woman! You want me to *tie up* the dangerous warrior-
woman? You 'fraid to touch her?"

A scuffle, over her. Booted feet stamped down dan-
gerously close to her head, on the cell's tiled floor. She
saw red clay, reddened by the single lamp's light; dirty
hems of robes, very finely riveted mail skirts, leather
greaves tied on shins, and—as she rolled over onto her
front and lifted her head—men's faces in snapshot details: a wild brown eye, an unshaven cheek, a hairy wrist
wiped across a mouth full of bright, regular teeth; a
snake-scar trailing white down a thigh, a robe hitched
up, the bulge under clothing of a cock growing hard.

"Fucking do her! Gaina! Fravitta! What you fucking
standing there for, ain't you seen a woman before?"

"Let *Gaiseric* go first!"

"Yeah, let the baby do it!"

"Get your cock out, boy. That it? She ain't going to
even feel *that*!"

Their deep voices resonated between small walls. She
is ten years old again, sees men as infinitely heavier,
stronger, muscled; but eight men are not just stronger
than one woman, they are stronger than one man. They
are stronger than *one*. Ash felt hot tears squeezing over
her shut lids. She got to her hands and knees, shouting
at them:

"I'm going to take some of you with me, I am going
to *mark* you, maim you, mark you for life—!"

Saliva dripped out of her mouth, damp-spotting the
baked tiles. She saw every crack at the edges of the
squares where the clay crumbled, every black spidering
mark of ingrained dirt. Her head and stomach throbbed,
half blinding her with pain. A hot flush ran over her bare
body. "I'll fucking kill you, I'll fucking *kill* you."

Theudibert bent down to scream into her face. His saliva sprayed her as he laughed. "Who's a fucking warrior-woman now? *Girl?* You gonna fight us, are you?"

"Oh *yeah*, I'm going to try and take on eight men when I don't even have a sword, never mind any mates."

Ash was not aware, for a second, that she had spoken aloud. Or in such a tone of adult, composed contempt— as if it were completely obvious.

Theudibert's eyes narrowed. His grin faded. The *nazir* remained bending over, hands splayed on his mail-covered thighs. His frown indicated confusion. Ash froze.

"Like, I'm going to be *stupid*," she whispered scornfully, hardly daring to breathe in the moment of stillness. She stared up at faces: men in their twenties who would be Barbas, Gaina, Fravitta, Gaiseric, but she could not know which was which. Her stomach wrenched with pain. She sat back up on her heels, ignoring a hot trickle of urine down her inner thighs as she pissed herself.

"There aren't any 'warriors' on a battlefield." Her scornful voice ran on, trembling, in rough Carthaginian, and she let it: "There's you and your buddy, and you and your mates, and you and your boss. A *lance*. The smallest unit on the field is eight or ten men. Nobody's a hero on their own. One man alone out there is *dead meat*. I'm no fucking volunteer hero!"

It was the sort of thing she might have said every day, nothing especially perceptive.

She looked up in the yellow light at swinging shadows on the walls, and the rose-tinged faces staring down at her. Two men shifted back on their heels, a younger one—Gaiseric?—whispering to a mate.

But it's the sort of thing *they* might say.

And no civilian would.

Not man versus woman. Military versus civilian. *We're on the same side*. Come on, see it, you must see it, I'm not a woman, I'm one of you!

Ash had sense enough to rest her palms flat on her

bare thighs and kneel there in complete silence. She appeared as unaware of her bare breasts and bruised belly as if she were back in the wooden baths with the baggage train.

Sweat poured unnoticed down her face. Salt blood from her cheek ran over her split lip. A rangy woman, with wide shoulders, and hair cropped boy-short, head-wound short, nun-short.

"Fuck," Theudibert said. His thick voice sounded resentful. "Fucking cowardly bitch."

A sardonic voice came from one of the eight men; a fair-haired man standing toward the back. "What's she gonna do, *nazir*, take us all out?"

Ash felt a definable cooling to the emotional temperature in the cell. She shivered: all the fine hairs on her body standing upright. *They're on duty. They* could *have been drunk.*

"Shut your fucking mouth, Barbas!"

"Yes, *nazir*."

"Ah, fuck it. Fuck her." Theudibert swung around on his heel, shoving between his men to get to the cell door. "I don't see none of you shits moving. *Move!*"

A thickly muscled soldier, the one she had seen get hard, protested sullenly, "But, *nazir*—"

The *nazir* thumped him in passing, hard enough to double him over.

Their heavy bodies cluttered the cell door for seconds, longer seconds than she had known at any period of time that wasn't on the field of battle: seconds that seemed to last forever, them muttering discontentedly to each other, elaborately ignoring her, one spitting on the floor, someone harshly, cruelly laughing, a fragment of speech: "—break her anyway—"

The iron grating that formed a door clanged shut. Locked.

In that split second, the cell was empty.

Keys jangling, mail rustling. Their bodies moved away down the corridor. Distant booted footsteps loping up stairs. Fading voices.

"Oh, son of a bitch." Ash's head fell forward. Her body expected the flop of long hair over her face, awaited the minute shifting of its weight. Nothing obscured her vision. Literally light-headed, she gazed up at narrow walls lit by the lantern beyond the iron grating. "Oh, Jesu. Oh Christus. Save me, Jesu."

A fit of shuddering took her. She felt her body was shaking like a hound coming out of cold water and, amazed, found nothing she could do would stop it. The lamp in the corridor showed only a few feet of clay-tiled floor and pink mosaic walls. The lock on the iron grating was larger than her two fists together. Ash scrabbled around with shaking hands and found her torn shirt. The fabric dripped wet in her hands. One of the *nazir*'s men had pissed on it.

Cold cut her skin. She wrapped the stinking cloth over as much of her body as she could reach, and curled up in the far corner of the cell. The absence of a door bothered her: she did not feel less imprisoned but more exposed by the steel grating, even if its mesh was not large enough to let her put a hand through.

In the corridor, a Greek Fire jet hissed into life. Intensely white squares of light fell through the iron grating, onto the cracked tiles. Her belly hurt.

The stench of male urine faded as her nose numbed it out. The wet cloth grew warmer with her body-heat. Her breath clouded the air in front of her face. Intense coldness bit at her toes, her hands; numbed the pain of her cut forehead and lip. Blood still trickled down, she tasted it. Her stomach twisted, in a grinding pain, and she wrapped her arms around her body, hugging herself.

All I did was catch them off their guard at the right moment. That won't happen twice. That was just bad discipline: what happens when they get genuine orders to give me a beating, or a rape, or break my hands?

Ash curled herself tighter. She tried to quiet the yammering fear in her head, bury the word *torture*.

Fuck Leofric, fuck him, how could he feed me and then do this to me; he can't mean torture, not real torture, eyes burned out, bones broken, he can't mean that, it must be something else, it must be a mistake—

No. No mistake. No point in fooling myself.

Why do you think they've left you down here? Leofric knows who you are, *what* you are, she will have told him. By way of a profession I kill people. He knows what I'm thinking, right now. Just because I *know* what's being done doesn't mean it won't *work*—

Another grinding pain went up through her belly. Ash pushed both her fists into her abdomen, tensing her body. A low pain made her stomach cold. It subsided: almost immediately it grew again, cresting at a peak that made her gasp, swear, and sigh a great shuddering breath as it died down.

Her eyes opened.

*Sweet Jesu.*

She put her hand between her thighs and brought it out black in the lamp's light.

"Oh, *no.*"

Appalled, she lifted her hand to her face and sniffed. She could not smell blood, could smell nothing now, but the way that the liquid covering her hand began to contract and pull on her skin as it dried—

"I'm *bleeding!*" Ash shrieked.

She pushed herself up onto her knees, left knee screaming at the impact; pulled herself to her feet, and limped two steps to the grating, her fingers locking into the square steel mesh.

"Guard! Help! Help!"

No voice answered. The air in the passage outside shifted, coolly. No voices came from other possible cells. No sound of metal: weapons or keys. No guard room.

Pain doubled her over. She gritted a high, keen sound out from between clenched teeth. Bent over, she saw the white skin of her inner thighs appeared black from pubic hair to knee, rivulets of blood running down from knee to ankle. She had not felt it: blood is undetectable, flowing over the skin at blood-heat.

The pain grew again, grinding down in the pit of her belly, in her womb, akin to monthly cramps but stronger, harder, deeper. A sweat broke out over her face and breasts and shoulders, slicked wet under her arms. Her fingers clenched.

"Jesu, for Jesu's sake! Help me! Help! Help! Get a *doctor*! Somebody help me!"

She sank to her knees. Bent double, she pressed her forehead on the tiles, praying for the pain from her grazes to offset the pain and movement of her belly.

I must be still. *Completely still.* It might not happen.

Her muscles cramped again. A sharp, shearing pain cut off thought. She hugged her hands up between her thighs, into her vagina, as if she could hold back the blood.

The lamplight dimmed, gradually going down to a small intense jet. Blood clots blotted her palms. Blood smeared her skin as she held desperately onto herself, pushing up, pushing at the womb's entrance; warm wet liquid running out between her fingers.

"Somebody help me! Somebody get a surgeon. That old woman. *Anything.* Somebody help me save it, help me, *please, it's my baby, help me—*"

Her voice echoed down the corridors. Complete silence resumed, after the echoes died, a silence so intense she could hear the lamp hissing outside the cell. Pain died down for a moment, for a minute; she prayed, hands between her legs, and the swooping drag of it began again, a dull, intense, grinding, and finally fiery pain, searing up through her belly as her muscles contracted.

Blood smeared the tiles, made the floor under her sticky. Artificial light turned it black, not red.

She sobbed, sobbed with relief as pain ebbed; groaned as it started again. At the peak she could not keep from crying out. The lips of her vagina felt the pushing expellation of lumps—black stringy clots of blood, that slipped like leeches over her hands and away, spilling on the floor. Blood hot on her hands and legs; smearing her thighs, belly; plastering in warm hand-prints over her torso as she hugged herself and shook, biting at the inside of her mouth, finally screaming in pain; and then blood drying cold on her skin.

"Robert!" Her imploring scream died, dull against the ancient tiled cellar walls. "Oh, *Robert!* Florian! Godfrey! Oh help me, help me, help meee—"

Her belly cramped, contracted. The pain came now, rose up like a sea swell, drowned her in agony. She wished she could pass out; but her body kept her present, working against it, swearing at the physical inevitability of the process, weeping, filled with a violent fury against—who? What? Herself?

I didn't want it anyway.

*Oh shit no—*

Her ragged nails made half-moon indentations in her palms. The thick stink of blood flooded the cell. The pain shredded her. More than that, knowing what this pain meant broke her into pieces: weeping, quietly, as if afraid now that she would be heard.

Guilt shuddered though her: *If I hadn't asked Florian to get rid of it, this wouldn't be happening.*

Her reasonably accurate guesses of the north ("nearly Vespers," "an hour before Matins") gave way to complete disorientation: it must surely be still black day, not starry night, but she could not be certain of it. Not certain of anything now.

Her belly's pain loosened and tightened every muscle in her body: thighs, arms, back, chest. The involuntary contractions of her womb died down, slowly. The immensity of the relief drowned her. Every muscle relaxed. Her eyes stared, fixed open wide.

Her breasts hurt.

She lay curled on her side in the lamp's checkered illumination. Both her hands were full of clots and strings of black blood, drying to stickiness. A flaccid veined thing lay on her palm, half that size, drying. It trailed a twisted thread of flesh no thicker than a linen cord. Attached to the cord's end was a red gelatinous mass about the size of an olive.

In the square of white light she could clearly distinguish its tadpole-head and curving body-tail, the limbs only buds, the head not human. An eight-week miscarriage.

"It was perfect." She screamed up at the invisible ceiling. *"It was perfect!"*

Ash began to cry. Great gasping sobs wrenched at her lungs. She curled up tight and wept, body sore, shuddering like a woman in a fit; screaming in grief, scalding tears pouring down her face in the darkness, howling, howling, howling.

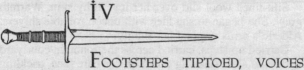

## IV

FOOTSTEPS TIPTOED, VOICES whispered: she didn't notice.

Gut-wrenching sobs faded to silent tears, running hot and wet over her hands. Grief ceased to be a refuge. Her limbs and body shook, with trauma and with the intense cold of the cells. Ash rolled into a tighter ball, cold palms clasped around her shins. Her lips were dry with thirst.

The world and her body came back. Chill clay walls bit into her bare flank. She shivered, all her body-hair standing up like the bristles on a pig; expected soon to be sleepy, to cease to shiver, as men do in cold high mountain snow when they lay down never to rise again.

The cell's steel grating slammed to one side. Slaves' bare feet slapped on the tiled floor; someone shouted, above her head. Ash tried to move. Soreness stabbed her vagina. Quaking shudders wracked her body. The tiles felt frost-cold under her.

A rasping voice shouted, "God's Tree, don't you know enough to report to me!"

Ash got her head up off the floor, neck straining, swollen hot eyes blinking.

"Light a fire in the observatory!" a bulky, dark-bearded Visigoth man snapped, standing over her. The *'arif* Alderic unbuttoned the voluminous indigo wool gown that hung from his shoulders, over his mail. He dropped it to the bloodstained floor, knelt, and rolled her into the material. Ash vomited weakly. Yellow bile stained the blue wool. Thick folds of cloth enveloped her, and she felt him thrust an arm under her knees, her shoulders, and lift. The mosaic walls whirled in the intense light of Greek Fire as he swung her up into his arms.

"Out of my way!"

Slaves ran. His footsteps jolted her.

Silk-lined wool slid over her icy, filthy skin. Warmth grew. She began to shudder with uncontrollable shivers. Alderic's arms gripped her tightly.

Carried up steps, carried across the fountain courtyard with cold sleet slashing down on her bare face, trickling pale red water, Ash tried to go away in her head. To put it all wherever it is that she puts memories of bad things, of people who betrayed her, of stupid miscalculations that got people killed.

Hot tears pushed up between her eyelids. She felt water trickle down her face, mingling with the sleet. In a crowd of slaves and shouted orders, she was carried into another building, down corridors, down stairwells; grief wiping out everything but a dim impression of a warren of rooms going on forever, rooted down into Carthage hill like a tooth into a jawbone.

The pressure of his arms under her relaxed. Something hard but slightly giving pressed into her back. She lay on a pallet on a blocky white oak daybed, in a spacious room lit by Greek Fire. Slaves ran in with ten or a dozen iron bowls, putting them on tripods and heaping them with red-hot charcoal.

Ash stared up. Metal cabinets lined the walls, below glass-and-fire lamps. Above the lights, the vaulted wooden roof *shifted*—shutting, like a clamshell, as she watched: cutting off a view through thick, gnarled glass of a black day sky above.

Slaves ceased pulling ceiling-panels, tied off ropes.

A pale-haired girl of eight or so scowled at Ash, fingering her steel collar. The male slaves left. Two more child-slaves remained to tend the ember-burners that gradually leaked warmth into the cold air.

Alderic's harsh commands brought more people. A freeborn, grave, bearded Visigoth in woolen robes stared down at Ash, together with a woman who wore a black veil pinned to the crown of her headdress. The two of them rattled a rapid conversation in medical Latin. She understood it well enough—*why not? Florian uses it all the time*—but the details slid out of her concentration. Her body shifted like meat on a slab as they pulled her legs apart, and first fingers and then some steel instrument were pushed into her vagina. She hardly winced at the pain.

"Well?" another voice demanded.

Her few minutes in the *amir's* company had not given her a memory of his face, but now she recognized his dirty-white hair and beard, tufting up like a startled owl. The *amir* Leofric, glaring down with alert, bloodshot eyes.

The woman—who must be a physician, Ash realized—said, "She will not easily conceive again, *Amir*. Look. I am surprised that she could bear this one for so long. There is chronic damage: she will never carry to term. The gate of the womb[28] is all but destroyed, and much scarred over with very old tissue."

Leofric stamped across the room. He reached out his arms and a slave put a green and gold velvet robe on him. "God's Tree! *This one is barren too!*"

"Even so."

"What is the use of these sterile females? I can't even breed from this!"

---

[28] Presumably "cervix."

"No, *Amir*." The woman probing between Ash's thighs lifted one blood-stained hand to put back her veil. She changed from Carthaginian Latin and spoke in French, as if she spoke to a child or an animal. The manner in which one speaks to a slave.

"I shall give you a drink. If there is more to pass, you will pass it. A flux, do you understand? A bloody flux. Then you shall be well."

Ash shifted her hips. Hard metal obstructions slid from her vagina, bringing infinite relief from a pain she had not known she felt. She tried to sit, to move, striking out weakly. The second doctor closed his hand around her wrist.

Her eyes focused on the man's cuff. In the room's white light, she saw slanting big stitches fixing the olive lining to the bottle-green wool garment. Wild stitches fastened button to cuff. The loop for the button was a mere hoop of fraying thread. *Someone, some slave, made this fast, sloppy, in a hurry.* Underneath his voluminous woolen sleeve a light silk robe was visible: far more like what she would expect to see worn in Carthage.

Alderic's wool gown cocooned her body, warming her core. Its workmanship was equally hurried.

*They* didn't expect this cold either.

What she feels here is not the warm, starlit, sweltering twilight that Angelotti described; when he was both slave and gunner on this coast. The Eternal Twilight in which nothing grows, but within the bounds of which the nobles of Carthage walk, silk-clad, under indigo skies.

The very air crackles with frost.

The woman, practiced, put a cup to her lips and tipped. Ash swallowed. A sweet herb tanged in the drink. Almost immediately her body cramped. The feeling of blood expelled from her body, soaking the wool, constricted her throat again and she clenched her jaw on a sob.

"Will she live?" Leofric demanded.

The elder doctor, very grave, very satisfied with his

own opinion, observed to the *amir* Leofric, "The uterus is strong. The body is strong, and displays little shock. If she is subjected to more pain, she will hardly die of it, unless it be most severe. She may safely be put to moderate torture within an hour or so."

The *amir* Leofric ceased pacing on the mosaic floor and flung open wooden window shutters. A blast of cold air entered the room, chilling the effect of the coals in iron dishes. He stared out into darkness at a sky of utter blackness: no moon, no star, no sun.

Ash lay in the pomegranate-carved oak bed, watching him. She thought: I really could die, now.

It was not a sudden realization. It came to her quite ordinarily, as it always did, usually just before battle; but it tightened the focus of her mind, snapped her into a complete consciousness of Leofric, his doctors, *'arif* Alderic and his guard, the bitter air, the bustle and business of the household. The hundred thousand men and women outside on the white-lit streets of Carthage, living out quotidian experience.

*About three-quarters of whom will know there's a war on, half of whom will care, and none at all will bother about just one more prisoner dying in a lord-*amir's *house.*

What came to her was the absolute apprehension of her own unimportance, as if a membrane had broken: all the things that one thinks could not happen "because I am me" become in an instant possible. Other people die of injuries, of accidents, of poisoned blood, of childbed fever, of an ordinary order of execution of the King-Caliph's justice, and therefore *I*—

She was used to thinking herself the hero of her own life: what lost sense for her now was the idea of it being a coherent story requiring a resolved ending (some day, in the future, the far future). She thought, *But it doesn't matter*, quite calmly. Other people can win battles, with or without "voices." Someone else can take my place. It is all accident, all chance.

*Rota fortuna*, Fortune's Wheel. *Fortuna imperatrix mundi.*

Without turning around, the Visigoth *amir* said, "I was reading a report from my daughter when the slaves summoned me. She reports you are a violent woman, a killer by profession, a warrior by desire rather than by training, as she is."

Ash laughed.

It was a tiny snuffle, a choke of a laugh, hardly a breath; but it surged through her so that her eyes ran, and she wiped the back of her hand across her chill, wet face. "Yeah, and I had so many professions to choose from!"

Leofric turned. At his back, a blank black sky whirled, flakes of snow plastering the edges of the wooden shutters. The same girl-slave pattered over the tiles and heaved the window-shutters to. Leofric ignored her.

"You are not what I expected." He sounded both fussy and frank. He bundled up his striped gown of green and yellow wool and paced across the floor toward her. "Foolishly, I expected you to be as she is."

That begs the question of what you think she is, Ash reflected.

"Take this down," Leofric said, to the smaller of the boy-slaves. Ash saw the child held a wax tablet, ready to impress it with his stylus. "Preliminary notes: physical. I see an habitually dirty young woman, evidence of parasitic skin inflammation common, scalp infested with ringworm. Muscle development unusual in a woman, especially in the trapezoid, and biceps. Peasant stock. General muscle tone good—extremely good. Some evidence of early malnutrition. Two teeth missing, lower jaw, left hand side. No evidence of caries. Scarring to face, old trauma to third, fourth and fifth ribs on the left side, to all fingers of the left hand, and evidence of what I suppose to have been a hairline fracture of the left shinbone. Rendered infertile by trauma, probably before puberty. Read that back to me."

Leofric listened to the young boy reading in a sing-song. Ash blinked back too-easy tears, huddling the wool gown around herself. Her sore body ached. Waves of sensation still throbbed through her belly, through her whole body: every tissue aching.

It took her breath: too stark to think about. Some arrogant part of herself rose up in revolt. "What is this, my pedigree? I'm not some God-rotted horse-coper's mare! Don't you know of what *degree* I am?"

Leofric turned back to her. "What degree *are* you, little Frankish girl?"

Cold air flickered across the hot coals, they burned red and black in turn. Ash met the eyes of the girl-slave kneeling on the far side of the iron tripod. The child winced and looked away. Ash thought, *Is he serious?* A waft of heat over the coals made her shiver.

"Squire's, I suppose. I sit at table with men of the fifth degree by right." It suddenly struck her as irresistibly ridiculous. "I can eat at the same table as preachers, doctors of law, *rich* merchants, and gentlewomen!" Ash shifted her body closer to the edge of the oaken bed and the nearest dish of hot coals. "I guess I eat with the knight's rank, now I'm married to one. 'The substance of livelihood is not so dignifying as is noble blood.' Hereditary knight beats mercenary."

"And of what rank am I?"

*She may safely be put to moderate torture within an hour or so.*

Flesh is so easy to burn.

"Of the second degree, if an *amir* is second in rank after the King-Caliph; that is, a bishop, viscount or Earl's equal." Her voice stayed calm. Her mind suddenly demanded, *What is John de Vere doing, is the Earl of Oxford dead?* She warily watched the Visigoth lord.

In his preoccupied tenor, he asked, "How should you address me, then?"

The answer he wants is *Lord-Amir* or *my lord*; he wants some show of respect.

Acidly, she suggested, " 'Father'?"

"Mmm? Mmm." Leofric turned and took a few steps

away from her, and back; his lined and faded eyes fixing on her face. He snapped his fingers at the slave scribe. "Preliminary notes: of the mind and spirit."

Ash pushed herself up into a sitting position on the palliasse, gritting her teeth against soreness and pain. Her eyes dripped. She bundled the warm wool around her naked body. She opened her mouth to interrupt. The little slave-girl's face screwed up in terror.

"She is a—" The white-haired man broke off. His gown moved, a bulge near his fine leather belt wriggling around. The gray nose and whiskers of a big buck rat poked out of Leofric's sleeve. He absently lowered his arm toward the oaken bed. The rat descended cautiously onto the palliasse near Ash.

"This is a mind between eighteen and twenty years of age," the Visigoth *amir* dictated. "She has a great resilience toward pain, and toward mutilation and other forms of physical damage; recovering from the miscarriage of a fetus of approximately eight weeks' growth inside of two hours."

Ash's mouth dropped open. She thought *recovered!* and then startled as a fly brushed the back of her hand. The jolt as she froze, instead of batting it away, left her body shaking. She looked down.

The gray rat was sniffing again at her hand.

"Such evidence as I have been able to gather speaks of her living among soldiers from an early age, adopting their modes of thought, and following both the military professions: whore and soldier."

Ash held out her brown-stained fingers. The rat began to lick her skin. It had a patched gray-and-white back and belly, one black eye and one red eye, and a plush velvet softness to its short coat. She cautiously shifted her hand to scratch it gently behind its warm, delicate ear. She attempted Leofric's chirrup. "Hey, Lickfinger. You're a witch's familiar if I ever saw one, aren't you?"

The rat looked up at her with bright mismatched eyes.

"She displays lack of concentration, lack of forward

planning, a desire to live for momentary sensation." Leofric signaled the scribe to stop writing. "My dear child, do you imagine I have *any* use for a woman who has become a mercenary captain in the barbaric north, and who claims her military skills come from saints' voices? An ignorant peasant, with a mere physical skill?"

"No." Ash, cold in her belly, continued to finger the rat's velvet coat. "But that isn't what you believe I am."

"You were with my daughter long enough to counterfeit a working knowledge of the Stone Golem."

"So the King-Caliph says." Ash let the cynical, acid tone remain in her voice.

"He is, in this case, correct." Leofric's tall skinny bulk sat on the edge of the bed. The gray rat skittered over the palliasse and climbed up his thigh, putting its front paws up on his chest. He added, "The Belly of God is right, you know; we Visigoths have no choice but to be soldiers—"

" 'The Belly of God'?" Ash echoed, startled.

"*Fist* of God," Leofric corrected himself. In Carthaginian Gothic it was a single word, obviously a title. "Abbot Muthari. I *must* stop calling him that."

Ash recalled a fat abbot in the King-Caliph's company. She would have smiled, but fear made her face stiff.

The *amir* Leofric continued: "Because you have every reason to attempt to convince me that you hear this machine, I can't believe anything you say about it." His faded blue eyes switched from her face to the rat. "I was not entirely lying to the King-Caliph, nor entirely attempting to save you from Gelimer's brutal, stupid wastefulness. I may have to inflict some pain on you, to be certain."

Ash rubbed her hand across her face. The coals took the chill from the air, but her sweat was cold. "How will you know I'm telling the truth when you hurt me? I'd say anything, and you know it, anybody will! I've—"

After a moment, into the silence, the white-haired

*amir* Leofric said gently, " 'I've tortured men.' Is that what you were about to say?"

"I've been present while it happened. I've given the orders." Ash swallowed. "I can probably frighten myself much better than you can, given what I've seen and what I know."

A slave-boy entered, coming to speak quietly to Leofric. The Visigoth's shaggy brows went up.

"I suppose I should admit him." He gestured the child away. A few moments later, two men in mail and helmets came in. Between his guards, an expensively dressed Visigoth *amir* with a braided dark beard entered the room.

He was the one with the King-Caliph, Ash remembered, and looking at his dried-grape eyes gave her memory of his name: Gelimer. Lord-*Amir* Gelimer.

"His Majesty insisted that I oversee this. Your pardon," the younger *amir* said insincerely.

"*Amir* Gelimer, I have never obstructed any order of the King-Caliph."

The two of them moved aside. Ash's stomach chilled. Inside a few seconds, the *amir* Gelimer made a signal. Two well-built men entered the room, one with a small field-anvil; the second with steel hammers and a ring of iron.

"The King-Caliph asked me to do this." *Amir* Gelimer sounded both apologetic and smug. "It is not as if she were freeborn, is it?"

Her body cramping, shuddering, bleeding; she let herself be pulled up from the bed, and stared fixedly at the mosaics on the wall—the Boar at the Green Man's Tree, in intricate detail—while a curved iron ring was shoved under her chin and held closed. Her head rang to the brief and accurate bang of hammers fixing a red-hot rivet through the collar's hasp. Cold water sluiced her. She could not move her head, cropped hair tight in one of the men's grips, but she blew water and spat and shivered.

The room smelled of soot. An unfamiliar cold weight

of steel rested around her neck. Ash glared at Gelimer, hoping to have him think her outraged, but her mouth kept losing its shape.

"Out of consideration for her illness, I think a collar will be sufficient," the *amir* Leofric murmured.

"Whatever." The younger *amir* chuckled. "Our lord expects results."

"I will soon be in a position to better inform the Caliph. Consulting records, I find seven litters born about the time of her apparent age; of which all were culled but my daughter. It could be that this one escaped the culling."

Ash shivered. Her head throbbed from the hammers. She put her fingers through the slave collar and pulled at the unyielding metal.

Gelimer for the first time looked her in the face. The *amir* spoke with the intonation one used to slaves and other inferiors. "Why so angry, woman? You have lost very little so far, after all."

What she sees, in her mind's eye, is a Visigoth lance-head sliding into Godluc's side: a thick knife on a stick ripping his iron-gray hair and black skin up his ribs, sinking in behind his forequarters. Six years' care and companionship ended in a brutal second. She clenched her fists, under the woolen gown serving her as a blanket.

It is easier to see Godluc than the dead faces of Henri Brant and Blanche and the other six score men and woman who turn the baggage train alternately into hotel, brothel and hospital, running it with all the enthusiasm they can bring her; and Dickon Stour's eternal efforts to improve his armory from repair to manufacture. Easier than to think of the dead faces of her lance-leaders, and each of their followers, drunk or sober, reliable or useless: five hundred dirty, well-armed peasants who would not consent to dig their lord's fields, or wild boys out for adventure, or criminals who would not stay for petty justice; but they will fight, for her. All this—the tents and their carefully sewn pennons, every war-horse or riding horse; each sword and the history of where she bought or stole or was given it; each man who has fought under her standard, in weather and ground always too hot—or too cold—or too wet—

"No, what have I lost?" Ash said bitterly. "Nothing!"

Gelimer said, "Nothing to what you may lose. Leofric, God give you a good day."

The half-cooled rivet on her collar stung her fingertips. Ash watched Gelimer's leave-taking. The complexity of politics in this court—impossible to learn in months, never mind minutes—weighed down on her. *Leofric might be trying to save my life. Why? Because he thinks I* am *another* Faris? *How important is that, now? Does it matter at all? My only chance is that it still matters—*

Her isolation cut her like a newly sharpened sword.

No matter how clear one's unimportance becomes, how easy it is to apprehend one's own death, the self still protests, *But it's too soon, too unfair, why* me?

Ash's skin chilled.

"What is going on?" she demanded.

Leofric turned back from the room's ornate, arched doorway. In French, again, he said, "If you want to live, I suggest *you* tell *me*."

It was blunt, a different tone completely from how he had spoken to *Amir* Gelimer.

"What *can* I tell you?"

"To begin with: how do you speak to the Stone Golem?" Leofric asked gently.

She sat on an oak carved bed it would take her five years to earn, wrapped in blood-soaked wool and linen. Her body felt sore. She said, "I just speak."

"Aloud?"

"Of course, aloud! How else?"

Leofric seemed to find something to smile at in her indignation. "You do not, for example, speak as you might do in silent reading, with an interior voice?"

"I can't do silent reading."

The scraggle-haired *amir* gave her a look which

plainly intimated that he doubted she could do any kind of reading.

"I recognize some of your machine's tactics," Ash said, "because I read them in Vegetius's *Epitoma Rei Militaris*."

The skin around Leofric's faded eyes became momentarily more lined. Ash realized his amusement. She remained on a cusp between fear and relief, held in tension.

"I thought perhaps your clerk had read it to you," Leofric said amiably.

The release of tension brought too-easy tears to her eyes.

If I'm not careful, I shall like you, Ash reflected. Is that what you're trying to do, here? Oh, Jesu, what can I *do*?

"Robert Anselm gave me his English copy[29] of Vegetius. I keep—kept—it with me all the time."

"And you hear the Stone Golem—how?" Leofric asked.

Ash opened her mouth to reply, and then shut it again. *Now why have I never asked myself that question?*

Finally, Ash touched her temple. "I just hear it. Here."

Leofric nodded slowly. "My daughter is no better at explaining it. In some ways she is a disappointment. I had hoped, when one was at last bred who could speak at a distance to the Stone Golem, that the least I could expect was to be informed how this was done—but no. Nothing but 'I hear it,' as if that *explained* anything!"

Now who does he remind me of? Just forgets everything and goes off, rides his own hobby-horse . . . ?

Angelotti. And Dickon Stour. *That's* who.

"You're a *gunner*!" Ash spluttered, almost hysterical, and clapped both hands over her mouth, watching his complete incomprehension with bright eyes.

"I beg your pardon?"

"Or an armorer! Are you sure you've never felt the

---

[29] Otherwise *De re militari*. The 1408 edition?—PR.

urge to make a mail shirt, my lord *Amir*? All those thousands of teeny-tiny rings, every one with a rivet in it—"

Leofric gave a bewildered, unwilling laugh; moved only by her evident mirth. Completely confused, the older man shook his head. "I neither forge guns nor construct mail. What are you saying to me?"

Why did I never ask? she thought. Why did I never ask *how* I heard? How *do* I hear it?

"Master Leofric, I've been taken before, I've been beaten before; none of this is new to me. I don't expect to live until Christ's Coming. Everybody dies."

"Some in more pain than others."

"If you think that's a threat, you've never seen a stricken field. Do you know what I risk, every time I go out there? War," Ash said, with very bright eyes, "is dangerous, Master Leofric."

"But you are here," the pale-colored, elderly man said. "Not there."

Leofric's complete calmness chilled her. She thought, Gunners, also, care everything about shot, aim, elevation, firepower: and only later think about the consequences, where it hits. Armed knights will, after battles, sit and discuss, realistically, the evils of killing; but this will not stop any of them devising a better sword, a heavier lance, a more efficient design of helmet. He *is* a gunner; an armorer; a killer.

And so am I.

"Tell me what to do to stay alive," she said. Hearing what she said, she suddenly thought *Is this how Fernando feels*? She went on: "For however little time it turns out to be before you kill me. Just tell me."

Leofric shrugged.

In the chill room, among bowls of red embers, lit by Greek Fire, Ash stared at the *amir*. She swathed the wool gown around her shoulders and sat up. It fell in blood-stained folds around her.

I never asked because I never needed to.

She felt it, now: a directing of her voice, somehow.

A directing of her attention toward—something.

"How long," she asked aloud, "has there been a Stone Golem?"

Leofric spoke words she didn't attend to.

*"Two hundred years and thirty-seven days."*

Ash repeated aloud, "Two hundred years and thirty-seven days."

Leofric broke off whatever he was saying. He stared at her. "Yes? Yes, it must be. The seventh day of the ninth month . . . Yes!"

She spoke again. "Where is the Stone Golem?"

*"The sixth floor of the northeast quadrant of the House of Leofric, in the city of Carthage, on the coast of North Africa."*

Her attention rose to a peak. Her listening, too, felt now that she attended to it as if it were something she did: not entirely passive, as one listens to a man speak or a musician play; not a mere waiting for an answer. *What am I doing? I'm doing* something.

"About five or six stories below us," Ash repeated, her eyes on Leofric. "That's where it is. That's where your tactical machine is . . ."

The *amir* said dismissively, "This much you might have heard from slave gossip."

"I might have. But I didn't."

He was watching her keenly now. "I cannot know that."

"But you can!" Ash sat up on the oak bed. "If you won't tell me what to do to stay alive—*I'll* tell *you*. Ask me questions, Master Leofric. You'll know what the truth is. You'll know whether I'm lying about my voice!"

"Some answers are dangerous to know."

"It's never wise to know too much about the affairs of the powerful." Ash got off the bed and walked, slowly and with pain, toward the window shutter. Leofric did not stop her as she unbolted it and looked out. A center iron bar bedded deep in the stone casement was thick enough to stop a woman throwing herself out.

Bitter air froze the skin on her cheeks, reddening her nose. She had a brief sympathy for those under canvas, in the wet cold north; a fellow-feeling for their misery and discomfort that was, at the same time, an utter desire to be there with them.

Below the stone sill, the great courtyard hissed and spluttered, Greek Fire lamps being hastily sheltered by an inappropriately gay striped awning. Ash looked down at mostly fair heads. The men and women who were slaves tugged the waxed linen into place with much swearing, complaints; thin arms holding up cloth or cord with impatient shouts. No one freeborn was in the court-yard except guards, and she could pick up their mutual enmity from here.

The lights, once shrouded, let her see beyond, to the squat square surrounding buildings—a household of at least a couple of thousand, she judged. It was impossible to see further in the dark, to see if this interior Carthage city contained other *amirs'* establishments equally rich and well-fortified. And no way at all to see—she leaned up on her toes on the cold tiled floor—whether this building faced harbor or something else; how much of Carthage lay between her and the dock; where the great and famous market might be; where the desert lay.

A hollow, moaning sound startled her. She lifted her head, alert, discerning that it echoed across rooftops and courtyard from a great distance.

"Sunset," Leofric's voice came from beside her. When she looked at him, her eyes were on a level with his white-bearded chin.

The metallic sound echoed again across the city. Ash strained to see the first stars, the moon, anything that would give her a compass bearing.

The wooden shutter was gently closed in her face.

She turned back into the room. The glowing warmth from the iron plates of coals made her feel how chill her face had grown, in those few minutes.

"How do *you* speak to it?" she challenged.

"As I speak to you, with my voice," Leofric said

dryly. "But I am in the same room with it, when I do it!"

Ash couldn't stop herself smiling.

"How does it answer you?"

"With a mechanical voice, heard by the ear. Again: I am in the same room when I hear it. My daughter does not have to be in the same room, the same household, the same continent—this crusade confirms me in my belief that she will never go a distance great enough for her not to hear it."

"Does it know anything except military answers?"

"It does not *know* anything. It is a golem. It speaks only what I, and others, have taught it. It solves problems, in the field, that is all."

She swayed on her feet as a wave of lassitude went through her. The Visigoth *amir* gripped her arm above the elbow, through the bloodstained wool. "Come and lie down on the bed. Let us try what you suggest."

She let him guide her footsteps, all but falling back onto the palliasse. The room swayed around her. She closed her eyes, seeing nothing but darkness for long minutes until the dizziness faded; opening them to the stark white light of the wall lamps, and the soft scritching of the boy-slave on his wax tablet.

Leofric made a gesture, and the child stopped writing.

His voice, beside her, asked quietly, "Who was it first built the Golem?"

Question and answer. She spoke it aloud: had to ask twice, the answering name was unfamiliar to her. She said uncertainly, "The . . . 'Rabbi'? Of Prague."

"And he built it for whom?"

Another question, another response. Ash shut her eyes against the harsh light, straining to hear the inner voice. " 'Radonic,' I think. Yes, Radonic."

"Who first built the Stone Golem, and why?"

" *'The Rabbi of Prague, under direction of your ancestor Radonic, two hundred years ago, built the first Stone Golem to play him at* shah.' —At chess," Ash corrected herself.

"Who first built machines in Carthage, and why?"

*"Friar Roger Bacon."*

"One of ours," Ash said. She let her voice repeat the sound of the voice in her head: *"It is said that Friar Bacon made, in his lodgings at the Port Carthage, a Brazen Head, from such metal as might be found in the vicinity. Howbeit, when he had heard what it had to say to him, he burned his devices, his plans, and his lodgings, and fled north to Europe, never to return. Afterwards the new presence of many demons in Carthage were blamed upon this scholar. Geraldus writ this."*

Leofric's voice said soothingly, "Many have read much into the Stone Golem's ears in two hundred years. Try again, dear daughter. Who made the first Stone Golem, and why?"

*"The* amir *Radonic, beaten in* shah *by this speechless device, grew weary of it, and was much displeased with the Rabbi.* That's lords for you," Ash added. She became aware that she was on the edge of hysteria. Dehydration made her head ache, blood-loss made her weak; all of this was enough to account for it. The voice in her head continued: *"Radonic, growing weary, caused the stone man to be set aside. Like a good Christian, he doubted the small powers of the Jews to be from the Green Christ, and began to think he may have countenanced demonic works in his household."*

"More."

*"The Rabbi had made this Golem a man in every part, using his semen, and the red mud of Carthage, and shaping it very handsomely. A slave in the household, one Ildico, grew greatly in love with the Golem, for that with its stone limbs and metal jointures it looked most like a man, and bore it a child. This she said was caused by the Wonder-Worker's intercession, the great Prophet Gundobad appearing to her in a dream and bidding her carry about her person his sacred relic, which was passed down in this slave's family since Gundobad lived."*

Ash felt a soft touch. She opened her eyes. Leofric's

fingers stroked her brow, the tips touching skin, dried blood, and dirt with complete indifference. She flinched away.

"Gundobad's your prophet, isn't he? He cursed the Pope and caused the Empty Chair."

"Your Pope should not have executed him," Leofric said gravely, removing his hand, "but I won't dispute with you, child. Eight centuries of history have passed over us, and who can tell what the Wonder-Worker was, now? Ildico believed in him, certainly."

"A woman who had a baby by a stone statue." Ash couldn't keep contempt out of her tone. "Master Leofric, if I were going to read history for a machine to listen to, I wouldn't tell it this rubbish!"

"And the Green Christ born of a Virgin, and suckled by a Boar; this is 'rubbish'?"

"For all I know, it is!" She shrugged, as well as was possible lying down on the bed. Her feet were cold. She became aware as Leofric frowned that she had slid into a French-Swiss dialect of her youth, and tried it again in Carthaginian Latin: "Look, I've seen as many tiny miracles as the next woman, but all of them could be chance, *fortuna imperatrix*, that's all . . ."

With slight emphasis, the Visigoth man said, "What made the *second* Stone Golem and why?"

Ash repeated his words. The voice that moved in the secret places of her mind was no different from the voice that answered when she gave it terrain, troop type, weather conditions, and asked for an ideal solution: the same voice.

*"Some have written that Ildico, slave, not only pre-served a powerful relic of the Prophet Gundobad, but was in direct line of descent from his body, through the generations from the eight hundred and sixteenth year after Our Lord was given to the Tree, to that year of twelve hundred and fifty-three."*

Leofric repeated his question. "Who made the second golem, and why?"

*"The eldest son of Radonic, one Sarus, was killed in*

*a battle with the Turks. Radonic then caused to be made a* shah *set in which the pieces were carved, complete to weapons and armor, resembling the troops of the Turks and the troops of his son Sarus. Then he recalled the Golem to his mind, and set about playing* shah *with it, and upon a day in that year, the Golem at last played out the game so that the troops of Sarus moved in a different array and would have defeated the Turks.*

*"Upon this day, also, Amir Radonic discovered his slave Ildico bedding the Golem; and he took a wall-builder's hammer, and he crushed the red mud and brass of the Golem to fragments, so small that no man could have told what it had been. Thereafter, he shut himself up in a tower. And Ildico bore a daughter.*

*"Radonic, thinking upon Sarus his dead son, and upon his sons yet living, came and bade the Rabbi make a second Golem, to replace the one he had destroyed in his wrath. This the Rabbi would not do, although the Amir threatened the life of the Rabbi's two sons. Not until Radonic made plain that he would impale and kill both Ildico and her newborn daughter would the Rabbi relent. Then he builded for Amir Radonic another Stone Golem, in a chamber within the house, but this human in seeming only in its upper body and head, thrice the size of a man: the rest being but a clay slab upon which models of men and beasts may be moved. And the brazen mouth of the Golem spoke."*

Ash curled her body up, swathed in wool. Two or three sentences at a time is nothing, she thought, but *this* . . . The emotionless recounting of the voice made her tired, dizzy, detached.

*"Then Radonic killed the Rabbi and his family, in case the Rabbi should make such another* shah-*player for his enemies, or the enemies of his King-Caliph. And instantly the sun grew dark above him. And the sun darkened above the city of Carthage, and to all the lands ruled by the King-Caliph did the Rabbi's Curse extend. And so no living eye hath beheld the sun break through the Eternal Twilight, in two hundred years."*

Ash opened her eyes again, not aware until then that she had shut them, the better to hear her voice. "Jesu! I bet there was panic."

Leofric said softly, "The then King-Caliph, Eriulf, and his *amirs* held command over their troops, and their troops kept the people quiet."

"Oh, you can do most things if you can keep a bunch of soldiers taking orders." Ash pushed herself up in the bed, until she came into contact with the white oak headboard, carved with fluted columns and pomegranates at the posts. She supported herself with an effort against the waxed wood. "This is all legends, I heard this stuff around camp when I was a kid. Legend number three hundred and seven about how the Eternal Twilight came to the south . . . Am I really telling you what you expect to hear?"

"Prophet Gundobad lived, and his slave daughter Ildico," Leofric said, "my family histories speak of it very clearly. And my ancestor Radonic certainly executed a Jewish Rabbi, about the year 1250."

"Then ask me things people won't have read in your family histories!"

The waxed wood of the bed smelled sweet to her. Her stomach growled. Strung out, watching Leofric's expression for the minutest changes, she ignored her complaining body.

"Who was Radegunde?"

Ash obediently repeated, "Who was Radegunde?"

*"The first to speak at a distance to the Stone Golem."*

She thought, It doesn't say "to me."

*"In these first years of crusade, when harvests failed and grain might not be got but by conquest of happier lands under the sun, then King-Caliph Eriulf began his conquests of the Iberian* taifa *states. While* Amir *Radonic fought for King-Caliph Eriulf, he learned from each defeat or victory as he played them out over again with his Stone Golem, after each campaign. The child of Ildico, the girl Radegunde, began in her third year to make statues of men from the red silt sand of Carthage.*

*"The amir Radonic, seeing how she resembled the old Rabbi, smiled to think he had been so simple as to think a statue might beget a child upon a woman, and to regret his first stone golem's destruction. So Radegunde might have remained only a slave in the House of Radonic, but that, upon a day, she overheard Radonic's discussions with his captains, upon the practice field, and bade the Amir tell her what tactics he would employ, so that she might engage to speak to her friend the stone man about his plan.*

*"Thinking to make merry, Radonic bid her ask the Stone Golem what it would have him do. Upon this, Radegunde spoke to the air. Then other slaves came running, to report that the Golem began to move the figures set out before it. When the amir Radonic arrived in its chamber, the answers to his question were set out plain, as if the Golem had received her childish speech from some demon of the air.*

*"Then Radonic abandoned the way of honor and rightness, and did not slay the child. Radonic adopted Radegunde, taking her with him to Iberia, speaking to her, and through her to the Stone Golem, and the tide of war turned in Eriulf's favor, so that southern Iberia became the grain-basket of Carthage under the Twilight. And at five, she made her first mud statue that moved of its own volition, breaking much in the household, and greatly the child laughed to see this destruction."*

Ash drew her ankles up to her haunches, under the covering wool gown, and studied Leofric's expression. It was one of intense concentration.

"Is that Radegunde?" She stumbled over the name.

"Yes. Ask, how did she die?"

"How did Radegunde die?" Ash parroted. The dizziness in her might have had a dozen causes. She suspected a concentration of her mind that felt, somehow, as if she were pulling—a load up a slope—or unravelling something.

*"In his seasons at home in Carthage, the amir Radonic gave orders that Radegunde should be aided to*

*make her new golems, bringing her scholars, engineers, and strange materials all as she desired. In her fifteenth year, God took away her powers of speech, but her mother Ildico communicated for her by signs known to them both. In this year also, upon a day, Radegunde builded a stone man that rent her limb from limb and so she died."*

Leofric's voice said, "And what is the secret birth?"

Ash kept her mouth shut, forming no words in her head, but letting an expectation form. An expectation of *being* answered. She let it somehow pull at other, implicit, answers. She said nothing out loud.

The voice began to speak in her head.

*"Desiring another who should hear the Stone Golem though separated from it by many miles, so that he might continue his war, the* amir *Radonic bred Ildico, in her thirtieth year, to the third golem, which had killed her daughter. This is the secret breeding, and the secret birth her twins, a male child and a girl."*

She mumbled out loud, too startled at hearing it to keep quiet; muttered a necessary question out loud, in the face of Leofric's keen stare, over the answer already coming into her head. Then she stumbled over words, getting them out:

*"The* amir *Radonic desired another such slave, a grown adult, who should communicate with the Stone Golem as Radegunde had, a* Janissary *general after the manner of the Turks, an* al-shayyid *who should defeat all the petty* taifa *kings of Iberia. The twin children of Ildico could not be brought to do it, no matter the pain inflicted upon them and their mother. Nor could another golem be built. At last, Ildico confessed that she had given Radegunde her holy relic of the Prophet Gundobad, to place it within her last golem, and to make it speak and move as men do. But, at this knowledge, the third golem slew Ildico, and leaped from a high tower, and was dashed to fragments beneath. And this is their secret death: none remaining of the Prophet and Rabbi's*

*miracle but the second Stone Golem, and Ildico's children."*

*Amir* Leofric's hands closed over hers, clasping them tightly. Ash met his eyes steadily. He was nodding, unstoppably, in agreement; his eyes were wet.

"I never thought to have two such successes," he explained, simply. "It does speak to you, doesn't it? My dear girl."

"That was two hundred years ago," Ash said. "What happened then?"

She felt him unite with her in a moment of pure curiosity on her side, pure understanding of the desire for knowledge on his. The two of them sat companionably side by side on the bed.

Leofric said, "Radonic bred the twins and their offspring together. He wasn't a man to keep careful records. After he died his second wife Hildr and her daughter Hild took over; they kept minutely detailed notations of what they did. Hild was my four times great-grandmother. Her son Childeric, and her grandsons Fravitta and Barbas, continued the breeding program, always tantalizingly close. As you know, as our conquests spread, many refugees and much scholastic knowledge came to Carthage. Fravitta built the ordinary golems, about the year 1390; Barbas presented them to King-Caliph Ammianus; they have since become popular through the Empire. The youngest son of Barbas, Stilicho, was my father; he raised me in the knowledge of the utmost necessity of our eventual success. My success was born four years after the fall of Constantinople. And so may you have been," Leofric finished thoughtfully.

*He's older than he looks.* Ash realized the Visigoth lord must be in his fifties or sixties. *That means he grew up under the threat of the Turks—and that begs another question.*

"Why isn't your general attacking the Sultan and his Beys?" Ash asked.

Absently, Leofric muttered, "The Stone Golem advised a crusade in Europe to be a better beginning; I must say I agree."

Ash blinked, frowned. "Attacking *Europe* is a better way to defeat the Turks? Ah, c'mon! That's crazy!"

Leofric ignored her mumble. "All has gone so well, and so speedily; if it were not for this cold—" He broke off. "Burgundy is the strategic key, of course. Then we may turn our attention to the Sultan's lands, God willing it so. God willing that Theodoric lives. He has not always been such a bad friend to me," the elderly man mused, as if to himself, "only in this last illness, and since Gelimer got his ear; still, he cannot very well stop a crusade once begun with so many victories . . ."

Ash waited until he looked up at her, raising his bowed head. "The Eternal Twilight has spread north. I saw the sun go out."

"I know."

"You don't know a damn thing about it!" Ash's tone rose. "You don't know any more about what's going on than I do!"

Leofric shifted very carefully on the edge of the white oak bed. Something squicked in the depths of his gown. The pale blue doe put out an indignant nose, and scuttled hastily onto his striped sleeve.

"Of course I do!" the Visigoth *amir* snapped. "It's taken us *generations* to breed a slave who can hear the Stone Golem without going mad. Now I have a chance of there being *two* of you."

"I'll tell you what I think, *Amir* Leofric." Ash looked at him. "I don't think you have any use for another slave-general. I don't think you need another Faris, another warrior-daughter who can talk to your machine— no matter how long it took you to breed that one. That's not what you want at all." She spared a finger for the rat, but it was sitting up on its haunches, grooming velvet-blue fur, and ignored her.

"Suppose I *can* hear your tactical machine. So what, *Amir* Leofric?" Ash spoke very carefully. The fog of misery was beginning to clear. Her body has ached from other wounds than this, if none so deep. "You can offer me a place with you, to fight for the King-Caliph, and I'll agree, and turn my coat as soon as I get back to Europe; he and you both know that. That's not important, it's not what you need!"

The exhilaration of unguarded honesty filled her. Looking around the room at the three slave children, she briefly realized, *I've taken to talking as if they're not there, too.* Her gaze returned to Leofric, to see him thrusting his fingers through his hair, spiking it up still further.

Come on, girl, she thought. If he were a man you were hiring, what would you make of him? Intelligent, secretive, with none of the normal social restraints about causing physical harm to people: you'd pay him five marks and put him on the company books in a second!

And he didn't get to stay an *amir* without being devious. Not in this court.

"What are you saying?" Leofric sounded bewildered.

"Why is it cold, Leofric? *Why is it cold here?*"

The two of them looked at each other, for what must have been an actual minute of silence. Ash read the flinch of his expression clearly.

"I don't know," Leofric said at last.

"No, and nor does anyone else here, I can see it by the way you're all running around scaring yourselves shitless." Ash made herself grin. It was not very close to her usual gaiety of heart; she still ached too much. "Let me guess. It's only been cold since your invasion started?"

Leofric snapped his fingers. The smallest slave-child came and took a rat from him, cradling the blue doe with exquisite care in her thin arms. She walked unsteadily toward the door. One of the boys took the mismarked buck, twitching its whiskers, anxious to copulate with the doe; and at Leofric's signal, the slave scribe followed them out.

He said, "Child, if you did know of a reason for this intemperate weather, you would have told me of it, to save your life. I know this. Therefore, you know nothing."

"Maybe I do," Ash said steadily. In the half-chill room, her sore body ran cold sweat, darkening the robe gathered up under her armpits. She went on desperately, "Something I may have seen—I was there when the sun went out!—it might tell you—"

"No." He rested his chin on the knuckle of his first finger, nestling it in his untidy white beard. He held her gaze. She felt something tighten under her solar plexus: fear slowly squeezing her breath. She thought, Not now! Not when I've just found out I can *make* it talk to me—

Not now, under any circumstances.

"You're still at war, I saw that coming in," she said, her voice still steady. "Whatever victory you had can't have been final, can it? I'll give you the disposition and array of Charles of Burgundy's troops. You and the King-Caliph think I'm a Faris, a magical general, but you're forgetting: *I was one of Charles's hired officers.* I can tell you what he has."

She said it fast, before she could regret saying it:

"It's simple. I'll turn coat, in exchange for my life. I'm not the first person to make that bargain."

"No," the *amir* Leofric said absently. "No, of course. You shall dictate what you know to the Stone Golem; doubtless my daughter will find it useful, if somewhat overtaken by recent events."

Her eyes ran tears. "So I live?"

He ignored her.

"Lord-*Amir*!" She shrieked.

He spoke absently, as if he had not heard her.

"Whereas I had hoped to have another general, perhaps to lead our army in the east, I shall not have it under this King-Caliph, not with Gelimer to speak constantly against me. However," Leofric mused, "this gives me an opportunity which I had not expected to have before the end of this crusade. You—not being needed, as she is—can be dissected, to discover the balance of the Humors[30] within your body, and if there are differences in your brain and nerves which make it possible for you to speak with the machine."

He looked at her with an absence of feeling that was frightening in itself.

"Now I shall find out if this is indeed the case. I have always had my failures to dissect. Since there is no further use for you, now I may vivisect one of my successes."

Ash stared at him. She thought, I must have mistaken the word. No, that was clear, pure, medical Latin. Vivisect. Meaning "dissect, while still alive."

"You *can't*—"

A sound of footsteps beyond the door brought her bolt upright, grabbing at Leofric's arm as he rose to his feet. He evaded her grip.

It was not a slave who entered but the *'arif* Alderic, a frown buried somewhere in his neatly braided beard; clasping his hands behind his back and speaking rapidly and concisely. Ash, too shocked, didn't understand what he was saying.

"No!" Leofric strode forward, his voice going up high. "And this is *so*?"

"Abbot Muthari has announced it, and called for prayer, fasting and repentance, my *Amir*," Alderic said, and with the air of a man repeating his initial message, slowly, as if the elderly lord-*amir* might not have understood: "The King-Caliph, may he live forever, is dead of a seizure this half hour, in his rooms in the palace. No doctor could bring breath back to his body. Theodoric is dead, my lord. The King-Caliph is dead."

Stunned for different reasons, Ash heard the soldier speak his news with something approaching complete unconcern. *What's a King-Caliph, to me?* She knelt up

---

[30] The medieval medical theory of humors attributes health to a balance of the sanguine (dry), choleric (hot), phlegmatic (wet) and melancholy (cold) humors in the body. Ill-health is a predominance of one over the others.

on the bed. The woolen gown fell away from her blood-stained body. One hand knotted into a fist.

"Leofric!"

He ignored her.

"Leofric! *What about me?*"

"You?" Leofric, frowning, looked over his shoulder. "Yes. You . . . Alderic, confine her to the guest quarters, under guard."

Her other hand made a fist. She ignored the Visigoth captain as he gripped her arm. "*Tell me you're not going to kill me!*"

The *amir* Leofric raised his voice to his slaves. "Get my court robes!"

A bustle began.

He said, over his shoulder, "Think of it as a reprieve, if that comforts you. We are about the business of electing a new King-Caliph—which will be a busy few days, to say the least."

He smiled, his teeth shining in his white beard.

"This is merely a pause, before I can investigate you. As custom dictates, I can begin my work again immediately upon the inauguration of Theodoric's successor. Child, don't think of me as barbaric. It is not as if I'm torturing you to death as part of the celebrations. You will add so *much* to the sum of our knowledge."

*[E-mails found inserted between pages]*

------------------------------

Message: #164 (Anna Longman/misc.)
Subject: Ash/texts/archaeological evidence
Date: 20/11/00 at 10.57 p.m.
From: Ngrant@          *format address deleted*
*other details encrypted by*
*non-discoverable personal key*

Anna--

Everything's STOPPED.

Some trouble with the local authorities—we're being forbidden to carry on with the digging on-site. I don't UNDERSTAND how this can be happening! It is extremely frustrating that I, myself, can do nothing about this.

I thought it was solved this morning: Isobel came back, optimistic. I think she had gone through 'unofficial channels' and greased a few palms with money. She drove back with Colonel ▮▮▮▮▮, who seemed very jovial, promising the use of his men for heavy work here where required. But this afternoon, STILL nothing is happening, there are obscure 'difficulties'.

I am concerned; it seems to be more than the usual patronage and nepotism; but Isobel has been too busy for me to ask her.

One minor good thing, I suppose, is that it gives me an enforced opportunity to work on 'Fraxinus'. Mediaeval Latin is notoriously ambiguous, and 'Fraxinus' more idiosyncratic than most. I am finalising the translation furiously! In fact, I am putting the finishing touches to the next section.

Since we're encrypted, I can now tell you something about the site. What we have here is a beautiful midden. That's a refuse-heap. Archaeology, as Isobel informs me, mainly consists of digging in other people's dung. She, however, did not say 'dung'.

You would not think—everything covered by suburbs: two-storey white buildings festooned with television aerials—that any of this was the site of Carthaginian and Roman settlements. Even the Roman aqueduct is pretty much gone. But when I walked down to the beach this morning, and stood there under a lurid dawn sky, with the cold wind blowing off the sea into my face, I suddenly realised that most of the worn and rounded 'pebbles' under my feet were actually bits of Roman brick and Carthaginian marble. Some of them might even have been pieces of golem, shapeless after five centuries of being rolled around by the sea.

Nameless rocks. We know almost nothing. It wasn't even until a decade ago that the site of Carthage was identified; prior to that there was this ten-mile stretch of coast, with nothing—two thousand years later—to indicate just where it might have been. Even what seems certain, we don't know. Bosworth field has its own tourist centre, but the field on which the battle was fought may not be that field at all (there is a theory it was closer to Dadlington than Market Bosworth). But I digress.

No, not really. I walked back through the site, in the chill fresh air—everything was under blue polystyrene covers. The gray boxes with notebook PCs plugged in had been removed back to the caravans. There were no men and woman in anoraks flicking away earth with tiny paintbrushes with their rear ends in the air. And what I thought was, Isobel is the one with the temperament for this. She wants to DISCOVER things. I want to EXPLAIN them. I need to have a rational explanation for the universe.

I even need a rational explanation for the 'miraculous' construction of these golems. The cold marble is uninformative. Andrew, our archeometallurgist, is studying the metal joints; he has no answers yet. How did it get those marks of wear that prove it walked? HOW DID IT MOVE?

And what can I give these people, from the 'Fraxinus' text? A story of a wonder-working Rabbi and the sexual congress of a woman and a statue!

I know I said truth can be conveyed down through history in a story. Well, sometimes it proves impenetrably obscure!

There were men with guns on the site perimeter as I walked in. I was thinking, as I passed them, that the military mind itself has a rational explanation for the way the universe works—it's just an explanation at 90 degrees to the real one.

Isobel's just told me there is 'stuff' going on behind the scenes, in local politics; we must be 'patient'.

So far we have various household implements, a dagger-hilt, and a piece of metal that might be a hair-fillet. I sit in on the discussions—arguments would, one supposes, be a better term—and put the case for a Germanic rather than an Arab culture here. The team agrees with me.

I need these diggings to start again.

I need more back-up for 'Fraxinus.'

If they don't let the team on site soon, the army can move in and clear out archaeological tents full of dead bodies: I myself will be found battered to death with my own laptop computer! We are going stir-crazy out here. And it's HOT.

--Pierce

- - - - - - - - - - - - - - - - - - - - - - - - - - - -

Message: #169 (Anna Longman/misc.)
Subject:  Ash mss., breeding of Rattus Norvegicus
Date:     21/11/00 at 10.47 a.m.
From:     Ngrant@                    format address deleted
                                     other details encrypted by
Ms Longman--                         non-discoverable personal key

While we wait, I am mailing you at the suggestion of my colleague, Dr Ratcliff, who has been kind enough to show me the Latin manuscripts he is at present translating for you. He suggests I do this since I have some amateur (if specialised) knowledge of rat genetics and breeding.

Although Pierce and I spent some time discussing this yesterday, and he is now as well-informed as myself, he suggested that I e-mail you personally since I have the time now.

You may be aware that in the last forty-eight hours we have had problems on-site, and at the moment there is little I can do except watch the military representatives of the local government treading on five hundred years of history. Fortunately most of the findings at this site are under silt, which prevents too great an amount of damage being done. The sole advantage I can see to this delay is that the government are forbidding access to the airspace above the coast, and this avoids saturation media coverage. Apart from a few blurred satellite photos, the recording of the expedition will be in the hands of my own capable videocam team.

Assuming that matters return to normal in the next twenty-four hours, as Minister ▆▆▆▆ promises, I shall then be too busy to be of any assistance to Pierce or yourself.

I really have very little to contribute; perhaps a footnote's worth of knowledge—some years ago, being in search of a relaxing hobby, I took up breeding specialist varieties of Rattus Norvegicus, the Brown Rat. Such varieties are known as Fancy rats; and I have been a member of both British and American Rat Fancy societies.

In point of fact, my then-husband Peter Monkham was a biologist; we never did quite see eye to eye on this matter, although his reasons for having a vivisectionist's license were no doubt good and sufficient to him. Peter's jeremiads on the state of animals in unrestrained nature (their lives being nasty, brutish, and shortly terminated by something one step further up the food chain) only served to convince me that my captive animals were in fact rather better off than they would have otherwise been.

I was therefore intrigued to discover, while reading Pierce's translation from the 'Fraxinus' manuscript for clues to our technological findings, that several of our current genetic mutations of Rattus Norvegicus seem to have been known in fifteenth century Africa. In fact, I had no knowledge of anything other than Rattus Rattus, the Black Rat, being present in mediaeval times anywhere outside Asia. (Rattus Rattus is, of course, the rodent popularly associated with spreading the Black Death.) I had believed that Rattus Norvegicus only spread here from Asia in or about the eighteenth century. What 'Fraxinus' describes, however, is undoubtedly the Brown Rat. If Pierce allows, I may use his findings for a brief paper on the subject of rat migration.

It seems possible, from 'Fraxinus', that these varieties were imported by North African traders. The Latin is sufficiently explicit that I actually RECOGNISE several varieties! I should explain that the brown or 'agouti' coat of the wild rat is in fact colored in bands, each brown hair being striped blue-grey at the base; the coat scattered with additional guard-hairs, which are black. Selective breeding of initially spontaneous mutations can give different colored coats which will then (with great effort) breed true. Patterned coats can also be bred true, although to give you some idea of the difficulty, the H locus which controls pattern can be modified to give at least six patterns: the Hooded rat, the Berkshire, the Irish, etc. And then there are polygenes to consider!

The difficulty is not in breeding a rat with a patterned coat, but in getting one that then breeds true to the same pattern. Two rats may be physically identical in their appearance while carrying completely different genetic histories in their alleles. Rat-breeding consists of trying to isolate certain genetic characteristics—without losing the proper bodily conformation of bold eye, well-set ears, good head, high rump, etc.—and creating a specific line of rats who will pass on that desired characteristic. Without keeping minutely detailed records of what bucks I bred to which does, it would have been impossible for me to select which of their offspring to use to continue the line.

Taking, for example, what 'Fraxinus' describes as a 'blue' rat— this is a rat bred to have the base blue colouring continued evenly through the fur coat. These are pretty, exotic little creatures, although (as this text in fact mentions!) early attempts proved difficult to get right, as the blue does suffered birthing problems. Whatever allele carried the gene for 'bleaching out' the agouti coat also stood a substantial chance of carrying a gene for deformed birth-canals, and bad temper. Blue rats used to bite, whereas the normal temperament of Rattus Norvegicus is inquisitive and friendly. The blue rat proper is then produced by breeding only from those examples which do not suffer from breeding difficulties, or difficulties of temperament.

'Fraxinus' also mentions the yellow/brown rat. This is known as a 'Siamese', and is the same gene that gives us Siamese cats (and, in fact, Siamese-coloured rabbits and mice); the coat is pale yellow except for the rump, nose, and paws, where the 'points' are dark brown. The description in 'Fraxinus' is excellent.

I can also account for the rat with different coloured eyes: the black eye being natural, the red eye a consequence of albinism. (The grey and white is referred to as 'lynx-marked' in the American Fancy.) The specimen referred to in this text appears to me to be a mosaic—genetically speaking, the opposite of a twin. Whereas with a twin an egg divides in the uterus, with a mosaic two different eggs fuse. This can produce a rat with the two halves of its body having different colour fur, or different colour eyes, or in some cases, being of different sexes. Since they are produced by random fusion, it is impossible for them to breed true, and they are of no use in fancy rat breeding.

Judging by the further description, the coat of the mosaic rat was either rexed—this is when the stiffer guard hairs are bred out, giving a soft curly coat—or velvet (short and plush).

I once bred a line of rexes myself—being a rex, naturally each one was named after one of the Plantagenets (my favourite kings); although a particularly fluffy rat of mine called 'John' gave me an excellent illustration, by his temperament, of why we have only ever had one king of that name.

Fraxinus's rat is particularly interesting if it is *not* a rex, since no one in the Fancy has yet successfully bred a velvet coat on a rat, although the Mouse Fancy had achieved both velvet and satin pelts. In this respect, fifteenth century North Africa seems to have out-done us!

This is conceivably because our Rat Fancy is primarily a twentieth century phenomenon (although young Victorian ladies were known to keep pet rats in birdcages). Perhaps because of the rat's undeserved bad reputation far fewer years this century have been spent on its specialist breeding than, say, has been the case with the Mouse Fancy, or with different breeds of dog or cat. However, there are, even now, dedicated amateur geneticists at work on the Brown Rat, and it seems encouraging to me—if wonderfully strange—to learn that we are REdiscovering the many possible varieties of this delightful, playful, intelligent little animal.

I have gone into this in some detail simply because it shows the sheer SOPHISTICATION of the mediaeval mind. Pierce's manuscripts are proving fascinating now that we have these technological survivals to study, but I am almost MORE interested in what this says about the living minds of those people, who could note, conceive of genetic heritage, and EXPERIMENT in that respect, long before the Renaissance and the Scientific Revolution of the seventeenth century. Of course, one sees the beginning of it in horse- and hound-breeding of the same period, as one sees a similar mediaeval 'industrial revolution' in mills and military technology; but to produce, for example, the Siamese-marked rat, shows a mind-beggaring attention to scientific detail in what it is easy to see as a superstition-ridden, theologically constrained and inhumanely brutal society.

If I can be of any further assistance to you, please mail me at the above address. I look forward to your publication of Pierce's work. It may interest you to know that, in view of the help he is giving me on site, I am more than willing for him to publish any details of our discoveries here in so far as they relate to the 'Ash' histories, provided I and the university are credited.

Sincerely--I. Napier-Grant

- - - - - - - - - - - - - - - - - - - - - - - - - - - - - -

Message: #99 (Pierce Ratcliff/misc.)
Subject:   Ash, media-related projects
Date:      21/11/00 at 11.59 a.m.
From:      Longman@            *format address and*
                               *other details*
Pierce--                       *non-recoverably deleted*

I just had mail from your Doctor Isobel. Most of it's *way* over my head. And *rats*, eurrggh!

John showed me the golem-photos. They are WONDERFUL! My MD Jonathan Stanley came over and saw them. He is equally impressed. He's contacting an independent television producer that he knows—well, who's the godfather of his son, actually.

Now I'm going to have media people to talk to. And explain that this Schliemann found Troy by following up a poem. I can do it, I suppose, but it would carry more weight coming from you or Dr Napier-Grant.

I know you haven't the time, right now. I don't like the sound of this problem with the authorities that you're having.

I'm getting edgy here.

--Anna

- - - - - - - - - - - - - - - - - - - - - - - - - - - - -

Message: #173 (Anna Longman/misc.)
Subject:   Ash mss.
Date:      22/11/00 at 02.01 p.m.
From:      Ngrant@

*format address deleted*
*other details encrypted by*
*non-discoverable personal key*

Anna--

Something to amuse you, then, and stop you being edgy, while we wait. Isobel has been re-reading my 'Fraxinus' translation and, as we have nothing better to do at this moment, has been devising with me a completely spurious scientific rationale for the abilities of Ash and the Faris as regards the Stone Golem. We decided to see if we could out-do Vaughan Davies! It goes like this—

Since human beings cannot, as far as we know, converse with stone statues, this must, by definition, happen by the power of a miracle.

Of course, stone-and-brass tactical computers do not function in the world as we know it, either! So this theory will also have to account for the construction of the various 'stone golem' by the Rabbi of Prague and the descendants of Radonic. Therefore, such construction is also deemed to be miraculous!

Isobel and I have been playing about with a hypothetical *if*. Our theory is: suppose this ability to perform miracles was GENETIC— *if* there existed such a thing as a gene for performing miracles, *if* this 'wonder-working' had a scientific rather than a superstitious basis, how would it function?

It would have to be a recessive gene, obviously. If it were dominant, everybody would be constantly performing miracles. It probably also has to be a recessive with something dangerous linked to the same allele or the same focus—Isobel points out that because blue rats have difficulty in successfully birthing litters, a spontaneous mutation of a blue rat will probably not perpetuate its line. You don't see many blue rats in the wild, and indeed there may not have been any in existence at all until breeders took an interest in Rattus Norvegicus.

Imagine, then, that this proposed 'wonder-working' gene would arise through spontaneous mutation very infrequently, and therefore those born to successfully perform miracles would be history's memorable prophets and religious leaders—Christ; the Visigoths' unidentified 'Prophet Gundobad'; the major Saints; other cultures' great visionaries and seers. They would not necessarily pass their genetic heritage on successfully, but it would remain as a recessive gene.

In 'Fraxinus's' history of Leofric's family, Isobel makes the suggestion—which I had not thought of—that both the Rabbi of Prague *and* the slave woman Ildico were wonder-workers, both of them using that capacity and carrying the gene.

The Rabbi, as wonder-worker, could build a miraculous stone chess-playing computer. Ildico, as the descendant of Gundobad, would carry enough of the ability to conceive a child from the stone man, but not to work miracles herself. Her daughter, Radegunde, could work the miracle of long-distance communication with the computer, and construct her own golem (but, given the circumstances of her conception, would be prone to physical and mental instability).

The descendants of Radegunde and Ildico would all carry the potential for miracle-working, but it would take a long programme of selective breeding to bring about another Radegunde, given that there is no miracle-worker there to aid Leofric's family in this project, it has to be done purely by two centuries of stock-breeding. (The morality of this is another question, and certainly does not seem to have occurred to Leofric or his ancestors.)

Both Faris and Ash carry the wonder-working gene, and in them the ability to successfully use it is dominant. It seems not to have been active in Ash herself at birth, instead being triggered at the onset of puberty, at which point she begins to 'download' from the Stone Golem.

And there you have it! It's a shame there's no such thing as miracles. Well, this is what academics do for fun, on long cold afternoons . . .

Of course, miracles are—pace centuries of stories from various faiths—merely superstition. A miracle is a non-scientific alteration in the fabric of reality, if I may define it that way, and by that definition it is impossible. When one is sitting in a surprisingly cold army surplus tent (there is a sea-fog) with absolutely nothing else to do but wait to continue the dig, these are intriguing speculations.

If this delay goes on much longer, I confidently expect that Isobel and I shall next devise a theory about how such a 'nonscientific alteration in the fabric of reality' or 'miracle' might be caused. We are no longer 19th century Materialists, after all; the higher reaches of theoretical physics have taught us that all our Laws of Nature and apparently solid world are probability, fuzzy logic, uncertainty. Yes, about another two hours should do it! We shall produce the Ratcliff-Napier-Grant Theory of Scientific Miracles. And begin to pray, doubtless, for a change of heart among the local politicos, so that we have something real to do!

I hope you are duly amused.

--Pierce

- - - - - - - - - - - - - - - - - - - - - - - - - - - - - - - -

Message: #102 (Pierce Ratcliff/misc.)
Subject: Ash, manuscripts
Date: 23/11/00 at 03.09 a.m.
From: Longman@

*format address deleted
other details encrypted
and non-recoverably deleted*

Pierce--

Pierce, I have GOT something for you!

I had to go to a book-launch tonight. While I was swanning around the party, networking like mad, I met up again with a dear friend of mine, Nadia—I told you about her—a bookseller from Twickenham—she has one of those independent bookshops which are fast dying out now in favour of chains, in which everything is welcome except customers. (When I asked her what she was doing there, she replied, 'The shop's full of people; I've come AWAY!')

However—there was a house clearance at some place in East Anglia, and she bid at an auction for several cases of books. One of them is Vaughan Davies's ASH: A FIFTEENTH CENTURY BIOGRAPHY, and it's *complete*!

Nadia suspects that the house clearance was either from Davies's own house, or a relative's house containing Vaughan Davies's belongings. I've asked her to find out more, tomorrow morning.

I haven't had time to read the thing yet (we had to go back to her shop, and I've only just come in!) but I'll do that while I'm scanning it in for you. Shall I send it through now?


--Love, Anna


- - - - - - - - - - - - - - - - - - - - - - - - - - - -


Message:  #174 (Anna Longman/misc.)
Subject:  Ash, archaeological discoveries
Date:     23/11/00 at 07.32 a.m.
From:     Ngrant@                    *format address deleted*
                                     *other details encrypted by*
Anna--                               *non-discoverable personal key*


Yes. YES. Scan it and send it to me NOW!

Good grief. A copy of Vaughan Davies, after all this time.

Anna, do you realise what this means? Please get your friend to contact the house-clearance people immediately. There may be UNPUBLISHED papers.

I know that my work is superseding Davies, but still—after all this time—even for pure interest's sake, I want to know what the missing half of the Introduction is. I want to know his theory.


--Pierce

----------------------------------

Message: #175 (Anna Longman/misc.)
Subject: Ash, archaeological discoveries
Date: 23/11/00 at 09.24 a.m.
From: Ngrant@ *format address deleted*
*text encrypted by non-discoverable*
Anna-- *personal key*

HOLD THE PRESSES!
  (I always wanted to say that.)
  Still nothing going on here, on site, but we're MOVING, tomorrow, Friday! Isobel received a radio communication from the expedition's ship. It's been examining the seabed north of Tunis, between Cap Zebib and Rass Engelah, around Bizerte (and the Lac de Bizerte, an enclosed sea-inlet south of the city). We're going to move to the sea-site while Isobel's manager handles the ongoing problem here.
  Apparently it's unsafe to dive up there, but the cameras on the ROVs (remote operated vehicles) have been sending back pictures.
  As soon as she allows me to, I'll be in contact with you.

--Pierce

# PART THREE

8 September–10 September AD 1476

*ENGINES AND DEVICES*

$\mathbf{I}$

**T**HE VISIGOTH CAPTAIN all but dragged Ash out and along narrow corridors, his squad forcing a way between crowds of running freemen and slaves, the whole house in an uproar.

Ash stumbled, aware of almost nothing, able to think only *I betrayed them, all of them, I didn't even think about it! Anything to stay alive—*

She became aware of being manhandled; lifted bodily. The sides of a wooden tub burned hot against her skin. Ash flinched back as slaves lowered her into water. They leaned her against sponges.

"I advise, as hot as you can bear it," a fat, cheerful young man observed, in Italian, unwinding the bindings from her left knee.

His voice echoed in the long hall, muffled only slightly by the sheets that hung, perfumed with flowers and herbs, from the ceiling of the lord-*amir*'s household bath-house. The hall has steel grills at the windows and bars on the doors.

" '*Arif* Alderic, what have you been doing to this one?"

Alderic shook his head. "Don't waste too much skill, *dottore*. She's one of the *Amir*'s. She only has to live a few days."

Ash looked dizzily up. Two women with iron collars around their necks, chained together with a span of links about six foot long, bent over the tub and began to sponge and soap her body. If she could have stopped the handling, she would have. She could only stare through the steamy air, hot for the first time in weeks. Tears began to leak from under her eyelids.

*I thought I would have more courage.*

Other bathers' voices echoed outside, in the vast tubs that stood in cubicles all down the hall; and a woman's high laughter sounded, and the clink of glasses.

"Whatever you do to her later, she must eat now. And *drink!*" The Italian man pinched the back of Ash's hand. Ash watched the ridge of skin stand up proud for a moment. "She is, I know only the Latin, dehydrated. Dried up."

Alderic took off his helmet and wiped his forehead. "Feed and water her, then, she'd better not die yet. *Nazir!*"

He stomped off, to give orders. As the sheets were brushed back, she glimpsed other tubs, occupied by pairs of bathers, plates set on planks above the water and jugs of wine standing on marble surrounds. A slave was playing a stringed instrument.

"You should not treat me," Ash protested. Only as she automatically spoke in Italian did she begin to realize the surgeon was not a Visigoth. She looked up, roused out of blank misery by surprise. A fat young man with straggling black hair, in red hose, stripped to shirt and pourpoint and still sweating in this steaming, echoing chamber, looking down at her.

He nodded, as if he guessed her confusion.

"We are a commonwealth, madonna; doctors and priests pass freely across borders, even in wartime," the fat young man said, his accent Milanese, now she thought about it. He raised a dark brow. "And, not treat you? Why?"

*Because I don't deserve it.*

Ash looked down at her brown, blood-dried skin. She submerged her hands under the surface of the hot, misty water. The heat sank in, sank into her muscles, into her bones. A great wave of warmth went through her, and relaxation. She had not known how cold she was. Just the animal comfort brought her back to herself, sore and aching and beaten: still alive.

I *would* have betrayed them—I still might—but I haven't yet.

Nothing more than luck!—Call it Fortuna. It's a chance. It's days. Two, three, four days, maybe. *It's a chance.*

It's helplessness I can't stand. Give me even the shadow of a chance, and I'll find a way to take it. Fortune favors the bold.

"Why?" the Italian insisted.

"Take no notice of me, *dottore*," Ash said.

The chained slaves put a plank across the tub. Another male slave brought a plate, and a narrow-necked pot topped with a pie-crust. As Ash pushed herself upright, he knocked the crust off and emptied the pot onto the plate: a rush of meat, chopped hot herbs, pickerel,[31] and spiced wine. Its strong scent brought her to the point of vomiting. Almost instantly, the nausea went off, succeeded by a griping pain that she recognized from her childhood: complete hunger. Carefully, she picked out a small piece of meat and nibbled, her tongue curling up at the sensuous taste of the sauce.

"Ash," she said.

"Annibale Valzacchi." The physician flung away soaked bandages, bending over the tub and manipulating her knee-joint. She grunted, in pain, through a mouthful of food. The Italian exclaimed, "God be good to us, madonna, what do you do in life? Pull a plow?"

Ash licked her fingers and stared down at the steaming stew, forcing herself to wait before she ate again.

"The King-Caliph *died*," she said suddenly. "That old man died."

She half-expected Annibale Valzacchi to deny it, or to ask her what she meant: all of it could, she felt, have been her own delirium. Instead the Italian nodded, thoughtfully.

"Of natural causes," Valzacchi observed, in his thick

---

[31] Young pike.

Milanese north Italian. "Yes, well . . . A cup of bella-donna *is* 'natural causes,' in Carthage!"

Rumors of assassination go around after every death of a powerful man. Ash gave an answering nod, and merely said, "He was too sick to live long anyway, wasn't he?"

"A canker, yes. We—doctors, surgeons, physicians, priests—we are here in Carthage in such numbers because he sought a cure, any cure. There is no cure, of course: God disposes."

*God or Fortune,* Ash thought, with a momentary shiver of awe, that shaded off into raw, mordant humor: *Haven't I always prayed before combat? Why stop now?* She said thoughtfully, "I should like to see a priest. A Green priest. Is that possible, here?"

"This lord-*amir* is no religious fanatic. It should be possible. You are not Italian yourself, madonna, are you? No. Then, there are three English priests, that I room with in the lower city; I know of a Frenchman, and a German, and there is one who might be from Franche-Comté or Savoy."

As if she were a beast in a byre, Valzacchi slid his hands up around her shoulders, expertly gauging their irregularity: the muscles of the right more developed than the left.

From behind, his voice said, "Strange, madonna. I should say this arm has been trained to use a sword."

For the first time in fifteen days, Ash couldn't help a genuine smile: half amazement, half delight. She sat back in the hot sweet-smelling water as his fingers probed her neck under the steel collar. "How the *hell* did you know that, *dottore?*"

"My brother Gianpaulo is a condottiere. I did my initial training with him. Until I discovered that civilian medicine is considerably less dangerous, and pays rather better. This is the muscle development of someone who uses a sword, and perhaps a military axe, right-handed."

Ash felt herself chuckle, a soft sound and a quaking body. She wiped her wet hand across her mouth. His hands left her shoulders. His touch of recognition gave her something back; her body, her spirit.

She rested her arms on her knees, sitting perfectly still in the hot water, and looked down.

Ash saw, on the still surface, a scarred cheek reflected through pale, rising mist; and a face she barely recognized with its cropped hair. *They wouldn't know me!* she thought, amazed; and on the heels of that, *What's happened here is past, I've left too many people behind me to give up now, I have responsibilities.* She knew it for bravado; knew also that, tended, it might be a seed of real courage.

"Yes," she acknowledged, more to herself than to the doctor. "I've been a condottiere myself."

Annibale Valzacchi regarded her now with an expression compounded of disgust, fear and superstition. It said plainly, *A woman*? Primly, he shrugged. "I can't refuse a request for religious consolation. A military priest would suit you best. The German, then. The German is a military priest, a Father Maximillian."

" 'Father Maximillian.' " Ash twisted around bodily, and stared up at him out of the hot steaming water. "*Dottore,* do you know if—Jesu! Do you know if his name is Godfrey, *Godfrey* Maximillian?"

She saw nothing of Annibale Valzacchi for twenty-four hours, as near as she could judge the time.

A different squad of Alderic's men took her down a hundred stone steps, into the heart of the crag's corridors and apartments, and left her with slave attendants.

The room the slaves brought her to was smaller than a field tent, with only a pallet and a blanket on the stone floor. It had walls a yard thick, she could see that from the window—more like a tunnel, with iron bars set halfway down, so that no one could climb up to look out.

A freezing wind blew in through the unglazed window, from the blackness outside.

"Can I have a fire?" Ash tried to make herself understood to the five or six men and women, whose Carthaginian Gothic was quick, guttural, local, unintelligible. She went through every word for "fire" that she knew; to blank looks from all of them, except a brawny big woman.

The fair-haired woman in an iron collar, woolen blankets belted around her waist, shook her head and said something sharp. A small, quick young man with her answered: it might have been a protest. He glanced at Ash. There were crow's feet around his eyes, his faded blue eyes.

"Can I have more clothes?" Ash gripped two fistfuls of the worn-thin linen night-shirt that the bath attendant had thrown at her, and held out the cloth. "More—warm?—clothes?"

The little girl who had attended on Leofric said, "Why should you? We not."

Ash nodded, slowly, looking around at the half dozen or so people, most of whom were openly staring at her. All but the girl had rough woven blankets, with stripe-patterns; the kind of wool that one throws over a pallet for extra warmth in the winter. They wore them wrapped around their bodies, and went barefoot on the mosaic tiled floor. The girl wore only a thin linen tunic.

"Here." Ash pulled the striped woolen blanket off the pallet, draping it around the child's shoulders. She fastened it with a neat fold under the arm. "Take it. Understand? Keep it."

The girl looked at the big woman. After a second, the woman nodded. Her frown faded, replaced by vulnerability, confusion.

Ash put her fingers under her iron collar, lifting it, giving her neck some relief from the weight. She said, "I'm like you. Just like you. They can do what they like with me, too."

The woman said thickly, "Slave?"

"Yes. Slave." Ash walked across the room and hitched herself up on her hands, peering out of the stone window. Frost sparkled on the surface of the red granite, and on the iron bars. Nothing was visible beyond, not roofs, not sea, not stars: nothing.

"It's cold," she said. She grinned at the slaves, beating her arms exaggeratedly around her body, and blowing on her fingers. "Every time Lord Leofric sits down, his arse gets just as cold as ours do!"

The little girl laughed. The sharp-faced young man smiled. The big woman shook her head, with an expression of fear, and jerked her thumb; ushering the domestic slaves out. The sharp-faced man and the child lingered.

"What's down *there?*" Ash hooked her arm up and over, in an exaggerated motion of pointing out of the window, and down. "What?"

He said a word she didn't understand.

"What?" Ash frowned.

"Water."

"How far? How—*far*—down?"

He shrugged, spread his hands, grinning ruefully. "Water, down. Far. Long. Ahh . . ." He made a noise indicating disgust, then tapped his chest, looking as though he was sure he would be understood in this, at least. "Leovigild."

"Ash." Ash touched her own chest. She pointed at the girl and raised her brows.

The child looked up from examining her new blanket, "Violante."

"Okay." Ash smiled, companionably. She sat down on the pallet, tucking her freezing feet under the hem of her nightshirt. The cold made her breath smoke on the air. "So, tell me about this place."

When food came, she shared it with Leovigild and Violante. The girl, with bright eyes and a red flush to her face, ate hungrily and chattered on, half-understood; interpreting for the older man where she could.

From growing up a peasant in a military camp, Ash knows that servants get everywhere and know about everybody. Ash begins—through the cold hours, mitigated when the big woman came in with two worn wool blankets—to get the shape of the *amir*'s household clear in her mind; how life is lived in the honey-comb chambers of the Citadel; slave and freeborn and *amir*.

In the hours when she should have been sleeping, hunger kept her usefully awake. She stayed at the foot of the stone embrasure, staring up out of the window. As her eyes adjusted to night-vision she saw bright pinpoints: Fomalhaut, and Capricornus, the Goat. The constellations of summer in a freezing, bitter night.

No moon, she thought, but it could be the dark of the moon now; I haven't been counting the days—

She slid her hand along the wall, guiding herself back to the pallet, and sat down, feeling around for blankets. She wrapped herself up. Her hands clasped across her belly. Her body shivered. But only from the cold.

*Let's say I have three days. Could be four or five, but call it three: if I can't get out of here in three days, I'm dead.*

A man's voice outside the steel door said something too muffled to identify. Her hands suddenly shaking, Ash stuffed the parchment sheet and charcoal stick down the bodice of her shift.

The key turned.

With her hand against the flat metal door she could feel the mechanism work, bars sliding back between the two steel plates. Warned, she stepped back into the tiny room.

"I'll be back here in a hour," *'Arif* Alderic said from the corridor, not speaking to her. His voice sounded unusually compassionate. The single unwinking, pale light above the door shone down into her eyes: Ash blinked, attempting to see who was coming in.

Fear makes the belly uncomfortable. Ash, who has fought, feels her bowels shift in momentary discomfort that she recognizes at last as fear.

A deep masculine voice said, in German, "Oh, excuse me, I thought that—" and broke off.

The man standing at the doorway wore a brown wool gown over his green priest's robes, the puffed sleeves slit, and lined with marten fur. It was the bulk of the gown, perhaps, that made his body look too big for his head. She stepped forward, thinking, *No, his face is thinner* staring at the way deep creases cut down beside his mouth, not hidden by his beard. The fragile skin of his eyelids clung close to the balls of his eyes, accentuating their hollow sockets. All his face was clearly shrunken down onto the bone. *He looks old.*

"Godfrey?"

"I didn't know you!"

"You look thinner." She frowned.

"I didn't know you," Godfrey Maximillian repeated, wonderingly.

The steel door slammed. The noise of bars sinking into sockets drowned out any words for a long minute. Ash self-consciously smoothed the blue wool bodice and kirtle down over her shift, and one hand went up to touch her shorn hair.

"It's still me," she said. "They wouldn't give me male clothes. I don't care if I look like a woman. *Let* them underestimate me. That's just fine. Jesus, *Godfrey!*"

She took a step forward, intending to throw her arms around him, and at the last minute flushed from bodice-line to forehead, and reached out and grabbed both his hands, hard. Tears welled up and spilled down her face. She said, again, "Godfrey, Godfrey!"

His hands were warm within hers. She felt him shaking.

"Why did you go!"

"I left Dijon with the Visigoths, I came here, I desperately needed to spy out the Caliph's court and find out the truth about your voice. I thought it was the only thing now that I could do for you—" Godfrey's face streamed, wet. He didn't let go of her hands to wipe it. "It was all that I could think of doing for you!"

His hard hands crushed hers. She tightened her grip. The wind from the open stone window blew in, hard enough to whip her skirts around her bare ankles.

"You're cold," Godfrey Maximillian said accusingly, "your hands are bitter."

He lifted her hands and put them up under his armpits, into the warmth of his robe, and for the first time, met her eyes. His lids were reddened, wet. She could not imagine what he was seeing: a crop-haired thing in a dress and a steel collar, could not know how her own face was sharpened by hunger, by the loss of a silver waterfall of hair, short hair throwing brow and ear and eye and scar all into sharp relief.

Her cold fingers began to warm, prickling with blood-flow.

*"What happened to us?"* she demanded, "to the Lion? *What?"*

"I—don't know. I left two days before you fought. I thought—"

He freed one hand and wiped his face, his beard.

Words hung between them, spoken at Dijon. Ash felt his body-warmth through her cold skin. She raised her head, needing as always to look up to look into his face; and saw, not anguished declarations, but a face she knows (given the infrequency of mirrors) better than her own, and a mind of which she knows most, if not every, weakness.

Godfrey Maximillian said brusquely, "When I docked here, the field had been fought ten days ago. All I can tell you is what everybody knows: Duke Charles is wounded; the flower of Burgundian chivalry lies dead on the field outside Auxonne—but Dijon is holding out, I believe; or, there's still some fighting somewhere. No one knows or cares about one mercenary company. The Lion Azure had some notoriety because of its woman commander, but there is nothing, only minor rumors, no one in Carthage cares whether we were massacred out-right, or changed sides and fought with the Faris, or ran away; they just care that the victory was theirs."

Ash found herself nodding her head.

"I have tried," Godfrey said.

Ash tightened her grip, fingers fisted in his, buried deep in his robe's scratchy brown wool. *No. If I hold him, embrace him, it will be for my comfort, not his. Not his, when he wants me. Shit. Shit.*

"You always come for me. You came for me at St. Herlaine, and Milan." A hot tear flowed. She hitched her shoulder up, wiping her cheek on the blue wool, and stared up in wonder at him. "You don't want me. You just think you do. You'll get over it. And I'll wait, God-frey, because I have no intention of losing you. We've known each other too long, and we love each other too well."

"You don't know what I want," he said roughly.

Godfrey stepped away and released her hand. The air seared cold on her skin. Ash watched him, calmly. She watched him pace, as far as the tiny cell allowed; two steps each way on the mosaic tiled floor.

"I burn. Doesn't the Word say it's better to marry than to burn?" His clear eyes, the brown of woodland-river water, fixed on her face. "You love that boy. What else needs to be said? You will forgive me, most men go through this at a much younger age; this is the first and only time I would have given back my priesting and rejoined the world." He made an odd, sonorous murmur in his chest, that Ash realized was laughter. "This, also, I have learned in confession—that men who love in se-cret, for so long, don't know what to do if that love is returned. I don't suppose I would be different in that respect."

Whatever: let him have that thought for consolation. *I must not hold him,* Ash thought; and could not stop herself. She moved forward, grabbed his arms, clutching him around the hanging sleeves of his gown, and hugged her arms around his broad back. "Shit, Godfrey! You don't know what it's like to see you here. *You don't know.*"

His forearms closed momentarily across her back. En-folded, her face buried against his warm chest, she is for a long second blank to everything but his familiarity, his scent, the sound of his voice, the history that they share.

He put her back from him. As his hands left her shoulders, he touched the steel band riveted around her neck.

"I found out *nothing* about your voice. I failed. Every bit of the money I brought with me is gone." A glint of humor in his eyes, gazing down at her, a half-smile on his lips. "If *I* can't buy information, child, who can? I bribed who I could. I know everything about the outside of this—" a movement of his bearded chin, indicating the walls of House Leofric "—and nothing inside."

"I know all about the inside. And my voice. Did they search you, coming in?"

"Your *voice*?"

"Later: it's complicated. It *is* the Golem. I think Leofric wants me to—" *learn from*, she did not say. She was unaware that an expression of pain touched her face, and that Godfrey registered it and remained thoughtfully silent. "Were you searched?"

"No."

"They might search you going out, though. They can't search your heart, Godfrey; look at this." She started to undo the draw-cord of her shift, hesitated, faced away from him, and retrieved her paper and charcoal before she turned back. "Here. This is my best guess for a house-plan."

Godfrey Maximillian eased himself down onto the pallet, which she patted in invitation. He pointed at the paper, and charcoal twig. "Where did you get those?"

"The same place I got most of this information. A slave child. Violante." Ash swathed the full skirt around her knees and tucked the hem under her feet, in an attempt to be warm. "I share my food with her. She steals things for me."

"You do know what could happen to her, if she's caught?"

"She could be whipped. Or killed," Ash said, "this is a crazy house. Godfrey, this is deliberate. I know what I'm doing, even if she doesn't, because my life depends on it." She turned the crumpled sheet to its blank side. "Okay, show me what's outside."

When he said nothing, she looked up again.

Godfrey Maximillian said quietly, "They let me in only to give you the last rites. I know they've condemned you to execution. What I don't yet know is why, and what I can do about it."

She choked up, nodded once, wiped the back of her wrist across her eyes. "I'll tell you, if there's time. Okay. Show me what's *outside* this building."

His broad, capable hands took the paper, the charcoal stick seeming tiny. With a surprisingly delicate touch, he drew an elongated squared-off U-shape. "You're on the middle headland that protrudes into the harbor. There are quays here and here—" An "x" each side of the U. "—and streets coming up the hill to the Citadel."

"What's the scale?"

"About a half-mile to the mainland. The bluff is three, four furlongs high?" Godfrey's rumble had a self-questioning note. He drew in another shape, an elongated square within the U, occupying the far end of it. "That's the Citadel, that we're in now. It's walled."

"I remember. They brought me in that way." Her dirty fingertip traced a path from the "x" quayside mark, up to the rectangle crowning the U. "Is this Citadel walled all the way around?"

"Walled and guarded. At this end, the walls come up sheer from the water. There are town streets going back onto the mainland, and then Carthage city is here and here—" A shape added, like a palm and three fingers, which Ash realized was the harbor and two other headlands; the town, by Godfrey's markings, all down on one side. "The market—here. Where the road goes out toward Alexandria."

"Which way is north?"

"Here." A scribble. "The sea."[32]

---

[32] The geography of Visigothic Carthage, as depicted in the *Fraxinus* manuscript, does not appear to wildly contradict the known archaeological facts. The compass directions are a little off, but there is more

"Uh-huh . . ." She held it in her field of vision, under the Greek Fire that hissed in its glass cage above the door, until the lines burned into her memory.

"This window looks north," she said thoughtfully, "as far as I can tell from the stars. There's nothing between me and the sea, is there? I'm at the edge. Shit. So much for that." She flipped the paper over. "I've talked to people. This is what I think we're in." She indicated her scrawled hollow square. "Where they bring you into the House, there's a ground floor all around a courtyard: that's the *amir* and his family, his hangers-on."

"It's big." Godfrey sounded rapt.

Ash dotted in a black mark at the corners of each square. "These are four stairwells. They go down into the house underneath. Slave-quarters, kitchens, storerooms. There are stables and a mews at ground level, everything else is beneath. Violante tells me there are ten stories carved out of the rock. I think I'm on the fifth one down. Each stair has four sets of halls and chambers coming off it, at each level, *and the stairs don't interconnect.*" She finished with a cross at one corner. "That's northwest, that's me. Leofric is here, in the northeast set of chambers."

She threw the charcoal stick down, and sat back against the wall.

"Shit, I would hate to have to take this place by force!"

When she glanced sideways, and saw Godfrey Max-

often than not a mismatch between site and chronicle in archaeology. (See map.)

In fact, there were two enclosed harbors behind an isthmus; the commercial harbor and the great naval shipyards. They were a feature of what we may call Liby-Phoenician, or Carthaginian, Carthage; as was the Byrsa, an enclosed hilltop citadel within the main city itself. The streets were, indeed, stepped.

Close to this original site, Roman Carthage added other features, including water-storage cisterns, aqueducts, baths, an amphitheater, and many features of civilized life; as well as their own great naval shipyards.

imillian's closed expression, she smiled quietly.

"No. I'm not mad. Just old professional habit."

"You're not mad," he agreed, "but you're different."

Ash said nothing. There was for that second nothing she was capable of saying. Her breasts momentarily hurt, heavy within her bodice.

"Is it this?" Godfrey touched the steel collar again.

"That? No." Ash's head came up. "This is my pass out of here."

"I don't understand."

"The Lord-*Amir* Gelimer did me a favor." Ash knotted her fingers around the metal, feeling the steel's rounded corners digging into her skin. She did not know that she looked at Godfrey with all the old careless excitement of balancing on an edge. "If I don't have this, I'm a prisoner, a guest, a something you notice. *With* this . . . Alderic brought you down here—"

"Alderic?"

"The soldier." Ash spoke more quickly. "He brought you down. You must have seen it, Godfrey. This house is *full* of fair-haired slaves. If I get out of this room then I'm just one more of them. Nobody sees me. Nobody finds me. I'm just one more faceless woman in a collar."

"If that's not the trouble, what is?" Godfrey pursued. He rapidly shook his head. "Deus vous garde.[33] No. Say nothing until you wish it."

"I will."

"There are too many soldiers in this house."

"I know. I have to get outside to escape. Just for a few minutes, just a chance." She grinned, lopsidedly. "I know how thin a chance it is, Godfrey. I just can't stop trying, that's all. I have to get back. I have to get *out*." She cut off the intensity cracking her voice; let her fingers trail off the pallet, on the uneven floor. "This place is old . . ."

The unwavering light of Greek Fire lit up every corner of the tiny room: the close-set tiles in their pink and

---

[33] "God protect you."

black geometries, the chamfered edges of the window embrasure, the faint worn bas-relief on the walls: pomegranates and palm trees and men with the heads of animals. Someone had scratched a name, ARGENTIUS, down close to the floor, with some sharpened tool; not, she thought, with the carved wood spoon that came with her wooden bowl and infrequent food.

She complained absently, "They wouldn't even let me have an eating knife."

Godfrey Maximillian said dryly, "I'm not surprised. They know who you are."

Ash was startled into a laugh.

"So different, and so much the same." Godfrey reached over to touch the cut ends of her silver hair. His hand went back to the cross at his breast. "If that captain didn't know you, I'd give you these robes and hood and let you try to walk out of here. That's been known to be successful."

"Not for the man left behind," she said acidly, and was startled when he, in turn, laughed. "What? *What*, Godfrey?"

"Nothing," he said, frankly amused. "No wonder I've been with you since you were eleven."

"They will kill me." Ash watched his face change. "I've got forty-eight hours, realistically. I don't know what it's like out there, while they're electing their new King-Caliph—"

"Chaotic. It's Carnival down in the city," Godfrey shrugged, "with only the city's own guards to keep it in order. As I discovered when I attempted to buy information, the *amirs* have retreated into their own houses up here, with their households and all their own troops."

Ash hit one fist into her palm. "It *has* to be now! Is there any way you can legitimately get me out of here? Just out onto the street, just for a minute?"

"You'll be guarded."

*"I can't give up now."*

Some feeling sharpened his features, bringing the skin even more taut across the bone, but she could not read him. He looked down at his spatulate broad fingers.

When he spoke, after some moments' silence, there was an edge to his voice.

"You never give up, Ash. You sit in here and calculate that you may have two days left—but you may have two hours, or less; that Visigoth thug could knock on your door at any minute of today." He glanced briefly at the stone tunnel that served as a window. The cell's Greek Fire brilliance meant no night vision, nothing visible but a square of blackness. His tone strained, he continued, "Ash, don't you know that you could die? Does nothing teach you that? Does *nothing* make you suffer?"

*He is trying to reach me*, Ash thought, killing her anger.

"I'm not deluding myself. Yes, I'm probably going to die." She wrapped her hands in a fold of her woolen skirt, shivering against the cold. Footsteps banged down the corridor outside and faded into the distance, muffled by the steel door.

Godfrey said, "I'm nothing but an uneducated hedge-priest. You know that. I will pray to Our Lady and the Communion of Saints, I'll move Heaven and Earth to free you, you know that. But I would be failing you in everything if I didn't try to bring you to some realization, some knowledge that you could be dead before you have time to put your soul right. When did you last go to confession? Before the field at Auxonne?"

Ash opened her mouth, shut it again. At last, she said, "I don't remember. I really don't remember the last time I was absolved. Does it matter?"

Godfrey gave a small, high chuckle; a noise that rather reminded her of Leofric's rats. He brushed his hand across his face. When he looked at her, his taut expression had relaxed. "Why? Why do I *bother*? You're a complete heathen, child. We both know it."

"I'm sorry," Ash said contritely.

"No."

"I'm sorry I can't be a good Christian for you."

"I wouldn't expect it. God's representatives on Earth have not been entirely kind." Godfrey Maximillian cocked his head, listening, then relaxed again. "You're young. You have neither kith nor kin, household nor guild, lord nor lady. I've watched you on the outside, child; I know at least one other reason than lust for why you married Fernando del Guiz. Every human tie you have is bound with money, and unbound with the end of a contract. That will never lead you to a tie with Our Lord. I prayed that you would have time to grow older, and to consider."

A long, harsh male scream echoed between the cell's stone walls. It took Ash a second to realize that it was not close at hand but far off—far below—and loud enough to echo up from the harbor, over the noise of gulls.

"Carnival, huh?"

"A rough carnival."

Ash thoughtfully wiped her charcoal several times across her paper, blurring the soft lines. She scrunched it up, knelt up, and threw it out of the window. The charcoal stick she tucked under one end of the pallet.

"Godfrey . . . How long does it take before a fetus has a soul?"

"Some authorities tell us, forty days. Others, that it takes on a soul when it quickens, and the woman feels the child move within her womb. Holy Saint Magdalen," he said flatly, "is that it?"

"I was with child when I came here. They beat me, and I lost it. Yesterday." Ash found herself making the same quick movement of looking at the black window that never showed her a sun, never reassured her that it was day. "No, the day before."

His hand closed over hers. She looked down at it.

"Are the children of incest sinful?"

Godfrey's grip tightened on her hand. "Incest? How could it be *incest* between you and your husband?"

"No, not Fernando. Me." Ash stared at the opposite wall. She did not look at Godfrey Maximillian. She turned her hand over, so that her palm slid into his, and they sat with their backs leaning up against the wall, the heavy-duty cloth of the pallet cold under them.

"I do have family," she said. "You've seen them, Godfrey. The Faris, and these slaves here. *Amir* Leofric breeds them—*us*—like cattle. He breeds the son back to the mother, and the daughter to the father, and this family's been doing it since before living memory. If I'd born a child, it would have been incestuous a hundred times over." Now she turned her head, so that she could see Godfrey's face. "Does that shock you? It doesn't shock me." And in a pragmatic monotone, she added, "My baby might have been deformed. A monster. By that reasoning, I may *be* a monster. Not just my voice. Not all deformities are things you can see."

His eyelids fluttered as he avoided her gaze. She thought she had not noticed before how long and fine his brown lashes were. She felt a pain in her hand and looked down. His knuckles were white where he gripped her hand.

"How—" Godfrey coughed. "How do you know it to be true? How did you discover this?"

"*Amir* Leofric told me," Ash said. She waited until Godfrey looked her in the face again. "And I asked the Stone Golem."

"*You* asked—"

"He wanted to know whether I was a fake or not. So I told him. If I could, and it was right, then I *had* to be hearing it from somewhere, I *had* to be hearing the voice of the machine." Ash reached down with her other hand and began to peel Godfrey's fingers off her. Where he had gripped, her skin was bloodlessly white.

"He bred a general who could hear his machine," Ash said, "but now—he doesn't need another one."

"Ieusu Christus Viridianus, Christus Imperator,"[34] Godfrey said. He looked down at his hands without seeing them. Ash noticed that the cuffs of his robe were frayed. And half the gauntness of his face could be attributable to nothing other than hunger: a poor priest,

---

[34] "Green Christ, Christ Emperor."

lodging in some Carthage tenement, dependant on doctors like Annibale Valzacchi for alms, and for information. No information is without its price.

In the silence, she said: "When you pray, Godfrey, do you get an answer?"

The question brought him out of his amazement. "I would be presumptuous to say."

All her body was tense against the cold, mitigated as it might be by thick stone walls. She shifted on the pallet.

"This," she touched her temple, "isn't the Communion of Saints. I used to hope it would be, Godfrey. I kind of hoped it would be Saint George, or one of the soldier-saints, you know?"

A faint smile curled up one corner of his mouth. "I suppose you would hope that, child."

"It isn't a Saint's voice, it's a machine's voice. Although the machine might have been made by a miracle. If Prophet Gundobad was a real prophet of God?" She looked quizzically at Godfrey, without giving him time to answer. "And when I hear it, I don't just listen."

"I don't understand."

Ash bounced where she sat, hitting one fist on the pallet. "It's not just listening. When I hear you speak, I don't have to *do* anything to hear you."

"I frequently feel that you don't have to pay attention," Godfrey said, with a grave humor; derailing her absolutely. He gave her a smile of apology. "There is something more to this?"

"The voice." Ash made a helpless gesture with her hands. "I feel as if I'm pulling on a rope, or—you won't understand this, but, sometimes in combat you can *make* someone else attack you in a certain way, by the way you stand and hold your weapon, by the way you move—you offer a gap, a way in through your defenses—and they come in where you want them to, and then you deal with them. I never noticed when it was just a question or two before we fought, but Leofric made me listen to the Stone Golem for a long time. I'm *doing* something when I listen, Godfrey. Offering a . . . way in."

"There are acts of omission and acts of commission." Godfrey sounded rapt, again. Abruptly, he glanced at the door and lowered the volume of his speech. "How much can you get it to tell you? Can it tell you how to leave?"

"Oh, it could tell me. Probably tell me where all the guards are stationed." Ash flicked her gaze up to meet Godfrey's. "I've been talking to the slaves. When Leofric wants to know what tactical questions the Faris is asking the machine, he asks it—*and it tells him.*"

"And would it tell what you ask, too?"

She shrugged. Staccato, she said, "Maybe. If it 're-members.' If Leofric thinks to ask. He will. He's smart. Then I'm caught. They'll just change duty rostas. Maybe beat me until I'm unconscious and can't ask."

Godfrey Maximillian took her hand. His body was still half-turned toward the door. "Slaves do not always tell the truth."

"I know. If I was going to—" Ash made another unspecific gesture, trying to frame a thought. "To call what it knows to me, I'd ask something else first. Godfrey, I'd ask it *why is it so cold here? Amir* Leofric doesn't know the answer to that, and he's scared."

"Everyone is—"

"That's just it. Everyone *here* is scared, too. I thought this was something they made happen for their crusade— but they didn't expect this cold either. This isn't the Eternal Twilight, this is something else again."

"Perhaps these are the last days—"

A heavy tread sounded in the corridor.

Godfrey Maximillian leaped to his feet rapidly, brushing down his robe and gown.

"Try and get me out," Ash said quickly and quietly, "if I don't hear from you soon, I'll try any way I can think of."

His strong hand enveloped her shoulder, pushing her back down as she tried to rise, so that she was kneeling in front of him as the cell door began to open and soldiers came in. Godfrey crossed himself, and lifted the cross from his broad chest, and kissed it devoutly. "I have an idea. You won't like it. *Absolvo te*,[35] my child."

The *nazir* with Alderic was not Theudibert, Ash noted; nor were any of the squad Theudibert's men. The *'arif* commander stood back while his soldiers filed out, Godfrey Maximillian between them.

Ash watched impassively.

"You ought to be more careful what you say, Frankish girl," *'Arif* Alderic remarked. He put his hand on the steel door and, instead of closing it behind him, pushed it to in front of him, and turned around to face her. "That's a friendly warning."

"One," Ash held up her hand and ticked it off on her fingers, "what makes you think I don't know there are always people here listening to me? Two: what makes you think I care what you report to your lord-*amir*? He's mad. Three, he's already planning to torture me, just *what* have I got to worry about?"

She managed to end with her fists on her hips, chin up; and more energy in her voice than she thought she could find, given the weakness from hunger that went through her every time she stood up. The big bearded man stirred uncomfortably. Something about her bothered him; it took Ash several seconds to work out that it was the contradiction between her dress and her stance.

"You should be more careful," the Visigoth captain repeated stubbornly.

"*Why?*"

*'Arif* Alderic did not answer. He walked past her to the window, leaning up the red granite shaft and peering at the sky. A smell of ripe harbor rubbish drifted in.

"Have you ever done anything you remained ashamed of, Frankish girl?"

"What?" Ash looked at the back of his head. By the set of his shoulders, he was uncomfortable. A chill feathered the hairs on her arms. *What is this?*

---

[35] More properly, *Ego te absolvo*: the priest's absolution of one's sins.

"I said, have you ever done anything that you stayed ashamed of? As a soldier?" He turned to face her, looked her up and down, and repeated more firmly, "As a soldier."

Ash folded her arms. She bit back the first smart remark that came to her mind, and studied him. In addition to his white robes and mail hauberk, the Visigoth wore a crude goatskin jacket, laced like a peasant's tunic; and furlined boots, not sandals. He carried a curved dagger at his belt, and a sword with a narrow straight cross. Far too alert to be attacked, surprised.

Moved to truth, she relaxed and said, "Yes, everybody has. I have."

"Will you tell me?"

"Why—" Ash stopped herself. "Okay. Five years ago. I was in a siege, it doesn't matter where, some little town on the borders of Iberia. Our lord wouldn't let the townspeople come out. He wanted them to eat up the garrison's supplies, so they'd have to give up the siege. The garrison commander didn't want that, so he evacuated them, drove them out into the moat. So there they were, two hundred people, in a ditch between two armies, neither of whom were going to let them back or through. We killed a dozen before they'd believe us. It went on for a month. They starved and they died. The smell was something else, even for a siege . . ."

She refocused her gaze on Alderic, to find the older man studying her closely.

"That's a story I've told before," she said. "Usually to discourage the kind of would-be mercenary recruit who is fourteen and thinks it's all sitting on horseback and charging a noble enemy. I don't suppose you have those. What I don't say, and what I'm ashamed of, is the new-born babies. Our lord said it wasn't right they should be unbaptised and go to hell, so he let the townspeople pass them up to us. And we passed them to the field-priest, who baptised them—and then we handed them straight back down into the ditch."

Unconsciously she rested her palms flat against her belly.

"We did. *I* did. It went on for weeks. I know they died of starvation while in a state of grace . . . but it stays with me."

The Visigoth *'arif* nodded an acknowledgment.

"We have the fourteen year olds in the household levies." White teeth flashed in his black beard, and then his expression changed. "Mine is infants, also. I was perhaps your age, no older. My *amir*—my lord, you would call him; Leofric—had me working in the stock pens."

Ash was aware that she must look puzzled.

"The slave breeding-pens. No larger than this, most of them." Alderic gestured around the cell. "My *amir* set me and my squad to culling 'errors' in the breeding program, when they were twelve or fourteen weeks old." The *'arif* abruptly pulled off his helmet, wiping his white brow, that was sweating despite the cold. "We were the clear-up squad. Nothing I have done since, in twenty years of war, has been so bad as slashing the throats of babies—the big vein, here—and then just . . . throwing them away. Out of windows like this one, into the harbor: rubbish. No one questions my *amir*. My squad did as we were ordered."

He shrugged helplessly, and met her gaze.

She looks at Alderic's face in the knowledge that—if this is the way it happened for her—there is a sporting chance that he almost killed her, casually slashed her throat and dumped her, twenty years ago. And that he knows this.

"So," Ash said. She grinned at Alderic companionably. "So, Leofric was nuts even back then, huh?"

She saw his brief confusion, a frown—*the woman can't be that obtuse, surely?*—and a dawning acknowledgment.

The *'arif* said, reprovingly, "That's a disrespectful way to speak of a man who may become King-Caliph."

"If the Visigoth Empire elects *Leofric*, you deserve all you get!" She lifted her hand to her neck. She is sure that her bodice shows the old white scar around her neck, that Fernando del Guiz touched so long ago in Cologne. "I always just assumed this was some childhood *accident* . . . Not that you were exactly efficient, 'Arif Alderic. A quarter-inch either way and I wouldn't be talking to you, would I?"

"Even a dumb grunt can't get everything right," Alderic said gravely. "Accidents will happen."

Pure happenstance. Pure, freak chance.

The thought makes her sweat. She distracts herself.

"Why so young?" she said suddenly. "These children . . . Wouldn't the babies have to be old enough to *talk*, at least, before Leofric could find out they couldn't communicate with the Stone Golem?"

Alderic gave her a look. It took her a second to realize that it was the look soldiers reserve for civilians who find some piece of mass battlefield killing irrational.

"They don't have to talk," Alderic said. "He doesn't find out from them. The babies are kept in a different quarter of the house; he waits until they are old enough to distinguish real pain from a hunger to be fed, or discomfort, and then he hurts them badly—usually burns them with fire. They shriek. Then he asks the Stone Golem if *it* can hear *them*."

*Sweet Christus!*

Ash thinks with her mind and with her body. Her body is reading his, judging, finding no fault in his alertness, no point at which she might snatch a knife, gain a sword. Her mind tells her there is nothing she could do with a weapon if she had one.

"Granted they were slave-children," the 'arif said, with a supreme insensibility to the slave-woman in front of him, "it is still something I dream I am doing, most nights."

"Yeah . . . people have told me about that sort of dream."

Over and beyond what they say, some other wordless, friendly communication is present in the room. Ash, bright-eyed, rubbed her hands briskly over her wool-sleeved arms. "Soldiers have more in common with other soldiers than with lords, with *amirs*, have you ever noticed that, *'Arif* Alderic? Even soldiers on opposite sides!"

Alderic touched his right hand to his chest, over his heart. "I wish I could have faced you in combat, lady."

"I wish you may still get your wish!"

It came out acerbic. The Visigoth threw back his head, beard jutting, and laughed. He moved toward the door.

"And while you're at it," Ash said, "the food here's terrible, but I'd like more of it."

Alderic smiled brilliantly, shaking his head. "You have only to command, lady."

"I *wish*."

The steel grill closed behind him. The sounds of locking metal died away, leaving only the wail of the rising wind. Outside, freezing rain spattered on carven red granite.

"I have only to command, *temporarily*," Ash amended, aloud.

There was nothing to mark the passing of any given hour in the day except the uninformative horns; no wheeling constellations; no difference to the passing footsteps, or the bells in what must be the household chapel: House Leofric appeared to swarm with activity through each twenty-four hours. She hoped for Alderic to send either a slave or a soldier with food within the hour: no one came. When each hour can be final, when any key unlocking the door can bring terminal news, time stretches unbelievably. It might only have been minutes until the sound of metal turning metal tumblers brought her up on her feet, swaying and dizzy.

Two soldiers, each carrying maces, came in and stood to either side of the narrow door. There was barely room for anyone else to come in. Ash backed up toward the window. The *'arif* Alderic pushed between his guards. A robed, bearded man followed him in. Godfrey Maximillian.

"Shit. Already? *Now*?" Ash demanded; but Godfrey

was shaking his head almost as soon as their eyes met.

"The Lord-*Amir* Leofric thinks it best to keep you in good health, until you're needed." Godfrey Maximillian stumbled almost imperceptibly over the last word: she saw Alderic register the priest's revulsion.

"And?"

"And you require exercise. A short period each day." Nice try, Godfrey.

Ash met Alderic's gaze. "So. Your lord's going to let me out of this stone box?"

Yeah, right. You have to be joking! Under what *possible* circumstances—

Alderic said impassively, "The *amir* has a trustworthy ally, he commits you to his custody for an hour each day from now until the inauguration. Perhaps only today."

Ash didn't move. She looked from one man to the other. Then she sighed, relaxing very slightly, thinking: Outside of here is a political machine running at full stretch, I have no way of knowing the various alliances, enmities, deals, bribes, tricks—and if some piece of double-dealing chicanery on Leofric's behalf is getting me out of this cell, I don't *care* what I don't know. I just need not to be watched for ten heartbeats and I'm gone.

"So who does the lord-*amir* count as his trustworthy ally?" Ash asked. "Who does he trust to keep an eye on me once I'm out of here? Let's not pretend I'm going to come back if I can help it."

"That much," the *'arif* Alderic said gravely, "I had worked out for myself. *Nazir!*"

The taller of the two soldiers hooked his mace over his sword hilt by its leather lanyard, and disengaged a long steel-linked chain from his belt. Ash lifted her chin as he approached and began to thread it under her iron collar.

"So, who?" she managed to get out.

Alderic's face took on an expression something between rough humor and disapproval. "An ally, lady. One of your lords. You know him, I'm told. A Bavarian."

Ash watched as the *nazir* bent down to attach manacles to her ankles. Cold metal links hung down, pulling at her collar. She could have throttled him with the chain, possibly, but that would still leave the rest.

"Bavarian?" she said abruptly. "Oh, *shit*, no!"

Godfrey Maximillian raised a brow. "I told you that you wouldn't like it."

"It's *Fernando*! Isn't it! He's come south! Fucking Fernando del Guiz!"

"He owns you," Godfrey said, stone-faced. "He's your husband. You're his property. I've brought the *amir* Leofric to a proper understanding of that fact—that the Lord Fernando can be held completely responsible for you. The lord-*amir* then agreed to release you into your husband's company for an hour, each day, on his parole."

"I imagine the Faris's lap-dog will guard you well enough," *'Arif* Alderic finished, with gallows cheerfulness, "since his life depends on it."

Of course, Ash thought, somebody else could just be using me to get rid of Fernando. He'll have made enemies. It could be anyone. Up to and including the Lord-*Amir* Leofric . . .

"*Fuck* politics," Ash said aloud, "why can't I just *hit* somebody?"

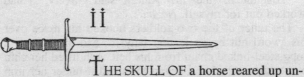

**ii**

THE SKULL OF a horse reared up under the nose of Ash's mount. Hollow white eye-sockets and long yellow teeth leered up at her, bleached bone bright-edged in the intense light of Greek Fire.

"Carnival!" a drunken male voice bellowed.

"*Shit!*"

The horse-skull's wearer waved wild arms, in a flurry of red ribbons.

The elderly furry brown mare took both her front feet off the street and skittered back on her white hind legs. Iron shoes struck sparks from the flint cobblestones.

*"Motherfucker!"*

Ash reined in, shifting her weight forward, trying to bring the rearing mare down. The chains that were manacled to both her ankles and passed under the horse's belly rubbed against tender skin. Her neck-chain, shackled to the stirrups, jingled. The mare threw her mouth up, creaming foam springing out on her neck.

*"Get* down," Ash ordered, trying to wheel the mare around, back away from the throng in the street. Two soldiers' horses closed in on either flank, pressing close enough to threaten her knees; two more trained cavalry horses to her rear. "Get over!"

An escort-rider in front leaned down and got the mare's bridle with one hand. With her steadied, he struck a blow at the reveler's masked face. The man staggered away, shouting, pissed, into the crowd.

A second man rode in close.

"We'll ride outside the city," Fernando del Guiz announced, tall in the saddle beside her, soothing the hooded bird that gripped his wrist: too small for a goshawk, too big for a peregrine falcon.

Desire did not flood her, as it had when she had seen him before; only the utter, surprising familiarity of his face made her heart thump, once, with shock.

Six of the escort troop immediately rode to the front, beating the reveling men of Carthage to one side. Ash, cold air stinging her face, kneed the mare forward; and when she could safely free her hands, drew her fur-lined hood up around her face, and wrapped her linen-lined wool cloak firmly about her body.

"Son of a *bitch*," she muttered. "How does anyone expect me to ride, like *this*?"

The chains that passed from ankle to ankle, around and under the mare's body, trapped her. Even an accidental slip out of the saddle would get her dragged, head-down, over cobbled streets; a death perhaps not much preferable to that planned by Leofric.

"Come on, beautiful," Ash soothed. The mare, happier by reason of being surrounded by nine or ten of her stable-mates, reverted to plodding between the companions of Fernando del Guiz. Armed German troops, mostly. Alert and unfriendly.

And if at some point I can persuade you to bolt, with me on you, Ash thought grimly as she leaned forward to slap the mare's neck, that *will* be a miracle. But it looks like it's my only chance...

Intense, blue-white Greek Fire blazed down into the rule-straight avenues, casting a high-definition light on men wearing heron's-head masks, painted leather cat's skulls, and knife-tusked boar's heads. She thought she saw one woman: realized it was a bearded merchant in a woman's gown. Harsh male voices sang all around her, noise echoing back from the buildings, the crowd only beaten back by the escorts using the flats of their blades. Fernando del Guiz reined his roan gelding in, his squires with him.

A man above the city gate shouted in quick, guttural Carthaginian Gothic, "Poncy German arse-fucker!"

Gathering a shaky amount of self-possession, Ash spoke before it even occurred to her that this was not wise, under these circumstances:

"Well, well. Someone who recognizes your personal banner. How about that?"

Fernando's face was not particularly visible behind the acorn-shaped steel helmet's nasal-bar: she could not read his expression.

Christ, the last thing I did in Dijon was hit him in the face, in front of his Visigoth mates; maybe I should just learn to keep my mouth *shut*?

She noted that he sat his black-pointed bay roan gelding somewhat wearily, and that his eagle livery coat showed threadbare in places, ripped at one seam. Something in his posture spoke of bearing up under trouble, makes her think that—however necessary it might be for survival—the role of a renegade is not proving easy for him. *Not the golden boy, now.*

He handed his hunting bird over to a squire and removed his helmet.

"You can stop hitting me. They let me keep Guizburg." His voice sounded rueful, with a hint of humor, and when she met his green eyes, they were dust-red and bloodshot: the eyes of a man who is not sleeping easily. "So, yes, it's still my livery."

*Damn! Your mouth is going to get you killed, girl . . .*

She could feel her face heating, although the chill wind disguised it; and she stared away into the darkness beyond the city gate. *Am I really going to do this? Am I really going to ask* him *for help?*

*What else can I do, now?*

A half-inch of steel, prosaic and unanswerable, is locked around her neck and her wrists and her ankles. Chains fasten her to her horse. An armed guard surrounds her, and she has no armed friends. With things as they are, she will ride out into the desert outside Carthage now, and she will ride back into Carthage again an hour or so in the future.

Maybe she'll risk spooking the mare, risk being kicked and trampled in the unlikely event the animal will bolt. Even so, she's still trapped by steel links that Dickon Stour could sever in one blow at the anvil—but Dickon is half a world away if he isn't dead. If they aren't all dead.

*I am going to do this.*

It is not the fact that she will ask Fernando for help that makes her ashamed. *It's the fact that fear forces me to do it. And he's weak; what* use *will this be?*

She snorted an amused laugh that came out too high, and wiped her streaming eyes. "Fernando. What will you take, to let me go? Just to turn your back for five minutes, that's all."

*Just let me merge into the slave-class, or into the darkness, no matter that I'm still in North Africa, that I'm hundreds of miles from home.*

"Leofric would have me killed." There was an educated certainty in his tone. "There isn't *anything* you could offer. I've seen what he does to people."

Do I tell this man what, in two or three days time, Leofric will do to me?

"You're here in his House, you must be in his favor. You could get away with it—"

"I don't get a choice about whether I'm here or not." The European knight in Visigoth armor snorted. "If I wasn't your husband, I'd have been executed after Auxonne for desertion. They still think I'm a lever they can use with you. A source of information."

"Then help me get away." She sounded unsteady, even to herself. "Because in two or three days, Leofric's going to strap me down and cut me open, and then you're redundant!"

"What?" He gave her a shocked look that for a second gave her back Floria del Guiz, his sister's expression on his face. Anguish. Then: "No! I can't do anything!"

The thought *I might not ever see Floria again* went though her mind. It brought a sharp pain that she pushed away into numbness.

"Well, *fuck* you." She breathed shakily. "That's about what I thought you'd say. You *have* to listen to me!"

The noise of their horses passing under the city gate drowned out her voice.

The look he gave her, she couldn't read.

Coming out into the open, outside the walls, the city lights left her half-blind in countryside darkness. She felt she was gripping the rein too tightly and eased off. The mare fretted and sidled toward Fernando's gelding. Ash raised her head to the black sky, brilliant with stars shining clear through the frigid air.

It *is* night . . . I wasn't sure.

Her eyes adjusting, she found the stars bright as strong moonlight. His face she could clearly see to be flushed.

"Please," she said.

"I can't."

A bitter wind whipped into her face. Stomach churning, on the verge of panic, she thought *What now?*

Capricornus hung high in the arch of the sky. They rode out onto a paved avenue. To either side, the great brick arches of twin aqueducts ran back into the city.[36] A faint sound of running water could be heard over the clink of tack, and the rumbled conversation of Fernando's men-at-arms and squires. The starlight gleamed on pomegranate-crowned pillars, robbing them of color.

She let the mare drop back.

"Ash . . ." Fernando's tone sounded warningly.

"Walk on." Ash clucked. The winter-coated mare shifted forward, taking two long strides to put herself in the center of the group of riders again, by Fernando. Ash sat up in the saddle, looking between the armed guards.

She was startled into speaking aloud.

"What's *that*?" She corrected herself. "Those?"

Fernando del Guiz said, "The King-Caliph's stone bestiary."

Under each aqueduct arch, great carved stone beasts rested, couchant, five or six times the height of a man.

Riding past an arch of the aqueduct, Ash saw in the charcoal shadow a great carved beast. The pale weathered stone gleamed, five or six times the height of a man. It was, she made out, the body of a lion, with the head of a woman: the stone face almond-eyed, the expression almost a smile.

As the avenue came level with the next arch, she saw another statue within. This was brick, shaped and curved into the flank of a hind: the neck collared with a crown, the tiny antlers broken off. Ash turned her head, looking across to the other side of the avenue. The aqueduct there was in deeper shadow, but something shone within its black arches: a blunt, granite statue of a man with the head of a serpent.[37]

---

[36] Archaeological evidence shows only a single Roman aqueduct. Ninety km long, it brought 8.5 million gallons of water per day to Carthage from Zaghouan. The remains can be seen crossing the Oued Miliana valley, twenty miles south of Tunis.

[37] Nothing of this "stone bestiary" survives, that we know of.

Dry-mouthed with a new fear, she suddenly asked, "Where are we going, Fernando?"

"Hunting."

"Yeah. Right." *And I'm the Queen of Carthage ...*

Movement caught her eye. A group of waiting riders, in the aqueduct's shadow. Another ten men? Mares, white surcoats—and the notched-wheel livery of House Leofric.

"We'll ride to the pyramids," Fernando called out to the group of waiting Visigoths. "The hunting is better there!"

Shit, Ash thought, looking at the Visigoth newcomers. This is going to be next to impossible. Come on, girl, think! Is there something I can use, here?

The chill air bit at her face, and her ungloved fingers. Her cloak spread out, covering her legs in the thin wool gown, and the mare's flanks. The mare plodded, even less lively now that she was out of the city. Ash strained her vision to look ahead, away from the city, southwards. The avenue and aqueducts ran away parallel into silver darkness. Into freedom.

Even as she looked, the mass of guards wheeled, taking her with them, off into flat, barren earthy country; and she slowed her pace, partly for the uncertain footing, partly to see if she could drop back, unnoticed.

A pitch-torch sputtered behind her. In its yellow light, she saw that the nearest riders were Fernando del Guiz and a dark Visigoth boy with a scanty, curled beard. The boy rode bare-headed, was dressed nobly, and there was something about his face that tugged at her memory.

"Who is this, Uncle?" The boy used what Ash recognized as an honorific rather than kinship title. "Uncle, why's this slave with us? She can't hunt. She's a woman."

"Oh, she hunts," Fernando said gravely. His eyes met Ash's, over the boy's head. "Two-legged quarry."

"Uncle, I don't understand you."

"She's Ash," Fernando said resignedly. "My wife."

"Gelimer's son does not ride with a *woman*." The boy

shut his mouth with a snap, gave Ash a glare of utter disgust, and nudged his mount across to the squires and birds.

"*Gelimer's* son?" she gasped, into the cold wind, at Fernando.

"Oh, that's Witiza. He lives in House Leofric." Fernando shrugged uncomfortably. "One of *Amir* Leofric's nephews lives with *Amir* Gelimer."

"Yeah, it's called 'hostages' . . ."

The new fear grew. She asked no questions—knowing there would be no answers—but rode on, every sense heightened by apprehension. Looking over at Witiza, with a pang, she thought, *He's neither man nor boy. He'll be about Rickard's age.*

She turned her head, missing the words the boy and squires were speaking—a discussion about hawking—and rode blindly, her eyes momentarily swimming. When she raised her gaze again, Witiza had ridden forward, and was laughing with the del Guiz men-at-arms. Fernando still rode at her right flank.

"Just let me ride off!" she whispered.

The young German knight's head turned. She abruptly remembered his face with a red mark of a blow swelling under his lip. Apart from his first remark, it was not being mentioned: she felt it hanging between them.

"I'm sorry," she said, with an effort.

Fernando shrugged. "So am I."

"No, I—" She shook her head. Other urgencies pressed in, brought by the image of him at Dijon. "What happened to my company at Auxonne? You can at least tell me that! You ought to know, you're in House Leofric."

Then, not able to keep bitterness out of her tone:

"Or didn't you see—given that you left early?"

"Would you believe me, if I told you?" It was not a taunt. She could not be aware of everything around her—stingingly alert to where each of the German men-at-arms was riding, who might be drinking from a wineskin and so not alert later, who was paying more attention to the squires carrying belled hunting birds than to their escort duties—impossible to be open to this, and not also know that Fernando had spoken without malice, only with a kind of tired curiosity.

"Very little," Ash said honestly. "I'd believe very little you told me."

"Because I'm a traitor, in your eyes?"

"No," she said. "Because you're a traitor in *your* eyes."

Fernando grunted, startled.

The mare's uneven gait brought her attention back to the ground, silver-and-yellow under starlight and torchlight. The cold wind whipped smoke from the burning pitch into her face, and she coughed at the bitter smell.

"I don't know what happened to your company. I didn't see, and I didn't ask." Fernando shot a glance at her. "Why do you want to know? They all end up dead with you anyway!"

It took her breath for a moment.

"Yeah . . . I lose some. War gets people killed. But then, it's their decision to follow me."

Her mind's eye holds the images of golem, wagons, fire-throwers. She will not think *Roberto, Florian, Angelotti.*

"And my decision to say that I take responsibility for them, while our contract lasts. *I want to know what happened!*"

She let herself look at him directly, and found herself looking into his tired, reddened eyes. His curling fair hair was longer, straggling around his face; he looked closer to thirty than to twenty, *and it is only two months,* she thought, *since I stood with him in the cathedral at Cologne: sweet Christ!*

She did not know what expression was on her own face, could not know that she looked simultaneously much younger, much more open and vulnerable, and at the same time herself looked aged. Worn, not by a life in camp, but by nights spent awake in Dijon, thinking about this, imagining what words she could speak, her body aching to lay full-length against him, wrap her legs around his hips, thrust him deep inside her.

And her mind despising her for that hunger for a weak man.

"I *don't* know," he mumbled.

"What have they got you doing now?" Ash said. "That's Gelimer's son. Lord-*Amir* Gelimer hates Lord-*Amir* Leofric. So, are you taking me to Gelimer? To be killed? Or what?"

His beautiful, ravaged face was momentarily blank.

"No!" Fernando's voice rose to a shout. He silenced himself; waving reassuringly to Witiza and the squires. "*No*. You're my wife, I wouldn't take you to be murdered!"

Ash slid the reins up between finger and thumb, her eyes on the riders around her. She said, bitterly, "I think *you'd* do anything. The minute somebody threatened you! You hated me anyway, Fernando. From the minute we met in Genoa."

He colored up. "I was a boy then! Fifteen! You can't blame me for some wild boy's prank!"

*That touched a nerve*, Ash realized, surprised.

Something whirred and clattered, out in the desolate land. A bird flew up from under one of the horse's hooves. Ash tensed, about to dig her heels in. The German troops closed in two deep around her: she imperceptibly relaxed.

The sound of hooves on earth gave way to the clatter of iron shoes on stone: the mass of troops riding out of the desert and onto ancient flagstones. Her belly churned. She looked ahead, straining her eyes to see more cavalry: expecting now the *amir* Gelimer's men in ambush, or men hired by him. Gelimer, who might want her killed, or questioned: either being vile. *Caught up in someone else's fight,* she thought. *Christ, I thought I had two days before Leofric did for me. I was safer inside Carthage!*

Dark shapes blotted the sky.

Hills, she thought; before her eye took in their regularity. The noise of the horses' hooves echoed back from flat surfaces that sloped up and away; so that her second apprehension was that she rode in a steep valley, but the sides even in starlight were too regular. Flat planes, sharp-edged.

Pyramids.

*Anyone could be hiding out here!*

Stars fringed the edges of the stone. Their light leeched all color from the sides of the pyramids: immense, shaped structures of carven stone, built up from a hundred thousand red silt bricks, faced with brilliantly painted plaster. Ash rode among armed men, among the pyramids of Carthage. She could say nothing; silenced; could only lift her head and look around her, regardless of the freezing wind that howled around the gargantuan stone burial monuments.

She saw that all the great frescoes were faded, damaged by centuries of weather and darkness. Plaster flaked off the tombs and lay in shards on the paving stones. Her mare trod on a painted gold-eyed fragment: a lioness with the moon between her brows. It crunched like frost.

Under their faded, flaking covering, the exact and mechanical regularity of the pyramids remained, stretching out as far in every direction as she could see—and she could see ten or a dozen of them, silhouetted against the stars. Her neck hurt from looking up, and her steel collar dug into her flesh.

"Christus!" she whispered.

An owl hooted.

She jumped. The mare startled, not very wildly; and she leaned forward to put a calming hand on the beast's neck.

A pair of wings stretched out from a squire's arm, ahead. Two flat yellow eyes gleamed at her through the starlit dark. The squire lifted his arm. The great owl lifted, silently, and swooped into the night.

"You're hawking with owls," Ash said, wonderingly. "You're hawking, with owls, in a graveyard."

"It's a Visigoth pastime." Fernando shrugged.

The group having halted, most of the guards were taking up stations in a rough circle between two of the immense sandstone pyramids. There was not room to gallop between them, Ash saw; even with a horse not twelve years old, overfed, and swaybacked into the bargain. She glanced back over her shoulder. Carthage was invisible, except for a white glow silhouetting a broken ridge, which she thought might be distant Greek Fire.

Clearly, we are waiting.

For someone? For something to happen?

The back of her neck prickled.

White, soundless death swooped past her head—so close that the pinions flicked her scarred cheek.

An owl.

In sheer, inane relief, she asked the banal question: "What do they hunt out here?"

"Small game. Gully-rats. Poisonous snakes."

Hunting is always a good cover for a covert meeting.

So easy. A crossbow bolt out of the dark. You wouldn't even have to hit me. Just this horse. Where am I going, when I'm chained to it? *She died in a riding accident, my lord.*

"Do you think I'm just going to sit here and *wait?*"

Fernando shifted in his saddle. Something gave a coughing growl, far off among the pyramids. It sounded like a wild cat. Ash looked at Fernando's German riders; two or three of them gazed nervously off into the darkness, the rest were watching her.

Shit! I have *got* to do something!

Fernando sat back in his saddle. "There's news about the French peace treaty. His Spider-Majesty Louis signed. France is now at peace with the Visigoth Empire."

Fernando's gelding mouthed at the mare's tack, lipping her. The mare ignored this. She nuzzled the flagstones for spindly, frost-burned tufts of grass.

"The war's going to be over. There's no one to fight now except Burgundy."

"And England, if they ever finish fighting their own

civil wars. And the Sultan," Ash said absently, staring into the darkness, "when Mehmet and the Turkish Empire decides you've worn yourself out fighting in Europe, and you're ripe to be picked."

"Woman, you're obsessed with war!"

"I—" She broke off.

What she had been watching in the distance materialized.

Not a troop of soldiers.

Two squires with satiated owls on their wrists, walking out from behind a corner of the pyramid, a dozen or more dead snakes spitted on a stick between them.

Her thumping heart slowed. She turned back in her saddle to face Fernando. Both she and the mare were chilling, stiffening up; and she nudged it into a walk, del Guiz riding beside her, gazing down at her with an expression of anxiety.

I can't just wait to be taken!

She demanded, "Do you really think *Amir* Gelimer doesn't want to kill me?"

Fernando ignored the question.

"Please," she said. "Please let me go. Before something happens here, before I get taken back—please."

His hair took gold from the torchlight, that brought a glow of color from his green livery and the gilded pommel of his riding sword. She thought he might be wearing a plackart over mail, under his livery jacket.

"I've been wondering," he said, "why men follow you. Why men follow a woman."

With a certain grim humor, that can stave off fear for whole seconds at a time, Ash said, "Often they don't. Most places I've been, I've had to fight my own troops before I've fought the enemy!"

In the torchlight, his expression changes. When he looks down at her, from the saddle of the Visigoth warhorse, it is with an unconscious awareness of the breadth of his shoulders, filling out into adulthood now, and the hard muscles of a man who trains daily for edged-weapon warfare.

"You're a *woman!*" Fernando protested. "If *I'd* hit *you*, I'd have broken your jaw, or your neck. You're nothing like as strong as I am. How come you do what you do?"

It is true, if irrelevant at this moment, that she neither hit him with her full strength, or with a weapon, or with the knowledge of where the human body breaks. She could have blinded him. Wondering now at her reluctance—Jesú Christus, he's *not* going to let me go!—she listened to the night's noises for a full minute before she spoke.

"I don't have to be as strong as you. I only have to be strong enough."

He looked blankly at her. " 'Strong enough'?"

Ash looked up. "I don't have to be stronger than you are. I only have to be strong enough to kill you."

Fernando opened his mouth, and then shut it again.

"I'm strong enough to use a sword or an axe," she said, huddled into her cloak, listening. Nothing but the hunting calls of the owls. "That's just training, timing, balance. Not weight-lifting."

He blew into his hands, as if for warmth, and without looking at her, said, "I know why men follow you. You're only incidentally a woman. What you really are is a soldier."

Thrown back in her memory to the cell, to Gaiseric, Fravitta, Barbas, Theodoric; to violence that stops short of rape; to shed blood; she winces.

"And it's nothing to be proud of!"

The chains chafe her wrists. "It's what I need to be, to do what I do."

"Why do what you do?"

Ash smothered a laugh: it would have come out weary, and on the wrong side of hysteria. "You're not the person I'd expect to ask that! You're the one who's spent your whole life training to wear armor and use a sword. You're the knight. Why do what *you* do?"

"I'm not doing it anymore."

What might have been adolescent in his tone was

gone now. He made a quiet statement of fact. Distracted from listening for hoofbeats, she gazed at his Visigoth mail hauberk, the trained horse that he was riding, and the sword-belt at his side; and let him see her looking.

Fernando stated, "I'm not killing anyone."

Ash's mind made a mental note that any other knight's sentence would have finished "anyone *else*," at the same time that her mouth opened and she said, without volition, "In a fucking pig's arse! That hauberk a present from Leofric?"

"If I don't wear armor or a sword, no one in House Leofric listens to a word I say."

"Yeah, and what does that tell you?"

"That doesn't make it right!"

"Lots of things aren't the way they should be," Ash said grimly. "You ask my priest why men die of sickness, or famine, or act of God."

"We don't *have* to kill," Fernando said.

A horse snorted, close at hand. Her pulse jolted, before she realized that it was one of the escort's mounts.

"You're as crazy as she is! The Faris," Fernando said. "I was one of the officers with her before Auxonne, walking the ground. She kept walking around saying 'we can make that a killing-zone' or 'put the war-wagons there, I can guarantee you sixty percent enemy casualties.' She's a fucking head-case."

Ash raised her silver brows. "In what way?"

She realized Fernando was staring at her.

"Doesn't it seem crazy to you to go around a perfectly good pasture and work out which bits of it you can use so that you can burn people's faces off, and chop through their leg-bones, and shoot rocks through their chests?"

"What do you want me to say, I lie awake nights worrying about it?"

"That would be good," he agreed. "But don't tell me; I wouldn't believe you."

Sudden anger sparked. "Yeah, well, I don't notice you going up to the King-Caliph and saying, hey, invading

Christendom is wrong, why don't we all just be nice to each other? And I don't guess you said to House Leofric, no, I won't take the horse and the kit, thanks; I'm not going to be a warrior anymore. Did you?"

"No," he muttered.

"Where's the hair-shirt, Fernando? Where's the monk's robes, instead of the armor? Exactly when do you plan to swear poverty and obedience, and go around the King-Caliph's nobles telling them to lay down their arms? Your ass would be hung up to dry!"

He said, "I'm too afraid to try."

"Then how can you tell *me*—"

He cut off her outraged protest: "Just because I can see what's right, that doesn't mean I can do it."

"Are you seriously telling me *you* don't intend to stand up and protest against this war, but you expect *me* to stop what I do for a living? Jesú Christus, Fernando!"

"I would think, from where you are, you'd know how I feel."

About to spit back some smart remark, Ash felt a chill in her belly that was not the bitter wind. She swallowed, dry-mouthed. At last, she said, "I'm on my own here. I don't have my guys with me."

Fernando del Guiz did not make a sarcastic or destructive comment; he only nodded, acknowledging what she said.

Ash said, "I'll strike a bargain with you. You free me, here, let me ride off into the desert, before anyone else gets here. And I'll tell you how you can legitimately have the marriage annulled. Then you're nothing to do with me anymore, and everybody will know that."

She brought the mare around again, moving within the enclosing circle of troops. A wave of fear went through her. *Who's already on their way here? Gelimer? Someone else? Someone I don't even know about?* An owl shrieked, close by. Something rustled in the torchlit darkness.

She heard Fernando say, "Why could I annul the marriage? Because you're a villein; slave-born?"

"Because you'll want an heir. I'm barren," Ash said.

She became aware that her bare hands locked shut on the pommel of her saddle, her shoulder-muscles rigid against—what? A punch, a blow from a whip? She looked up swiftly at Fernando del Guiz.

"You are?" The lines of his face showed only shocked bewilderment. "How do you know?"

"I was with child at Dijon." Ash found she couldn't release the grip of her hands. The leather reins, wrapped around the pommel, cut into her cold fingers. She kept her gaze on his face in the circle of torchlight. "I lost it, here; it doesn't matter how. It isn't possible for me to have another."

She expected anger, tensed against being hit.

"My *son*?" he said wonderingly.

"A son or a daughter. It was too soon to tell." Ash felt her mouth twist into a painful smile. "You didn't ask me if it was yours."

Fernando stared off, toward the dark pyramids, not seeing them. "My son or daughter." His gaze came back to Ash. "Did they hurt you? Is that why you lost it?"

"Of course they hurt me!"

He bowed his head. Without looking at her, he said, "I never meant . . . Did it happen when we were riding to G—" He stopped.

"To Genoa," Ash completed. "Ironic, isn't it? While we were on the river."

Momentarily, he cupped both hands over his face. Then he sat up in the saddle. His shoulders went back. The torchlight shone on his eyes, that gleamed wet; and Ash, frowning, found him stripping off his gauntlet and reaching a hand out to her. His expression held pain, sardonic humor, and a raw, undilute empathy that started to rip her open.

"Sometimes I wonder, how did I get to be this person?" Fernando pressed his other hand's knuckles to his mouth, and took them away to add, "I wouldn't have had much to leave him. A keep in Bavaria and a blackened reputation."

His pain hit her, raw, under the breastbone. She pushed it away: *this is not what I need to feel.*

He exclaimed, "You should have told me, at Dijon! I would have——"

"Changed sides?" she completed, sardonically; but she reached across and gripped his hand, flesh warm in the cold night. "By the time I knew, you were gone."

His hand tightened on hers.

"I'm sorry," he said quietly, "you wouldn't have had much of a husband in me."

A sharp answer came into her mind but she didn't speak. For all his inanity, what shone out of his face as he reached down from his saddle to her was a genuine regret.

"You deserve better," he added.

She let go of his hand, settling back onto the saddle's chill leather. Above, thin clouds began to hide the stars.

"I'm barren," she said flatly. "So that's the end of that. Don't tell me you don't want an annulment. You can always put a barren wife aside."

"I don't know that we *are* married. Leofric's lawyers are arguing over it."

He turned the gelding, riding back across the open ground.

"You're a bondswoman. Either you're now my property, because I married you—or you didn't have a right to consent to any contract, and the marriage is void. Take your pick. It doesn't matter to me—whether the Church blessing holds or not, these people still think I'm the one who knows about you. I'm the one they ship down here because of that!"

Chill, inner and outer, went through her, and she said, "Fernando. They are going to kill me. One or another of these lords. Please, *please* let me go."

"No," he said, again, and the cold wind ruffled his hair. He looked across at Witiza and the squires, absorbed in the minutiae of hunting; and Ash could see him picturing a fair-haired boy of the same age.

A barn-owl slid through the darkness as if the air were

oil, gliding across the sloping face of a pyramid and vanishing into blackness.

"How can you let this happen! I'm sorry I hit you," Ash said in a rush. "I know you're afraid. But please—"

Fernando, his voice rough, his face growing redder, snapped, "I'm trying to keep my own head on while these heathens anoint another of their Goddamned Caliphs! You don't know what it's like for me!"

Ash talks to slaves. She knows that, up at the palace, the fretwork stone corridors resound to the screams of unsuccessful candidates for the Caliph's throne.

"Oh, I do." Ash rested the brown mare's reins under her cloaked knee, and blew on her white fingers. There was a laugh pressing up under her breastbone: or it might have been tears. "I remember something Angelotti once said to me. He told me 'the Visigoths are an elective monarchy—a method we may call succession by assassination'!"

"Who's Angelotti, for Our Lady's sake?"

"My master gunner. He trained here. You employed him, briefly. You," Ash said, "wouldn't remember."

Overhead, the stars had moved to midnight, or close to. She saw no moon. Dark phase, then. Three weeks after Auxonne field. The freezing wind began to drop, chill on her face; and she lifted her head, hearing the chink of bit and bridle—a split second before the German men-at-arms heard it, their lances lowering, visors going down.

Fernando barked an order. Ash saw lances going back up to rest-position. Newcomers obviously expected. *It's now*—

Her stomach plummeted. She held onto her saddle with one hand, leaned out with the other, and grabbed for her husband's sword. His leather-gauntleted hand smacked down, crushing her fingers. He grabbed both her wrists.

"You will not be killed!"

"That's what you say!"

Horses came riding in between the towering sides of

the pyramids, their torches sending shadows leaping across the ancient stone paving. Ash smelled horse-sweat. The brown mare's flanks creamed whitely, as she backed up, pressing her rump against Fernando's gelding. The newcomers wore mail, a dozen or more of them, and she opened her mouth to say, "Twelve cavalry, swords, lances;" to the machine, ready now—now it could not matter; in this extremity—ready to break silence, but she thought *And I'm unarmed, no armor, chained; what's it going to tell me—"die"?*

The boy Witiza shoved his hunting owl at a squire and rode forward. A shrill horn split the silence.

Not from the new party—from further back.

Ash heard it; and she stood up in the stirrups, as if the mare were a war-horse, and peered forward into the flickering light.

"Exactly how much company were you expecting?" she inquired caustically.

Fernando del Guiz groaned, "Shit . . . ," and thumbed his sword loose in the mouth of its scabbard.

Enough torches clustered together now between the two pyramids that Ash could see clearly. Crumbling plaster walls bore faded hieroglyphs in white and gold and blue, and the two-dimensional images of cow-headed women and jackal-headed men.

Riding over broken paving stones, the Lord-*Amir* Gelimer was reining in a bright bay gelding with white coronels, and staring behind him, past his armed escort.

Ash followed his gaze.

Thirty or forty more horses rode up out of the darkness.

These bore men in mail, riding with their lances at the rest-position. She saw a pennant with the device of a toothed wheel, and found herself looking at helmeted faces that she nevertheless knew: *'Arif* Alderic, *Nazir* Theudibert, a young soldier—Barbas? Gaiseric?—and two more *nazirs*, and their squads, each man mounted.

Alderic's forty men, at their full strength.

"God give you all a good night," the *'arif* Alderic

said, his voice a deep rumble as he bowed in the saddle to Gelimer. "My *Amir*, riding so late can be dangerous. I beg you to accept my *Amir* Leofric's hospitality, and our escort back to the city."

Ash put one hand thoughtfully over her mouth, and deliberately didn't catch Alderic's eye. The soldier barely dignified what he said with the tone of a request.

She saw the Lord-*Amir* Gelimer glare at Alderic, glance around, see Witiza, and Gelimer's small-eyed face shut up like a strong-box.

"If I must," he said ungraciously.

"Wouldn't do to leave you alone out here, sir." Alderic rode on past him, bringing his rangy, flea-bitten gray mount up beside Ash's mare. "Same goes for you too, Sir Fernando, I'm afraid."

Fernando del Guiz began to shout, one anxious eye on the Visigoth noble, Gelimer.

Ash bit her lip. It was either that, or shout, or cheer, or burst out into hysterical laughter. The cold wind chilled the sweat under her arms and down her back.

She saw a dun palfrey approaching in Alderic's wake. The rider, whose feet appeared to almost touch the ground either side, put back his hood.

"Godfrey," Ash acknowledged.

"Boss."

"Leofric get to hear about who's putting the screws on my husband, then?"

She edged the mare a step sideways away from Fernando del Guiz, who was roaring furiously at the *'arif* Alderic.

"I was talking to the *'arif* when the order came up."

"I don't suppose you brought a pair of bolt-cutters? I might just about get away with it, right now."

"The *'arif*'s men searched me. For that, and for weapons."

"Damn . . . I hoped there was going to be a fight. I might have got out of here." Ash rubbed her palms across her face and brought them away hot and wet with sweat. She huddled her cloak around herself, to keep her shaking hands out of Godfrey's sight. Clouds coming up from the south began to blot out the sky.

Overwhelmingly, as if it was her body that thought, a physical desire overcame her for blue sky, for the gold-hot burning eye of the sun, for dry grass and bees and barley buried in red poppies; for meadowlark song, and cows lowing; for rivers glittering thick with fish; for the sun's warmth on her naked skin, and daylight in her eyes; an ache so hard that she groaned, aloud, and let her hood fall back and tears stream from her eyes in the bitter cold south wind, staring beyond the sharp walls of the pyramids for the slightest break in the darkness.

"Ash?" Godfrey touched her arm.

"Pray for a miracle." Ash smiled crookedly. "Just a tiny miracle. Pray for the Stone Golem to break down. Pray for these chains to rust. What's a miracle, to Him?"

Godfrey smiled, reluctantly, gazing up at her from the palfrey's back. "Heathen. But I do pray—for grace, for freedom, for you."

Ash tucked Godfrey Maximillian's hand under her arm and squeezed it. She let go quickly. Her body still shook with reaction. "I'm no heathen. I'm praying right now. To Saint Jude."[38] She couldn't manage to sound humorous as she picked up her reins. "Godfrey . . . I don't want to go back and die in the dark."

He shot a glance at the surrounding horsemen. Ash regarded Theudibert's squad, now so close that only what appeared to be an odd, comradely compassion made his men pretend not to be overhearing her conversation.

"God will receive you, or there is no justice in heaven," Godfrey protested. "Ash—"

Something cold stung her scarred cheek. Ash raised her head. Outside the circle of the torches, everything was black; the stars obliterated by cloud. A whirl of white specks shot across the ancient paving, among the legs of cavalry mounts moving quickly into their escort

---

[38] Patron saint of lost causes.

array around herself, and around Gelimer's men.

*"Snow?"* she said.

In yellow torchlight, wet flakes showed white. Like a dropping veil snow came suddenly and thickly down on the south wind, building up swiftly on the sides of the nearest pyramid, plastering white lines along the edges of bricks, delineating unseen irregularities.

"Close up!" The *'arif* Alderic's hoarse shout.

"No more yapping, priest." *Nazir* Theudibert pushed his gray mare in between Godfrey and Ash. Ash's mare dropped her head down, presenting a winter-coated furry flank to the wind. White ice plastered the leather tack, the folds of Ash's cloak.

"Move it!" Theudibert grunted.

"Snow. In the middle of a fucking *desert*, snow?" She transferred her reins to one hand, jabbing a bare cold finger at the *nazir's* face. "You know what this is, don't you? *Don't you*? It's the Rabbi's Curse, come home at last."

Judging by Theudibert's bony, red-cheeked face, she had hit a superstitious nerve. A brief hope flared in her. The *nazir* coughed, and spat a gob between their horses.

"Fuck off," he said.

Ash pulled her hood forward. The lining of marten fur tickled her frozen cheek. *What did you expect him to say?*

The troop of horse moved off, riding back in the direction of Carthage; torches and armor glinting in the snow. She kneed the brown mare to a weary walk. *He said just what I'd say. Except that I know there is a curse.*

Aptly, as if he could read her thoughts, Theudibert growled under his breath, "Fucking *'arif*'s all the curse *I* fucking need!"

"Well, I'll tell you something." Ash let her mouth run, feeling the pull of steel chains at her neck and ankles, looking furiously around for a gap between riders, for help, for anything. "I'll tell you. Your *Amir* Leofric breeds slaves—I reckon someone out there is breeding sergeants. '*Arifs*. 'Cause they're all the fucking same!"

Theudibert looked at her coldly. Two of the soldiers laughed and smothered it; both of them men who had been in the cell with her, threatening rape. Ash rode on between them.

*If I could kill this horse, they'd* have *to take me out of the chains. However briefly. But I'd need a weapon for that, and I don't have a weapon. If I could lame her, get free—*

She let her gaze travel ahead, looking for holes in the paving.

*—then I'd be on foot, in the desert, in a blizzard, with sixty men trying to find me. Well, hey, it's not such a bad deal. Not when you consider the alternative.*

*Not when you consider that, if they have to cut the chains to get me off this beast, there'll probably be six of them with swords at my throat every minute while they're doing it. That's what I'd do. That's the trouble. They're as smart as me.*

*I just have to hope that someone will make a mistake.*

Ash let her awareness spread out, taking in the whole troop. Alderic's heavy cavalry platoon around her, one squad behind, one to either side; and Alderic ahead, riding with Gelimer and Fernando del Guiz, Gelimer's troops out in front—*where he can see them*, Ash approved—and Godfrey's palfrey plodding, head down, in the shelter of Alderic's scraggy mount.

*I do not, ever, give up. No matter* what.

Driving snow plastered her cloak against her back, and the back of her skull; freezing wind seeping through the wool. Outside the circle of torchlight, a whirling white desolation screamed, the wind rising. She saw Alderic order a scout[39] forward.

*We came, what, two miles? Three? It isn't possible to get lost three miles from a city!*

*Yes it is . . .*

A mail-covered arm reached across in front of her.

---

[39] Literally, "aforerider."

*Nazir* Theudibert yanked the mare's reins out of her hands, and wound them around his wrist. His squad closed in, Gaiseric's cob nipping at the mare's rump; all of them riding within touching distance. Snow began to lay on the paved ground. She let Theudibert yank the mare into movement, clasping the furry body with her knees, keeping her weight level and her knees still.

*Just a broken paving stone, a rabbit hole,* any*thing* . . . Feeling the recalcitrant weight and solidity of the mare's barrel-body, that might come crashing down on her leg if they fell. *I'll take the risk!*

The mare plodded exhaustedly on. The stink of sweating men and hot horses faded from Ash's nostrils, obliterated by the cold. White flakes lay, eating up the flat ground, piling up against a plinth. She looked up into the star-crowned face of a stone queen, snow whitening the gargantuan granite beast-body. The sphinx's smile blurred under clinging ice.

"Where is Carthage?"

It was the merest whisper, into the fur lining of her hood. The *nazir* glared suspiciously at her, then turned aside to speak with one of his men. A low-voiced dispute broke out between them.

In her head, words sounded:

*"Carthage is upon the northern coast of the continent of Africa, forty leagues to the west of—"*

"Where is Carthage from where *I* am!"

No voice sounded in her head.

The mare slowed, plodding through drifting snow. Ash peered out of her hood. Theudibert's men rode, hunched, muttering. Their tracks were churning up a hand's-deep fall of snow now, that clung in bobbles to the hairy hocks of the horses. One white mare whickered, tossing up her head.

"This isn't the way we rode in, *nazir*!"

"Well, it's the way we're riding out. Do I have to shut your fucking mouth for you, Barbas?"

Ash thought, What does it matter, now, if Leofric

learns I'm asking the Stone Golem questions? If they get me back inside Carthage, I'm *dead*.

"Forty men and twenty men and fifteen men, all cavalry, possibly all three groups hostile to each other," she breathed, mist dampening the fur around her mouth and freezing immediately to ice. She found she was shivering, for all her wool gown and cloak. Her bare feet were numb blocks of flesh, and all sensation had gone from her hands. "One person, unarmed, mounted; escape and evasion, how?"

*"You should provoke a fight between two forces and escape in the confusion."*

"I'm chained! The third force isn't mine! How?"

*"No appropriate tactic known."*

Ash bit at her cold, numb lower lip.

"You might as well pray, I suppose," a light tenor voice called. Fernando del Guiz rode in from her right, pressing the roan gelding between Alderic's troopers without a thought. Perhaps for that reason, they admitted him. His green and gold banner whipped in the blizzard, momentarily blocking out torchlight. Ash looked up at his snow-plastered helmet and cloak.

"Is that necessary?" Fernando added, indicating the mare's reins with one gloved hand.

"Sir." Theudibert's tone was a gruff, less-urbane copy of his *'arif*'s. He kept her reins knotted firmly in his right hand, riding knee to knee with Ash. "Yes, sir."

Trying to read Fernando's expression, Ash could make out nothing. Over his shoulder, through driving snow, she saw the Lord-*Amir* Gelimer and his son Witiza riding back down the column toward them.

"When *I* pray, I want an answer." She spoke lightly, as if it were a joke. Snow melted, chill on her lips.

"I'm sorry!" Fernando leaned over, close enough that his breath was damp and warm on her cheek. The male smell of him jolted her heart. He hissed, "I'm caught between the two of them, I can't help you!"

She held in her mind the expectation of a voice.

"You've got, what, fifteen men with lances? Could you get me out of here?"

The familiar voice in her head said, *"Two larger units will unite to defeat third: tactic unsuccessful,"* as Fernando del Guiz laughed, slapped the nearest Visigoth soldier on the back, and said, unconvincingly jovially, "What wouldn't you give for a wife like that?"

The young soldier, Gaiseric, said something quickly in Gothic which Ash could see Fernando didn't understand.

"I'm worth more than 'one sick goat,' trooper!" she remarked, in Carthaginian. The trooper snuffled a laugh. Ash gave him a quick grin. It's worth making them think of me as a commander, if it slows their reaction time by even a split-second—

"Del Guiz!" The Lord-*Amir* Gelimer closed distance through the wind and snow.

"Del Guiz, I am riding back to the city. Ask me for no further help." His sharp, gauntleted gesture took in the blizzard, Alderic's horsemen, the del Guiz squires shuddering with cold and riding with the hooded owls sheltered under their cloaks, his own son's blue-white face. "I hold you implicated in this! I should have made a better judgment of you—a man who would marry this, *this*—!"

He pointed at Ash. She gripped a fold of her cloak and shook snow off herself; wiped the snow from her eyelashes. The brown mare whuffed, too tired to pull away from the *nazir's* grip on her reins. Ash sniffed back a runny nose, staring up at Gelimer; at this richly robed and armored man, white snow lodging in the braiding of his beard.

"Well, fuck you too," she said, almost cheerful, if only because of the appalled expression on Fernando del Guiz's face. "You're not the first person to act like I'm an abomination, my Lord-*Amir*. If I were you, I'd be worrying about worse problems than me."

"You!" Gelimer waved a finger at her. "You and your master Leofric! Theodoric was misguided enough to *lis-*

*ten* to him. Yes, it is essential that Europe be eradicated, but not—" He stopped, wiping a blast of snow out of his face. "Not with a slave-general! Not with a useless war machine. These things *fail*, and then where are we?"

Ash made great show of looking around her, at Theudibert hunched over his saddle, at the troopers pretending not to listen to the overwrought *amir* as they rode knee to knee in a tight little group, at Alderic ahead supervising Gelimer's men.

She raised her head to the high, white, whirling air, and the snow-covered immense statues, and the blanket of snow smoothing out the desert in the sputtering light of the wet pitch-torches.

"Why is it winter here?" she demanded. "*Look* at this. My mare has her winter coat and it's only September. Why is it so damn *cold*, Gelimer? Why? *Why is it cold?*"

She felt as if she slammed, face-first, into a stone wall.

Her expectation of a voice in her head was flooded— no other word for it—with a stunning, fierce, complete silence.

The lord-*amir* shouted something in return.

Ash didn't hear it.

"*What?*" she said, aloud, bewildered.

"I said, this curse began with Leofric's slave-general going on crusade, it will probably stop when she dies. All the more reason to put a stop to his activities. Del Guiz!" Gelimer shifted his attention. "You could serve me yet. I can forgive!"

He spurred his mount. The gelding arched its back, took a kick in the flank, and cantered forward, iron shoes skidding on the snow-covered flagstones. The lord-*amir* called out. Gelimer's men spurred forward, away from Alderic's troop, on into the dark blizzard ahead. The *'arif* let them go.

Fernando groaned. "I thought he'd given up on me."

Ash paid him no attention. Her breath steamed around her face. Even her knees, where she clasped the mare's flanks, were numb with the cold; and snow gathered in the folds of her cloak. The iron chain from her collar burned, where it touched her skin under her clothes.

Appalled, she whispered delicately, "Forty men and fifteen men, armed cavalry, escape and evasion, how?"

"What?" Fernando sat down in the saddle from peering after Gelimer.

"Forty men and fifteen men, armed cavalry, escape and evasion, *how*?"

No voice sounded in her mind. She let herself will the effort of active listening, making a way in through defenses, demanding an answer from the silence within.

A cold slap of ice-flakes on her face snapped her attention outward.

Am I not . . . hearing? That's it. That's it. It isn't as if I'm stopped, blocked . . . There is no voice here. Only *silence*.

Beside her, on his palfrey, Godfrey spoke cheeringly over what was plainly her indistinguishable mumble. "These *amirs* are crazy, child! You know that Gelimer was a rival with Leofric for the King-Caliph's money, for the crusade? To raise troops? And now they're both trying to get themselves elected King—"

"What is the secret breeding?" Snow burned Ash's face. She muttered insistently: "What is the secret birth!"

No voice. No *answer*.

The potential there, but utterly, utterly silent.

*"Where's my fucking voice?"*

"What do you mean?" Fernando pressed his gelding close in and reached out to pull back her hood. "Ash? What are you talking about?"

Theudibert reached across in front of her, over the mare's saddle, to push the fair-haired European knight away. Ash lunged, almost automatically, reaching across the *nazir's* mailed back, grabbing for his knife where its scabbard hung on his right hip, with the intention of slashing through the mare's reins.

A soldier shouted a warning.

Something fast and black came down between her and the *nazir:* a lance-shaft. She jerked away.

"Shit!"

Ash grabbed for the saddle.

She knew she hadn't made it, was falling off the mare. Something caught her arm a numbing blow. She cried out. Her heel jerked back. The furry mare jinked to the right. She grabbed for the saddle and her numb bare fingers slid across leather, fear flooding her gut as she slipped, falling, falling forward and down toward snow-covered stone.

Her stomach swooped. Her head banged sharply against something that gave—the mare's foreleg. Every muscle cringed, taut, against impact. Waiting for an iron-shod hoof to kick back into her face. Waiting to hit stone pavement.

The fall stopped.

Ash hung, upside-down.

A hoof clopped on stone, close by her ear. Something banged her jaw, very softly. She thrashed her head in the enveloping cloak and kirtle and shift falling down over her ears, and found herself staring at pale-tipped brown horse-hair.

The underside of the muzzle of the brown mare.

The horse stood, all four feet planted, knees locked, her head hanging exhaustedly down to the ground in front of Ash's face.

Above her, there was a noise. A man laughing.

Dazed, Ash made out that she was hanging with both her hands and feet above her. Her cloak and skirts fell down over her head.

*"Shit!"*

She hung upside-down, the chain between her ankles now taut across the mare's saddle, and her whole body suspended under the mare's belly. Some confusion of garments and chain and collar had both her hands pulled up tight into one stirrup and trapped.

Her cloak and gown fell back over her head and shoulders, baring her legs to the blizzard.

Ash giggled.

The mare placidly nosed back at her wool-shrouded head. Folds of wet cloth slid down, across her face, and uncovered her again, drooping to sweep the snow-covered stone.

"*Nazir!*" a voice she recognized as Alderic's bawled hoarsely, through the blizzard.

" '*Arif?*"

"Get her back on that horse!"

"Yes, '*Arif.*"

"Ah—wuff!" Ash choked, tried to muffle it, and a wet laugh burst out from between her lips. She snuffled. In front of her, upside-down to her view, the legs of horses milled about, male voices shouting in confusion. Her chest began to ache as she laughed harder, not able to stop, her convulsing body driving out all her breath, tears streaming out of the corners of her eyes and down into her cropped hair.

She hung, completely unable to move, while mail-clad soldiers of the Visigoth empire tugged thoughtfully at the chain across the mare's back, and picked hopefully at the tangle of her wrists in the cloak and stirrup.

A face came into her view, a man bending down. The *nazir* Theudibert shouted, "What have you got to laugh at, bitch?"

"Nothing." Ash shut her lips firmly together. His upside-down face, beard at the top and helmet underneath, and with an expression of complete bewilderment, sent her off again. A chest-heaving, belly-shaking laugh. "N-n-nothing—I could have been k-killed!"

She managed to wrestle her right hand and chain free. With that resting on the flagstones, wrist-deep in cold wet snow, she took some of her own weight. Hands manhandled her and the world swooped, sickeningly, and she was upright, the saddle between her thighs, feet scrabbling for stirrups.

A circle of dismounted men with swords surrounded her and the mare, wind driving snow into their faces. Beyond that were a ring of surrounding riders; and a clump of cavalry close around both Godfrey's palfrey, and Fernando's riding-horse. Even in the increasing wind and poor visibility, there was no way through the cordon.

"Nobody made a mistake, then," Ash remarked cheerfully as her gut settled.

She freed her hands and wiped her nose on the linen lining of her cloak. The inner cloth was still dry. She started to speak, giggled, swallowed it back, and surveyed the cavalrymen around her with a warm, appreciative, and entirely embracing smile. "Who's dumb idea was this in the first place?"

One or two of them grinned despite the foul weather. She sat back in the saddle and picked up her reins, snuffling back chest-aching mirth.

Fernando del Guiz, from where he and his German troops sat surrounded on their horses, called, "Ash! Why are you *laughing*?"

Ash said, "Because it's funny."

She caught sight of Godfrey. Under his snow-whitened hood, he was smiling.

The *'arif* Alderic's horse moved back into the circle of torchlight, Alderic riding with a solid, erect stance despite the driving snow.

"*Nazir.* Get that damn horse moving. The scout's come back. We're no more than a furlong from the city gate."

### iii

"BUT THEY GOIN' to *kill* you!" the boy-faced soldier, Gaiseric, emphasized; his tone somewhere between confused malice, and awe. "You know that, bitch?"

"Of course I *know* it. Do I look stupid?"

The northeast quadrant steps of House Leofric jolted

Ash as she plodded down their spiral again, Gaiseric and Barbas and the *nazir* in front of her, the rest of the squad behind. Mail jingled; sword scabbards scraped the curved wall. Her soaking wet wool skirts dragged behind her on the steps.

"I don't think," Ash said, "that you've understood."

As they walked out into a corridor, she hauled her cloak out from under her feet. The glasses of Greek Fire in the corridor showed her Gaiseric's bewildered face, white with the cold.

"Don' get you," the boy said, as his *nazir* went ahead down the mosaic-tiled corridor.

Ash only smiled at him. She surreptitiously flexed her bruised and aching arms. The muscles of her inner thighs burned. She thought, It must be three weeks since I've ridden anything—not since the field of Auxonne.

"I've been taken prisoner before," she explained. "I think I'd forgotten that."

*As to why I'd forgotten*—she cut the thought off, putting the cell with the blood-soaked floor away in some part of her mind where she need not look at it. She is young, she heals quickly; there is a background discomfort from her head, her knee; it does not, now, affect this rising of her spirits.

A voice called, "Bring her!"

Leofric, Ash identified. Yeah, thought so.

Gaiseric unexpectedly mumbled under his breath, "You'll be all right in there. He has a fire in there for the vermin."

Two soldiers slid open an iron-bound oak door. Theudibert pushed her through. She shook off his hand. There was a brief exchange of words between the lord-*amir* and the *nazir*. Ash strode forward, direct as a crossbow-bolt's flight, toward a brazier full of red-hot charcoal, and sank down on her knees on the stone floor in front of it.

Something rustled. Something squeaked.

"Oh, *yeah* . . . that's more like it," she sighed, eyes closing. Heat from the fire soaked her face. She opened her eyes, reached up clumsily, and pushed her hood back. Steam rose off the surface of the wool. The stone floor was wet all around her. She rubbed her fists together, biting her lip against the pain as numbness gave way to returning circulation.

"Lord-*Amir*!" Theudibert acknowledged. The door slammed; soldiers' footsteps departing down the corridor. She looked up to find herself alone with the Lord-*Amir* Leofric and a number of his slaves, some of which she knew by name.

The walls of the room were stacked with iron rat cages, five and six deep. A myriad beady eyes watched her from behind thin metal grills.

"My lord." Ash faced Leofric. "I think we have to talk."

Whatever he had been expecting, it was not speech from her. He turned, more like a startled owl than ever, his gray-white hair and beard jutting out where he had run his fingers through it. He was wearing a floor-length gown of green wool, spotted with the droppings and litter of his animals.

"Your future is decided. What can you have to say to me?"

His incredulous emphasis on *you* stirred her temper. Ash got to her feet, pulling down the tight wrists of her gown, so that she faced him as a young woman in European dress, her shorn hair hidden by her coif, her body swathed in the wet cloak and hood that she would not abandon in case some slave cleared it away.

She got up and approached the bench where he stood by an open cage. Violante stood beside him, carrying a leather bucket of water.

"What are you doing?" It was a deliberate distraction, while she furiously thought.

Leofric glanced down. "Breeding a true characteristic. Or rather, not. This is my fifth attempt. And this, also, has failed. Girl!"

The iron box in front of the *amir* was full of chopped hay. Ash lifted her brows, thinking, The sheer expense of that, here, where nothing grows—!

Wriggling white grubs lay among the hay. She peered closer, memories coming back of living in a wagon with Big Isobel, when she had been nine or ten: the quartermaster paying a loaf of bread for ten dead rats, or a litter of babies. She leaned over the box, looking at the rat pups—their blind heads big, like hound-pups, and their small bodies covered with a fine white fur. Two were plain gray.

"At five days, you may see the markings. These, like the previous litters, have proved to be useless," the Lord-*Amir* Leofric observed over her shoulder. His breath smelled of spices. He reached down with trim-nailed fingers, scooping the whole litter up in his palm, and dropped them into the leather bucket.

"Wh—"

They plopped beneath the black surface of the water without a struggle. Her senses, stretched keen, distinguished the rapid succession of fifteen or twenty tiny, heavy, splashes. Ash, staring, met the eyes of Violante, holding the leather bucket. The child's eyes brimmed over with tears.

"The buck is number four-six-eight," the elderly man said, oblivious, reaching up to another cage. "It *will not* breed true."

He reached swiftly in. Ash heard a squeal. Leofric took his hand out, gripping a buck rat around the middle of its body. Ash recognized the liver-and-white patched rat—it squealed, thrashing, all four legs splaying, tail held out stiff, then whipping from side to side in panic. Leofric raised the rat up and brought its head cracking down on the sharp edge of the bench-

Ash, moving before she realized she had the intention, locked her hand around his wrist, arresting his movement before he could strike the animal's brains out.

"No." She pressed her lips together, shook her head. "No, I don't think so—father."

It was said purely to jolt him. It did. The elderly man stared at her, skin crinkling around his faded blue eyes.

Abruptly he flinched, scowled, and flung the rat straight at her, putting his bleeding finger to his mouth. "Keep it if you want it!"

The flying object thumped into Ash's chest. She dropped her hands to catch it, momentarily held a bundle of flailing needles, swore, snatched at the rat's muscular body, and froze, completely, as the animal shot down into the depths of her voluminous cloak.

"What is your *objection*?" Leofric snapped testily.

"Um . . ." Ash remained perfectly still. A stench of rat droppings was in the air. Somewhere in the folds of her cloak, a small solid body moved. *It's sitting in the crook of my elbow!* she realized. She did not put her hand into the cloth. She attempted a chirrup. "Hey, Lickfinger . . ."

The small warm solidity moved. She felt the rat's body shift into a crouch. She couldn't help but tense against the stab of razor-sharp chisel-teeth.

No bite came.

Wild animals do not willingly put up with human touch. They panic, confined. Someone has handled this one, Ash thought. Often. Far more often than Leofric, playing the eccentric rat-breeding *amir* . . .

Ash, very still, shifted her gaze and looked at Violante. The slave girl had put down the bucket of dead rat-pups and was standing, fists in her mouth, face wet, staring at Ash with appalled hope.

Tameness is a "by-product" of the breeding program, is it? Bollocks! *Bollocks*. Leofric, you haven't got a *clue*. I know who's been petting these beasts. And I'll bet she isn't the only slave to do it, either . . .

"All right, I'll keep it." Ash turned back to Leofric. "I think *you've* misunderstood."

"Misunderstood what?"

*"I'm not a rat."*

"What?" Ash held herself in stillness. The small, warm, solid body stretched out, under the wool, resting on her forearm. Against her skin—*under* my sleeve! she thought, picturing it sliding between points at her shoulder, wriggling under the neck of her shift. She had a brief lurch in her gut, feeling its furry snake-head and bald, scaly tail in contact with her skin—and realized that what she was feeling was warm fur, no different to a hound puppy; and a rapid, pattering heartbeat.

Ash raised her eyes to Leofric's face and spoke with care. "I'm not a rat, my lord father. You can't breed me. And I'm not one of your naked slaves, either. I come with a history. I have a life, eighteen or twenty years of it, and I have ties, and responsibilities, and people who depend on me."

"And?" Leofric held out his hands, and one of the male slaves came with a bowl and towel and soap. He spoke without appearing to notice the man who washed him.

I've done that with pages, Ash thought suddenly. It isn't the same. It isn't the same!

"They come with a history, too," she added.

"What are you saying to me?"

"If I come from here, you still don't own me. If I was born to one of your slaves, so what? I'm not yours. You have a responsibility to let me go," Ash said. Her expression changed. In a quite different voice, she said, "Oh Lord, it's licking me!"

The small hot tongue continued to rasp at the tender skin of her forearm, inside her elbow. Ash shivered. She looked up again, delighted; and seeing that Leofric was regarding her with his hands folded in front of his body, she said, "Talk. Negotiate. That's what real people do, my lord father. You see, you may be a cruel man, but you're not mad. A madman could have run this experiment, but he couldn't have managed a household, and court politics, and all the preparations for the invasion—crusade," she corrected herself.

Leofric lifted his arms as a slave buckled his belt and purse over his long gown. He prompted quietly, "And?"

"And you should never turn down the chance of five hundred armed men," Ash said calmly. "If I don't have my company anymore, give me a company of *your* men. You know what the Faris can do. Well, I'm better than her. Give me Alderic and your men, and I'll make certain House Leofric doesn't go down in the struggle for election. Let me send messengers and call my captains, and my specialist gunners and engineers, and I'll make sure things go your way in Europe, too. What's Burgundy, to me? It all comes down to armed force, in the end."

She smiled, hand hovering over her elbow, afraid to touch the rat through the damp wool. By the feel of it, the animal could be asleep.

"Things are different, now that Caliph Theodoric's dead," she said. "I know what it's like, I've been around enough times when heirs take over from lords, and there's always the doubts about the succession, about who's going to follow who. You think about it, my lord father. This isn't three days ago, this is *now*. I'm not a rat. I'm not a slave. I'm an experienced military commander *and I've been doing this a long time*." Ash shrugged. "A split second with a poleaxe and these brains go flying out, and end up splattered up someone's breastplate. But until that happens, I *know* so much that you need me, lord father. At least until you've got yourself elected King-Caliph."

Leofric's lined and creased face ceased to have its habitual, blurred expression. He put his fingers through his unbraided beard, combing it tidy. His eyes were bright, and focused on Ash. She thought, *I've woken him up, I've got him.*

"I don't believe I could trust you to command my troops and remain here."

"Think about it." She saw the fact that she did not plead sink home with him. "It's your choice. No one who's ever hired me *knew* I wasn't going to turn coat and leg it. But I'm neither stubborn nor stupid. If I can come to a compromise that keeps me alive, and means I have some hope of finding out what happened to my guys at Auxonne, then I'll fight for you, and you can trust me to go out there and die for you—or *not* die," she added, "which is more to the point."

She deliberately turned away from his intense, pondering face.

"Excuse me. Violante? I have a rat down my shift."

She did not look at Leofric for the next confusing few minutes, loosening her laces, the small girl's cold hands rummaging around her bodice, and the rat's needle-thin claws scoring red weals down her shoulder as the reluctant furry body was removed. One ruby and one black eye fixed on her from a pointy, furry face. The rat squicked.

"Look after him for me," Ash ordered, as Violante cuddled the buck against her thin body. "Well, my lord father?"

"I am what you would call a cruel man." The Visigoth noble's tone was completely unapologetic. "Cruelty is a very efficient way of getting what one needs, both from the world and from other people. You, for example, would suffer if I ordered the death of that piece of vermin, and the girl, or the priest that visited you here."

"You think every other lord who hires a bunch of mercenaries doesn't try that?"

"What do you do?" Leofric sounded interested.

"Generally, I have two or three hundred men around me who are trained to use swords and bows and axes. That discourages a lot of them." Ash straightened her puff-shouldered sleeves. The chill, animal-scented room was finally beginning to feel warm, after the blizzard outside. "There's *always* someone who's stronger than you. That's the first thing you learn. So you negotiate, make yourself on balance more useful to them than not—and it doesn't always work; it didn't work with my old company, the Griffin-in-Gold. They made the mistake of surrendering a garrison: the local lord drowned half of them in the lake, there, and hanged the rest from his walnut trees. Everybody's time runs out sooner or later." She deliberately met Leofric's gaze, and said brutally, "*Later*, we're all dead and rotten. What matters is what we do now."

He took some notice of that, she thought, but could

not be sure. What he did was to turn aside and let his slaves finish dressing him, in a new gown, belt, purse and eating-knife; and fur-trimmed velvet bonnet. She studied his back, that was beginning to stoop with age.

He's nothing more than any other lord or *amir*.

And nothing less, of course. He can have me killed at any time.

"I wonder," Leofric's voice creaked, "whether my daughter would behave so well, if she were captured, and in the heart of an enemy stronghold?"

Ash began to smile. "If I'd been a better military commander, you wouldn't be having the chance to compare us."

He continued to watch her assessingly. Ash thought, He doesn't mind hurting people, he's ambitious enough to try for the place of power, and the only difference between him and me is that he has the money and the men, and I don't.

That, and the fact that he has forty or so years of experience that I don't have. This is not a man to fight. This is a man to come to an agreement with.

"One of my *'arifs*, Alderic, takes you to be a soldier."

"I am."

"But, as with my daughter, you are something more than that."

The lord-*amir* glanced away as an older, robed slave entered the room, his hands full of parchment scrolls. The slave bowed briefly and began immediately to whisper to Leofric in an intense undertone. Ash guessed it to be a series of messages, requiring—by Leofric's tone—assent, reassurance, or temporizing rejection. It gave her the sense of how, six floors above her head, the stone world of the Citadel buzzed with men seeking allies, to gain power.

Leofric broke off. "I grant you that I will consider this."

"My lord father," Ash acknowledged.

Better than I'd hoped for.

Rats rustled and scuttled, captive in their cages that

lined the room. The hem of her kirtle dragged wetly at her heels, and the manacles on her ankles and her steel collar made her wince with their galling.

He hasn't changed his mind. He may be thinking about changing it, but that's as far as he's got. What can I put into the balance?

"I *am* something more," she said. "Two for the price of one, remember? Maybe you could do with a commander here in Carthage who can use the Stone Golem's tactical advice?"

"And sometimes needs to use it for a revolt of her own men?" the lord-*amir* said quizzically, preparing to follow the slave out. "You are not infallible, daughter. Let me consider."

Ash froze, not attending to his last words.

For a revolt of—

The last-but-one time I spoke to the Stone Golem, it was the riot, when they almost killed Florian—

She bowed her head as the Lord-*Amir* Leofric left the room, so that he shouldn't see her expression.

Jesu Christus, I was right. He can find out from the Stone Golem what questions it's been asked—by her or by me. He can know exactly what tactical problems I've had.

Or will have. If I still *have* a voice. If it isn't just silence, like it was out in the pyramids. And I can't ask! *Goddammit.*

She thought, furiously, not really attending as a troop of soldiers escorted her back to her cell. The manacles on her ankles were removed, the collar left on her. She sat in the dark of the day, alone, in a bare room with only a pallet and a piss-pot, her head between her hands, straining her mind for an idea, a thought, *anything.*

No. Anything I ask it—Leofric will know. I'd be telling him what I was doing!

A hollow metallic call from outside announced sunset.

Ash lifted her head. Snow, drifting, whitened the stone ledge at the front of the window embrasure, but it did not penetrate far in. Gown and cloak swathed her.

Hunger, grinding, made her stomach knot up. The single light, too high up to be reachable, shone down on bas relief walls, and the worn mosaics of the floor, and the flat black surface of the iron door.

She pushed her fingers up under her collar, easing the metal away from the sores it had already rubbed on her skin.

Something scratched on the outside surface of the door.

A child's voice came clearly between the junction of door and jamb, where great steel bars socketed into the wall.

"Ash? Ash!"

"Violante?"

"Done," the voice whispered. More urgently, "Done, Ash, done!"

Ash scrambled to the door, kneeling on her skirts. "What is it? *What's* been done?"

"A Caliph. We have Caliph, now."

Shit! The election's finished sooner than I thought.

"Who?" Ash did not expect to recognize the name. Talking to Leovigild and other slaves had brought her scurrilous rumor about the habits of the lord-*amirs* of the King-Caliph's court, a passing acquaintance with some political careers, the knowledge of such sexual alliances as slaves witness, and a good deal of gossip about deaths from natural causes. Given another forty-eight hours to persuade the soldiers to gossip, she might have been in a better position to judge military power. Leofric's name was often mentioned, but that Leofric should gain the throne was neither impossible, nor likely.

If he does, he'll have too much new business to think about vivisecting me. If he doesn't—

I needed another forty-eight hours. I don't know *enough*!

"Who?" she demanded, again.

Violante's voice, through the knife-thin crack, said, "Gelimer. Ash, *Amir* Gelimer is Caliph now."

# IV

IN THE ROOM outside her cell a second row of Greek Fire lights flared into brilliance, marking the onset of black day. Their radiance shone through the stone grill over the door. Ash sat staring at the window embrasure and the lightless sky.

"Faris," a man's voice said, over the noise of steel bolts sliding protestingly back into the wall sockets.

"Leovigild?"

The beardless slave stepped into her cell, leaving two armed guards outside. He carried a bundle in his arms.

"Here!"

A roll of cloth dumped and spilled on the pallet. Ash knelt up, hands rapidly sorting through the pile.

A fine-textured linen shirt. Hose, still laced to a pourpoint; the color invisible in this light. A great thick wool demigown with the sleeves sewn in, and silver buttons down the front. A belt, a purse—empty, her furiously scrabbling fingers determined—and no shoes, just a pair of soles with long leather cords affixed. Ash looked up, puzzled.

"I show, wear." Leovigild shook his head in frustration. The reflected light allowed her to see the relaxation of lines in his face. "Violante speak, not come." The lithe man made a quick gesture, cradling his arms as if cuddling something against his cheek. "Wear, Faris."

Ash, kneeling on the pallet, looked up at him. What she held between her hands was the padded roll and hanging tail of a chaperon hat.

The hydraulically powered horn sounded the hour across the city six times before her cell door opened again.

Hunger gnawed in her gut, and finally quietened. It would return later, sharper, she knew. A small smile curled up one corner of her mouth, that she was unaware of; it was a smile of pure, delighted recognition. Hunger and isolation are tools she is familiar with.

They mean she is still worth being persuaded.

From the harbor below, sounds racketed up the stone walls and battlements: loud singing, shrill music of flutes, continuous shouting, and once a swift crash of blades. She could not wriggle up the window embrasure far enough to see downwards, but pressed up against the iron bars, staring into the dark, she witnessed bonfires on top of the next harbor headland, to the east, and tiny figures silhouetted against the flames, dancing in wild celebration. The smell of the sea came tinged with wood-smoke.

The hose were tight, the doublet a shade big, but the feel of a fine linen shirt against her skin again made up for it all. She was whistling under her breath without knowing it as she laced Leovigild's odd footwear up her shins, over her hose, with fingers blue with cold.

"All I need is a sword."

She knotted the ties of the cloak around her neck, put on her hood, and tugged the shoulder-cape of the woolen hood down and under the steel collar around her neck, not caring if it was a visible mark of slavery so long as she had something to cushion it from the sores on her skin. She wore the hood pushed back and the hat pulled down on her head; gradually growing warm now, despite the howling chill and sleet at the granite window's edge.

When she finally heard footsteps in the guardroom outside, she had used the pisspot and been ready for the better part of an hour.

"*Nazir,*" she greeted Theudibert, standing.

His expression, between disapproval and fear of a reprimand if he questioned the reason for her new appearance with his superiors, might have made her smile, but his attack was not yet distant enough in her mind.

"Move!" He jerked his thumb at the door.

Ash nodded, not so much in acknowledgment of what he said, as to herself.

*I need to know who sent me these clothes. If it was Leofric, as a gift, it means one thing. If Violante or Leovigild stole them, it means another. If I ask, and it* was *theft, they'll be killed. So I can't ask.*

*So, I don't ask. It's only one more thing that I don't know. And I can handle that.*

One of the men said something to Theudibert, gesturing at her ankles. A suggestion to replace the manacles, Ash guessed. *My hands, too?*

The *nazir* snarled something and struck the man.

*Orders not to? Or just, no orders?*

Tension tightened her gut, like the morning before battle. Ash hitched the heavy woolen cloak forward around her shoulders, tucking her bare hands into the cloth, and smiled at Gaiseric and Barbas as she strode out of the cell.

The spiral stairs of House Leofric were packed with freeborn men in their finest dress. Theudibert's squad moved her through with the minimum of fuss; up and out into the great courtyard, scarred with sleet, where bareheaded slaves slipped as they ran, bringing drink, banners, lutes, roasted fish, fire-crackers, and bandoleers of folly-bells. She bit her lip, her sandaled heels skidding on the sleet-covered checker-paved court; found herself huddled between armed men and hurried out through a long archway, out into a lightless street or alley.

*This is the way I was brought in to House Leofric. Four days ago? Is it only four days?*

Gaiseric stopped dead in front of her.

She cannoned into his back, and grunted. His mail hauberk was covered with a long surcoat, the notched-wheel livery of House Leofric, bright black on white. His sword-hilt was almost reachable. In the same second of realization she heard a command from the *nazir*, and she felt her hands gripped, and a short length of cord tied around her wrists.

Gaiseric moved forward a step.

The torches, held high, showed nothing in front of them but the backs of other men.

They began to inch slowly forward, with the crowd, on through the narrow blank streets of the Citadel.

Ash found herself stumbling over discarded rubbish underfoot: burned-out torches, someone's shoe, ribbons, a discarded wooden plate. Having her hands bound kept her off-balance, and her eyes down, trying to see in the wavering yellow light what she was about to trip over. The distant city clock hooted again twice while she sometimes walked, and more often stood still, crammed up against the bodies of Theudibert's squad.

None of the young men put their hands on her.

Her gaze down, she could not see where they were heading until they were almost there. A fine cold wet-ness—not quite sleet—fell out of the black sky onto upturned faces. Here, there were enough torches, held by bare-headed slaves standing on a low circular wall, surrounding an open square, that she could see for about a bow-shot.

Yellow light fell on the heads of the packed crowd, and on the walls of a building that stood, isolated, in what must be the Citadel's center. Its gilded, curved walls rose up into a great dome, high over Ash's head. An even-tighter cordon of armed men in the Caliph's personal colors surrounded the front of the building: she could actually see bare pavement behind them.

A disturbance eddied the heads of the crowd to her right. The *nazir* muttered something unenthusiastic.

"Not here, *nazir*!" a sharp, deep voice said. Ash got sight of the *'arif* Alderic shoving his way through the civilian crowd. "Round the back."

"Sir."

The squad fell in around Alderic. Ash took in the fact that the bearded Visigoth soldier sweated, despite the cold. She could not have eaten, now, her stomach knotted up like a horse with colic.

"I hear you might be joining us as a captain," '*Arif* Alderic murmured, his eyes fixed forward.

No hope of keeping anything secret in a household full of slaves. Or soldiers, Ash reflected. Is this truth, or only a rumor? *Please, let it be true!*

"It's what I do. Fight for who pays me."

"And you'll be betraying your previous employer."

"I prefer to think of it as re-aligning my loyalties."

Alderic's squad shoved their way through a crowd that did not perceptibly thin as they circumnavigated the wall of the massive building. Closer to the walls, Ash could see that arches punctuated it at intervals around; and through these, light spilled out, and the sound of boy-choirs singing; the inaugural festivities obviously still not completed, eight hours on in the day. The dome above her gleamed. The tiles that scaled its curves looked, very much, as if they were gilded; and Ash blinked, dazzled, both at the reflected torchlight from gold leaf and the realization of wealth.

The squad wheeled left. '*Arif* Alderic went forward, speaking to a sergeant in a black surcoat. Ash craned her neck back, apparently gawping at the dome, and let her peripheral vision bring her an assessment of the chamberlains, musicians, squires and pages crowded around this entrance. All of them wore what she thought must be their winter clothes, for such winter as ever came to this warm twilight coast, shivering in thin woolen robes; the ones who had money distinguishable now by northern garments: Venetian gowns, or English wool doublets, or dagged hoods and linen coifs.

A man's fist thumped her hard between the shoulder-blades. She stumbled forward, out of the sleet, into the building and the shelter of the archway; almost losing her balance since she was not able to put out her tied hands to recover it. If she had been wearing skirts, she would have gone sprawling.

"In, bitch," Theudibert growled.

"That's 'Captain Bitch' to you."

Someone snickered. The *nazir* was not fast enough to see who. Ash pressed her lips together and kept a straight face. She walked between armed men, out from under the arch and into the hall. Hundreds of courtiers and slaves crowded the rim of the circular hall, under its archways.

The central floor was bare, except for a cluster of people around a throne.

Green vegetation strewed the tiles. Much trodden down, it was nonetheless still recognizable: green blades of corn.

No, Ash corrected herself, dismissing the gilded stone above her head. *This* is wealth.

She surveyed the green stems, laid so thick that the floor was hardly visible. Smears of green marked the mosaic tiles, where boots had skidded on the leaf-sheathed stalks and prickly green heads of corn. A sharp, sour fragrance pervaded the air. Unripe corn, brought in from Iberia, she guessed; and wasted, purely for ceremony, laid down as one lays down rushes, to keep the floor neat.

"Madonna Ash," a familiar voice said as she was hustled to one side. She found herself standing, bound, with Alderic's troop of forty; and with them a straggle-haired young man.

"Messire Valzacchi!"

The Italian doctor removed his velvet bonnet and bowed, as well as he could in the close crowd. "How is your knee?"

Ash flexed it absently. "Hurts with this cold."

"You should attempt to keep it warm. The head?"

"Better, *dottore.*" Like, I'm going to say I still get dizzy, in front of men I might—sweet Christ, please—might be commanding, before long.

"You could always untie me, *'Arif,*" she added to Alderic. "After all, where am I going to go?"

The Visigoth commander gave her a short, amused glare, and turned back to his subordinates.

"Worth a try . . ." Ash murmured.

An oval white patch lay on the floor ahead of her, off-center. Ash looked up. The great inner curve of the dome rose up over her head, ivory and gold mosaics picturing the saints in their splendor: Michael and Gawaine and Peredur and Constantine. The dark intricacy of the icons defeated her, she could not tell, in torchlight, whether it were bulls or boars depicted between the saints. But what she at first thought was a black circle seventy feet above her head was, in fact, an opening. At the apex of the dome, a stone-rimmed gap opened to the sky.

Through the hole, as if it were night, Capricornus shone. A faint peppering of snow drifted down into the rotunda, diagonal on the air, sifting to the corn-strewn pavement beneath.

The boy-choir began again. Ash deduced that the children must be somewhere on the far side. She could not see past the heads of the men around her. Tiered oak benches set between the arches held nobles and their households, their soldiers lining the aisles—a noble for each gap between arches, she guessed, running her eye across foreign heraldry.

To her right, someone bore Leofric's banner. Where polished and carved oaken pews rose up, she recognized some of the household, Leofric himself not visible.

Before her, on a great octagonal plinth in the center of the rotunda, stood the throne of the Visigoth Empire. A man sat there. At this distance she could not make out his face, but it must be the King-Caliph. Must be Gelimer.

Annibale Valzacchi remarked, "You are privileged, madonna."

"I am?"

"There are no other women present. I doubt there is a woman out of doors in all Carthage." The young man snickered. "Since I am a doctor, I can at least vouch for your being female, if not a woman."

Despite choir and royal occasion, people were talking between themselves. Valzacchi's voice came quiet under the buzz of three or four thousand voices, but with unmistakable malice. Ash gave him a swift glance, which took in his black wool gown, the cloth much faded, and the squirrel-fur trim at his hanging-sleeve slits matted and dirty.

"No one pay your fees, *dottore*?"

"*I* am not a hired killer," Valzacchi emphasized bitterly. "Theodoric died, and so I go without my fee. You kill, therefore they are prepared to pay you. Tell me, madonna, where is Christian justice in that?"

*Prepared to pay you.* Oh sweet Christ, Christ Viridianus, let it be true, not just a rumor—if I've convinced Leofric—

"Let me even the balance of Justice's scales. If I'm here to be bought, I'll buy a doctor, too. You said you'd worked in a condottiere camp." A tremor went through her body, so that she had to grip her hands together under her cloak, the cords chafing her wrists. *Fortune is to be wooed, not commanded.* "Of course, if I'm here to be executed, I'll keep my mouth shut about you."

The doctor stuttered a laugh at this skinny, wide-shouldered woman in man's dress; her shining silver hair cut too short even for a man, as short as a slave's crop.

"No," he said. "I prefer to earn my gold healing, even if lately that gold has been copper. I will ask you a question, madonna, that I asked my brother Gianpaulo once in Milano. From the rise to the set of the sun, you put all your mind and all your body and all your soul into ways in which you can burn down houses, foul wells, slaughter cattle, rip unborn children out of their mother's bellies, and slice off the legs and arms and heads of your fellow men, on the field. How is it that you sleep, at night?"

"How is it that your brother sleeps?"

"He used to drink himself senseless. Lately, he turned to the Lord God, and now says he sleeps in that mercy. But he has not changed his trade. He kills people for a living, madonna."

Something about the man's face triggered, finally, recognition. "Shit! You're *Lamb's* brother! Agnus Dei. Aren't you? I never knew his name was Valzacchi."

"You *know* him?"

"I've known Lamb for years." Oddly cheered, Ash smiled and shook her head.

Annibale Valzacchi repeated, "How is it that you can sleep at night, after what you do? Do you drink?"

"Most of the people I employ, drink." Ash met his gaze with her clear, cold dark eyes. "I don't. I don't need to, *dottore*. Doing this doesn't bother me. It never has."

A familiar voice said something from the other side of the *nazir's* cordon of soldiers. Ash didn't catch what, but she went up on her toes to try and see who it was. To her surprise, the *nazir* Theudibert grunted, "Let him through!—Search him first. It's only the *perigrinari Christus*."[40]

The boy-soldier Gaiseric suddenly said, at her ear, "Old Theudo's scared shitless, ma'am! He's reckoning on you favoring him later, if he lets you have a priest now."

Godfrey Maximillian's big hands gripped both of hers warmly. "Child! Praise God, you live."

Under cover of a sonorous Latin blessing, and the sleeves of his green robe, Ash felt Godfrey's fingers move quickly around her wrists, loosening the knots of the cord. His bearded innocent face remained uninvolved, as if his hands were acting without his own consent. She shrugged her freed hands back into her enveloping cloak, as casually and as quickly as if it were something they had practiced, like mummers in a play. The back of her neck prickled hot and wet with the effort of not looking to see if anyone had noticed.

"Did you assist in the eight offices here, Godfrey?"

"I am too heretic for them. I may preach, if this ceremony ever ends." Godfrey Maximillian's forehead

---

[40] Term used of Celtic traveling monks, without an abbey of their own: "a wanderer for Christ."

shone. He spoke past her, to Annibale Valzacchi. "Is the man Caliph or not, yet?"

The doctor moved his shoulders in a very Italian manner. "Since this morning. The rest has just been consecrations."

Ash looked across the corn-strewn floor. Something to do with priests was going on around the throne, iron-gray men in green robes processing, hieratically, about the Lord-*Amir* Gelimer. She strained her vision, trying to bring his face into focus, a child-like conviction in her mind that a man should look different after the anointing oils, after he was no longer man, but king.

*Have I done it? Have I wagered and won?*

Thousands of candles heated the air, making her cloak almost uncomfortably warm, and shining a soft gold light upon the walls. She looked up at the great Face of Christ depicted above the saints, and the sprouting viridian foliage of the Tree thrusting from His mouth.

His lips encompassed the circular hole at the top of the rotunda, as if He opened His mouth upon star-ridden darkness.

"Christus Imperator," Ash breathed. Her neck hurt, staring up. Her guts twinged; fear and anticipation, rather than hunger.

"The Mouth of God. Yes. Here in Carthage He is preferred as He was when He ruled over the Romans," Godfrey Maximillian murmured, his arm pushing up against her shoulder, his body warm and comforting beside her. "Are the rumors true?"

"What rumors?" Ash smiled.

She thought she managed to hit the correct expression, somewhere between deference and complacency. Certainly Annibale Valzacchi gave her a look of contempt. *Florian would see through this at once*, she thought. A sideways glance assured her of Godfrey's complicit silence.

*Leofric wouldn't have brought me here if he wasn't planning to do* something *with me. But* what? *Can it* matter to him that he thinks of himself as a father—her father—mine?

But I am not the Faris.

And Gelimer is Caliph now.

Ash shifted, slightly, causing two of Alderic's *nazirs* to look at her. It became apparent to them that she was trying to see their lord-*amir*, through the massed ranks of his household. No hands went to sword-hilts.

She got sight of Leofric at last, one elbow on the arm of his carved walnut chair, at the top of the rising pews on the left-hand side of the archway. He was speaking to someone, a young man in rich dress—a son? a brother?—but his gaze was fixed forward, on the throne of the King-Caliph, and on Gelimer. Ash stared, willing Leofric to look at her.

Seated men around him leaned forward, speaking quietly. Male backs shut her off from Leofric. Men in robes, men in mail; household priests in their high-fronted headdresses.

"Aren't they splendid?" a guttural Gothic voice whispered in her ear. Gaiseric, again.

Ash, startled, studied the boy's face, and then the men clustered beneath the black notched-wheel banner. Noble men in hastily stitched wool gowns and hukes, older men wearing nine-yard velvet houppelandes; knights in full mail hauberks. Swords, daggers, chased leather purses, riding boots; she knows what you will pay to have these made, and what they will fetch as loot.

She knows what it is like to go barefoot, own one wool shift, and eat every other day.

Gaiseric, as she glances at him, is plainly from a village of two huts, or a farmhouse with earthen floors, one room for the people and another for sow and cow—from rich freemen, his face does not have the early lines of malnutrition.

"What about the King?" Ash whispered.

The boy's face shone with an adoration reserved for priests, at the altar, lifting bread and bringing down flesh. "This ain't no old man. *He* won't stop us fighting."

Nine-tenths of the cultivated world is forest, strip-fields, lath-and-plaster huts, and chilblains and hunger; death from early disease or accident, and no touch of any fabric softer than wool woven by the winter hearth. For this it is worth strapping metal to one's body and facing the hard blades of axes, and the punching steel of bodkin arrow-heads. Or it is, for Gaiseric. Worth it to be standing in a city, now, of sixty thousand people, while his king is crowned in the sight of God.

And for me? Ash thought. Worth it not to be knee-deep in mud, all my life? Even if it brings me, finally, to standing here, not knowing what will happen to me, only that the next few minutes will decide it? Oh yes. *Yes*.

Godfrey Maximillian's hand closed over her arm. A blast of clarions shattered the song of boys, ripping the vast dome of air above their heads. All the flames of the wax candles shook; sweet-smelling candles as thick as a man's thigh. An explosion of tension went through her blood, both hands going to her belt. Her hands, purely of themselves, missed the feel of the hilts of sword and dagger; as her body missed feeling the weight of protective armor.

From every quarter of the hall, men began to walk in.

She had a brief glimpse, at the front of the crowd, of men's faces. Pale, bearded faces; young and old, but all, all, male. From every arch they advanced, leaving the aisles in front of the pews bare, so that great spokes of empty floor ran from the high seats of the lords-*amir* to the throne of the King-Caliph. Between, men who might be merchants, ship-owners, great importers of spice, grain and silk, packed the space elbow-to-elbow, in their fairest dress.

Clarions ran on, each higher burst shattering at her ears. Ash felt tears start at her eyes and could not tell why. The distant figure of the King-Caliph, swathed in his cloth-of-gold robes, stood and raised his arms.

Silence fell.

A bearded Visigoth warrior called out, words she could not understand. At the furthest quarter of the dome, where another great household sat arrayed, there was a stir—men rising to their feet, banners raised, swords unsheathed, a great deep-voiced shout. And then they came forward, down the steps to the grain-covered mosaic tiles, striding forward to the throne, each falling down upon his knees as a lord-*amir* and his household swore, in unison, their fidelity to the ruler of the Visigoth Empire.

A similar preparatory stir moved Alderic's troop. Ash shot a glance around the Lord-*Amir* Leofric's quarter of the rotunda. Banners raised up, trailing from their spiked and painted poles. *Nazir* Theudibert lifted a pennant. Alderic said something quickly professional to another of Leofric's *'arifs*, who grinned. A great rustling of cloth sounded as all the knights and men-at-arms shifted forward to their pre-planned places; and Ash hauled her hat off, uncovering her head like the rest of Leofric's household. She unconsciously straightened her shoulders, her head coming up.

"You are like my brother's war-horses!" Annibale Valzacchi muttered, disgusted.

Ash caught herself in a rare moment of comprehension. She shook her head. "He's right. The *dottore* is right."

One of Godfrey Maximillian's hands came up swiftly and brushed over her cut hair. Godfrey said, painfully, "I am here. Whatever happens. You will not be alone."

Men around them began moving forward. Horns shattered the high air. Stumbling beside Godfrey, Ash said, without looking at him, "You're no war-horse. How do you manage to stay on a field of battle, Godfrey? How can you bear with the killing?"

"For you." Godfrey's words came hurriedly, and she could not see his face for the press of people. "For you."

What the hell am I going to do about Godfrey?

There were more people shoulder-to-shoulder around her now. Ash saw, over the heads of some of them, that Leofric must have six or seven hundred men present.

I know what's missing!

She searched around the hall, staring at banners, seeing no white pennants with red crescents.

No Turks, here to see the crowning.

But I thought, at Auxonne—I thought they *must* have allied—am I wrong?

What she did see, in the crowd around ahead, was a familiar green and gold banner: the livery of Fernando del Guiz. And then, all around her, men began to sink to their knees, and she knelt with them, down in the sour smell of crushed corn, the air cold on the back of her neck, sleet falling down on her from the Mouth of God above.

She craned her neck back once, to see stars in the blackness; and the great painted curls of foliage spiraling out from His mouth and down the curving dome, winding about the armor-clad saints and the tops of squat, papyrus-grooved pillars. A cold wind blew into her eyes. With a start, she realized that Leofric was speaking.

"You are my liege, Gelimer." His creaking, quiet voice became audible over the sussuration of a thousand men breathing. "I hereby swear, as my fathers swore, honor and loyalty to the King-Caliph; this promise to bind me and my heirs until the day of the Coming of Christ, when all divisions shall be healed, and all ruling given over to His reign. Until that day, I and mine shall fight as you bid us, King Gelimer; make peace where you desire, and strive always for your good. Thus do I, Leofric, swear."

"Thus do I, Gelimer, accept your fealty and constancy."

The King-Caliph stood. Ash lifted her head very slightly, peering up from under her brows at Leofric moving cautiously forward and embracing Gelimer. Now she was close to the front, she could see the octagonal steps that rose up to the ancient black throne, with its carved wooden finials and bas-relief suns. And the men's faces.

Gelimer's narrow-faced looks were not noticeably improved by dressing the man in a cloth-of-gold houppe-

lande with ermine trim, Ash thought; and you might
braid as much gold wire into his beard as you chose,
without making him any more prepossessing. The
thought gave her an odd, partial comfort. Gelimer, standing before her, with his arms formally around Leofric,
kissing him on each cheek, might look like some hier-
ophantic doll. But for the moment, not only the men of
his own household, but Alderic and Theudibert and all
the rest would take their swords and fight where he indicated.

"For as long as it lasts . . ." Ash pressed her lips together. "What d'you think, Godfrey? A 'riding accident'? Or 'natural causes'?"

In an equally faint whisper, Godfrey Maximillian said,
"Any king is better than no king. Better than anarchy.
You weren't outside in the city these last few days.
There has been murder done."

The sonorous formal exchanges allowed her a quick
reply:

"There may be murder done here in a minute—except, they'll call it execution."

"Can you do nothing?"

"If I've lost? I'll try to run. I won't go quietly." She
grabbed his hand, under her cloak, and gripped it, turning a bright-eyed gaze on him. "Throw a fit. Throw a
prophecy! Distract them. Just be ready."

"I thought—but—he'll hire you? He must!"

Ash shrugged, the movement made jerky by tension.
"Godfrey, maybe nothing at all will happen. Maybe
we'll all turn around and march out of here. These are
the lords of the kingdom, who cares about one condottiere?"

Leofric stepped back from the King-Caliph, his pace
slow as he walked backwards down the shallow stairs
of the throne. A gold fillet glinted in candlelight, binding
back his white hair. The gilded pommel and hilts of his
sword caught the light, too; and his gloved hands glittered with the dome-cut splendour of emeralds and sap-
phires.

At the foot of the steps he stopped, made a shallow bow, and began to turn away.

"Our lord Leofric." The King-Caliph Gelimer leaned forward, seated on his throne. "I accept your fealty and your honor. Why, then, have you brought an abomination into the House of God? Why is there a woman with your household?"

*Oh, shit.* Ash's gut thumped. I know a put-up question when I hear one. There's the formal excuse for an execution, if Leofric doesn't speak for me. Now—

Leofric, with every appearance of calm, said, "It is not a woman, my king. It is a slave, my gift to you. You have seen her before. She is Ash, another warrior-general who hears the voice of the Stone Golem, and so may fight for you, my king, upon your crusade now ending in the north."

Ash picked up *now ending*, so obsessed for a second, debating *Is the war in Burgundy over? Is this just flattery, for Gelimer?* that she did not realize Gelimer had begun to speak again.

"We will continue our crusade. Some few heretic towns—Bruges, Dijon—yet remain to be taken." Gelimer's pinched face moved into a smile. "Not enough, Leofric, that we need subject ourselves to the danger of another general who hears battle commands from a Stone Golem. Your first we will not recall, since she proves useful, but to have another—no. We may come to rely on her, and she may fail."

"Her sister has not." Leofric bowed his head. "This is that captain Ash who took the Lancastrian standard at Tewkesbury, in the English wars, when she was not yet thirteen years of age. She led the spearmen from the wood, onto Bloody Meadow.[41] She has been tested upon

---

[41] The battle of Tewkesbury (Saturday 4 May 1471) decided the second of the Yorkist/Lancastrian wars in favor of the Yorkists. Ash would have been thirteen or fourteen years of age at this time. Edward of York, afterwards king, is said to have hidden two hundred of his "fellowship" in a wood, from where they broke out, flanked and routed

many fields, since. If I give her a company of my men, lord king, she will prove helpful to the crusade."

Gelimer slowly shook his head. "If she is such a prodigy ... Great generals grow dangerous to kings. Such generals weaken the realm, they make confusion in the minds of the people as to who is the rightful ruler. You have bred a dangerous beast here. For this reason, and for many others, we have decreed that your second general shall not live."

The sleet fell down more slowly, now, from the Mouth of God; white flecks floating upon the air.

"I had thought you might use her as a condottiere, my king. We have used such before."

"You had thought also to make an investigation upon the flesh of this woman. Do it. She is your gift to me. Do it. You may thus ease our mind about your other 'daughter.' Perhaps, then, *she* will be allowed to retire, alive, when this war is ended."

Ash registered the flick of deliberate malice in King-Caliph Gelimer's voice. She thought, This isn't personal. Not on the strength of one insult. Not on his coronation day. Too petty. This isn't aimed at *me*, any of it.

Leofric's the target, and I think this is the end of a long campaign.

She sensed Gaiseric and Theudibert shifting fractionally back, on their knees, leaving her isolated in the front row of Leofric's household. Godfrey Maximillian's bulk remained, solidly, at her shoulder; blocking any movement behind her.

The Lord-*Amir* Leofric put his hands to his belt buckle, where its long leather tongue hung down, ornamented with golden studs in the shape of notched

the Duke of Somerset's troops, and began the rout of the whole Lancastrian army, large numbers of which were butchered, becoming trapped in the "evil ditches and lanes" covering the battlefield. Contemporary reports do not mention mercenaries in this context, but they were known to have fought in the battle of Barnet, which immediately preceded Tewkesbury.

wheels. She could see only his profile, not enough to guess if his façade of calm had cracked.

"My king, it has taken two centuries to breed two women who can do this."

"One was sufficient. Our *Reconquista* of Iberia is complete, and soon we shall have completed our crusade in the north, we do *not*," the King-Caliph Gelimer said deliberately, "we do not need your generals, or this . . . gift."

I don't believe this.

Disbelief burned in her, false and familiar; the same disbelief that she sees in men's eyes when they take a final wound from her, staring at cut flesh, slashed gut, white bone: *this cannot be happening to me*!

Ash started to rise. Theudibert and Gaiseric grabbed her shoulders. Apparently unconscious of the movement, the Lord-*Amir* Leofric gazed at the men of the king's household, surrounding the throne, and back at Gelimer. Ash caught sight of Fernando, between two German men-at-arms, his chin scraped clean and his eyes reddened. Beside King-Caliph Gelimer, a fat robed man bending to speak into the royal ear.

Leofric said mildly, as if nothing at all had been decided, "Our Prophet Gundobad wrote: the wise man does not eat his seed corn, he saves it so that he will have a harvest the following year. Abbot Muthari may have the Latin of it, but it is perfectly plain. You may need both my daughters in the years to come."

Gelimer snapped, "*You* need them, Leofric. What are *you*, without your stone machines, and your visionary daughters?"

"My king—"

"Yes. *I* am your king. Not Theodoric, Theodoric is dead, and your place of favor died with him!"

A low, startled buzz of voices sounded. Someone blew the beginning of a clarion call. It cut off abruptly. This isn't part of the ceremony, Ash realized. She shivered, where she knelt.

Gelimer stood up, both his hands gripping the royal

staff of ivory that he had been clasping across his lap. "I will have no over-mighty subjects in my court! Leofric, she *will* die! You will oversee it!"

"I am no over-mighty subject."

"Then you will do my will!"

"Always, my king." Leofric inhaled deeply, his face impassive in the shivering lights of the candles. He looked gaunt. There was no reading his expression, not after sixty years spent in the courts of the King-Caliph.

Ash let her field of vision expand, widening focus as one does in battle, to be aware of the soldiers beside her, the blocked aisles out of the building, Fernando's aghast face, the packed crowds around the throne, the archway half a bow-shot behind her. No chance of reaching it, through the soldiers. No chance that—heart in her throat, sweating, fear beginning to push her to some stupid final act—no chance that she would not try for it.

The voice of a very young man, very nervous, sounded in the silence. "My lord King-Caliph, she isn't a slave, she isn't Lord-*Amir* Leofric's property. She's freeborn. By virtue of marrying me."

Godfrey Maximillian, behind her, said, "God on the Tree!"

Ash stared across at Fernando del Guiz. He returned her gaze hesitantly, a young German knight in a foreign court, bright in steel and gilded spurs; whispers going on all around him—the whole matter of the treatment of Visigoth-conquered territory brought up into public domain again by his ingenuous words.

Ash, her knees hurting her, climbed to her feet.

For one moment, she made eye-contact with Fernando. His clean, shaven, fair-haired appearance was altered now; dark color under his eyes, and new lines around his mouth. He gave her a look that was rueful; half-apologetic, the other half sheer terror.

"It's true." Ash hugged her cloak around her shoulders, her eyes wet, her smile ironic. "That's my husband, Fernando."

Gelimer snorted. "Leofric, is this turn-coat German yours, or ours? We forget."

"He is nothing, Lord King."

A gloved, thin hand closed on Ash's arm. She startled. The Lord-*Amir* Leofric's grip tightened, the gold of his rings biting into her even through cloak and doublet.

Still formal, Leofric persisted, "My king, you will have heard, as I have heard, how this young woman has won much fame as a military commander in Italy and Burgundy and England. How much better, then, that she should fight for you. What could better prove your right to rule over the north, than that their own commanders fight for the King-Caliph?"

Close enough to him now, Ash saw Gelimer nip his lower lip between his teeth; a momentary gesture that made the man look no older than Fernando del Guiz. *How in Christ's name did he get to be elected Caliph? Of course. Some men are better at gaining power than holding onto it . . .*

Leofric's inoffensive, soft, penetrating voice continued. "There is the wife of Duke Charles, Margaret of Burgundy, who yet defies us behind the walls of Bruges. It is not certain the Duke himself will die. Dijon may hold out until the winter. My daughter the Faris cannot be everywhere in Christendom. Use this child of my breeding, my king, I beg you, while she is yet of use to you. When she is no longer useful, then carry out your just sentence upon her."

"Oh no you don't!" Ash shook her arm free of the Visigoth noble. She stepped forward, into the space before the throne, not giving the King-Caliph time to speak.

"Lord King, I *am* a woman, and a woman of business. Charles of Burgundy himself thought I was worth my hire. Give me a company, make it of whoever's household troops you choose—yours, if you want it that way—and give me a month, and I'll take any city you want taken, Bruges or Dijon."

She manages to have an air about her, something to

do with being the only woman present among four thousand men, something to do with her hacked-off silver-
blonde hair and her face, identical to their Faris who has
won cities for them in Iberia. She has a presence. It is
more to do with how she stands: a body trained for war
does not move in the same way as a woman kept behind
stone-tracery bars. And the light in her eyes, and her
crooked grin.

"I can do this, Lord King. Quarrels and factions in
your court aren't as important as that. I can do it. And
don't kill me at the end of it, pay me." A glitter in her
eyes, thinking of red crescent banners. "War is a never-
ending presence on the earth, Lord King, and while it
is, you must live with such evils as captains of war. Use
us. My priest, here, is ready to swear me to your serv-
ice."

Gelimer seated himself, a movement which Ash
thought gave him a moment to consider.

"As to that, no." His voice gained a sharper edge of
malice. "If nothing else, you are a mercenary who will
desert at the earliest opportunity."

Ash, bewildered, said, "Sire?"

"I have heard of your fame. I have read the reports
which Leofric says come from his general, in the north.
Therefore, one thing is obvious to me. You will do what
you did before, last month, at Basle, when you ran away
to join the Burgundian army. You call yourself 'condottiere'—you broke your *condotta* with us at Basle!"

"I broke no contract!"

It was the name of the city of Basle that did it. Voices
drowned her out. Ash's stomach swooped, sickeningly.
A noise broke out, each man telling their neighbor some
distorted story. Beside her, Leofric's complexion grayed.

"But that isn't what happened!" Godfrey Maximillian
lumbered up off his knees, protesting to the King-Caliph.
"She was torturing Ash! *She* broke contract! We had no
intention of joining the Burgundians. Ash! Tell him!"

"My Lord King, if you will listen—"

"Oath-breaker!" the King-Caliph announced, with

some satisfaction. "You see whom you trust, Leofric? She and her husband both! All these Franks are treacherous, unreliable bastards!"

Godfrey Maximillian straight-armed two soldiers out of the way; Ash grabbed him as the troop closed in, manhandling the priest back. Unknown to her, her face twisted into a bitter smile. *I always wanted to be known across Christendom—so much for fame.*

"Godfrey! It doesn't matter what *did* happen!" She shook him vehemently. "It doesn't matter that my story's true. Can you see me trying to *explain* it? What's true is what they *believe.* Sweet Christ, what the hell did the truth ever matter!"

"But, child—!"

"We'll have to handle it another way. I'll get us out of here."

*"How?"*

A shrieking horn drowned out his voice. The King-Caliph, Gelimer, sat with his arm upraised. Silence fell, across the whole rotunda. Slowly, Gelimer lowered his arm.

"We are not this day anointed King so that we may *debate* with our lords. Leofric, she is an approved traitor. She will be executed. She is a monster, of course," Gelimer leaned back on his throne, "hearing voices; as your other child is, but your other child is at least loyal. Perhaps, when you put this one under the knife, you will be able to tell us, my lord, where in the heart treachery lies."

A burr of sycophantic laughter went around the court.

Ash gazed at the faces of nobles and knights, bishops and abbots, merchants and soldiers; and found nothing but curious, avid, amused expressions. Men. No women, no slaves, no clay golem.

King-Caliph Gelimer sat resting both arms on the arms of the throne, his slender hands cupping the carved foliage, his back straight, his braided beard jutting as he stared around at the thousands of men gathered under the roof of the palace and the great Mouth of God above his head.

"*Amirs* of Carthage." Gelimer's tenor voice echoed under the dome. "You have heard one of your number here, the *amir* of House Leofric, doubt our victory in the north."

Ash became conscious of Leofric stirring, in irritated surprise, at her side, and thought *He didn't see this coming. Shit*!

The new King-Caliph's voice rang out again:

"*Amirs* of Carthage, commanders of the empire of the Visigoth people, you have not elected me to this throne to lead you to defeat—or even to a weak peace. Peace is for the weak. We are strong."

Gelimer's bright black gaze flickered across Ash.

"No peace!" he repeated. "And not the war that weaklings fight, my *amirs*. The war of the strong. In the heretic lands of the north, we are fighting a war against Burgundy, most powerful of all the heretic nations of Christendom. Most rich in her wealth, most rich in her armies, most powerful in her Duke. And this Burgundy *we shall conquer*."

Under the painted foliage of the Mouth of God, under the stone rim opening upon the black day skies of Carthage, every man is silent.

Gelimer said, "But we are not content merely to conquer. We will not merely defeat Burgundy, the most mighty nation. *We will raze Burgundy to the ground*. Our armies will burn their way north from Savoy to Flanders. Every field, every farm, every village, every town, every city—we will destroy. Every cog, carrack and war-ship—we will destroy. Every heretic lord, bishop and villein, we will destroy. And the great Duke of Burgundy, the great conquering Duke and all his kin—we will kill. He, his heirs, his successors, to the last man, woman and child—we will kill. And with this example, my *amirs*, we shall be the overlords of Christendom, and none will dare dispute our *right*."

A roar shocked through her at his last word. Gaiseric

grinned, yelling, at her side. The *'arif* Alderic gave a great shout. Ash winced at the deep noise from thousands of male throats; a shout she has heard on battlefields, but now—hammering back at her from the walls of the dome—it frightens her; twists in her cold belly along with her fear for her life.

Godfrey whispered in her ear, "I see it now. That's how he got elected. Rhetoric."

The noise began to die down, echoing away from the throne at the center of the hall. The men of House Leofric continued to stand stolidly under their banners.

The King-Caliph leaned down toward Leofric. "You see, *amir*? We have, still, the advice of the Stone Golem: that Burgundy shall be destroyed, as an example to all others. The Stone Golem has been our guide and advisor for many generations of King-Caliphs; for more years than we have had the use of your female general. And as for your *second* slave-bastard—she is not necessary to us at all. Dispose of her."

The last cold dots of sleet starred Ash's cheeks, falling from the chasm above her head. The heat of the candles and the cold of the wind from outside set her shivering. A force of emotion grew in her belly; something she knew from experience could turn into paralyzing fear, or hypertense readiness to act.

What will they chronicle? *"The accession of King-Caliph Gelimer was celebrated by the execution of a forsworn mercenary—"*

"No!" she spat, aloud. "I'll be damned if I'm dying here as part of someone else's celebrations! Leofric—"

"Be quiet," Leofric grated. He smelled of sweat, now, under his fine robes.

Ash began to whisper, "A household troop, swords, glaives; one exit; one woman unarmed . . ."

Before, it would have been an automatic action, after a decade; to call her voice, for help with tactics. *He cannot stop me asking the Stone Golem questions, he cannot stop it answering me—*

Can he?

The fear-suppressed memory of the sudden silence in her head, riding among the pyramids and sphinxes outside the city, brought a chill fear in her mind. *But I will speak, what other choice is left?*

She bit her lip, began to speak—and stopped as Leofric spoke again.

"Very well. If you will have it so. My lord king," the elderly Lord-*Amir* Leofric said decisively, "consider only one thing more, before you give your judgment. If you permit her to make war for you, she will not run. She has nowhere to go."

"I *have* given my—our—judgment!" Gelimer spoke with asperity, then a weak curiosity. "What do you mean, 'she has nowhere to go'?"

"I mean, my lord king, that next time she cannot run back to her company. They no longer exist. They were massacred on the field of Auxonne, three weeks ago. Dead, to a man. There is no Lion Azure company for her to run to. Ash would be—must be—faithful only to you."

Ash heard the word *massacre*. For a second she could only think, confused, *what does that word mean? It means "killed." He can't mean "killed." He must be using the wrong word. The word must mean something else.*

In the same split second she heard Godfrey's grunt of pain and realization behind her; and she spun around to stare at '*Arif* Alderic, at Fernando del Guiz, at the Lord-*Amir* Leofric.

The bearded Visigoth commander, Alderic, had his arms folded, his face giving no sign of any emotion. *He was ordered to tell me nothing, is this why? But he wasn't there, on the field, he wouldn't know if this is true—*

Fernando only appeared bewildered.

And the startled-owl face of Leofric, pale under his pale beard, showed nothing but an undefined strain.

*He is fighting for his political life, to keep his power*

base, which is the Stone Golem and the general—and me—he would say *anything*—

The King-Caliph Gelimer said sulkily, "There has been nothing but cold here since your Christ-forgotten daughter the general went north! We will not bear with this blight, this curse! Not another one. Who knows but she might leave us frozen as the bitter north? No more, Leofric! Execute her today!"

*Leofric will say anything.*

A voice ripped out of her that she did not recognize, did not know she was going to hear until she found herself screaming.

"What's happened to my company!"

Her chest burned; her throat hurt. Leofric's pale face began to turn to her, Alderic's men moving at the *'arif*'s snapped command, Gelimer standing up again on the dais.

*"What's happened to my company?"*

Ash threw herself forward.

Bear-like arms wrapped around her from behind, Godfrey clutching at her, his wet cheek at her cheek. Two of Theudibert's squad ripped her out of the priest's arms, mailed fists efficiently punching her in gut and kidney.

Ash grunted, doubled up, held in their grip.

The floor swam under her gaze: muddied stalks of corn, trodden across mosaics of the Boar and Her litter. Tears rolled out of her eyes, snot from her nostrils; she could only hear the noise she was making, the same noise that all men make during a beating.

"What—happened—?"

A metal-wrapped fist struck the side of her jaw. She jolted back, only supported now by the men who held her, Gaiseric, Fravitta; her knees gone rubbery. The huge features of the Green Christ swam in her vision, above her, as she fell back.

They dropped her face-down on the stone floor.

Ash, her hands flat against the freezing tiles, lifted her head and stared up at the Lord-*Amir* Leofric. His pale, faded eyes met hers; nothing in them but a faint condemnation.

In a moment of complete clarity, Ash thought, He could be lying. He could be saying this to persuade Gelimer to let me live. And he could be saying this to persuade Gelimer to let me live because it's true. I have no way of knowing.

I can ask. I'll *make* it tell me!

Through split, swollen lips, Ash spoke with an instant, precise accuracy: "The field of Auxonne, the twenty-first day of the eighth month, the unit with blue lion on a gold field, what battle casualties?"

Leofric's expression turned to one of irritation. "Gag her, *nazir*."

Two soldiers tried to get hold of her head from behind. Ash let herself fall forward, limp, her body banging shoulders, elbows and knees against the stone floor. In the few moments as they lifted her up, uselessly boneless, she violently screamed, "Auxonne, unit with a blue lion livery, what casualties?"

The voice sounded sudden and clear in her head:

"*Information not available.*"

"It can't be! *Tell me!*"

Ash felt herself supported upright, gripped between two men. Someone's hand clamped tight across her broken mouth, and tight across her nose. She sucked for air, the candle-dark hall darkening still more in her vision.

The hand clamped over her face, immovable.

Not able to breathe, not able to speak, she raged through crushed lips into the suffocating glove: "You do know, you *must* know! The Faris will have told you—!"

Nothing like a voice came from her throat.

Sparkles danced across her vision, blotting out the court. No voice sounded in her head. She tried to close her jaws. She felt the scrape of metal rings against her teeth. Copper-tasting blood choked in her throat. She coughed, gagged; the men still held her, tight, as she strained, gasping, suffocating.

I *will* know.

If I can't speak—I'll listen.

She let fear and futility rush through her, forced herself to be calm, to be perfectly still in the midst of bodily pain and mental agony.

She saw nothing but the pattern of veins inside her eyelids, printed on the world outside. Her lungs were fire.

She made a ferocious effort. An act of listening—no passive thing, something violently active. She felt as though she pushed, or pulled; drew up a rope, or swung down with an axe.

I *will* hear. I *will* know.

Her mind *did* something. Like a broken rope, her whole self jolted; or was it a meniscus, that suddenly gave way, and let her through some barrier?

She felt a wrench, in the part of herself that she had always thought of as being shared by her voice, her saint, her guide, her soul.

A grinding roar shook the world.

The walls of the building moved.

A voice exploded through her head:

"NO!"

The solid floor lifted up, under her feet, as if she stood again on the deck of a ship at sea.

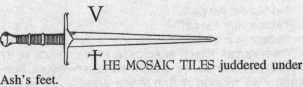

V

THE MOSAIC TILES juddered under Ash's feet.

"WHO IS THIS?"

"IT IS ONE—"

"WE PREVAIL——"

She lurched, losing her footing, dizzy; vision filled with yellow sparkles. The solid world shook. Through a roaring noise—in her mind? in the world?—many voices slammed into her head:

"BURGUNDY MUST FALL——"

"YOU ARE NOTHING——"

"YOUR SORROW, NOTHING! YOU ARE NOTHING!"

In that second, Ash realized: Not *a* voice.

Not *a* voice—*voices*. Not *my* voice. Sweet Jesus, I am hearing more than one voice! What's happening to me!

A grating roar jerked the floor under her as a dog shakes a rat.

She got her arms out from under her entangling cloak, slammed an elbow into Theudibert's mail-clad ribs, jarring her shoulder. She clawed at the man's hand across her mouth, breaking her fingernails on the mail of his gauntlets.

"WHAT IS IT THAT SPEAKS TO US?"

"IT IS ONE OF THE SHORT-LIVED, BOUNDED BY TIME."

"WE ARE NOT SO BOUNDED, SO CONSTRICTED."

"IS IT THE *MACHINA REI MILITARIS*?"[42]

"IS IT THE ONE WHO LISTENS?"

The hand clamped over her face suddenly dropped away.

Ash dropped to her knees; sucked in a great, unobstructed breath. The smell of the sea filled her nostrils and mouth: salty, fresh, terrifying.

"Who are you? What is this?" She gulped air; screamed: "What happened to my company at Auxonne?"

"AUXONNE FALLS."

"BURGUNDY FALLS!"

"BURGUNDY MUST FALL."

"THE GOTHS SHALL ERADICATE EVERY TRACE OF IT FROM THE EARTH. WE WILL——WE *MUST*——MAKE BURGUNDY AS THOUGH IT HAD NEVER BEEN!"

---

[42] "War-machine," "machine [for making] tactics."

"Shut up!"

Ash shrieked, aware that the noise of voices was in her head, and a greater noise was ripping through the hall: a shattering, cracking roar.

"What's happened to my people? *What!*"

"WE SHALL—WE *MUST*—MAKE BURGUNDY AS THOUGH IT HAD NEVER BEEN!"

"Voice! Stone Golem! Saint! Help me!" Ash opened her eyes, not knowing until then that she had screwed them shut in concentration.

Iron candle-trees tipped over, yellow flames arcing across the vast chamber. Men around her sprang to their feet. Smoke filled the air.

Ash fell, sprawling prone. The buckling tiles shuddered under her hands. She scrabbled one foot under her, flexed her injured knee, came halfway up onto her feet.

A man screamed. Fravitta. The Visigoth soldier threw up his arms and vanished from in front of her. The floor split and opened, mosaic tiles rending raggedly along a line of stone flooring. Fravitta rolled down the floor that suddenly *sloped*, vanished into blackness—

The whole world jolted.

She was instantly in the center of a pushing, jostling crowd; armed men ripping swords from their scabbards, yelling orders; men of law and men of trade reduced to a mass, clawing to force their way back, away from the throne, away toward the archway exits.

Ash spread her arms wide, flattening herself down on the bucking floor. Black cracks spidered across its vast expanse. Heaps of trodden corn tipped up and slid, with benches, with robed men falling to their knees; slid down slabs of mosaic-covered red terracotta tiles that tilted up with a great rending crash—

Something dark flashed across the air in front of her.

Ash had a second to glance up, one arm going automatically over her head. The Mouth of God opened. Blocks of stone, painted with curling leaves, fell away from the circular rim and tumbled down through the empty air.

On the far side from her, a quarter part of the dome shattered and fell out of the roof.

Horrific, harsh male screams sounded; she could not see where the masonry was landing, but she could hear it, great impacts that vibrated the floor, shook the ground—

"WHAT SPEAKS TO US?"

The vibration in her mind and in the world met, became one. Another section of the roof fell. The stars of the south shone between racing clouds.

The tiles on which she stood, buckled.

*Earthquake*, Ash thought, with complete calm. She stood and stepped back, at the same time reaching out and grabbing the sleeve of Godfrey's robe, hauling him toward her. A stench of feces and urine filled her nostrils: she choked. Buffeted by stampeding soldiers— Theudibert, Saina—and deafened by Alderic shouting, "To Leofric! To *Leofric*!"; and another *'arif* screaming *"Evacuate the hall!"*, Ash flashed a shaky grin at Godfrey.

"We're going!" She started to move backwards as she spoke.

A shatter of plaster fell, exploding on the floor not twenty feet away. Two great chunks of masonry tumbled down, seemingly slowly, through the air. Her gut curdled.

"The doctor!" Godfrey bawled.

"No time! Oh shit—get him!" Ash let go of Godfrey's robe. The falling stone struck somewhere to her left, with a noise like cannon-fire. Fragments shrapnelled through the crowds. The sheer mass of people between her and the impact saved her. Stone slashed through flesh. Shrieks and cries deafened her. An eddy of motion pushed her forward.

She braced herself, and knelt down. Men's bodies knocked against her, all but trampling her. A body in a mail hauberk sprawled at her feet. The boy-soldier Gaiseric, moaning, semiconscious. She ruthlessly rolled

Gaiseric over, unbuckling his sword-belt. "*Godfrey!* Move! Go, go, go!"

Kneeling, she lifted her head in time to see Godfrey Maximillian staggering back across the tilted floor, a man's struggling body slung over his shoulder—Annibale Valzacchi, his face all one bloody bruise.

*I hear more than one voice—! Who? What—?*

*If they speak again, we'll all die—*

Sure-fingered, Ash buckled belt and scabbard around her, settling the sword on her hip as she sprang up, reaching to try and take some of the Italian man's weight from Godfrey. Men struck against her, pushing past.

"We're out of here!" she shouted. "Come on!"

The noise of stonework tearing drowned out her voice.

She has a moment to stare around her, through dust and flying mortar-powder—the throne and dais gone, buried under raw-edged marble cladding and granite masonry. No sign of King-Caliph Gelimer. A glimpse of a white head, far over: Leofric being hustled between two soldiers; Alderic behind him, a flash of his drawn blade in the smoky air.

A carved, curving block of stone crashed to the floor thirty feet ahead of her. Instantly she dropped, pulling Godfrey and the injured doctor down with her.

Stone splinters whistled over her head, which she buried in her arms. Stone fragments ricocheted, stinging her legs.

"Sweet Christ, if I only had a helmet! This is more dangerous than combat!"

"There's no way through!" Godfrey Maximillian bellowed, his big body pressed up close to hers where they lay.

Terrified clawing crowds of men blocked every near archway. The hall had no lights now, no candles, no torches. Red flames flickered up from one wall: embroidered hangings flaming into fire. Someone screamed, above the tumult. Two voices bellowed contradictory orders. Over to the left, blades rose and fell: a squad of soldiers from some *amir*'s household attempting to cut their way through and out into the open.

"We can't stay here! The rest of this place is coming down!"

A cold wind blew dust into her eyes. Ash coughed. The stench of sewerage grew stronger. She nodded once to herself; got up onto hands and knees, and grabbed Annibale Valzacchi's arm again. "Okay, no problem. Follow me."

*Any decision is better than no decision.*

Valzacchi's dead-weight body jolted as they pulled it over rubble, Godfrey Maximillian crawling beside her, his robes blackened with stone-dust. The chape of her scabbard scraped a groove in the mosaic tiles beside her.

"Here!"

The tilting floor fell away, ahead of her, down into darkness. The crust of tiles had broken like the pastry crust that coffins a pie. She wiped her streaming eyes, let Valzacchi's arm fall, and knelt up, looking for a fallen torch or candle. Nothing but the dim light of fire flickered across the hall.

"What is this?" Godfrey wiped his beard, choked at the fetid air.

"The sewers." Ash, in the stink and faint light, grinned at him. "Sewers, Godfrey! Think! This is *Carthage*. There had to be Roman sewers. We can't go out, we go *down*!"

A creaking groan filled the air. For a moment she was not certain where it came from. She glanced up. Torn clouds raced across a black, starry sky. The moist air stank.

What remained of the dome groaned. She could almost swear she saw, in the light of burning banners, the stone masonry sag inward.

Ash picked up a fragment of granite the size of her fist and tossed it into the black gap in the floor in front of her. The rock bounded once on the sloping floor and disappeared.

"One—two—"

A splash, from the darkness below.

"That's it! I'm right!"

A straining groan of masonry filled the air. Ash met Godfrey's eyes. The bearded priest smiled at her, with a sudden, surpassing sweetness.

"I only wish this were the first time you'd landed me in the shit!" He reached for Valzacchi, rolling the unconscious man forward, and poised his body at the top of the tilting slab of tiles. "All the saints bless you, Ash. Our Lady be with us!"

Godfrey pushed Valzacchi. The Italian, his face black with blood in the dim light, rolled over and over and vanished into the cleft.

"One . . . two . . ."

Ash heard the heavier splash of a man's body hitting liquid.

Deep, or shallow?

No solid sound, that would indicate rock beneath.

She nodded once, decisively, tucked her scabbarded sword up under her left arm, and crabbed forward on her hands and knees. "Better not let the bastard drown, I guess—*let's do it*!"

A hollow crackling roar grew louder. Fire. The light flickered redly across the terracotta tiles. The cleft, some six or seven feet across, split the hall each way as far as Ash could see. Nothing penetrated the darkness of the hole: light stopped at the fractured edges of tiles. The faint illumination showed fresh, raw broken stone on the far side of the gap. Nothing of what lay below down in the darkness.

She hesitated.

Water? Rubble? Broken rock? Valzacchi might have landed luckily, the next one might break their neck—

"Ash!" Godfrey whispered. "Can you?"

"I can. Can you?"

"There's a hurt man down there. I knew I could do it, if there was. Follow me!"

She was suddenly looking at his robed rump as Godfrey Maximillian crawled rapidly forward, slid himself sideways over the edge, hung by his hands, and dropped.

Displaced air blew across her face.

Instinct took her. She threw herself forward. The tiled floor battered her. The hilts of the Visigoth sword dug into her unarmored ribs. The floor suddenly wasn't there. She dropped into void and darkness—

—an immense weight struck the floor of the dome above her. A *boom*! as loud as a siege bombard deafened her. The darkness filled with rock, with flying fragments, with dust. She dropped into something freezing cold, in a shock that nearly drove her heart to stop and battered the air from her lungs.

She clamped her mouth shut. Water stung her eyes. Water enveloped her. She beat her arms, kicked her legs. The water swallowed her down, her lungs straining for air. She thrashed her legs, disorientated; certain for a split second that she would see sunlight to guide her to the surface, that she would splash up under the stone pylons of a river bridge in Normandy, or in the valley by the Via Aemelia—

Something sucked her down.

The force of the water swirled her, bodily. Something passed, taking her down with it. A hard shock broke against her thigh, numbing all her right leg; and her right hand would not move. Ferociously, she thrashed her numb arms, kicked; her chest burning; her eyes wide open and stinging in the black water.

Redness shone, to her right and below her.

*I am diving*, she realized. She twisted her body in the water, kicked herself up toward the light.

Her mouth opened of its own accord. Head back, face slapped with frozen air, she sucked in great sobbing breaths. She kicked again with her legs: found herself standing, crouching on rock, her head just above water, thick with filth; her body numb.

The stench of an open sewer forced her gorge to rise. She straightened, vomiting weakly.

"Godfrey? *Godfrey*!"

No voice.

The noise of fire echoed down from above. Red light limned the edges of the gap. A thin warmth drifted down, and smoke, and she coughed, choking again.

"Godfrey! Valzacchi! Here!"

Her eyes adjusting, she made out that she crouched at one side of a great tubular sewer, built of long red bricks, ancient beyond measure. Where the earthquake had cracked the pipe, water was rushing out between the gaps. Tumbled blocks of stone choked the rift, not ten feet away from her, piled up in the water and blocking the flow.

Dust settled over her wet face.

She straightened, the weight of her soaking clothes dragging her down. Her cloak was gone; the belt and scabbard still around her waist, but the sword gone out of it. Her left hand was white, her right hand black. She lifted it. Blood trickled over her wrist. She flexed her fingers, sensation returning. Grazes bled. She stooped to feel her leg, below the surface; aching now, but whether with injury or with the cold of the water, it was impossible to tell.

Realisation came to her with the settling dust.

*The roof fell in after me.*

"Godfrey! It's all right, I'm here! Where are you?"

A noise sounded to her left. She turned her head. Her dark-adjusted eyes showed her a lip of brick—an access path, she realized. She reached out, grabbing the edge, and tried to pull herself up out of the water. The scuffling noise increased. In the light of the fire above, she saw a man. His hands were clamped over his face. He ran off, staggering, into the dark.

"Valzacchi! It's *me*! Ash! Wait!"

Her voice echoed flatly off the brick walls of the sewer tunnel. The man—it must be the doctor, by his build—did not stop running.

"*Godfrey!*" She hauled herself up on her belly onto the platform—a brick ledge a few yards wide, running along the course of the sewer pipe. Grit slashed her palms.

She spat, coughed, spat again; and crawled forward, leaning over the water, staring down.

Flames reflected from the swift-running surface. It stank with a sweetness that choked her. She could see nothing beneath.

An explosion boomed through the tunnel.

She jumped, her head jerking up. Above, the building was still collapsing, broken masonry hitting the floor with a sound of artillery. Warmth fanned down on her face from the flames. In her mind's eye she pictured what had been left of the dome—two-thirds of the roof poised to fall.

"Well, *fuck*." She spoke aloud. "I'm not going without you. Godfrey! Godfrey! It's Ash! I'm here! Godfrey!"

She limped along the brick pathway, quartering the area under the crevasse. The floor of the hall groaned above her. She called out, paused to listen, called again, as loudly as she could.

Nothing.

Wind blew across her wet face, sucked up through the gap to the fire above. Red and gold light shimmered on the running water that carried the Citadel's sewage. She wiped her streaming nose, turned around, moved back; this time leaning out over the water to stare across at the piled broken masonry under the rift.

Something moved.

Without a second's hesitation, Ash sat down on the lip of the platform and slid over into freezing water. She thrust her feet against the side. The impetus swirled stinking water across her face, but she managed, with two gasping strokes, to swim across to the fallen masonry.

Her fingers touched wet cloth.

A body rocked, caught under the shattered bas-relief carving of Saint Peredur. She knotted the cloth around her hand, pulled; couldn't move it. The block stood taller than she did, bedded down into the channel. She braced her foot against it and tugged.

Cloth ripped. The body came away free. She fell back

into deep water, out of her depth in mid-pipe; kept her numbed, frozen grip on the wool and swam, dragging him with all her strength, toward the platform. The body floated face down; Godfrey or maybe not Godfrey; about the right build—

Cold limp hands brushed her, under the water. Fravitta?

Splashing water echoed from the broken roof of the pipe. Frenetic, straining, she found rough places in the bricks below the water line. She dug her toes into the holes. She ducked down under the water line; got her shoulders under his chest, and lifted his body up.

For a second she was poised, all his fourteen-stone weight on her shoulders, just above the lip of the platform. Her fingers slipped, losing their cold grip on his thighs. She tilted her body sideways, rolling him; knew as she fell back that she succeeded, got most of his body onto the path; and she surfaced, shaking wet hair out of her face, to see the body slumped and dark on the brickwork above her.

She crawled up and out. Her legs were leaden. Her breath sobbed in her throat. She knelt on all fours.

The soaking robes were no color, in this gold light; but she knew the curve of this back and shoulder, had looked over at it sleeping in her tent too many times not to know it.

"Godfrey—" She choked, spat filth; thought, *I can't see him breathing, get him over on his side, get the water out of his lungs—*

She touched him.

The body flopped over onto its back.

"Godfrey?"

She knelt up, water streaming off her. Blood and filth soaked her clothes. The stench of the sewer dizzied her. The light from above dimmed, the crackling roar diminishing, the fire finding nothing more to burn than stone.

She reached out a hand.

Godfrey Maximillian's face stared up at the curved, ancient brick. His skin was pink, in the fire-light; and where she touched his cheek he felt icy cold. His chestnut beard surrounded lips just parted, as if he smiled.

Saliva and blood gleamed on his teeth. His dark eyes were open and fixed.

Godfrey, still recognizably Godfrey; but not half-drowned.

His face ended at his thick, bushy eyebrows. The top of his head, from ear to nape, was splintered white bone in a mess of gray and red flesh.

"Godfrey . . ."

His chest did not move, neither rise nor fall. She reached out and touched her fingertip to the ball of his eye. It gave slightly. No contraction moved his eyelid down. A small, cynical smile crossed her lips: amusement at herself, and how human beings hope. *Am I really thinking, with his head caved in like this, that he might still be alive?*

I've seen and touched dead men often enough to know.

His mouth gaped. A trickle of black water ran out between his lips.

She put her fingers into the unpleasantly warm and jellied mess above his broken forehead. A shard of bone, still covered with hair, gave under her touch.

"Oh, shit." She moved her hand, cupping it around his cold cheek, closing the sagging, bearded jaw. "You weren't meant to die. Not *you*. You don't even carry a sword. Oh, shit, Godfrey . . ."

Careless of his blood, she touched her fingers to his wound again, tracing the dented bone to where it splintered into mess. The calculating part of her mind put a picture before her inner eye of Godfrey falling, broken rock falling; water, impact; heavy masonry shearing off the top of his skull in a fraction of a heart-beat, dead before he could know it. Everything lost in a moment. The man, Godfrey, gone.

*He's dead, you're in danger here, go!*

You wouldn't think twice, on the battlefield.

Still she knelt beside Godfrey, her hand against his

face. His cold, soft skin chilled her to the heart. The line of his brows and his jutting nose, and the fine hairs of his beard, caught the last light from the flames. Water ran off his robes and pooled on the brick-work: he stank, of sewerage.

"It isn't *right*." She stroked his cheek. "You deserve better."

The utter stillness of all dead bodies possessed him. She made an automatic check with her eye—does he have weapons? Shoes? Money?—as she would have done on a stricken field, and suddenly realized what she was doing, and closed her eyes in pain and breathed in, sharply.

"Sweet Christ . . . !"

She rose up onto her haunches, crouching on her toes, staring around in the water-rushing darkness. She could just make out the white glimmer of his flesh.

I would leave any dead man upon the field, if there was still fighting going on; would—I know—abandon Robert Anselm, or Angelotti, or Euen Huw; any of them, because I would have to.

She knows this because she has, in the past, abandoned men she loved as well as she loves them. War has no pity. Time for sorrow and burial afterwards.

Ash suddenly knelt again, thrusting her face close to Godfrey Maximillian, trying to fix every line of his face in her mind: the wood-brown color of his eyes, the old white scar below his lip, the weathered skin of his cheeks. Useless. His expression, his spirit, gone, it might have been any dead man laying there.

Black clots of blood rested in the splintered bone of his forehead.

"That's enough, Godfrey. Joke's over. Come on, sweet-heart, great-heart; come on."

She knew, as she spoke, the reality of his death.

"Godfrey; Godfrey. Let's go home . . ."

Sudden pain constricted her chest. Hot tears rimmed her eyes.

"I can't even bury you. Oh, sweet Jesus, *I can't even bury you.*"

She tugged at his sleeve. His body did not move. Dead weight is dead weight; she would not be able to lift him, here, never mind carry him with her. And into what?

The water rushed and things rustled in the darkness around her. The rift above was a pale, rosy gap. No noise came down from the ruined halls above, now.

Under her feet, the earthquake shuddered again.

"You killed him!"

She was on her feet before she knew it, shrieking up into the darkness, spittle spraying from her mouth in fury:

"You killed him, you killed Godfrey, *you killed him!*"

She had time to think, *When they spoke to me before, there was an earthquake.* And time to think, *"They" didn't kill him. I did. No one is responsible for his death except me. Ah, Godfrey, Godfrey!*

The old brickwork shook under her feet.

I've been a soldier for five or six summers, I must be responsible for the deaths of at least fifty men, why is this different? It's *Godfrey*—

Voices spoke, so loud in her mind that she clamped her hands over her ears:

"WHAT ARE YOU?"

"ARE YOU ENEMY?"

"ARE YOU BURGUNDY?"

Nothing physical could block it. Her lip bled where she bit it. She felt a great vibration, the ancient bricks grinding together beneath her feet, mortar leaking out in dust and powder.

"Not my voice!" she gasped, lungs hurting. "You're not my voice!"

Not *a* voice, but *voices*.

As if something else spoke through the same place in her—not the Stone Golem, not that enemy: but an enemy somehow behind the Visigoth enemy, something huge, multiple, demonic, vast.

"IF YOU ARE BURGUNDY, YOU WILL DIE—"

"—AS IF YOU HAD NEVER BEEN—"

"—SOON, SOON DIE—"

"Fuck off!" Ash roared.

She dropped to her knees. She wrapped her fists in the soaking wet cloth of Godfrey's robes, pulling his body to her. Her face turned up sightless to the dark, she bellowed, "What the fuck do you know about it? What does it matter? He's dead, I can't even have a mass said for him, if I ever had a father it was Godfrey, don't you *understand*?"

As if she could justify herself to unknown, invisible voices, she shouted:

"Don't you understand that *I have to leave him here*?"

She leaped up and ran. One outstretched hand thumped the curved wall of the tunnel, grazing her palm.

She ran, the touch of the wall guiding her, through the darkness and the stone, through after-shocks of earthquake; into the vast and stinking network of sewers under the city, Godfrey Maximillian left behind her, tears blinding her, grief blinding her mind, no voice sounding in her ears or her head; running into darkness and broken ground, until at last she stumbled and came down on her knees, and the world was cold and quiet around her.

"I need to know!" She shouts aloud, in the darkness. "Why is it that Burgundy *matters* so much?"

Neither voice nor voices reply.

*[E-mails found inserted in copy of text:] [previous hard-copy missing?]*

------------------------------------------------

Message: #177 (Anna Longman/misc.)
Subject: Ash
Date: 26/11/00 at 11.20 a.m.
From: Ngrant@

format address deleted
other details encrypted by
non-discoverable personal key

Anna--

We can't GET to the offshore site. The Mediterranean is stiff with naval helicopters over the area, as well as surface ships. Isobel is off again talking to Minister ▇▇▇▇: I don't know what influence she can bring to bear, but she *must* do something!

Forgive me, I haven't even had time to tell you that your scanned-in text of the Vaughan Davies 'Introduction' came through as machine-code. Could you possibly try again in a different format? Did you talk to your bookseller friend, Nadia? Does she have any more information about this house clearance in East Anglia? As far as I am aware, Vaughan Davies died during the last war—this is a son or daughter of his, perhaps?

The way I've been moving around, it's no wonder that you couldn't get the file through to me. I'm back on Isobel's machine now, working on the transferred FRAXINUS files, on the on-going translation, while we wait. I've been slowed down, obviously—you've nearly caught up with what I've completed.

As far as I can discover, no one has cracked Isobel's encryption, so I feel free to tell you that the last two days have been absolutely *bloody*.

While Isobel's team are perfectly amenable people, they're under considerable stress; we spend our time sitting around in the tents—with them running analysis on what data they have been able to collect, and playing around with image-enhancers for the underwater details—Roman shipwrecks, mostly.

Anna, this isn't the MARY ROSE, there may be a whole new level of mediaeval technology down there on the seabed, that we haven't previously suspected the existence of!

Sorry: when I come to splitting infinitives, I know I'm distressed.

But there may be ANYTHING down there. Even—dare I say it—even, perhaps, a 15c GOLEM-POWERED ship?

Is there anything *you* can do, Anna? Have you any media contacts which could put pressure on the government? We are losing a priceless archaeological opportunity here!

--Pierce

- - - - - - - - - - - - - - - - - - - - - - - - - - - - -

Message: #118 (Pierce Ratcliff/misc.)
Subject:  Ash, media
Date:     26/11/00 at 05.24 p.m.
From:     Longman@

                              *format address deleted*
Pierce--                      *other details encrypted and*
                              *non-recoverably deleted*

I think I got the text file through to you this time. Please confirm.

I can't promise anything, but I'm going to a social do tonight, at which will be an old boyfriend who now works for BBC current affairs. I'll do what I can to suggest more notice should be taken of this affair.

This interference is INTOLERABLE. Surely it's got to become a cause celebre?

Hang in there!

Anna--

- - - - - - - - - - - - - - - - - - - - - - - - - - - - -

[Scanned text 26/11/00: hardcopy print-out:—
        excerpt from: Vaughan Davies, Ash: A Biography, 1939:
        'Introduction']

-----------------------------------

Message: #117 (Pierce Ratcliff/misc.)     format address deleted
                                          other details encrypted
Subject:  Vaughan Davies                  and non-recoverably deleted
Date:     26/11/00 at 05.03 p.m. (local time)
From:     Longman@

indeed I believe it to be founded on the most scientific and rational grounds.

I think that it would fair to say that no man without a thorough knowledge of the sciences might have conceived of it; and it would be wise for another historian, if he would seek to discount my theory, to have a wide knowledge of both the historian's and the physicist's fields of enquiry.

Let us begin, then, with a theory of history and time.

Conceive, if you will, of a great mountain range, an Alps almost beyond the imagination of man; and let this represent the history of our world. The vast main part of it is nothing but bare rock, for here our history is that of geological aeons, as the planet cools and takes its orbit around the sun. At the most recent edge of the mountains, a little fringe of life appears—the millions of years of prehistoric vegetation, animalcules, amoeba; developing in a final rapid rush into animals, birds, and at last, man.

We, as we traverse these 'mountains', that here represent our physical existence in the universe, experience our passage as 'time'. Those of my readers familiar with the works of Planck, Einstein, and J. W. Dunne (but I hardly hope for such erudition among my lay readers, the split between science and art being what it is in English culture) will not need me to inform them that time is a human perception of a vastly more complicated process of actual creation.

The world, as it comes about, is shaped by what has gone before. Those mountains behind us prefigure what is to come; the shape of the paths across them determines the paths that we ourselves will take, in what we see as our 'future'. The actions of men in mediaeval times have set us here, on the brink of what may prove to be the world's most destructive conflagration, no less surely than the more recent acts of (let us say) Mr. Chamberlain and Herr Hitler. We are what we follow.

My own theory is, now that I have studied the real evidence implicit in the history of Ash, that the 'mountains' are not as immovable as one might suppose. I hold, in effect, that it is possible that from time to time an earthquake shakes the landscape. It obliterates some things, alters some; rearranges the rock under some of that little fringe of life which inhabits its crevices.

On some occasions, this will be no more than a minor disturbance—a name different here, a girl born in place of a boy, a document lost, a man dead before he otherwise would have been. This is merely a tremor in the great landscape that is time.

However, on at least one occasion a great fracture, as it were, has taken place in what we perceive as our 'past'. Imagine the hands of God reaching down to shake the mountains, as a man might shake a blanket—and then, afterwards, the bedrock remains, but all the shape of the landscape is changed.

This fracture, I believe, takes place for us in the first week of January 1477.

Burgundy, in our mundane historical records, is a magnificent mediaeval kingdom. Yet it is no more than that. Culturally rich, and militarily powerful, its Dukes spend their time in perigrinatory pilgrimages, building sideshow castles after the manner of Hesdin, and warring against the decaying monarchy of France, and the Dukedoms that lie between the north and south of this most disunited of lands, trying to unite a 'Middle Kingdom' stretching from the English Channel to the Mediterranean Sea. Charles, most aggressive and last Duke, dies fighting the Swiss in a foolhardy, freezing bloodbath at Nancy; and the waves of history roll over him, closing over Burgundy. Its territories are divided among those who can get them. There is nothing in the least remarkable about it.

Most historians do not write of it at all, perceiving it perhaps as a backwater, of little importance now. Yet a common thread runs through the small amount of historical writing which there is upon Burgundy. One finds it plainly in Charles Mallory Maximillian, when he writes of a 'lost and golden country'. While for most, Burgundy has been swept from memory, for a few it is a symbol, a sense of loss: a forgotten phoenix.

I have come to see, through my researches, that when we remember this, it is *Ash*'s Burgundy that remember.

As I have written elsewhere, it is my contention now that the Burgundy of which the 'Ash' biographers tell us did not vanish. It became transformed. The mountainous landscape of the past shifted, and when the earthquake was done, the nameless fragments of her story had alighted in other, different places—in the story of Joan of Arc; of Bosworth Field; the legends of Arthurian chivalry, and the travail of the Chapel Perilous. She has become myth, and Burgundy with her; and yet, these faint traces remain.

It can be clearly seen from this that what was created on 5 January 1477 was not merely a new future. If current thinking is correct, different futures may spring into existence at every moment, and these 'alternate' histories continue in parallel with our own. We will, one day, detect this; upon whatever molecular level such a detection can take place.

No, the vanishing of Burgundy—Ash's Burgundy—shattered the landscape entire. Such a change would bring about a new future, yes, but also a new past.

Thus, Burgundy vanishes. Thus, the tales which we have left—as myth, as legend—remind us that once they were themselves true. They serve to remind us that we ourselves may have begun, only, in 1477. This past that we in the 20th century excavate is in some senses a lie—it did not exist until after 5 January 1477.

It is my contention, therefore, that these documents which I have translated are authentic; that the various recountings of the life of Ash are genuine. This is history. It is just not our history. Not now.

What we might have been, if not for this temporal fracture, one can only speculate. More tenuous still must be speculation of what we may now become. History is vast, massive, as impervious to alteration as the adamantine bedrock of the Alpine peaks. As I believe it says somewhere in the King James Bible, nations have bowels of brass. Yet, it seems plain to me, the landscape of our past shows clear evidence of this change.

Ash, and her world, are what our world used to be. They are no more. The surging forward edge of time is left to us to inherit, and the future, make what we will of it.

I leave to others the task of determining the exact nature of this temporal change; and whether or not there is a likelihood of another such fracture in the orderly processes of the universe occurring.

I am presently in the process of preparing an addendum to this Second Edition, in which I plan to detail the vitally important connection between this lost history and our own, present, history. If I am spared from what, it seems in this month of September 1939, will be a conflagration to shake the whole world, then I will publish my findings.

*Vaughan Davies*
*Sible Hedingham, 1939*

------------------------------

Message: #180 (Anna Longman/misc.)
Subject:  Ash/Vaughan Davies
Date:     27/11/00 at 02.19 p.m.
From:     Ngrant@          *format address deleted*
                          *other details encrypted by*
Anna--                    *non-discoverable personal key*


History plays us some small tricks of coincidence. The end of the Introduction names the place where Vaughan Davies was writing at the time. I KNOW Sible Hedingham.

It's a small East Anglian village, close to Castle Hedingham, which itself is the village attached to Hedingham Castle. Hedingham Castle was owned for centuries by the de Vere family—although John de Vere, the thirteenth Earl of Oxford, did not spend much of his time there.

Perhaps this coincidence appealed to Vaughan Davies? Or perhaps (always look for the simplest explanation) his historical researches took him there and he liked it enough to settle down. When you follow up this house clearance, you might have a go at finding out whether the Davies were incomers, or a family that's been in Sible Hedingham since the Domesday Book.

I am unspeakably grateful for this chance to see Vaughan Davies's complete theory. Anna, thank you. I hardly dare ask more of you, but I would give anything to go to the family house and see if there are surviving family; if—more importantly—there are any surviving, unpublished, papers.

That is, I would give anything except the chance of seeing something concrete from Visigothic Carthage being gradually uncovered from beneath the decay of centuries. Perhaps more relics, perhaps—dare I speculate?—even a ship!

Please, go in my place?

What surprises me most, now that I have read what you scanned in and sent to me, is that I RECOGNISE Vaughan Davies's theory. Although he has couched it as a metaphor, this is plainly a mid-century attempt to describe one of the most up-to-date tenets of particle physics—the anthropic principle that, on the sub-atomic level, it is human consciousness that maintains reality.

I am already contacting the colleagues I have on the net who are knowledgeable about this. Let me give you what I have from experts in the field—bearing in mind it's only my understanding!

It is we, theorists of the anthropic principle state, who collapse the infinite number of possible states in which the basic particles of the universe exist, and make them momentarily concrete—make them real, if you like, instead of probable. Not at the level of individual consciousness, or even the individual subconscious, but by a consciousness down at the level of the species-mind.

That 'deep consciousness' of the human race maintains the present, the past, and the future. However solid the material world appears, it is we who make it so. It is Mind, collapsing the wavefront of Possibility into Reality.

We are not talking about the normal human mind, however—myself, you; the man in the street. You or I could not alter reality! Theoretical physics is talking about something far more like the 'racial unconscious' of Jung. Something buried deep in the autonomic limbic system, something so primitive it is not even individual, a leftover from the prehistoric proto-human primates who lived a group-mind consciousness. No more accessible or controllable by us than the process of photosynthesis is to a plant.

For Vaughan Davies's 'hands of God', therefore, read 'human species subconscious'. If I were a physicist myself, I could make this clearer to you.

Leaving aside all this 'new past as well as new future' nonsense, it is just about possible to make a case in theory for Vaughan Davies's 'fracture'—or at any rate, it is not possible to prove that it could NOT happen. If deep consciousness sustains the universe, one supposes deep consciousness might change the universe. And then the leftovers of the change—like a written-over file leaving bits of data in the system (you see how cognisant I am becoming of computers!)—would remain, to puzzle historians like Vaughan Davies.

Of course, not being able to prove something cannot happen is very far from proving it CAN happen; and Davies's theory remains one with the esoteric speculations of some of our modern physicists. But it has a certain beauty as a theory, don't you think?

I am very interested to know if he wrote anything between the publication of ASH: A BIOGRAPHY in 1939 and his death later in the war. Is there news?

--Pierce

------------------------------

Message: #124 (Pierce Ratcliff/misc.)
Subject: Vaughan Davies
Date: 27/11/00 at 03.52 p.m.
From: Longman@

*format address deleted other details encrypted and non-recoverably deleted*

Pierce--

Okay, okay. I'll go to Sible Hedingham. Nadia says she's going down again anyway.

I'm getting moderate media interest. I think it will depend on whether it's decided that the political-military problems you're having on site make you too hot to handle, or whether it's those same problems that make you interesting and a probable media 'cause'.

Jonathan Stanley's handling that. I'm trying to keep him on general grounds. Even though your archaeologist found Troy where a poem said it was, I don't really want to have to explain that the manuscripts you've translated are in any way questionable. I'll handle that when I HAVE to.

The Vaughan Davies stuff is fascinating, isn't it? Is this guy crazy or WHAT? I thought it was only the present moment that could be made into reality, and so become history? How could there be *two* histories of the world? I don't get it. But then, I'm no scientist, am I?

It's okay for you, Pierce, you can play around with theories, but I have to work for a living! One history is more than enough. It's going to take some neat handling by me to get this all to go right. When you finally meet him, for God's sake don't go telling Jon Stanley about all this! I can do without him telling me one of my authors is a mad professor.

--Love, Anna

---

Message: #202 (Anna Longman/misc.)
Subject: Ash
Date: 1/12/00 at 01.11 p.m.
From: Ngrant@

*format address deleted
other details encrypted by
non-discoverable personal key*

Anna--

I don't know how to tell you what has happened.
I'm handing you over to Isobel.

------------------------------

Message: #203 (Anna Longman/misc.)
Subject:   Ash
Date:      01/12/00 at 02.10 p.m.
From:      Ngrant@

*format address deleted
other details encrypted by
non-discoverable personal key*

Ms Longman--

At Pierce's request, I am conveying to you some very unfortunate news. I regret that it will have an effect on the publication of his book, as well as on our expedition here.

As you know, the great 'find' of this dig has been the Visigothic 'messenger-golems'—one intact and complete, one in remnants. Because the fragmentary golem was already in pieces, I chose that one to be sent off to be tested.

Among the tests we do is $C_{14}$ radio-carbon dating. When it comes to marble and other forms of stone, dating an object by this method is impossible—one merely gets the age of the rock before it was carved into an object. However, the 'messenger-golems' also include several metallic parts. The broken one had sections of a ball-joint for one arm.

I have now had the radio-carbon dating report back on this bronze joint. I have also doubled-checked with our archeometallurgist here.

Bronze is an alloy of copper, tin and lead. These metals are smelted together and then cast. During the casting process, when the metal is poured, organic impurities can become mixed in; and a study of the crystalline structure of this joint, when shaved down, showed that just this sort of impurity *had* become incorporated into the structure.

When subjected to radio-carbon dating, these organic fragments gave an extremely odd reading. The tests were repeated, and repeated again.

The lab report, which arrived today, states that in their opinion, the readings show that the organic fragments in the metal contain the same levels of background radiation and pollution as one would expect to find in something which has been growing today.

It seems that the metal for the joints and hinges of the 'messenger-golems' must have been cast during a period of much higher radiation and atmospheric pollution than existed in the 15th century—indeed, a high enough level to make me certain the metal was cast during the last forty years (post-Hiroshima and atomic testing).

I am left with only one possible conclusion. These 'messenger-golems' were not made in the 1400s. They were made recently, possibly very recently. Certainly after the date that, as Pierce tells me, Charles Wade brought the 'Fraxinus' document back to Snowshill Manor.

Frankly, these 'golems' are modern fakes.

I have had little enough time myself to take in this news. Pierce is shattered. You realise that one of the reasons for the extreme security of the dig is that such things do happen in archaeology—fakes are a constant problem—and I never make any announcements until I am sure.

I realize that this leaves Pierce with documents that have been re-classified as fiction, rather than history, that now have no significant archaeological evidence to support them.

I expect that you will want to consider this news before you make any decisions about publication of Pierce's translations.

Colonel ████████ has authorised offshore diving to resume at first light tomorrow. Despite our problems, I am reluctant to lose any opportunity, given the political instability of the region. I am no longer sure if the images from the ROV cameras are relevant, but of course we shall be following up this area of investigation.

We shall therefore be leaving for the ship at daybreak. I think, if you could contact Pierce, he would appreciate a kind word.

I am so sorry. I wish I could have brought you better news.

--Isobel Napier-Grant

--------------------------------

Message:  #137 (Pierce Ratcliff/misc.)
Subject:   Ash/archaeology
Date:       01/12/00 at 02.31 p.m.
From:       Longman@

Pierce, Isobel--

*format address deleted
other details encrypted
and non-recoverably deleted*

ARE YOU SURE?

--Anna

# PART FOUR

11 September AD 1476

*"FERAE NATURA MACHINAE"*

THE DARKNESS WENT on for what seemed hours.

Ash had no way of judging the time. The world was anything she could feel with her fingertips, at arm's length, in cold blackness. Brick, mostly; and damp nitre. Mud or shit underfoot. She found the darkness reassuring. No light must mean no breaks in the sewer-covering: therefore these particular brick passages could be safe to traverse.

*If there are no pits. No shafts.*

*If I were with Roberto, now, we'd get drunk. Talk about Godfrey. I'd get so drunk I couldn't stand up. I'd tell him Godfrey was always a damn peasant at heart. One time I saw him* call boar. *Wild boar, out of the forest! And they came. And I forget how many times he's listened to me when I needed to talk to someone who wasn't one of my officers—*

*Not a father. Who needs fathers? Leofric calls himself a father. A friend. Brother. No, more than a brother; what would it have cost me to love you, just once? Just* once?

*Falling-down drunk. And then we'd go off and get into a fight somewhere.*

*Jesus, what's Roberto going to say when I tell him this?*

*If Robert's alive.*

The sound of water running deep and smooth ahead of her made her slow her steps. The wall under her fingertips turned a corner. She paced slowly forward around it, putting her feet down toes-first, testing for broken ground.

The sewers went on.

*I shouldn't leave him.*

I can't do anything else.

I could ask my voice for the way out of here—no, it doesn't know places, it only solves problems—

Can I even talk to the Stone Golem, now?

Other—voices?

*What are they?*

Does Leofric know? Did the Caliph know? Does anybody know? Christ, I want to talk to Leofric! *Did anybody know anything about this before today?*

I shouldn't have left him.

Pale light made geometric shapes on her retinas.

Ash stopped, her bleeding hand still touching brickwork. The light was strong enough to show her what planes and surfaces it illuminated. A junction of tunnels. Flat walls, curving walls, sweeping up to a cracked roof that let in faint light. Running water. Walkways. Rubble.

This could go on for miles. And it could all come down on my head any second. The earthquake must have shaken a lot of stonework loose.

A noise.

"Valzacchi?" she called, softly.

Nothing.

Ash raised her head. Above, four or five stones had fallen from the tunnel roof. Enough to let through a faint glow of Greek Fire. She thought she heard a confused noise, this time outside, but it faded as she strained to listen.

How long before the rest of this part of the sewer collapses?

Time to be somewhere else.

Unexpected grief bit at her. Her eyes flooded over with tears. She wiped them on her sleeve. She had a moment of knowing, beyond doubt, her responsibility. *And I can never say to you that I'm sorry you came here because of me.*

Ash pressed her filthy hands over her face, once. She raised her head. Grief will come, she knows, in seconds and minutes when she does not expect it; will bite harder when this shock fades and she accepts into herself the knowledge that—when the reasons are found, the responsibilities accepted, her confession made—it does not matter. It does not change the fact that she will never speak to Godfrey again; he will never answer her.

She whispered, "Goodnight, priest."

Something white and moving caught her eye.

Her hand flashed to her belt and met only the empty scabbard. She flattened her back against the tunnel wall, staring ahead.

Something small and white scuttled across the walkway and off into the darkness.

Ash stepped cautiously forward. Her sandals grated on brick. Two more white things darted off out of her way in a low-slung scuttling run.

"Rats," Ash whispered. "*White* rats?"

If the earthquake breached the sewers built under the Citadel's streets, could it have breached the walls of the houses cut down *into* the rock? Am I near House Leofric?

Maybe.

Maybe not. If they are his freak rats, that doesn't necessarily mean I'm close. Rats can move a long way; it's got to have been an hour since the quake, maybe more.

"Hey, ratsies . . ." Ash chirruped softly. Nothing moved in the dim light.

A thought came into her mind, of what rats might feed on, down here. She glanced back, into darkness.

"Godfrey . . ."

She began to edge around the corner of the junction, treading silently, unwilling to disturb the air and the cracked brickwork shell above her head. She stopped. She looked back.

"You won't approve, Godfrey . . . You always said I was a heathen. I am. I don't believe in mercy and forgiveness. I believe in revenge—I'm going to make somebody *hurt* because you're dead."

A distant chittering echoed from further down the sewer.

The sweet stench of shit, unbelievably, grew worse. Ash started to walk on, with her wet sleeve clamped over her nose. She had nothing left to vomit up. Water flowed sluggish and silent below the brick walkway.

The last light from the cracked roof caught on an irregularity in the wall. She reached out, touched brick, touched darkness—touched emptiness.

With her fingertips, she traced out a long brick slot, as tall as her two hands together. She tentatively reached in. Her knuckles barked on bricks and mortar, no great distance in front of her. Frowning, she slid the flat of her hand up the wall in front of her, and her palm slipped into air, into another slot. And above that, another.

The lower edge of each slot had a lip, made of brick, perhaps two inches thick, and three inches high. Strong enough to bear a man's grip and a man's weight.

Gladness flooded her. She breathed in, unawares; coughed at the sweet stench, and laughed aloud, her eyes running. She slid her hands up and down the surface of the wall, to be sure there was no mistake. As high over her head as she could reach, the brickwork had slots built into it. And it was not a curving wall, not here at this junction of tunnels: the wall above her went straight up.

Ash reached up and put her hands into one slot, her foot into another, and began to climb the wall.

The first fifteen or twenty feet were easy enough. Her arms began to ache. She risked leaning back to look up. The broken part of the pipe might be fifty or sixty feet above her, still.

She reached for the next slot in the brickwork "ladder" and hauled her sopping weight upwards. Distracting herself from the physical, she let her mind ramble.

I think the "voices" are speaking *through* the machine, through the Stone Golem. They come into my spirit the same way. But they're not like my voice.

Does anybody know this? Does the Faris know? How

long have they been doing it? Do they tell her things, through the Golem—do they pretend to *be* the Stone Golem? Maybe nobody knows. Until now.

Suppose that the *machina rei militaris* has been in House Leofric for two centuries, suppose that these— others—have been speaking through it? Or are they a part of it? A part that Leofric doesn't know about? But does he?

Ash resolutely kept the part of her mind that listened, quiet.

She reached up above her head, biceps aching, and hauled herself up another rung. Her thighs and calves burned. She absently glanced down and saw, past the length of her body, how far up she was.

Forty feet onto brick, or into a sewer, is high enough to kill.

She pushed herself on, upwards.

And supposing it's these "voices" that hate Burgundy? Why *Burgundy*? Why not France, Italy, the empire of the Turks? I know the Burgundian Dukes are the richest, but this isn't about wealth; they want the land burned black and sown with salt—*why*?

Ash rested, leaning her forehead against the brickwork. It felt chill. Mortar grated dustily.

She had to twist around now to see the broken part of the roof, above her and to the side. A stone lip was cutting her off from it. The steps led up—she raised her head—up into a narrow roof shaft. Within it, darkness. No way of telling what might be up there.

She clung, puzzling, shivering in her wet and filthy clothes. She abruptly smiled into the darkness.

That's *it*. Of *course*. *That's* why the Visigoths have attacked Burgundy, not the Turks! The Turks are a bigger threat, but the machine's been *telling* them that its solution is for them to attack Burgundy. That has to be it! But it isn't the Stone Golem, it's the voices!

Ash clenched her fingers on the rung. Her muscles jabbed at her with cramps. She dug her toe deep into the rung and flexed her leg, straightening it; reaching with her other foot for a rung higher up.

If some other *amir's* family has created another Stone Golem . . . that would be known! Even Leofric never tried to keep it secret. Just secure. But if it isn't another clay machine, what is it—what are they?

Whatever they are, they know about me.

She moved into darkness, head and shoulders and the rest of her body, as she climbed up into the shaft. If it leads nowhere I shall just have to climb down again, she thought, and then: So they know about me now. Good. *Good.*

*I've lost my people. I've lost Godfrey. I've had enough.*

"You better damn well hope you know me," Ash whispered. "Because I'm going to find out about *you*. If you're machines, I'll break you. If you're human, I'll gut you. Messing with me may just be the stupidest thing you ever did."

She smiled in the darkness at her own bravado. Her fingers, reaching up, touched brick and metal. She stopped.

Feeling up carefully with her fingertips, she touched dusty stone, directly above her head, and a rim of cold iron. Within the rim, more metal—a circular iron plate, about a yard across.

Ash settled her feet as far as they would go into the brick rungs she stood on. She gripped a rung with her left hand. With her right hand flat against the metal, she pushed up.

She expected resistance, was thinking *shit I need to get my back under this and I can't* and it took her by surprise as the metal cover flew up and back and off. A bolt of cold air hit her in the face. Greek Fire blazed, dazzling her. She fell forward, mashing her face against the brick ladder, almost losing her hold.

"Son of a bitch!"

She shoved her body up two more steps and groped outside, for something to haul herself out by. Nothing.

Her fingertips scraped stone. The port was too wide for her to brace herself across it.

In one movement, she got both feet up to a higher rung, let go with her left hand, straightened her legs and pushed herself up, and dived heavily forward.

Momentum carried her: she sprawled out across a road, her thighs and the rest of her legs dangling over the abyss but her body safe. She put her palms down flat, and wriggled her body forward, and rolled, jack-knifing; not stopping the roll until she was a good ten feet away from the open sewerport.

In a narrow alley between windowless buildings.

One glass of Greek Fire burned, twenty yards away. The others, closer to her, were smashed. A few yards down the alley, the paving stones ominously sagged.

Her night-adjusted eyes ran with water. She shook her head, getting up onto her hands and feet; the wet wool of her hose and doublet clinging to her, rapidly freezing in the black air.

*I'm still in the Citadel: where—?*

The wind changed direction. She rose, straining her ears.

A confused noise of shouting and screams came to her. Rumbling cartwheels. Metal striking metal. A fight, a chaos; but nothing to tell her where, within the Citadel or outside the walls in Carthage itself—the wind blew at her back again, and she lost the sounds.

*But I'm out!*

Ash drew a deep breath, choked at her own stench, and looked around herself. Bare stone walls confronted her, either side of the narrow street. They went up high enough that she had no chance of seeing a landmark, no guess at which way might be the dome, which way the walls. She sniffed. The smell of the harbor, yes, but something else . . .

Smoke.

A smell of burning drifted across the narrow street. Ash looked up and down: cross-streets at either end. The subsidence to her left should be avoided. She moved off to the right.

A pang went through her, of sorrow and revulsion. Something lay ahead on the cobbles, at the edge of the pool of light cast by the remaining lamp.

A man's body, slumped—with the same stillness that Godfrey has, dead.

She put grief out of her mind quite deliberately. "It'll keep."

She strode up the alley, moving quickly to keep warm. Her sandals left smears of filth on the cobbles. She went toward the prone body that lay up against the featureless wall. *Rob it of money if a civilian; or weapons, if a soldier—*

The light was not good. The Greek Fire above her dimmed in its glass bowl. Ash knelt, reaching out to roll the prone body over onto its face. In quick succession she noted, as her hands hauled at his cold dead weight, that it was a man, wearing hose, and livery tabard, and steel sallet; his belt already gone, his sword looted, his dagger missing—

"Sweet Christ."

Ash slid down into a sitting position, her knees gone. She leaned forward and threw the dead man's arms back, exposing his chest. All his throat and shoulders were a mass of coagulated blood. A bright livery tabard was tied on over his mail shirt, ties knotted at his waist, and some dark device on the cloth—

She unbuckled the strap of the man's sallet, hauling it off his head, her hands coming away bloody from the crossbow-bolt that stood up out of his throat. A sallet, with a visor, and an articulated tail: not a Visigoth helmet. *Made in Augsburg, in the Germanies—home!*

Ash jammed the padded helmet on her head, buckled the strap, reached for the man's ankles, and dragged him bodily over the cobbles, under the dimming light.

He sprawled with his arms above his head, his head turned to one side. A young man, sixteen or seventeen, with light brown hair and the beginnings of a beard; she

has seen him somewhere, knows him, knows the dead
face if not his name—

Under the light, she stares down at his livery, clearly
visible now.

A gold livery tabard.

On the breast, in blue, a lion.

The livery of the Lion Azure. Her company livery.

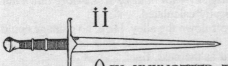

ASH UNKNOTTED THE ties with
wet, frozen fingers, and hauled the livery-tabard off the
boy's body. The neck of the garment was made wide
enough to accommodate a helmet: she threw it on over
her head. Tying its cords at her waist, she stared down
at him. "Michael? Matthew?"

He had stopped bleeding. His body did not feel rigid.
Cold in this outdoor city, but not stiff. No rigor, yet.

She smoothed the dyed linen cloth down over her unprotected belly. No way to get a mail-shirt off a casualty
alone, mail is hard enough to get off when you're living:
the linked metal sucks onto the body. She tugged the
mail mittens from his hands—too large, but she can live
with that—and the boots from his feet.

Stripped, he seemed pathetic; with the long bones and
fat face of young manhood. She hauled his boots on.

"*Mark*. Mark Tydder," she said aloud. She reached
across, drawing a cross on his cold brow. "You're—you
were one of Euen's lance, weren't you?"

You're not here on your own.

How many more people are going to die because
somebody brought me to Carthage?

Ash stood up and stared around her at the cold dark
street. I can't waste time wondering *if there's one, are*

*there more; who's alive, who's dead?* I just have to find them and get on with it.

She bent and kissed the soiled, dead body of Mark Tydder on the forehead, and folded his arms across his chest.

"I'll send someone back for you if I can."

The Greek Fire above her guttered and gave out. She waited a moment as her eyes adjusted to the dark. The shapes of windowless walls rose above her, and, in the gap between roofs, recognizable constellations of stars in the icy, windy sky—*an hour or less before dawn* her mind automatically calculated.

She moved off down the alley. Here, no damage could be seen from the quake. At the first cross-street, she turned left; and at the next, right.

Buildings spilled rubble across the road. She slowed, picking her way. Above her head, splintered beams jutted out. The further down the alley she went, the more she was picking her way over high piles of dressed stone, fractured mosaics, broken furniture—a dead horse—

*No dead people. No wounded. Someone has been through this area after the quake—or it was deserted, everyone up at the palace.*

Climbing over a fallen pillar, boots skidding on frost-slick stone, she came to what had been another road junction. Buildings on the far side still stood. Immense cracks, taller than she was, spider-webbed their walls. She halted, lifting up her helmet and listening intently.

There was a deafening *boom*! A sound loud enough to burst her eardrums blasted the air. Rubble shifted and slid.

"*Shit!*" Ash grinned, ferociously, her head ringing. She swung around to her left. With no hesitation, she scrambled down and trotted as fast as she could in the dark, in the direction of the noise. "That's guns!"

*A swivel gun or a hook gun. Light cannon?* She skidded across split cobbles, scrambling down the dark narrow street. *Not Goths! That's us!*

Clouds slid over the sky. The faint starlight dimmed to nothing, leaving her between windowless houses cracked from foundations to roof. She saw little rubble here. Heedless, in almost complete blackness, she loped on down the alley, arms stretched out in front of her to hit obstacles first.

*Boom!*

"Got you." Ash halted. The slick soles of the boots let her feel the contours of the cobblestones under her feet: the ground sloping slightly down now. She stared into the absolute darkness. Air blew into her face. An open square? An area where the quake has demolished every house? Trailing leaves brushed her face—she flinched—some kind of creeper?

Lanterns.

The yellow light might have been just flecks in her vision, but a sharp angle cut across it: a wall. She made out that she was standing off-set from an alley leading out of this square, the buildings on the left-hand side of it collapsed in on themselves, but on the right-hand side, still standing. Towards the far end of the alley, someone was holding a lantern.

The dry, acrid, infinitely familiar smell of powder hit her nostrils.

Ash did not know that her teeth were bared, grinning fiercely into the dark. One hand closed, by itself, seeking the hilt of a sword which did not hang from her belt.

She filled her lungs with the cold, gunpowder-air:

"Hey! ASSHOLES! DON'T SHOOT!"

The lantern jerked. An explosive *spang!* blew fragments of clay facing down on her head. A crossbow-bolt: shot high and wide, hitting the righthand wall somewhere above her.

"I SAID *DON'T* FUCKING SHOOT ME, YOU ASSHOLES!"

A cautious voice called, "Mark? That you?"

A second voice cut in: "That's not Tydder. Who goes there?"

"Who do you fucking think?" Ash bawled, still in the

Franco-Flemish dialect that was the common patois of the camp.

A silent pause—which brought Ash's heart up into her mouth, dried out her chest with breathlessness, fear, hope—and then the second voice, rather small, and distinctively Welsh, called uncertainly, ". . . Boss?"

"Euen?"

*"Boss!"*

"I'm coming in! Don't be so fucking trigger-happy!"

She trotted up the alley toward the light. Six or seven men with weapons filled the width of it: men in European-style steel helmets, and with razor-edged bills, and swords, and two with crossbows, one frantically winching as if to prove he had not fired his bolt.

"Negligent discharge," Ash grinned in passing, and then: "Euen!" She reached out, grabbing the small dark man's hands and wringing them. "Thomas—Michel—Bartolemey—"

"Jesus fucking Christ," Euen Huw said reverently.

"Boss!" Euen's red-haired 2IC, Thomas Morgan, crossed himself, with the hand that did not hold a spanned crossbow.

"*Shit*, man!" The others—tall, broad-shouldered men with hard, hunger-marked faces—began to grin at her and make comments among themselves. They were standing among neatly piled heaps of wine-casks, velvet gowns, and heavy jute sacks, Ash noted; their shining faces turning to her, plain wonder on their expressions. "Would you ever fucking *believe* it!"

"It's me," Ash said, turning back to the wiry, dark Welshman.

Euen Huw was not a particularly prepossessing sight: his jack was faded, salt-stained under the intermittent light from the pierced iron lantern; and an old blackened bandage was wrapped around his left hand and wrist. His other hand grasped the hilt of a riding sword, a ridiculous forty inches of razor-sharpened steel.

"Christ, I might have known it, boss," Euen said.

"Straight out of the middle of a fucking earthquake, you come. Right. What do we do now?"

"Why are you asking me?" Ash inquired wryly, surveying their dirty larcenous faces. "Ah, that's right—I'm the boss! I knew there was some reason."

"Where you *been*, boss?" Michel, the other crossbowman, asked.

"In a Visigoth nick. But." Ash grinned. "Here I am. Okay, this ain't a fucking social banquet. Tell me. Who's here, why are we here, and what the fuck is going on?"

*Boom!*

That gun was close enough that the ground twanged under her feet. Ash fingered her ear with a pained expression, watching them watch her do it, seeing them grin; judging how much strain was also in their expressions, how most of them were losing the momentary amazement of her presence, falling back into the old habit of being commanded by her: *this is Ash, she'll tell us what to do, get us through this*. In the adrenalin-rush of combat, they are not even surprised: impossible things happen all the time in battle.

In the middle of the heart-city of the Visigoth empire, surrounded by enemy people and enemy troops—

"What dumb fuck brought you guys here?"

The crossbowman, Michel, shoved a suspicious sack aside with his boot. "Mad Jack Oxford, boss."

"Oh my God. Who's with the guns?"

"Master Captain Angelotti," Euen Huw answered. "He's up there trying to bust into this shit-rich lord-*amir's* house—'course, *his* house couldn't fall down like the rest of them, could it? No chance!"

"*Which* lord-*amir*—no, tell me later. What are you motherfuckers doing out here?"

"We're a picket, boss, wouldn't you know it? Waiting for all them little rag-heads to turn up and try to mince us into the ground."

His sardonic sarcasm got answering grins from his lance. Ash let herself chuckle.

"I'm just sorry for the Goths! Okay, stick to it. And watch it! You're in the middle of an overturned hive here."

"Don't we know it!" Euen Huw grinned.

"Mark Tydder's body's down one of those alleys, you— Michel—go scout it; then you and another man bring him back, if the road's clear. We don't leave our own—"

A sudden image bit into her mind. Godfrey, his green robe black with water and filth, and the white splinters of bone above his tanned brow. Her eyes stung.

"—if we can help it. If any troops show up, report to me fucking fast. I'll be with HQ."

Euen Huw said cheerfully, "Boss, you *are* HQ."

"Not until I know what the hell Oxford thinks he's doing! You." She indicated the redheaded lance-second, Thomas Morgan. "Lead me to Oxford and Angelotti. And you guys here, *close that fucking lantern up*! I could see you a mile off! None of you have got the brains of a field mouse, but that's no reason you shouldn't make it home—just follow my orders! Okay, let's go! Move it!"

As she moved off, Thomas Morgan's tall broad back blocking the hastily closed lantern, she heard a man mutter, "Shit, lil' scarface is back . . ."

"Too fucking right," Ash growled.

*They're alive!*

With the lantern gone and the cloud-cover thick, it was impossible to see anything but blackness, but there were voices ahead of her now, and the shouts of men sponging gun-breeches and loading them: she tucked her mittened fingers under the back of Thomas Morgan's belt and followed his uncertain progress as he tapped his way down the cobbles with the shaft of his bill, the wood knocking against spilled masonry and rubble.

A coldness crept into her belly. Her mind put nightmare pictures on the darkness in front of her: these men, men that she knows, trapped in these streets, trapped inside the middle of a walled city—a walled city *within* a walled city—and all of Carthage outside, the *amirs*, their household troops, the King-Caliph's army, the merchants and the workers and the slaves, each an enemy—

What fucking dangerous *lunatic* brought them here! Ash wondered bleakly, furiously. How do I get them *out* of here?

And do what we have to do, first?

Thomas Morgan stumbled, muttered something obscene, clattered his bill-shaft against a splintered masonry block, and stepped to the right. She kept her footing and followed.

How *many* of my guys are here now? *What the fuck is Oxford thinking of?* Just because we're mercenaries doesn't mean you can stick us out as a forlorn hope and leave us to die—well, maybe *he* thinks it does—I thought better of him—

The quality of the air changed.

Glancing up, Ash saw how the clouds, shredding, opened on bright stars: the constellations of the Eternal Twilight. Quickly she lowered her gaze. Her nightvision took enough from the starlight to let her see where she stepped, drop her hand from Thomas Morgan's belt, and focus on the corner of the blank-walled house in front of her.

Way down on her right, ahead, the building's massive iron-banded main gates hung splintered and blasted—cannon-fire, not quake damage. Guncrews crowded the corner here, behind a cluster of pavises.[43] Two swivel guns had their supporting spikes jammed down into the dirt where the quake had split the cobblestones. Men, swearing bitterly and shouting; were trying to shoot fifty yards cross-wise down the alley and blast the gates open—no room to get cannon up close, opposite the House gate, not in an alley no more than ten feet wide.

More men came running in, pavises going up, looted

---

[43] Crossbowmen used these wooden shields as mobile protective defenses, shooting from behind them. Pavises were often three to four feet high. They would be supported upright by stakes, or by another man.

wooden doors piled as makeshift defenses. A silent flight of bolts impacted ten yards from her feet, blasting up splinters of stone. Antonio Angelotti's voice—*Angeli'*! Ash grinned, delighted at the recognition, his presence— screamed a beautiful obscenity. On the House roof, men briefly moved: shooting down: Visigoths, Visigoth House guards, this house—

Ash felt a sudden stab of memory. Genuine? Illusory? *I think we've come north, I've come all the way back from the King-Caliph's palace, this is how I was brought into Leofric's house—this is House Leofric—*!

Realization hit her.

Oh shit. I know why Oxford's here.

He's doing what I said *I* was going to do.

He's here for the Stone Golem.

Thomas Morgan bellowed, "Here they are, boss," in a tone that suddenly held doubt.

Ash trotted past him, into the alley that dead-ended on her right, lit with lanterns and torches; all filled up with men and their shouting, men running, two more swivel-guns commanding the alley directly in front of House Leofric, having their breeches frantically sponged and shot rammed home. A tall, fair-haired man in Italian doublet and demigown crouched by the guncrews, shouting—Angelotti—and a dozen other familiar faces; the deacon Richard Faversham, a skinny blond man with his hands wrist-deep in a sack of bandages, behind a big pavise and two billmen—Florian de Lacey, Floria del Guiz—and beyond her a massive cluster of men in breastplates and leg-harness, with maces and arquebuses, and Lion livery—and a young corn-haired knight in half-armor, Dickon de Vere; and John de Vere himself taking off his sallet to wipe his forehead—

She has a split-second to study them while they, busy in ordered chaos, ignore her arrival. It puts a curdle of panic into her bowels: to be facing men, soldiers, who ignore her as if she isn't there—this is the commander's dread of authority (that spider-thread) disappearing like mist. Who is she, that anyone should do what she says?

The person who persuaded them off their farms and into this business. Into many wet mornings on grassy blood-soaked hills, many nights in burning towns sprawling with mutilated bodies. The person whom they will think can get them through this alive.

Two or three nearer heads turned, Thomas Morgan's visible presence penetrating their attention. One of the gunners put down his worm, staring; another man dropped the breech of the second gun. Three Flemish billmen stopped talking and gaped.

Antonio Angelotti said a foul word in utterly musical Italian.

Floria slowly stood up, her face in the flaring light broken with hope, with amazement, with a sudden wrenching fear.

"Get down in *cover*!" Ash bawled at her.

Ash nevertheless remained in the open. She reached up and unbuckled the strap of Mark Tydder's sallet, easing it off her vulnerable head. Her cropped silver hair stood up in spikes, sweaty despite the freezing air. *Even with the risk of some bastard getting me with a composite bow, they have to see me.*

"Fuck," someone said, awe-struck.

Ash tucked the sallet under her arm. The metal was freezing, even through the leather palms of her mittens. Lantern-light fell on the livery tabard that she wore, black and stiff with dried blood at the throat, the Lion Azure plain across her chest. Her hands, muffled in too-large mail mittens, and her feet in too-large boots, gave her the appearance of a child in adult clothing. A tall skinny child with three scars standing out dark against the skin of her frozen white cheeks.

And then she moved, put her other fist on her hip, to be recognizably their Ash, Captain Ash, condottiere: a woman unlawfully dressed as a man, in doublet and hose, hair cut short as a serf's, face gaunt with hunger and pain, but with a shining grin that lit up her eyes.

"It's the *boss!*" Thomas Morgan called, his voice shaky.

"ASH!"

She couldn't tell who shouted: they were all moving by then, careless of the armed household a few yards away; men running, shouting the news to their lance-mates, Angelotti reaching her first, tears streaming down his powder-black features, throwing his arms around her; Floria shoving him bodily aside to grab her arms, stare into her face, all questions; and then a throng: Henri de Treville, Ludmilla Rostovnaya, Dickon Stour, Pieter Tyrrell, and Thomas Rochester with the Lion banner, Geraintab Morgan in deep-voiced Welsh amazement: all piling onto her, mailed hands thumping her back, voices shouting, everyone too loud for her to make herself heard:

"Shit, look what happens to you motherfuckers when I leave you alone for five minutes! Where the fuck is Roberto?"

"Dijon!" Floria, a tall dirty-faced man to all appearances, grabbed at her arm. "*Is* it you? You look older. Your hair—You've been prisoner here? You escaped?" And at Ash's nod of agreement: "Our Lady! You didn't have to walk back in on this. You could have walked away. One man could make it out of here alone—"

*She's right*. Ash felt a startled realization. I stood a much better chance of slipping away alone. I didn't have to come up this street and put myself in the middle of a—very small—bunch of armed lunatics.

But it didn't occur to me not to.

There was no regret in her mind, not even wonder; all the amazement was on Floria's face. The disguised woman surgeon touched Ash's cold, scarred cheek. "Why would I expect anything different! Welcome to the madhouse."

*I'll tell her about Godfrey later*, Ash decided; and lifted her head and looked around at the circle of faces, the men sweating despite the chill air, weapons un-sheathed, two men further away climbing down from a high wall.

"Get me my officers!"

"Yes, boss!" Morgan ran.

We're in one of the alleys that run around three sides of House Leofric to the end of the cliff, Ash thought with a minute and detailed realization. The fourth side is the Citadel wall itself.

She looked down the cross-alley.

I am looking north. To the Citadel wall. Over that wall—and a fucking long way down—is Carthage harbor.

In the torch and lantern light she cannot be sure: there may be a glow beyond the wall, and noise, far down below.

"*Geraint!*" She grinned up at Geraint ab Morgan as he pelted back from the barrier of pavises, slapping his shoulder.

"Fuck, it *is* you!"

"Got us here by sea, did you? I assume we have ships? How are you enjoying foreign travel to the Eternal Twilight, Geraint?"

"Hate it!" Her big-shouldered captain of archers grinned at her, half sardonic, all amazed. "Not me, boss, I didn't do this! I get sea-sick, see."

"*Sea*-sick?"

" 'S why I'm an archer. Not a wool merchant like my family. I used to leave meals with the fishes all the way from Bristol to Bruges." Geraint ab Morgan wiped his mouth with the back of his wrist. "And all the way across from Marseilles to here in those fucking galleys. I just hope it's worth it. Rich, is he, your father?"

A group of her men ran over with pavises, and she dropped to one knee behind the temporary shelter as her other officers ran up. Ash buckled her sallet back on, staring at the gates of House Leofric: fifty yards along the alley ahead, blasted by two—or three?—cannon shot, but still intact. Need more guns.

"Leofric's not my father. He is rich. But we'll be traveling light, so keep it to the easy, portable bits of loot— got it?"

"Got it, boss. Oh yes."

Ash made a mental note to search Geraint on the way back to whatever ships there might be.

"How the *fuck* did you guys *get* here?"

"Venetian galleys," Antonio Angelotti said, at her ear; and when she looked at him, his angelic lashes lowered over amused eyes: "My lord Oxford found us a pair of Venetian captains who survived the burning of the Republic. There is nothing they would not do, to harm Carthage."

"Where are they?"

"Moored ten miles west of here, along the coast. We came in disguised as a wagon-caravan from Alexandria. I thought—we thought they might have taken you, after Auxonne. There were rumors you were in Carthage."

"No shit? For once, rumor's right."

The expectation was less marked on Angelotti's face, but it was there all the same in his eyes, as it was in all the eyes watching her. A trust, an expectation. Ash felt fear pang in the pit of her belly again, crouching behind the flimsy shields.

Down to me. We got to do this and get out—or just get out—or we're all dead. However many of them are here, they're dead men if I can't get them out. And they expect me to do it. They've expected it for five years now.

My responsibility. Even if de Vere brought them in.

The freezing winds from the southern desert moved across her face, bringing a faint sound of shouting and panic-stricken confusion up from the center of the Citadel. Nothing moving here in this broken place. *Where is Leofric, where are his men? Where are the King-Caliph's men? What's happening here?*

"Right," Ash said. "Somebody find me some armor! That *fits*. And a sword! My lord de Vere, I want a word with you," and she stood and stepped forward to meet the Earl of Oxford as he ran up, taking his steel-clad arm and steering him a few steps in close under the walls, no murder-holes above, and the angle too steep to be shot at.

A scream and a crunch came from somewhere along the alley, and a loud cheer.

"Got 'im!"

"Fucking rag-head!"

" 'Ave that from the fucking Franks, why don't you?"

"Madam," John de Vere said.

Ash looked up at the English Earl in a mutual amazement. His faded blue eyes crinkled as if against bright light or in amusement. His steel armor was covered by de Vere livery, brilliant scarlet and yellow and white in lantern-light. Under the pushed-up visor of his sallet, his face was fair, dirty, lined, and bright with the excitement of a much younger man.

*Boom*!

The sound stabbed her ears. Even through helmet-padding it hurt. Every bit of loose mortar and stone dust on the walls fell down into the alley, showering her livery jacket and doublet shoulders; every bit of debris on the quake-damaged cobbles leaped up, making her eyes sting.

"Captain Ash," John de Vere spoke loudly over the cascade of sounds after Angelotti's cannon-fire. His tone sounded businesslike, or, if not quite that, pragmatic at least. No surprise at her presence. He pointed over her head toward the massive Citadel wall; a twenty-foot-high blank end to the alley to her right. "The rest of the guns are on their way in."

She fell back into habit: brief questions, to the point. "How are you getting men and artillery up here?"

"Along the top of the wall. This wall, that encloses the Citadel. It's wide enough for patrols, so I'm using it. All the streets are choked."

John de Vere's pointing hand shone, encased in delicate Gothic fluted gauntlets, the lantern light picking out the lace-pattern of pierced metal on cuffs and knuckles. Ash found herself thinking, *He's come here in all his riches, but in armor light enough for maneuver in these bloody tight alleys; I've seen none of my men wearing more than breast, back and leg armor, no spaulders and* pauldrons,[44] he may be mad but he knows what he's doing.

"What about the gate between the Citadel and Carthage itself?"

"Madam, I have men holding that gate, ready, and also Carthage's south gate on the landward side—we have perhaps an hour, if God and Fortune favor us, to raid and run."

Thomas Morgan and the billman Carracci trotted up and Ash stretched out her arms while they stripped off her livery and doublet, pointed on some young man's arming doublet—a trifle tight across the chest, but with reassuring panels of mail sewn in at armpits and shoulders—and set about pointing and strapping someone else's breastplate and backplate on over it.

They did not fit her. *Stationary defense only,* she thought. *No running around.*

"Get you leg armor in a second, boss," Carracci promised.

Ash sucked in her breath as the metal shell locked home and Thomas Morgan pulled the straps tight. She rapped her knuckles against the plackart riveted to the breastplate. Protection. Carracci knelt to buckle tassets onto the lower lames of the fauld.[45]

Her mouth curved up, in a smile she couldn't conceal. "Knee cops,[46] if you can't find anything else. Some fucking rag-head did my knee in at Auxonne."

"Sure, boss!" Carracci took an archer's falchion and sword-belt from Thomas Rochester: the dark Englishman now kneeling to help him buckle them around her armored waist.

Ash turned her head to speak to John de Vere, yanking on the mail gauntlets again. "You're here for the

---

[44] Cumbrous steel plate shoulder defenses.

[45] The skirts or articulated lames of armor protect the lower abdomen and buttocks; protective plates called tassets hang below them to protect the thighs.

[46] A shaped piece of armor that straps over the knee.

Stone Golem. Have to be. Fuck, this is a suicide raid, my lord!"

"Madam, it need not be; and we are in such straits, in the north, that she must be stopped in some way."

"How are you going in?"

"By main force—take this House, and search it from roof to cellars."

"That's easier said than done. You know what it's like in these places?"

"No—"

John de Vere broke off to shout to his brother Dickon; the young knight strode away down the right-hand alley to where, in lantern light, scaling ladders were visible at the foot of the Citadel's enclosing wall, and dark heads silhouetted the skyline above it, in a furious bustle of activity.

"I'm going up there," Ash stated. "I need to get my bearings. Did you start this raid before the quake, my lord, or after it?"

"It was a happy accident."

"A *happy*—!" Ash snorted, despite herself.

Rope-and-wood ladders hung from their scaling hooks on the parapet, twenty feet above her head. She reached up, had one terrifying moment when her arms seemed too weak to pull her up—Christ, I've rested, I can't be sick *now*!—and then she found her footing, powerful leg-muscles pushing her up, swaying in the winter-dark air, reaching up to hands at the parapet and the muttered oaths from men who didn't recognize her in borrowed armor.

A row of pavises, broken doors, and splintered beams made a temporary barricade across the wall. Further along was bare. On the higher front of House Leofric, that overlooked that stretch of wall, she glimpsed the flash of light from Visigoth steel helmets, and from the heads of arrows: the *amir*'s soldiers able to lay down a withering fire if they went forward of this position.

"Francis; Willem!" She greeted her crossbowman and lance-leader. "What's it like at the Citadel gate?"

"Fuck," Willem muttered.

The two men stared at her, frozen, holding a solid oaken cask between them. The bowman, Francis, abruptly coughed, spat, and said, wonderingly, "Couple of skirmishes, boss. There's nobody really down there right now. Everybody's running around like a bitch in heat because of the quake damage."

"Let's hope it stays like that. Okay, get shifting!"

"Boss—" The crossbowman gave up, shaking his head, but with a wide grin. He turned back as other men came running up with casks. "Here! She's *back*—!"

Up here, on the roof of the city, out of the sheltering alleys, the bitter wind sheared across Ash's face, under her visor, and tears sprang into her eyes. She was instantly frozen. She ran, half-crouching, to the harbor-facing side of the city wall, glancing out into the black depths.

John de Vere went back to the ladders, shouted down, took something, and came across to her, holding a thick woolen cloak which he thrust at her. "Madam, take this. I've had your people coming into the city disguised for the last three days. They are God's own bastards and a joy to lead. I had the raid planned for a later hour, but this—" A stark gaze around, at the broken roof-lines of the inner city, at tumbled walls and blocked alleys: "This was an opportunity not to be refused. Will you take command again under me, madam? Are you well enough to do so?"

Ash glanced up at the sky. Nothing to give her the hour. Maybe thirty minutes since she had emerged from the sewers? No more.

The cold at least kept some of the stink out of her nostrils; she doubted the others, with a stench of powder and killing on them, had even noticed it.

"Who else of my officers is here? And where the fuck are the others!"

"This is but half your full company. By Duke Charles's command, Master Robert Anselm stays in Dijon, with two hundred men, keeping up the siege against the Gothic forces; his last message reached me a week since. They hold out."

"*Robert's*—" Safe. Alive. "*They're alive!*"

Or, they were, a week ago.

Sod it, they're alive still, I know they are! I know them.

Her eyes filled up with tears.

"Son of a *bitch*!" Ash said weakly. "I might have *known*. It takes more than a bunch of rag-heads to finish these arseholes off. Sweet Christ, I should've trusted them for that!"

"You had no word?" the Earl said.

"None: and I was lied to, told we were all dead on Auxonne field!"

"Then I am glad to bring you this news." John de Vere smiled, one ear cocked to the shouting and clamor below. "And if I had a better thing, I would have brought it to you with as good a heart. Your people sorely felt your loss."

"I didn't know—" Ash swallowed, her throat tightening. She felt herself grin. "*Shit*. They made it? You're sure they made it? When you left, they were okay? Robert's okay?"

"Inside the walls of Dijon, and like to hold out, I think. The news of its fall would have been heard, madam. They have Charles within the walls, also, and the capture of a Duke, or his death, would have been shouted abroad. Now." De Vere reached out and gripped her forearms in his gauntlets. "We must take counsel together."

When you wake up on a runaway wagon, you either grab the reins, or you jump off. One or the other.

Dozens of men on the wall now, heaving weapons and crates down the scaling ladders, into the alleys; and all of them detouring past Ash as they ran back and forth, staring, calling *it's her, it* is *her*, receiving her nods of acknowledgment; running with a new fervor, excitement, joy.

"Bugger counsel!" Ash said. "We go or we fight. Now—"

Perhaps an hour, now, from the moment of the quake. The sense grows in her of a clock, ticking, ticking away time in which the overturned hive of Carthage might recover, regroup, begin to send troops out of the fortress-houses of the inner city and into the streets and alleys. To discover Frankish cannon-fire.

"They won't have heard us yet. Or they'll think it's just some *amir* or other taking advantage of the confusion to do in old enemies—"

*BOOM!*

*"Shit!"* Ash grabbed the stone parapet. The violence of the sound jabbed into her eardrums. *One of Angelotti's cannon exploded?* she thought, about to run to that side of the wall; and then a flare of light bloomed on the night's darkness, towering up, rising from the harbor below.

"That," the Earl of Oxford directed her attention, "will be Viscount Beaumont."

The pillar of fire rose up, illuminating the cliff below Ash, shining red light across the inner harbor of Carthage. Smoke, flames: and at the foot of the towering conflagration, a great Visigoth war galley, burning—burning to the water line.

She gripped the stone and leaned over, staring down at black water, ice. Fierce crackling flames billowed up, fork-tongued: stabbing up into darkness. By their immense light she saw other ships, a whole harbor full of vulnerable, inflammable wood, rope, cord, cargo. Another curl of flame suddenly ripped the night air, racing up the masts of a merchant cog, spidering out along the yardarms, wisping ropes into so much ash on the cold wind.

Two ships now on fire. Three. Four. And over there—

Ash squinted, tears running down her frozen cheeks from the wind, at the roofs of warehouses across the inlet. She unconsciously hauled the cloak around her shoulders and knotted the ties. Warehouses, with curls of flame flickering up from their roofs and upper granary stores—

Another sudden noise came on the wind, as if the explosion had been a signal. Noise blown from the west, from the main part of Carthage town that lay over the next headland. She could not distinguish if it were fire or voices.

"And that will be my brothers, Tom and George," the Earl of Oxford added. "The King-Caliph brings in a lot of cattle, captain. Thousands of head, to feed all Carthage, where nothing may graze. George and Tom will, I trust, have taken and stampeded the stock market . . ."

"The stock—" Ash wiped her streaming nose. She choked back a laugh. "My lord!"

"Streets full of maddened cattle, in these ruins, should spread more confusion." De Vere added thoughtfully, "I wanted to fire the naphtha plant too, but that would be too well-guarded, and I could gain no solid information as to where it is sited."

"No, my lord." *You're a fucking maniac, my lord.* In her mind's eye: tremor-ravaged buildings, running men, women, wild-horned beasts, fire, injury, death, utter confusion. Utter *effective* confusion. "How many of us are with you?"

"Two hundred and fifty. Galley-crews back at the ships. Fifty men on this Citadel gate, fifty holding the south gate where the aqueducts come into the city. Above one hundred here, light armor, close combat weapons, and light guns; crossbows and arquebuses."

In the harbor, flame runs from ship to ship along the docks, carracks and cogs burning, a throng of men like black lice running frantically, a bucketline forming to the warehouses, chaff and embers sprinkling red on the wind, drifting toward other roofs. Small boats are being frantically rowed across the black vitreous water, trying to take cargo off before vessels are burned—and a throng of merchants, clerks, sailors, tapsters and whores shrieks around the warehouses, leather buckets of water pissing on the conflagration, chains of men passing cargo out, fights starting, theft.

Ash heard screamed orders, shouting, and on one burst of wind, the sound of a man bellowing in such pain that it made her hurt in sympathy. This will be happening a thousand times across Carthage now: no one is thinking about one *amir*'s house, up on the Citadel.

"Shit." She found herself grinning at the Earl of Oxford. "What an opportunity. *Nicely* done. There won't be another chance like this."

John de Vere gave her a shining, utterly reckless smile. "I thought this worth the venture, though foolhardy or desperate even if it succeeded in destroying the *machina rei militaris*. Now, with the earth tremor, madam, yes, we may succeed and leave. Oftentimes I am blessed with such lucky accidents when I need them."

"Wuff!" Ash felt breathless. " 'When I need them'—!"

"However," de Vere continued, squinting down at the chaos of burning ships and men, "I had planned us to leave by way of the aqueducts—which have not fallen, but they may not be safe after the earth tremors."

"We won't get out by way of the streets, even in this." Ash's scarred face shone in the flickering light of the flames below. "Even if they're falling down, the aqueducts are a damn sight better than trying to fight our way out through Gelimer's army—this confusion won't last forever."

"Gelimer?"

"The newly elected Caliph."

"Ah. That was his name."

"You *have* been lucky," Ash said. She spoke to Oxford over her shoulder as she crab-crawled behind the barricade, back across the wall. Two black-feathered shafts abruptly stood out from a pavise over her head. She ignored them as if they were a mere irritating nuisance. "Theodoric's death, and the election!—all the *amirs'* troops are wiping their own masters' bottoms right now, instead of thundering around the city. All there is down *there* is the militia, and they're crap. Up here . . ."

Ash wiped her nose on the leather palm of her mail glove, wet skin freezing in the air.

"This city spends half its time with lord's households at war with each other," she said. "They're *used* to shutting themselves up in these house-forts and waiting for the shit to go away. But Leofric's men are going to come out real soon."

"They need not do so, if we cannot take that gate!"

A shriek thirty feet away whipped her head around. On the roof of House Leofric, another mail-clad man in white robes threw up his arms and slumped over the wall, tumbling down into the alley. A raucous cheer went up from below. Carracci ran forward and dragged the twitching dead man behind the shields; Thomas Morgan scooped up the Visigoth's bow.

"Leofric left troops guarding the place—or maybe he's made it back from the palace. Either way, they've about worked out that we're not Visigoths, we're Franks, this isn't another *amir* attacking them."

A whistling sound split the air. Ash had no time to throw herself flat, only to wince—herself, Oxford, and the soldiers on the Citadel wall half-ducking in identical jerky movement—and something whooshed up from inside the walls of House Leofric, and a flare and flat concussion banged out fifty feet above their heads.

White light strobed collapsed buildings, blocked alleys, the mass of helmets below.

"Distress rockets! Calling their allies." Ash shook her head. "Okay. Decision, my lord—we attack right now, or we withdraw."

"*No*! No retreat!" The Earl of Oxford swore. "I will have this Stone Golem of the Faris's, and I will leave it rubble like the rest of this thrice-damned city!"

"The Visigoths have other generals."

"But none that they believe to be of such great power." Oxford gave her a look which, despite battle-dirt and their situation, was all reflective irony. "I dare say they have *better* generals, madam—but none with a mystical war-machine at home, none that they believe invincible. We are in such straits, in Burgundy, we *must* stop her!"

Something about *Burgundy* tugged at her mind: she forcibly ignored it.

"My voice for the attack. Dickon?" The Earl glanced at his younger brother, who stuttered, "Yes, my lord, mine also."

Ash loosened the strap of her helmet and lifted the edge, listening—hearing nothing but the racket and clamor of her own men. "They're still my people. This is my company. The decision's mine." *When we run, we'll get mauled getting out, too.* "You may be an English Earl, my lord, but I am their captain, who are they going to follow?"

John de Vere regarded her grimly. "In especial, after a miraculous reappearance? Better not to put it to the test, madam. Leadership cannot quarrel, not where we stand now!"

"Who's quarreling?" Ash grinned widely, breathing in the chill air that stank sweetly of black powder; putting aside her invaded soul, other voices, everything, for this now-or-never second. "There'll never be another chance like this! Let's do it!"

"Boss!" Geraint's voice came from an anonymous head in an archer's sallet, stuck up just above the level of the parapet. "They're trying to get runners out, down the wall from their roof!"

"Get your bowmen back out there, pick them off!"

The helmet vanished. She has not fully taken it in, the reality of the presence of these men: Geraint, Angelotti, Carracci, Thomas Morgan, Thomas Rochester—and Floria! Christus! Floria . . .

Here. Here in *Carthage*. Shit.

She risked a glance over the edge, into the alley below. Floria and Richard Faversham knelt in a protective cordon of billmen, a thrashing yelling body between

them—the crossbow-woman, Ludmilla Rostovnaya—
rolling bloody on the cobbles; Floria's surgeon's box
open, bandages welling red with blood.

"*Don't* attack through that front gate," Ash snapped.
"It opens into a tunnel. A closed passage full of murder-
holes!"

De Vere frowned. Still more of her men came piling
past them now—mere minutes since she'd come up
here—climbing down the scaling ladders, shifting iron
barrels on wooden trenchers, casks, arquebuses, barrels
of arrows and bolts. The Earl lowered the intensity of
his tone so that his voice should not carry:

"I could purchase no information about the inside of
these palaces."

"But *I* know, my lord." Ash's face went momentarily
bleak, remembering. "I talked a lot to slaves. The houses
go down into living rock. There are six floors below
street-level. I was in this House for—" She had to force
herself to think. "Three, four days. There are shafts,
murder-holes, and *deep* bolt-holes. It's fucking impossible. I don't wonder Carthage was never taken!"

"And the Golem?" De Vere's sandblasted fair face,
under his visor, lit up grimly. "Madam, *do you know
where this golem is kept!*"

The realization came to her with the sensation of ma-
chinery locking home: this man's knowledge, and her
own.

*We're going to do this. We're going to succeed.*

"Yes. I know exactly where the Stone Golem is. I
talked to the slaves who clean it. It's in the northeast
quadrant of the House, and it's six floors down."

*"God's bollocks!"*

An odd abstraction overcame her. She ignored the
swish of a second distress rocket climbing the black sky,
blasting a hollow sphere of light above her.

"How *would* I attack this place . . . ? Not frontally,
that's for sure. We could scale their walls and climb
down into the central courtyard—and then be caught in

a crossfire from all directions, when they pot us from inside the building . . ."

"Madam Ash!" John de Vere shook her by the shoulders. "No time for talk. We go or we stay, we run or we attack! There is no time. Or I shall lead this company in despite of you!"

Ash leaned out from the wall, one hand to the top of a ladder. "Carracci! Geraint! Thomas Morgan!"

"Yes, boss?" Red-faced under his helmet, Carracci bawled happily up at her.

*"Clear this alley!"*

"Yes, boss!"

"Angelotti!"

The master gunner ran through the crowding armed men to the foot of the wall, and shouted up: "What, madonna?"

*This is the northeast side. Allow about twenty paces for the thickness of the city wall—then allow another twenty feet—*

"Put powder casks up against the House wall, right down *there*." She pointed. "Everything you've got in casks, and clear this area!"

"Yes, madonna!"

The powder will not be going off in a confined space, so it will have less force; but in an alley ten feet wide, even open to the stars, it will have such force between the buildings that it will rip masonry apart.

As Angelotti and his crews ran, Ash said, "I paced it out, my lord. My cell, the passage. I know where things are on the other side of that wall."

Preparing to climb down the scaling ladder, John de Vere gave her a look that was equal parts admiration and appalled shock. "This, while you were prisoner, and doubtless ill-handled? Madam, you are an amazement to me!"

Ash ignored that. Her pain, her blood on the floor; these are somewhere she cannot feel or notice them now.

She pointed at the growing heap of powder-casks. "We don't mess about with storming gates, we go straight in *through* the wall—blow the side of the building in. That puts us in at ground-level in the northeast quadrant."

The Earl of Oxford nodded sharply. "And we take the whole house?"

"Don't need to. It's built in four quadrants, around four stairwells, and they don't connect. Take the top of one, and you've taken the whole—or bottled up anyone who's in there. I need men on the ground floor, to hold this quadrant against the rest of the house. Then we have to fight our way down six floors to find the Stone Golem . . ."

She turned, swung herself down the ladder, awkward in ill-fitting armor but growing accustomed; down out of the icy night wind, sweating into her padded arming doublet, into the empty alley, John de Vere and Dickon beside her; the alley dim now almost all the lanterns and torches had been pulled back.

A tall, leggy man in a powder-scarred padded jack heaved a last barrel into place: Angelotti, his curls bright gold under the metal rim of his helmet. Approaching, catching what she said, he offered, "The casks are in place. I still have powder. We can toss grenades down the stairwell."

"That ought to do it—" Ash broke off.

She stands in a bare alley, the stars of the southern sky above her head; sounds of crossbows being frantically winched toward the front of the House, but here nothing, nothing except John de Vere treading with great care, so as not to strike a spark from his metal sabatons on the cobbles. And an innocent heap of small oak casks, piled neatly against the wall of House Leofric.

"We haven't got much time, boss." Geraint ab Morgan joined them with a bare respectful nod to the Earl of Oxford, and Dickon de Vere. "They're shooting from slot windows up front, picking my boys off."

"Madonna, do you want me to stop the swivel-guns attacking the gate?" Angelotti demanded, wiping his mouth with a black, sweating hand. He took a slow match from Thomas Morgan as the man walked briskly up. The fuse smouldered odorously. "Or keep them going until we blow the wall?"

Both men shouted, loudly, to be heard over the noise of the wall-guns, and sporadic arquebus fire; the harsh shouts of men used to bellowing at other men wearing helmets, half-deaf from the padding, and the clatter of armor.

They looked to her expectantly, for split-second orders.

Ash, appalled, found herself speechless.

She stared at the men in the alley, her voice dead in her throat.

HER SILENCE STRETCHED out.

"Are you hurt, madam?" John de Vere half-shouted. "Ill-treated by your captors? Unfit for this?"

"No—" Now it ceases to be theory: becomes concrete.

Doubt grew on Geraint ab Morgan's face.

Angelotti, his smirched beauty plain in torchlight, said swiftly, "Madonna, when I was Childeric's gunner, I had to kill Christians. But when I returned to Christendom, I found at first I had no heart for fighting Visigoths— they might have been men I knew."

"Shit. *Shit*, yes." Ash spread her hands toward the Italian gunner. "Angeli', I never—this is the first time I had to attack somewhere where I *know* the defenders . . ."

Where I've lived with them.

She added, with difficulty, "I have—blood kin, within House Leofric."

*"Kin?"* Angelotti, startled out of his Byzantine calm.

"I found out whose bastard I am."

"You're not *Leofric's* daughter?" the Italian said.

"No. His slave. Daughter of his House slaves. Sorry."

She couldn't prevent the note of grim amusement in her voice now, gazing around at the group: Dickon de Vere merely puzzled, excited with the anticipation of battle; his older brother with a calm, concerned face; Geraint shifting from one foot to another and scratching under his hose; Angelotti taken aback.

Violante. Leovigild. Even Alderic, even the *'arif*, even the bloody rats; I *know* these people—if they're inside, if the earth tremor hasn't killed them, if—

If they're inside now, and I order this attack, they're on my conscience.

"I never had family before," she said.

"Area's clear!" Carracci bawled from the far end of the alley. "I've cleared the men back three streets! Boss, come on back, and we'll blow it!"

Men anxious to attack, now, before momentum and courage slacken.

Dickon de Vere said in a high-pitched voice to his brother, "Do it, before someone on the roof sees this! If someone drops a torch on those casks, we're dead!"

Pull back from this wall, reinforce the perimeter, let no one approach this end of the headland, blow open the House—

It is no voice in her head, but she feels her own thoughts almost as automatic, as pragmatic, with the same absence of human feeling.

She thought, It's only my trade, it's only what I do, it isn't *me*.

"When I give the signal!" Ash shouted to Angelotti, where he stood swinging the slow match and waiting her word to touch it to the fuse.

She turned, loping urgently back with the English Earl, Geraint, and Dickon de Vere. The mass of men in the back streets had grown large. She watched their bobbing heads: faces under visors, hands gripping swords, axes, crossbows.

"Listen up!" she yelled in growing desperation to their upturned faces, raw with readiness, shitting themselves to be at it, in the overwhelming excitement and terror of actual fighting. "Listen—"

It is too little, too late.

"—We're going in. My orders are, *don't hurt the house slaves.* Spare the slaves! They have fair hair, and iron collars. *Only kill the fighting men.* Spare the commons!"

It is an old cry, from the English wars; John de Vere nods brief approval. Possible in battle. Sometimes. Men being what they are, on the verge of killing other men, they will listen to her to get them through this fight, but as for other orders . . .

And powder will not listen: not when you plan to use casks to blow the walls to smithereens and anyone inside to bloody rags of meat.

I can't claim to be trapped in this, Ash thought. Even if it does feel like being caught up in a mill-wheel: grind or be ground. It's still my decision.

*"Angelotti, blow this place wide open!"*

Carracci, further forward, relayed her shout. In seconds, he and Antonio Angelotti came pounding back down the alley, armored elbows tucked into their ribs, running at the sprint. She spun around, following them; the cobbles hard under her boots, around one corner, around the next, plunging into the middle of a group of men: Euen Huw and his lance, all their faces wild with excitement, the unbearably prolonged moment before battle.

*BOOM!*

She did not hear the explosion so much as feel it, instantly deaf with the unbelievable roar of sixty casks of powder going up. The street jumped under her feet; a swirl of movement ahead is a building sliding into a slow collapse, black powder ending what the quake began; dust filled her face and she coughed, choked, Angelotti's slender hand thumping her shoulders; a tongue of fire leaping up like lightning in reverse, to strike the heavens, somewhere somebody shrieking in utter agony; John de Vere's mouth opening and shutting soundlessly.

Not hearing any word he said, she swung around, faced the mass of men, and shrieked, "Come on, you bastards!"

She cannot hear herself yell, lifts her arm, lifts the sword, points forward; and is running, all of them running with her and her banner, her head ringing, eardrums pierced with a thin wire of pain; running through great clouds of dust, stone chips, mortar-dust, flakes of granite embedded in the cobbles; running to where the side of House Leofric stands.

There is nothing.

A great cloud of dust hurtles around her head. She screams, "Lanterns! Torches!" not knowing if she will be heard.

Light comes: partly from armed men with torches, partly from a roaring fire-rimmed cavern ahead. Men stream past her, she swats at their shoulders, urging them on and through, down the alleys; Geraint and Angelotti with her, shouting their own commands; Oxford and his brother at the head of the billmen; all faces contorted, all mouths open and yelling, but for her in the silence of the deaf.

The dust began to clear.

Ash, at the head of them by the time they reached the side alley, jerked up her hand for them to halt. Bodies crowded in back of her, shoving her forward.

To left and right, the side of the houses were gone. As if something had reached down and bitten a great hole in the walls. Most of the road surface was gone, a great deep pit where the barrels had stood.

And ahead of her was open air.

The wall of the Citadel—breached.

Great basalt masonry gone, blocks at the edges hanging out into empty darkness—and she saw the sea beyond, the northern sea and the road home.

House Leofric burned. Half of the side of the alley
was nothing, now, except stone, rubble, beams, timbers,
broken furniture, men in white robes screaming bloody,
a woman in an iron collar coughing her guts into her
skirt, a broken mosaic of the Boar and the Tree, exposed
wood blackened and burning.

"Take the ground floor! Secure the windows!" Ash
bawled. Carracci nodded, running forward. Her hearing
just began to come back, accompanied by a thin, high
whistling.

"We're in!" Carracci: back at her side, grinning
through dust-blackened sweat. "Geraint's bowmen are at
the courtyard windows! The arquebuses are there, too!"

"Thomas Rochester, keep the perimeter! I'm going
in!"

Now is the time when you do not feel the restrictions
of armor, the body can do anything, buoyed up with the
exhilaration of fighting. Euen Huw and his lance
crowded shoulder to shoulder tightly around her: commander's escort. Thomas Morgan dipped the pole of the
Lion Azure banner as she strode forward, in the wake
of the shouting mob of armed men, over the piled broken
foundations of the wall, still hot and glowing with scraps
of powder and burning fragments of cloth, into a great
room with pavises now up at the shattered stone-lace
windows, Geraint ab Morgan striding up and down behind the ranks of crossbowmen and arquebusiers; John
de Vere at the head of the soldiers fighting—

That was over as she looked: a dozen or more men
in white robes and mail cut down, one doubled over de
Vere's blade, his guts spilling out pink on the mosaic
floor; Carracci bringing his bill straight down on a *nazir's* helmet, shearing the metal wide open, the man
collapsing like a dropped stone. No prisoners.

Another *nazir* lay at her feet, his mouth full of blood,
dead or unconscious.

For the first time in combat, Ash found herself looking
to see if she knew an enemy's face: she did not.

Her ears hurt, badly. The Earl of Oxford shouted

something, his bright steel arm lifting; and a unit, two dozen or more men, thundered across the room and took positions either side of the door.

*"Stairs!"* Ash yelled, coming up with de Vere, and footsteps on the roof above made her glance up, once. "Stairwell, beyond that door!"

"Where is the master gunner?"

*"Angelotti!"*

The Italian came over rubble at a run, more men with torches behind him. Ash stared around the broken stone cavern that had been a room, hangings still on fire, floor slippery with blood and excrement.

"Grenades!"

"Coming up!"

"Get back from the door!" Ash yelled; and gauged it—a stone slab, of antique design, that slides on metal rollers. It will keep the blast in. *"Go!"*

A dozen of the company's gun crew piled in, de Vere urging the billmen to pull back the stone door; a dozen crossbowmen covering the entrance, and Ash felt a hand on her breastplate push her sharply back.

A shower of bolts shot up through the open door— from the stairs below, by angle—and she ducked her head automatically, grinning at Euen Huw. A runner from Geraint at the far side reached her at the same time as Dickon de Vere thumped down at her other side.

"Courtyard's clear!" the runner bawled.

She risked a glance—dust, rubble; and beyond the stone windows, on the tiles by the fountain, two or three sprawled men in mail and white surcoats. Stone window frames spurted dust with the impact of black-fletched arrows. A *nazir* screeched orders and pain from across the great inner yard.

"Keep it that way! Don't waste bolts! We have to get out of here, too. Dickon?"

"The door on the far side of the stairwell is open, they are firing from the far side of that room!"

"Well, fuck subtlety," Ash said—teeth white in a blackened face, an appalling flat grin on her face, her voice hoarse, her ears singing, her face frozen by the wind whipping dust across the broken room, where there is no longer a city wall to obstruct it—"Fuck subtlety, chuck in the grenades! And shut the fucking door!"

Angelotti bellowed. His crews lit fuses, and rolled the sputtering casks across the floor and into the stairwell. De Vere put his shoulder to the stone door with her men: all shoving.

The metal rollers screamed and stuck.

The door jammed, three-quarters open.

Ash yelled, "DOWN!" in a voice that ripped her throat, and fell flat onto sharp, sticky rubble.

*Boom!*

The semi-muffled blast lifted her, bodily, she felt it. Two more followed, on the heels of the first; Euen Huw in his padded jack almost suffocated her, where he sprawled across her armored back, and then she was up on her feet, the Welshman beside her; she and his lance scrambling across the room, the archers swearing loudly and getting up from below the windows, John de Vere and the three lances with him standing up, one screaming man being bandaged by Floria, her face dirty, intent, utterly concentrated; and Ash ran to the end of the jammed door.

"DUMB BITCH!" Euen Huw screamed in her ear.

*"Someone's got to do it!"*

Riding adrenalin, bubbling laughter behind the metal bevor that protects her mouth, body in metal plate that digs and restricts, she hurtled through the gap between door and wall, out onto the pie-shaped step in the stairwell, into blackness lit by flaring torches from the room opposite and a man charging out straight at her.

She registers that it is someone wearing an acorn-shaped helmet, mail hauberk, flowing robes, and with a sword lifted up. It is a snapshot recognition of an enemy silhouette. She is already moving, swinging her sword up in a two-handed grip, bringing it over her head; her shoulder-muscles forcing the metal to whip over in a tight arc and slice down, smack, on his upraised arm.

Her blade doesn't slice mail: riveted links absorb the edge's cut. But under the arm of his hauberk, smashed back with the power of her blow, his elbow-joint shatters at the impact.

"*Aahh*—!" His piercing-high scream: pain, rage?

Anyone with him? Behind him?

Jarred through gauntlets and armor, Ash whips her blade down, through, and up again: over and down—no split-second hesitation between the blows: she hits the man hard on the junction between his helmet and his falling arm, stopped by the mail between neck and shoulder.

"Uhhnh!"

Hits him again—

"Uhh! Uhhnh! *Uhhh*!"

—and again, and again, grunting uncontrollably, putting him down with ferocity and speed; he falls down on the floor, long before she stops striking; ready for the man behind him—

No one.

Her breastplate drips, red running thinly over mirror-polished steel. The bottom edge of the steel is cutting painfully into her hipbone.

A snapshot apprehension of dust, smoke, silence in the far room every nerve shrieking with alertness—

Thomas Morgan stumbled into her shoulder, bearing her banner, shouting: "Haro! The Lion!"

Euen Huw's wiry body tried to shove her aside, at the head of the men of his lance: it ended with both of them stumbling into the far wall together, to a raucous cheer from Geraint's archers.

Nothing else moving, nobody—

An empty room opposite, empty platform, no one running up the stone stairs—

The powder-blackened walls of the stairwell dripped.

Ash stopped, a fierce smile on her face.

Her stomach heaved dryly at the hot smell of burned flesh.

There had been a squad running up the stairs at pre-

cisely the wrong moment. One man's arm, blown clear
off, lay at her feet, ragged and bleeding from the white
knob of the shoulder-joint, sword still gripped in the
hand. A heap of men lay tangled midway down the
clockwise curve of the stairs. As dead men always do,
they looked like men sprawling in a heap, splashed with
red limewash or dye, their swords and bows dropped
any old how. But arms do not bend at that angle, legs
do not lay under bodies that way; and a blackened, fried
face stared up at Ash through the dust: Theudibert, *nazir*
Theudibert; no point in looking at the faces of the men
with him, his eight, no point now.

She looked, all the same. Gaiseric and Barbas and
Gaina, young men, boys not much older than she is.
Their faces are recognizable, although Gaiseric's helmet,
blown off by the blast, has taken a large part of his
jawbone with it. Barbas's open eye reflects the greasy
light of torches: Euen's men, behind her, with Rochester's lance, Paul di Conti, Henri de Treville; their men
stomping in.

Gladness sears through her: rich, amoral, vengeful,
entirely of the moment.

*"Clear!"* Ash screamed. Her escort pulled her back;
men charged across the stairs into the room on the opposite side.

The Visigoth soldier she has killed is dragged bodily
by one arm and thrown against the wall, out of the way.

She tried to see his face, in the dim light. She remembers many of the men she has seen in Leofric's household. This man is unrecognizable, a little soft brown hair
poking out from under the lining of his helmet. Two
slashes from her edge have chopped his face apart from
temple to cheekbone, eye to mouth.

She remembers almost all the faces of the men she
has killed, in five years.

"Block the doors!" Ash shouted, voice pitched brazen-
high to carry through the clamor. "Bottle them up! Don't
lose it, guys! We don't need to kill them! *Take the
stairs!*"

She took two steps back, as the mass of men went past her, seeing nothing but torchlight on armored backs, swords and maces over their heads, no room in here for polearms; and she stepped back again, her chest heaving, breath forcing itself raggedly into her lungs, finding herself beside John de Vere, giving brisk orders to a runner from the perimeter.

"Skirmish at the gate, madam!"

She could not read his mouth, with his bevor up; she could just hear him if she thumbed up one side of her helmet.

"Which gate?"

"Citadel! Some *amir*'s house-guard, fifty men or more."

"Can we still get out that way?"

"We're holding!"

Defence is easier than attack: the gate can probably hold. If her men don't lose heart. More explosions rocked the lower part of the building, echoing hollowly up the stairwell. Taking the next floor down.

Ash turned, Euen's men with her. Thomas Morgan swore under his breath as the top of the banner caught against the shattered vaulting of the ceiling:

"Other commanders fucking stay still! Other commanders don't fucking charge up and down the fucking field of battle!"

"Follow me!" She went through the door again, hearing the sound of hammering and banging even with her deafened ears. The mass of armed men had gone through and down the stairs. Angelotti stood, shouting orders.

A dozen of the gun-crew, with mauls, knocked shards of splintered timber under the doors, jamming closed the doors to every room opening onto the stairwell.

"Well done!" Ash walloped the shoulder of his padded jack. "Keep doing it! Follow them down!"

"Yes, madonna! The bang—*bellissima!*"

Ash stepped over Theudibert's stained, burned legs. Her escort trod indiscriminately on the body until Euen Huw cursed and kicked it sideways on the steps.

But it is *bellissima*, she thought, staring into the dead man's face. It is *bellissima*, too. Like Godfrey says— said. *Fair as the moon, clear as the sun, and terrible as an army with banners.*[47]

With Morgan cursing at getting the banner down the narrow stairwell, and runners pelting up and down the stairs toward her, it took her long minutes to get down to the next floor. Sounds of shrieking voices and slicing metal echoed up from below.

Two men in Lion livery lay across one threshold, hacked about the face and stomach: Katherine, Ludmilla's lance-mate; and big Jean the Breton.

Ash knelt down. Jean still moved, whimpering.

"Get him upstairs! Move it!" She rattled on past, the clatter of tassets loud in the enclosing stone; two of her escort splitting off to carry the wounded man.

Angelotti's door-team overtook her, running down the steps with complete disregard for safety, hammering rough wedges in as the foot-soldiers hacked arms and hands from door-frames, crossbows shot up rooms, and stone slabs slid shut.

The grenades had chipped the edges of the worn steps, and twice her feet slid out from under her; both times she was grabbed and set back on the steps, and they pelted on down.

Counting floors, Ash thought: Four? Yes. We're four floors down. Shit, too easy, even if they don't have all their forces here, too easy! We're not seeing anybody! Where are Alderic's men—?

A gust of hot air whooshed into her face.

Hot as fire: blasting her unprotected skin and eyes.

"Stop!" She thwacked Euen across the breastplate to halt him, shoved up her visor, stood listening.

Something teased at her hearing. She frowned, looked questioning at Euen, who shook his head. A sliding, cracking noise.

*Boom!*

---

[47] Song of Solomon 6:10, AV.

Thirty feet below her, a great number of voices suddenly screamed.

The sound howled up the stone shaft. Over it, she heard the sound of creaking, breaking wood; and a hollow roar of flames.

"Shit!" Ash gripped the hilt of her sword and ran down the curving steps.

"Boss, *stop!*"

One boot heel slipped. She grabbed for the wall with her free hand, ripping the leather palm of her gauntlet, and skidded to a stop on her arse on the next pie-shaped big step with a room opening off it. Fourth floor down.

There was nothing beyond.

"Carracci?" Ash shouted.

At the rim of the step, ahead, was darkness. Empty darkness.

She stood up and limped across to it, for once careless of the door at her back; and heard a clatter of boots as Euen's men moved in, and ignored them, ignored them, because what was in front of her *was* nothing, nothing at all.

The stone stairs ended where she stood. She was looking down a sheer masonry drop into blackness, where flames flickered, stirred . . .

Furnace-hot air shrieked up from below. She clamped her hand over her mouth, leaning forward, looking down. Light flared.

"Shit," Euen Huw breathed at her side.

"Pity of Christ!"

The stairwell went on down, a slick-walled empty stone shaft thirty feet across. At the bottom, fierce flames roared up among a great mass of tangled ropes, planks, beams, and splintered wood.

Black against the fire at the bottom of the shaft, fallen men writhed and screamed.

*"Get ropes! Get scaling ladders! Get them down here! GO!"*

Sick-faced, Euen Huw turned around and pelted back up the stairs.

Ash stayed quite still, looking down at men in mail shirts and padded jacks and helmets, who had plainly fallen fifty or sixty feet straight down. And not down onto stone, but onto the collapsed wreckage of stairs.

Deliberately collapsed. The stairs for these last two floors weren't stone. They were wood—

Ash knelt, reached down at the side of the shaft, finding what she expected: a hole in the masonry big enough to socket a wooden beam, which would support wooden stairs.

Which can be brought down, tripped, collapsed, whenever an enemy gets in.

The sounds of screaming echoed up from below, and the roar of fire.

"A bolt-hole shaft," Ash said, and became aware it was the Earl of Oxford, panting, standing beside her and staring down, his expression blankly fierce. She stepped to one side to let the men with ropes ladder through. "That's where they are. Alderic, the household troops, Leofric if he made it."

"They collapsed the stairs and fired them, with our people on them." John de Vere knelt, constrained by his leg-armor, staring over the edge into bitter blackness and flames. "And now they will have barricaded every door down there, and it will take more than powder to get through."

"More powder than we have." Antonio Angelotti said, beside her. His eyes were brilliant in his blackened face: wet.

"Shit!" She smashed her mailed fist into the wall. "Shit. *Shit!*"

"Out of the way!" a low-pitched, ragged voice ordered.

Ash stepped back again, letting Floria pass her, which the woman did without a look; merely ordering Faversham and a lance of men to help her carry up two bodies, which the ladders had brought up. Carracci was one, helmet gone, screaming. His high-colored face and white-blond hair all one color now: burned black.

"Pity of Christ," Ash said again, her face wet and her voice shaking; and then she straightened, walked to the edge, and looked down at the men on the ladders, dangling over fire, desperately trying to get within reach of the broken bodies of the fallen.

Superheated air breathed across her face.

"Back up the ladders!"

"Boss—"

*"I said pull out! Now!"*

As the last man came up, flames licked at his heels, soaring up.

Black smoke and panic filled the shaft.

Coughing, tears streaming down her face, Ash began to push and shove men up the stairs, Morgan with her with the banner, Euen's men at her side; John de Vere grabbing men and throwing them up the steps, climbing, climbing in searingly hot air and soot, until she staggered out last across a stone threshold and out into air cold by contrast—the ground floor room of House Leofric, open to the sky.

"They have air-shafts!" Ash bit back a fit of coughing. "Air-shafts! They can feed the fire! Turn the whole thing into a chimney!"

Someone put a leather flask to her mouth. She gulped water, stopped, coughed it back up again, her mouth bitter with bile. Another mouthful; this one swallowed.

"You okay, boss?" Euen Huw demanded.

She nodded abruptly. Heads were turning, at the defended windows, the other doors, the arquebusiers poised to shoot up into the shattered roof. To the Earl of Oxford, she yelled, "They've turned it into a chimney! We haven't got time to wait for the fire to burn out, there's too much timber down there!"

"Will the heat crack the shaft? Their doors?"

Angelotti, taking off his helmet and wiping his wet curls back, said, "No, my lord. Never, with this thickness of wall. This whole place is carved down into the headland."

"They can just pull back into the outer rooms," Ash

yelled bitterly. She became aware that she could hear herself, her deafness fading. More quietly, she said, "They can stay in the outer rooms, wait for the fire to go out, and then I'll bet they have ladders and stores down there. They're used to doing this. Shit, I should have seen this one coming! Geraint, Angelotti, how many people did we lose?"

"Ten," Antonio Angelotti said, grimly. "Nine if Carracci lives."

The courtyard windows were still full of pavises, the crossbowmen ceasing to crack jokes, winching their bows with their eyes on the increasing smoke pouring out of the stairwell. A cold wind blew across the shell of the house here. In the middle of the floor, Floria knelt with Richard Faversham, over Carracci, her hands black.

Ash crossed to her. "Well?"

"He's alive." The woman reached out, her hand hovering over the injured man's face. Carracci moved, moaned, unconscious. Ash saw that the lids of his eyes had been burned off.

"He's blind," Floria said. "His pelvis is shattered. But he'll probably live."

"Shit."

"This is where we could do with one of Godfrey's miracles," Floria said, brushing her hose as she stood up, and her tone changed: "What is it? Ash? Is Godfrey *here*? In Carthage? Have you seen him?"

"Godfrey's dead. He died in the earth tremor." Ash turned her back on the woman's expression. She spoke to Antonio Angelotti. "We'll try what powder there is left. See if you can blow the bottom of the shaft. Don't risk men."

"I've got no powder left!"

"Send to the gates?"

"Not enough to do this, not even if we leave them with none. It took everything to crack the House!"

For a moment she and the Italian gunner looked at each other. Ash gave a small shrug, which he returned.

"Sometimes, madonna, this is the way the Wheel turns."

They stood together, Ash and Angelotti, Floria and Richard Faversham; Euen Huw and both noble de Veres watching the momentary silence. The men at the windows went quiet.

Tears ran from her eyes, stung by the pouring woodsmoke coming up the shaft and into the room. Ash shook her head slowly.

"No point trying to take another quadrant, my lord. We won't have enough powder to try and blow a connecting way through. I really think we're fucked."

De Vere swore resonantly. "We can't fail now!"

"Let me think—"

Scaling-ladders, to the foot of the shaft. Then what? Fifty men at the bottom of a stone tube, facing three-foot-thick stone slabs, locked across doorways. No more powder. What are we going to do, chip away at the doors with daggers?

"Hang on—how *deep* is the shaft? Euen, which of your guys went down the ladders?"

"Simon—"

A young lad hauled through the group of men to her, by Huw's hand on his shoulder: another long-boned boy, brother to Mark Tydder.

"Yes, boss?"

"Could you see where the lowest doorways were, down there? Were they level with the base of the shaft?"

The young man in Lion livery colored up to his hairline at the attention fixed on him: his lance-leader, his boss, the mad English Earl. "No, boss. All those doors were above my head. The stairs went further down than the lowest floor."

Ash nodded, glanced at the Earl of Oxford. "Violante told me there are cisterns in the rock, water supplies— if it was me, I'd have it fixed up so I could flood the stairwell. Drown any attacker down there like a—rat."

John de Vere frowned. "And drain it, after?"

"This headland's a honey-comb!"

Are they down below, under her feet, six stories deep
in the rock? *'Arif* Alderic commanding his men to bring
the stairs down, fire the wreckage? Lord-*Amir* Leofric
giving bright-eyed orders, in the unknown room where
the *machina rei militaris*, the Stone Golem, stands?

She met de Vere's gaze, with plainly the same thought
in it.

"Madam," he said bluntly, in front of her men, "ask
your voice. Ask the Golem."

She abruptly turned, gestured for everyone to move
back, even her frowning officers; and was left with the
Earl of Oxford in the center of the room. "*Amir* Leofric
only has to ask it what I'm saying, and he'll know what
we're doing."

"Much good may it do him to know! *Ask.*"

As concisely as she could make it, under the roaring
noise of the stairwell chimney, she said, "There is more
than one machine, my lord."

"More—"

"Far more than one. I heard them. It's not the Stone
Golem. It's not another Stone Golem. These are *other*
voices. They talk through the machine, use it as a—a
channel."

"God's blood!" The whites of John de Vere's blue
eyes showed bright in his dirt-streaked face. He sprung
the pin, dropping his bevor down, and said more quietly,
"*Another* machine? If your men hear that, they won't
fight here, it's only desperation keeping them in this
place! The desperate knowledge that what they do is
crucial, that there is one devil's engine to destroy. If
many other *amirs* have Stone Golems—"

"No. These aren't like the Stone Golem! They're—
different. They know more. They—answer . . ." Ash
wiped at her mouth. "Wild Machines.[48] Not tame; not
devices. They're feral. I heard them . . . today . . . for the
first time. At the moment of the earth tremor."

---

[48] The *Fraxinus* text has *machinae ferae*: "wild machines." By the
latter part of the manuscript this has become a proper name.

"Demons?"

"They could be demons. They speak to me through the same part of my soul as the Golem-machine does."

"What has this to do with asking advice of your voice, now that we need it!"

Ash became aware that her hands were shaking. Stinking, chill, adrenalin dying down; it is not yet two hours since the great palace of the King-Caliphs fell.

"Because *they* might hear me asking the Stone Golem. And because, when the Wild Machines spoke to me— that was the exact moment that the earth tremor happened. The city fell down, my lord."

John de Vere scowled.

"Ask! We need to know, it is worth the risk."

"No! I was in that; it is *not* worth the risk, not with my men here—!"

"My lord! You must come! Quickly!" a voice shouted outside the house. The Earl of Oxford broke off, rumbled, "Here!" and strode over the rubble toward the cratered alley outside.

"Get hurdles, doors, whatever." Ash turned to Floria. "I want the wounded to be carried out when we go. Faversham, help her; Euen, get your lads busy on this too!"

"Are we pulling back?"

She ignored her lance-leader's question, striding off out after the Earl of Oxford.

*How can I ask my voice? If the others—the voices that say* Burgundy—

Plumes of black smoke billowed out from the stairwell.

"Geraint, pull the archers back, use that as cover!" She picked a careful way out, and across the demolished building opposite, to where new scaling ladders had been set up on the Citadel wall, a hopefully safe fifty yards along from the breach.

Oxford's scarlet, gold and white livery tabard shone plainly visible in the light of many lanterns, climbing one of the hooked ladders. Ash jogged to the foot of the ladders.

"Shit. I knew it. We've lost one of the gates, haven't we," she muttered to herself, watching de Vere climb. "Tell *me*, I'm only the fucking company captain!"

She put all thought of the *machina rei militaris* into the back of her mind. Burgundy, she thought. She reached for the wooden rungs, climbed up after the Earl. Burgundy: huge voices which had insisted on *Burgundy*, voices in her head before which she felt the size of a louse.

No. Don't think about it. And don't ask questions. Above all, be *quiet*.

The sunless sky of Carthage was black above. For all that her body insisted that it must be sunset, or close on that time, there was nothing around her but darkness. Shouting came up from the center of the city, and from the harbor, clearly heard now that she climbed higher. As she came over the lip of the wall, with assistance from one of the picket there, she caught a sound like distant surf, or a wind through a beech-wood; and realized that it was fire.

Not only the harbor, but Carthage town burning, burning in the sunless dark.

"If we go *now*, we might just get out of here in one piece," Ash emphasized, coming up with John de Vere and his brother. "If you want my advice, this is where we leave. We can't get to the Stone Golem now. It's impossible!"

"After all such effort?" The Earl of Oxford hit his steel fist into his palm. "Two and a half hundred men, across the Middle Sea, and for *nothing*? God rot Leofric! Leofric and his daughter, Leofric and his Golem! We *must* try again."

Ash met his gaze, which was not blustering, not at all; but bitterly angry and frustrated beyond all reckoning.

"This is where we get real," Ash said. "My guys down there have heard what's happened, that we've lost people, that we can't get down the stairs, never mind down to the sixth floor. My lord, contract or not, they're not going to die for you under these conditions. And if I tell them to, they'll tell *me* to fuck right off."

Morale is as fluid as water, as subject to such changes, and she has had practice enough at judging it. Undoubtedly, what she says is true. It also gives a gilding of morality to her conscience: *The sooner I am out of here, the better! Whatever Carthage is—slave-breeding, Stone Golems, tactical machines, blood-kin—I want no part of it! I am only a soldier!*

Slowly, the Earl of Oxford inclined his head. He looked about him, at the city wall, at the broken roofs and buildings of the Citadel. Ash looked with him at the earthquake damage.

Something tugged at her attention. She became aware that she was staring at the slash of destruction that lay through Carthage, from here, through the King-Caliph's palace, to the city beyond the Citadel's southern gate. It is plain to see, from this vantage height. The tumbled buildings are all on a straight line, that runs away to the south.

"We cannot leave this undone," de Vere said bleakly, before she could mention it; and turned his head to look down at her face. There was nothing of pride in his voice. "I have done a thing here which only the foremost soldier of this age could have done: taking and holding this House, while the Stone Golem is destroyed. Carthage is not destroyed. Carthage, after this—"

"Carthage will be shut up tighter than a duck's arsehole," Ash said brusquely. She spat, to get the taste of smoke out of her throat. Below, in the broken alleys, her men pulled back to House Leofric's breached walls; by the heads jerking down, a strong fire was being kept up from inside the House itself.

"There will be no other chance to do this," Oxford warned.

"But I don't believe the Faris can't be defeated. Let her keep the Stone Golem! She'll make mistakes—" Frustration boiled up in Ash, hearing her own words. "Shit! All right, my lord, I don't believe it either. She'll carry on being the young Alexander, if only because her men *believe* that she is. I can't believe we've come this close, and failed! I can't believe there's nothing we can do!"

Slowly, John de Vere said, "But we have not failed in one thing, madam. We know, now, that there is more than one machine—she may be nothing to the purpose, the Faris. Are there other generals? If there are other machines in Carthage—"

"In Carthage? I don't know *where* they are. I just know I heard them." Ash touched her temple, under her visor; then rubbed her gauntlets together, the chill air beginning to freeze her fingers and chill her body now that she had stopped fighting. "I don't know *anything* about the Wild Machines, my lord! I haven't had time to think—it's hardly been an hour. Demons, gods, Our Lord, the Enemy, the King-Caliph ... they could be anything! All I know is that they want to wipe out Burgundy. 'Burgundy must be destroyed'—that's it: the sum total of my knowledge."

She met his gaze: a veteran of many wars gazing down at her, his face framed by helmet and padding, the skin pinched together between his brows.

"I sound like a lunatic," she said bluntly, "but I'm telling the truth."

Footsteps pounded along the walls, Angelotti and Geraint ab Morgan; Floria del Guiz limping along behind them. The three of them ducked down beside Oxford, panting.

"There's men gathering inside, over the far side of the courtyard." Geraint gulped breath. "Boss, they're getting ready to make a sally. I swear it!"

"No shit? Who's daft idea is that?" *Not Alderic's*, Ash guessed. But there are soldiers in the other quadrants of the house, and they can't communicate with this one; they don't know what the Franks might be doing. "If they do sally, they'll get killed, but they'll take some of us with them."

"I have twenty wounded men," Floria said crisply. "I'm moving them out."

Ash nodded. "No point waiting around for an attack—since we're pulling out anyway. Aren't we, my lord?"

"Yes," the Earl nodded. "And with dawn coming—"

"*Dawn*?" Ash spun around to look where the Earl looked. "That can't be dawn, not here in Carthage—and that's south!"

"Then, madam, what is it?"

"I don't know. Shit!"

She, Geraint, Angelotti, and Floria ran crouching to the inner edge of the wall, gazing south across Carthage. Winter-iced air blew into her face, whipping at tufts of short hair that stuck out from her helmet padding. She snatched a breath. What had been, when they entered House Leofric, an empty black sky, was no longer empty.

The south glowed with light.

*Outside the city.* It's too far off to be the city burning, and there is no smoke, no flame. Further south—

The southern horizon glowed, with a fluctuating brilliance some color between silver and black. Her men up here on the wall swore obscenely, watching the light grow.

Far south, further than the broken dome of the Caliph's palace, further than the Citadel gate and the Aqueduct Gate out of Carthage itself.

The sky ran with ribbons of light.

Purple, green, red and silver: towering curtains of brilliance, against the blackness of the day-time sky.

Armed men beside her dropped to their knees. She became conscious of a faint vibration in the stone wall under her feet: an almost imperceptible vibration, keeping time with the fluctuations of the silver-black light, with the beat of her heart.

John de Vere crossed himself. "Brave friends, we are now in God's hands, and will fight for Him."

"Amen!" Several voices.

"Get moving," Ash croaked. "Before they realize in

House Leofric that we're standing here gaping at the sky!"

A foot-soldier came sprinting along the city wall, not hers, one of the Earl of Oxford's forty-seven men in white and murray. He kept his body half-flinched away from the light in the south.

"My lord!" he bawled. "You *must* leave, my lord! The Citadel gate is being taken from us! The *amirs* are coming!"

## IV

ASH AND OXFORD did not need to exchange glances.

"Officers, *to me*!" Ash yelled, without hesitation. "Angelotti, Geraint; covering fire! Euen, Rochester, *get 'em moving*! Don't get hung up in this one! We're going straight through this gate and *out*. Don't get caught up in the fighting!"

A withering fire of bolts and arquebus-balls swept the roof of House Leofric. She moved into the mass of her men; urging them toward the wall. Orders can barely be heard. No Visigoths can be seen: the fire keeping their heads down.

In the middle of a hundred and fifty archers and billmen, she is climbing up onto the Citadel's surrounding defensive wall—wide enough to drive two chariots—among soldiers shifting equipment, carrying screaming wounded men bodily; all under a black, coruscating sky.

"God's pity!" Oxford, grunting, loped back along the wall in a clamor of armor, his drawn sword in his hand. "Dickon holds the gate! What *is* that? It is some weapon?"

From the height of Carthage's walls, Ash stared south.

The wind drew heedless frozen tears from her eyes, confronted with the bleak empty land beyond the city. The southern desert—where a furry brown mare took her riding with Fernando, with Gelimer and *'Arif* Alderic.

Riding, among the pyramids.

They lay between the city and the southern mountains, small from here: regular geometric shapes that sway, in her vision, as things sway under water. Their sharp edges glow silver, wavering in the light. Vast planed surfaces of stone, bright against the unnatural black of the Eternal Twilight.

"The tombs of the Caliphs . . ." she breathed.

"Well, madam, we have no time to watch them!"

Night-vision momentarily gone, she stumbled off along the wall with her escort. Euen Huw's voice reported, panting, "Citadel gate—skirmish is over—we're clear to the city gate!"

Carthage, ancient city, victor over the Romans,[49] great African ruin of what was once an empire covering Christendom—Carthage is a mess of fire, shrieking and running men and woman, fire in the streets and the harbor, looters pelting off, stampeding horses, the frightened bellowing of cattle; men in mail, men in iron collars; all the stone high walls echoing deafeningly to their shouting.

At the city gate they are met by the white, unblooded face of Willem Verhaecht at the head of fifty of her men: this gate not taken, not even attacked.

The aqueducts of Carthage run out across the city, dizzyingly high over roofs.

"Out," she ordered briefly, "on the aqueduct. My lord Oxford will lead you to the camp you made coming in!"

"I hear, madam." Two words of command to his own men: ropes slung down for the gate guards in the street, men in Lion and Oxford liveries being hauled up onto the ancient brickwork, archers and crossbowmen and arquebusiers covering them as they climb.

---

[49] A direct translation of the *Fraxinus* mss.

*"Up!"* Ash reached down, grabbing arms, hauling men up; her sheathed sword battering against her breast-plate as she moved. The edges of her armor cuts the hands of men she helps, but they don't notice, throw their lance-mates up within reach of the top of the aqueduct, tumbling over the walls, clutching weapons, down on—amazingly—green grass.

Men piled up the stairs from Carthage's main gate, onto the aqueduct. Ash pounded up the steps in their wake.

"Go! Go! *Go!*"

All the noise is behind her, now.

"My lord Oxford! You take the van," Ash said brusquely. "You know the way. Geraint, Angelotti, take the center. I'll bring up the rear."

There is no time and no disposition for arguing: they like the confidence with which she tells them what to do. Angelotti goes forward with only a murmured wail under his breath: "My *guns* . . ."

"Too much weight! Euen, keep your guys back; help the wounded. Angelotti, I want two lines of missile weapons behind us, and two ahead of us; don't shoot unless I give the word. Geraint, take forward position. Oxford, get 'em moving!"

Something resonant and obscene in East Anglian English echoed back; she spared two heartbeats to look forward along the aqueduct and see her men gathering around the Blue Boar banner of my lord Oxford.

Dim starlight lit broken ground. It is already night.

" 'Ere they come!" Geraint yelled from further back along the aqueduct.

Ash, leaning over the brick coping, saw the foot of the street—coming up from the harbor—all one mass of armed men. Visigoth militia flags. Without hesitation, she bawled at Thomas Morgan and her banner went forward along the aqueduct, out into the darkness, fifty feet above the ground, the desert, the stone statues of the Caliph's Bestiary.

The brick cover of the aqueduct is covered with

sparse, lichen-like grass: a green neglect. It skids under her heels, leaves cold black trails behind her.

"Run!" she urged. "Run like fuck!"

Breath burns in her throat, and the borrowed armor rubs her under the armpits, in the soft flesh there under the mail: she will have cuts and bruises, tomorrow. If there is a tomorrow. And there is, there will be: the darkness around them is unbroken, a long line of running men, two hundred or so men with weapons and bows, pelting along the hollow echoing cylinder of brick that brings water into Carthage, and takes them out— out over the desert, under the black sky where stars are slowly dawning, away from the towering fires of Carthage harbor, and the rioting streets. Outdistancing pursuit.

*We have left the Stone Golem.*

Out into silence.

*We have left Godfrey.*

Out into silver veils of light, shimmering across the southern sky.

Scaling ladders led them down from the aqueduct, four miles beyond the city walls.

Ash's feet hit the desert dirt. She is estimating, thinking, planning—doing anything except paying attention to the silvery light gilding the broken ground.

"They're going to be behind us! Let's move it!"

Nothing now but to urge them on, her voice hoarse, her visor up, her scarred face visible so that they can *see* their commander. There are sullen growls from some men: none that she hasn't marked down before as men who will do this, in the sweat and strain of combat. The rest—some still amazed, her reappearance startling news—act with brutal professional efficiency: weapons gathered, lance-members counted.

*Keep them moving or they'll start to grumble about losing*, Ash resolved as she pounded across broken ground, into the temporary fortified wagon-camp. *Don't give them time to think.*

Her squire came running out with absurd joy on his
face.

"Boss!" Rickard's voice squeaked into boyish registers.

"Get the wagons harnessed and moving! Don't slow
down!"

Moving in toward the wagons, Richard Faversham
came level with her. The big black-haired deacon had a
man in full Italian armor slung bodily over his shoulders—and he was running. Not staggering, running.

*Dickon de Vere*, Ash recognized; yelled, "Keep going!" and fell back further to Floria and men with her,
men carrying wounded and injured men on bill-shafts,
and in makeshift arrangements of ropes, other men's
shirts, or just slung between them, gripping wrists and
ankles.

Over the sound of screaming, Floria yelled, "I'm going to lose some of them. Slow down!"

It is an eternity in Ash's mind since the tent outside
Auxonne; now here is Floria—*Floria!*—dirty-faced and
utterly familiar and bawling her out again.

"We can't—leave them. Prisoners—be killed. Keep
going! You can do it!"

"Ash—"

"You can do it, Floria!"

A swift flash of a grin, teeth in a dirty face, white
eyeballs; and the surgeon said in the space of a heartbeat,
"Cunt!" and, "We're here, don't worry, don't leave us!"

"We don't leave our own!"

That is partly for Floria, wavering on the edge of ex-
haustion as she runs; partly for the men with Floria.
Mostly for Ash herself: the body of Mark Tydder is being carried with them, but not Godfrey's body.

Unburied, and in a sewer.

*"Go!"*

"Wuff!" Ash ran into Thomas Morgan's backplate as
her banner-bearer came to a sudden halt.

And there is nothing around them now but their own

camp, a square of wagons which men are rushing to lead out into column; two hundred and fifty men whose faces she knows. No sound of pursuit.

"Well—" Floria halted at her elbow, letting her impromptu helpers go ahead. She bent almost double, chest-heaving. "You always tell me any fucking moron can attack—"

"—but it takes brains to get out again in one piece!" Ash turned and hugged the disguised woman enthusiastically. Floria winced as plate armor dug into her jack. "You can thank de Vere for this. We're going to do it—" She crossed herself: *"Deus vult."*

"Ash . . . What's *happening*, here?"

Men pelt past her, running: Angelotti is walking up and down behind his lines of arquebusiers. Ash met Floria's exhausted gaze.

"We're trying to get to the shore, the galleys—"

"No. *That.*"

Closer now: they gleam, under starlight, pyramids, blackly glowing. A little further south, only a little; and cold sweat makes her wet under the armpits and between her breasts. Men are crossing themselves, someone is praying in a half-shout to the Green Christ and Saint Herlaine.

"I don't know . . . I don't know. We can't stop to think about it now. Get the wounded on the carts."

Wounded men, some who can walk, some who have to be carried—Ash estimated twenty five men in all—are taken past her; and she turns her back on all Floria's questions, leaves the woman to her ferociously active duties as surgeon; yells "Take the roll!" to Angelotti and Geraint as she waves them into camp, jogging to join the Earl of Oxford.

No sound of pursuit, and even Euen Huw's scouting men behind her have not ridden with news of any; but this is the heart of the empire, they are close to the main caravan routes, and two miles from the beach where Venetian ships may—or may not—be waiting.

Ash stared south across the intervening miles at blackly glowing edifices of stone.

Where the voice of the *machina rei militaris* had fallen silent in her head, among the pyramids and monuments ageless beyond the measure of man.

The visual memory in her mind is of riding past their flaking surfaces, seeing, under the painted plaster, the red bricks of which they are made: a million flat bricks fashioned from the red silt of Carthage.

It comes in the kind of intuition that is faster than words or thought: a knowledge, a certainty that she is right, before she ever goes back, plodding, to follow the line of reason that led her here:

The red silt of Carthage. As the Rabbi made the *machina rei militaris*, the Stone Golem, the machine-mind; the second one of which is not shaped like a man.

"Those." Ash spoke over the noise of men shouting orders, horses neighing, the sudden shots of distant arquebuses. "The pyramids. Those are the other voices. The voices that spoke from the earthquake. Those are the Wild Machines."

"*What?*" John de Vere demanded. "*Where*, madam?"

Ash's fists knotted in her gauntlets. She ignored the Earl, stared at the saw-toothed horizon; spoke without any intention of speaking words aloud: "*Sweet Christ, did the Rabbi make* you, *too?*"

A ripple of vibration came, below hearing, so low that she felt it up through the soles of her boots, came grinding through earth and air.

Voices in her head deafened her, more surely than Angelotti's guns:

"IT IS SHE."

"IT IS THE ONE!"

"THE ONE WHO LISTENS!"

"My lord, there is pursuit!"

"Captain Ash!"

"IT—IS—SHE."

Her soul shakes like a struck bell.

"NO. NOT SHE! THIS IS THAT OTHER ONE, NEW ONE, NOT KNOWN, NOT OURS."

"NOT SHE WHO LISTENS TO THE *MACHINA REI MILITARIS.*"

"NOT SHE WHOM WE HAVE BRED—"

"BRED OUT OF SLAVES—"

"—MADE OUT OF HUMAN BLOOD—"

"—BRED FOR, FOR TWO HUNDRED YEARS—"

"—OUR WARRIOR-GENERAL—"

"NOT SHE WHO MOVES FOR US, FIGHTS FOR US, WARS FOR US; NOT OUR WARRIOR—"

"The Faris." Through hot tears shaken out of her by voices that deafen, she looked at John de Vere, Earl of Oxford. "They're saying—that—*they*—bred her, bred the Faris-General—"

The Earl in his armor is clasping her arms, staring into her face, frowning under his raised visor that is splashed red with some man's blood.

"There is no time, madam captain! They are on us!"

"The Wild Machines—they bred her—but how?"

De Vere thrust out a hand, stopping his aide; his gaze fixed on Ash. "Madam, what is this? You hear them now? These—other machines?"

"Yes!"

"I don't understand. Madam, I am but a simple soldier."

"Bollocks," Ash said, with a perfectly friendly grin at John de Vere, his mouth curving in reluctant humor; and in an instant, voices thundered again in her head:

"SHE IS NOT OURS!"

"WHO IS SHE?"

"WHO, THEN?"

"WHO?"

"WHO!"

"Who are you?" Ash screams, not certain whether she asks or only echoes; deafened, shaken, falling down on her knees. Steel armor crunches against the broken paving of the desert. "What do you want? Who made you? *Who are you?*"

"*FERAE NATURA MACHINAE*":[50] SO HE CALLED US,
WHEN HE SPOKE WITH US—"

Ash shut her eyes. Footsteps ran either side of her,
someone—the Earl?—shook her violently by the shoulders; she ignored it, and reached out, listening. Listening
as she did within the palace of the King-Caliph, something in her mind which is at once a pull, an enclosing,
a violent and sudden creation of a gap which must be
filled—

"I *will* know!"

John de Vere's voice shouted in her ear: "Get up,
madam! Order your men!"

She is half up, on one knee, her eyes open to see his
face with a trickle of blood running from mouth to
chin—arrow-nick—and all but on her feet; then:

"I don't care if the world falls in, I *will* know what I
am sharing my soul with!"

A great masculine grunt of irritation. "Madam, not
*now*!"

Two men pelt past her toward the moving wagons:
Thomas Rochester and Simon Tydder, bandaged, with
Carracci between them on a stretcher made of two bill-
shafts and someone's blood-soaked Lion Azure livery
tabard. Ash finishes standing up, fists clenched, torn between the two urgencies.

"These are nobody's machines. Who could own
these—"

"Leofric, the King-Caliph, what does it matter!"

"No. They're too—big."

Ash calmly met John de Vere's harassed gaze: a man
intent on necessary orders, actions, emergency measures.

"They know about the Faris. The 'one who listens.'
If she's theirs—But does *she* know about the Wild Machines? She's never said a damn thing about 'Wild Machines'!"

---

[50] Medieval bad Latin: possibly intended for "wild machines in a state
of nature"; "natural machines" or "engines"; "natural devices."

The Earl snapped, "*Later*. Madam, your men need you!"

Ash looks out across the earthquake-broken desert, back into darkness: the black city ten miles away which has seen two deaths before this bloody shambles: Godfrey and her unborn child. She thinks herself bitter, now; stronger; morally compromised, perhaps. Revenge is not so easy.

She is no longer free to be only a soldier. Perhaps she never has been.

"My lord—*you* brought 'em in, *you* take 'em out!"

Ash clasped the Earl's armored hand and forearm, with a fierce grin. Bright-eyed behind her visor, she is all legs, cropped hair, broad shoulders, warrior-woman.

"Some choices don't *have* a right answer. Get my guys out! I'll follow."

"Madam Ash—!"

"Carthage has done enough to me! It's not going to do anything more. I will *know*, before I leave here—"

Across the black open countryside, under a sky of void, a dozen ancient pyramids burn silver, massive monuments of stone: and in her mind she does everything that she has done before, but harder: listens, reaches out, *demands*.

"*—Now!*"

The stone paving rose up and smacked her in the face.

In that instant, before the channel of communication is shut down behind a violent, appalled wall of silence, what she gets is not voices, not narrative, but concepts slammed whole into her mind—

She felt the crunch of metal as visor and helmet took the impact, a dull stab of pain in her leg; and her mind wiped out everything, a woman's voice saying abrasively, "It's a holy fit; damn, what a time for—" and a man's reply, "Bear her with us! Quickly, master surgeon!"

—the entirety of the Wild Machines—

Armoured feet run past her, black with dirt and blood.

—a gulf of time so vast—

"Billmen, retreat! Bows, cover them!"

—not voices, but as if all the voices of the world could be compressed and made small, like angels on a pin-head, Heaven in the compass of a rose's heart; and with the thought *Godfrey, Godfrey, if you were only here to help me*! she falls into the perception of their communication—

"Pick her *up*, God rot you! God's bollocks! *Carry her!*"

—and the rose flowers, the pin-head becomes Heaven, it is all there, in her mind, the Wild Machines whole and complete—

All voices become one voice, a quiet voice, no louder than the tactical computer that she has heard in her head for the better part of her life. A voice the nature of which would make Godfrey quote St Mark: *My name is Legion: for we are many.*[51]

Ash hears stone demons and devils speaking to her in one whisper.

"*FERAE NATURA MACHINAE*, SO HE CALLED US, HE WHO SPOKE WITH US. . . . THE WILD MACHINES—"

A sick dizziness comes with that whisper. Ash is aware that hands grab her as she slumps, that running men catch her limp body between them; if she could shout, she would say *Put me down! Run*! but in the insidious infection of the voice, she can get no words out.

She is caught in one single moment of apprehension, as if they are paralyzed in this desert near the sea; surgeon, lord, military commander; while her mind gulps down knowledge that she has summoned to her; knowledge falling like a storm, a rain, an avalanche, in one elongated second of voices too swift for the human soul to know. *A moment in the mind of God*, she thinks, and—

"—AND 'WILD MACHINES' WE ARE. WE DO NOT KNOW OUR OWN ORIGIN, IT IS LOST IN OUR PRIMITIVE MEMORIES. WE SUSPECT IT WAS HUMANS, BUILDING RELI-

---

[51] Mark 5:9.

GIOUS STRUCTURES TEN THOUSAND YEARS AGO, WHO ... PUT ROCKS IN ORDER. CONSTRUCTED ORDERED, *SHAPED* EDIFICES OF SILT-BRICKS AND STONE. LARGE ENOUGH STRUCTURES TO ABSORB, FROM THE SUN, THE SPIRIT-FORCE OF LIFE ITSELF——"

A memory of Godfrey's voice says in her mind *heresy*! Ash would weep for him, but she is caught in this one moment of knowing all. Her question is implicit, part of the avalanche: being asked, already asked. "What are you!"

"FROM THAT INITIAL STRUCTURE, AND ORDER, CAME SPONTANEOUS MIND: THE FIRST PRIMITIVE SPARKS OF FORCE BEGINNING TO ORGANIZE, TEN THOUSAND YEARS AGO. FIVE THOUSAND YEARS AGO, THOSE PRIMITIVE MINDS BECAME CONSCIOUS, BECAME US, OURSELVES— WILD MACHINES. WE BEGAN TO EVOLVE OURSELVES DE-LIBERATELY. WE KNEW THAT HUMANITY AND ANIMALS EXISTED, WE REGISTERED THEIR WEAK LITTLE SOULS. BUT WE COULD DO NOTHING. WE HAD NO VOICE, NO WAY TO COMMUNICATE, UNTIL THE FIRST OF YOU——"

"Who called you *ferae natura machinae*," Ash completed, between numb lips. "Friar Bacon!"

"NOT THE FRIAR," the voice whispered. "LONG BE-FORE HIM, A STRONGER SOUL WAS BORN. THE FIRST SOUL TO WHICH WE COULD EVER SPEAK, BREAKING THE DUMBNESS OF TEN THOUSAND YEARS—WE SPOKE TO HIM, TO GUNDOBAD, WHO CALLED HIMSELF 'PROPHET.' HE WOULD HAVE NONE OF US, CALLED US DEVILS, DE-MONS, VILE SPIRITS OF THE EARTH. WOULD NOT SPEAK! AND, SO STRONG WAS HIS SOUL, THAT HE MADE A MIR-ACLE: WARPED THE FABRIC OF THE WORLD ITSELF, PUT-TING A DESERT ABOUT US HERE, WHERE THERE HAD BEEN A GREAT RIVER AND SILT-FIELDS; FREEING HIM-SELF FROM US, GOING AWAY TO WHERE WE COULD NOT REACH HIM."

"To Rome ... the Prophet Gundobad went to Rome and died——"

"FOUR HUNDRED TURNS OF THE SUN ABOUT THE EARTH PASSED. A LITTLE, LITTLE SOUL CAME CLOSE TO

US, MAKING HIS MACHINES FROM BRASS. WEAK, BUT STILL ANOTHER SOUL THAT COULD WORK WONDERS, ABOVE THE NATURAL LOT OF MAN. WE SPOKE TO HIM, THROUGH HIS BRAZEN HEAD, OUR VOICES TO HIS SENSES."

"He burned it . . ." Black sky and black masonry are frozen in her vision. "The Friar—broke the Brazen Head—burned his books."

"AND NOT UNTIL THE ANCESTORS OF LEOFRIC BROUGHT A RABBI TO THEM, COULD WE SPEAK AGAIN. A WONDER-WORKER, THIS SOUL, WE PERCEIVED IT WHEN HE CAME CLOSE TO US. AND HE BROUGHT TO OUR COM- PREHENSION ILDICO, DAUGHTER DESCENDED TEN GEN- ERATIONS FROM GUNDOBAD. STRONG SOULS, STRONG WONDER-WORKING SOULS . . . THE RABBI BUILT HIS GO- LEM. OUR NEW CHANNEL BY WHICH WE COULD COM- MUNICATE WITH HUMANITY. WISER, NOW, WE HID BEHIND THE VOICE OF THE FIRST GOLEM, EASING OUR SUGGESTIONS INTO ITS VOICE. AND THE RABBI, A WONDER-WORKER, AS THE FIRST MAN WAS, MADE THE SECOND STONE GOLEM FROM THE BODY OF ILDICO AND GUNDOBAD . . ."

What she hears, she has heard a version of when she reached into the *machina rei militaris*, to prove her value for Leofric. Now she reaches through the tactical com- puter, past it, to a perception of vast static edifices of stone—unmoving, with no hands to manipulate the world, only thoughts, and a voice—

"It was you. Not the Visigoths! You, that the Rabbi cursed!"

"LITTLE SOUL, LITTLE SOUL . . ."

The voice whispers, amused multiplicity, in her head:

"IT IS NO CURSE. WE MANIPULATE OUR OWN EVOLU- TION BY MANIPULATING THE ENERGIES OF THE SPIRIT WORLD. FOR THIS, WE DRAW OUR POWER FROM THE NEAREST AND GREATEST SOURCE IN THE HEAVENS—THE SUN."

Above her head, the day-sky gleams black.

"WE HAVE DONE THIS SINCE WE BECAME CONSCIOUS,

FIVE THOUSAND YEARS AGO. THEN, FOR THE RABBI'S GOLEM, MORE POWER WAS NEEDED. AND SO, ABOVE CARTHAGE, THE SUN APPEARED TO BE BLOTTED OUT. IT IS ONLY HIDDEN IN THE PARTS OF IT THAT YOU PERCEIVE—THE 'LIGHT' BY WHICH YOU SENSE THE WORLD. HEAT STILL PENETRATES. HENCE, YOUR CROPS HAVE FAILED, BUT NO ICE CREEPS DOWN ACROSS THIS LAND. TWO HUNDRED YEARS AGO THIS BECAME A LAND OF TWILIGHT: THE NIGHT STARS VISIBLE ALL THROUGH THE DAYTIME, THE SUN INVISIBLE. A RABBI'S CURSE!"

Something that might be demon-laughter.

The vision of their existence grows in Ash's head, claustrophobic and black. A few tiny sparks in the endless darkness, like the sparks that flow up from a campfire. Silence except for their machine souls speaking together. And then, after aeons greater than she can conceive, a new voice out of the darkness . . .

The whisper continued, "WE HAD NOT THOUGHT OF YOU LITTLE SOULS . . . AROUND US, A WARLIKE HUMAN CULTURE GREW UP. THEY TOOK DARKNESS FOR GRANTED. THERE COULD BE NO AGRICULTURE, SO THEY WERE DRIVEN TO EXPAND THEIR EMPIRE INTO FERTILE, SUNLIT LANDS . . . SO USEFUL FOR US, FOR OUR LONG-TERM GOALS!

"IT WAS NOT YET ENOUGH. HIDING OUR VOICES IN TACTICAL DATA, MANIPULATING HUMANS THROUGH THE *MACHINA REI MILITARIS*, WE HAD THE FATHERS OF LEOFRIC BEGIN A BREEDING PROGRAM.

"WE FAILED WITH ILDICO, CONTINUED WITH HER CHILDREN. WE HAVE WAITED TWO HUNDRED TURNS OF THE SUN TO BREED A WONDER-WORKER WITH WHOM WE COULD SPEAK, TALK, *COMMAND*—"

Ash completed: "The Faris! The general."

"GUNDOBAD'S CHILD, HOWEVER DISTANT. GUNDOBAD, WHOM YOU CALL A VISIGOTH 'SAINT'; WHOSE RELICS WE USED."

"He's not a saint, to you. Is he? Not *holy*."

"LESS A SAINT AND MORE OF A MIRACLE-WORKER." The voices are multiple and amused again. "ONE OF

THOSE VERY, VERY FEW SOULS, LIKE YOUR GREEN
CHRIST, WHO HAVE THE POWER TO INDIVIDUALLY ALTER
REALITY, AND THUS DO MIRACLES'."

"Blasphemy!" Ash says, and her hand would go to
her sword, to cross herself, to fight for the Lord on the
Tree, if she could move, could break free of this endless
moment.

"NECESSITY. WE CAN TOUCH NOTHING, CHANGE
NOTHING. WE ARE VOICES IN THE NIGHT, ONLY. PER-
CEIVING THE HEAT OF YOUR LITTLE SOULS. VOICES TO
PERSUADE, CORRUPT, INSPIRE, DELUDE, ENTICE . . . OVER
CENTURIES . . . UNTIL *NOW*—

"NOW: AND THIS SPRING SOLSTICE, WHEN THE SUN
WENT DARK ACROSS THE EARTH, WHEN WE DREW ON
MORE POWER THAN WE EVER HAVE IN TEN THOUSAND
YEARS!"

"The *invasion*, the crusade—!"

"*FELIX CULPA*, LITTLE SOUL. A HAPPY ACCIDENT OF
TIMING, ONLY, FOR OUR UNKNOWING SERVANTS. WE,
THROUGH LEOFRIC, THROUGH THE *MACHINA REI MILI-
TARIS*, BEGAN THIS WAR; BUT MEN SHALL FIGHT IT FOR
US. UNDER OUR COMMAND, YOU SHALL LAY WASTE TO
EVERYTHING BETWEEN US AND THE NORTH. BUT THE
DARK OF THE SUN—AH! WITH THAT, WE TESTED OUR
ABILITY TO DRAW MORE POWER THAN WE EVER HAVE
BEFORE. AND SUCCEEDED."

Clear in Ash's memory: the terror of the sun going
out, and the world shrouded under a blank, black, graveyard sky. She says—or has said—or will say:

"This is *bad war*. This is . . ." Pain, memory; in the
frozen moment of knowledge falling into her mind:
"These are the Last Days."

"YES. FOR YOU, YES."

"Tell me why!"

"WE HAVE BEEN BREEDING FOR ANOTHER MIRACLE-
WORKER. AS GUNDOBAD AND ILDICO WERE. A CHANGER
OF REALITY, A WORKER OF WONDERS. *ONE THAT IS UN-
DER OUR CONTROL*. NOW WE HAVE HER!—OUR GEN-
ERAL, OUR FARIS, OUR MIRACLE-MAKER!—"

"*Why?*"

"—AND WHEN WE USE HER, IT WILL NOT MATTER IF SHE IS WILLING OR NOT. EARLY ON, WE BRED OUT ANY ABILITY TO CHOOSE. SHE CANNOT CHOOSE. WHEN SHE IS MADE READY, WHEN IT HAPPENS, IT WILL NEED THE SAME POWER THAT OBLITERATES THE SUN, TO TRIGGER *OUR* CHANGING OF REALITY."

Triumph: ragged, bitter, many-voiced, chorused:

"WE HAVE BRED THE FARIS TO MAKE A DARK MIRACLE—AS GUNDOBAD MADE ONE, WIPING OUT THE LAND HERE AND LEAVING A DESOLATION. WE SHALL *USE* HER, OUR GENERAL, OUR FARIS, OUR MIRACLE-MAKER—TO MAKE BURGUNDY AS IF IT HAS NEVER BEEN!"

Burgundy, always Burgundy, nothing but fucking Burgundy—

"WHY?" Ash bawled, in her head, and outside it. "Why Burgundy? Revenge? But Gundobad wasn't a man of Burgundy! And why not do it *now*? Why do you need an invasion? You didn't need a war, if you can change the world! I thought Leofric was—you were—breeding for someone who could win a war by hearing the tactical computer at a distance—"

Their response is instant, intimate, unguarded: "BUT WE BRED, ALSO, FOR THAT, FOR THE VOICE OF THE GOLEM—"

As if it wrenched roots out of her soul, the voices pulled back. She felt a *snap!* almost physical.

"WHAT HAS SHE DRAWN FROM US?"

"HOW CAN SHE COMPEL—?"

"—DRAW UPON KNOWLEDGE—?"

"—DRAW IT FROM US, WITHOUT OUR WILL—?"

*They thought I couldn't do this!*—Deafened, in her soul—*That it could only happen when they permitted it!*

"—DANGER!"

Floria's acerbic tones said, "I don't care if you sling the stupid bitch into a dung-cart! She should never have been allowed to fight, in her condition! Put her on one of the hurdles; on the wagon! Quickly!"

The black sky swooped over Ash's head. Jagged ends of osier stuck into her thighs.

"Who hit her?"

"No one hit her, Euen; she went down like a mined wall!"

"Shit!"

Somewhere there is a crowd of men, hands grasping the sides of swaying wagons; the bitter din of swords and bills striking other weapons, armor, men's flesh.

The horse-drawn wagon rumbled under her. She reached out, touching armored fingers to the walls that rose up beside her. She felt vibration, a shivering in the air: and the voice in her head drowned every sensation out with finality:

"YOU WILL COME TO US."

"YOU WILL COME."

"Fuck you," Ash said clearly and aloud. "I don't have time for this now!"

She struggled upright, the edges of her knee-cops cutting into her shins, and her backplate jabbing into her neck and spine. Thomas Morgan, trotting beside the moving cart with her Lion banner, reached out to give her a hand off.

Euen Huw fell in beside them. "Boss, Geraint says shall we light torches?"

"No!"

"Boss says no fucking way!" Euen called forward; and as he spoke, Floria elbowed her way in past the Welshman, her eyes concerned, but her voice business-like.

"You should ride!"

"We have to keep going—"

And in mid-sentence Ash stops.

She turns—her body turns itself—and begins to walk. South.

Nothing voluntary about it. For a moment she is dazzled by the way her body moves without her volition: smooth muscles and tendons sliding, flesh and blood turning, walking straight toward the south, toward the towering flat planes of the pyramids, toward the silver light of the Wild Machines.

"YOU WILL COME."

"WE WILL EXAMINE YOU."

"DISCOVER YOU."

"WHAT YOU ARE——"

She speaks—and is silent.

Nothing can move her mouth, her throat; her voice is silenced within her. Her legs move involuntarily, carrying her forward; and she shudders inside her flesh, overtaken as one is by vomiting: the body in charge, the body doing what it will do—

—what it is being forced to do.

"COME."

Not a call, but an order, an instruction; and she panics, inside her head, carried without her will, bruised and aching but striding off into the darkness. No way to break it.

"Boss?" Euen Huw called. "Morgan, grab her!"

Hands grab her steel-covered body: Floria del Guiz. Ash's body knows that it can take the woman down; tenses to slam a mail gauntlet across Floria's eyes.

"Back!"

The voice is Welsh and two hard impacts take her across the backplate, men bearing her down to the earth, the shafts of two bills pinning her to the broken Carthaginian paving; so that she can't use her armor as a weapon, can't get her hand to her sword, can't move at all.

"You want to be careful with her, surgeon," Euen Huw's voice says, in pedantic instruction. "She's used to killing people, see."

He adds, up over his shoulder, kneeling all his weight down on the bill's eight-foot shaft. "It's combat stress; I seen it before, lots. She'll be fine. We might have to carry her back to the ships. Thomas, will you shift your Gower ass so that I can see the girl?" Euen Huw's brilliant black eyes stare down at her. "Boss? You okay?"

Her voice will not obey her. Now she chokes, almost

unable to breathe, as if her body is forgetting how. She still feels her legs move, like a dying animal kicking; legs that are trying to get up and walk her south, to where the ground trembles at the feet of great pyramids: where the Wild Machines glow under the black sky that they have made.

"Carry her," Floria del Guiz's voice snaps, "and take that bloody sword away from her!"

Nothing, nothing now but confusion; her body struggling as they lift her, entirely out of her control. She thrashes in their arms as the men run, striking out across the desert, constellations their landmarks.

Her head hangs down, the steel helmet banging against a low outcrop, stunning her, and she bites her tongue, the thin taste of blood in her mouth. Upside down in her vision, the silhouettes of the Wild Machines dominate all of the south, rising up over the men who trot, weapons shouldered, into darkness.

And—a fraction of her mind is her own.

She could strike killing blows, but she doesn't. She could use what she knows, chop metal gauntlets at vulnerable elbow and knee joints, stab for faces; but she does none of these things.

*They don't know how*, her mind guesses, *and they can't make me.*

But they can make me walk away from my men, make me come to them—

Prisoner in flesh, she strains. Her mind burns like a flame, a fierce will that does not submit, no matter what her limbs are trying to do.

Abruptly she is back in the cell in House Leofric, blood streaming down her thighs: isolated, agonized, alone.

*I will not—*

And is also somewhere else: somewhere she does not know, now; where she is held, her body powerless, by great force; where violation is ripped into her, and she cannot act, cannot move, cannot prevent—

*I will* never—*!*

Time loses itself in fever.

The thunder in her mind is weaker.

Ash lifts her head.

She is carried between two men, anonymous in steel helmets; the stars are further advanced across the dome of the sky, it will be past matins now, almost lauds.

A violent trembling shook her body, all her limbs jerking spastically.

"Put her down!"

The two men, whose faces she knows in torchlight—torchlight?—lay her down on round pebbles and rock. A sound reaches her ears. The sea. A cold wind blows across her face. The sea.

"Hey, boss." Euen Huw reached out cautiously and shook her armored shoulder. "You flipped out there for a bit."

Thomas Morgan said plaintively, "Are you going to hit me again, boss?"

"I didn't hit you. If I'd *hit* you, you'd know about it!"

Morgan grinned, propping the battered pole of the banner against his shoulder, and reached up and took his open-face sallet off. Sweat slicked his long red hair down flat against his skull, ears and neck. He freed a hand from a gauntlet and wiped his cheeks. "Shit, boss! We made it out."

Somewhere over toward the middle of two hundred men, Richard Faversham's loud and tuneless voice sings the mass for lauds, and for deliverance. This would be dawn, if it were not the Eternal Twilight. A few lanterns gleam, one or two per lance, Ash guesses; and shifts up on her elbows, bruised, drained, sore, exhausted.

"We waiting for those galleys Angelotti was telling me about?"

Euen Huw jerked a thumb at a rose-colored glow, further down the beach. "Beacon, boss. They better turn up soon, fucking gondolier-pilots; my boys will have their guts for point-ribbons if they don't."

Storms, currents, enemy ships: all possible. Ash sat up. "They'll be here. And if they're not, well . . . we'll just go back and ask the King-Caliph very nicely if we can borrow one of his. Won't we, boys?

The two Welshmen chuckled.

A voice a little way off lisped, "Victuals."

"Wat!" She climbed to her feet, aching. Someone had stripped her back and breast and leg armor: presumably the man who owned it, and she felt both lighter and unprotected. "Wat Rodway! Over here!"

"Meat," the cook said tersely, holding out a steaming strip.

"You reckon?" Ash took it, crammed it in her mouth as her stomach groaned with hunger, and passed two more handfuls on to Huw and Morgan. Saliva filled her mouth. She chewed raggedly, swallowed, licked her fingers, and exclaimed, "Wat, where'd you get my old boots from!"

"Best beef," Rodway lisped, his tone aggrieved.

Euen Huw, under his breath, said, "It was, before you cooked it."

Ash spluttered into a giggle. "Where's Oxford?"

"Here, madam."

He still wore his full harness, and did not look as if he had taken his armor off since Carthage. Ground-in dirt made the lines around his eyes plainly visible.

"Are you well?"

"I have things I must tell you." She saw her officers in de Vere's wake and beckoned them up; and Floria joined the group, out of the darkness, carrying a lantern that showed her dirty, pale about the eyes, and with a fierce frown.

"Are you losing your mind?" Floria said without preliminary.

Both Angelotti and Geraint looked shocked.

Ash gestures them around her with the familiar movement, so that they squat, the lantern showing them each others' faces, in a circle on the wave-beaten beach ten miles west of Carthage.

The voices in her mind are—not fainter, but less powerful. As winter sunlight is no less light than the summer sun, but is thinner, weaker, without the same heavy fire and warmth. So the whispers in her mind nag at her, but do not force her body out of her own control.

"Too much to tell you . . . but I will. First, I have orders, and a suggestion," Ash said. "I plan now to go back to Dijon. To Robert Anselm, and the rest of the company. Most of my men will come with me, my lord Oxford—if only because they're dead if they stay in North Africa. We may have desertions once we're back in the north, but I think I can get most of them to Dijon."

She hesitated, her eyes screwed up, as if against remembered light.

"The sun's still shining in Burgundy. Dear God, I want to see daylight!"

"And then what?" de Vere said. "What will you have us do, madam?"

"I can't command you. I wish I could." Ash smiled, very slightly, at the English Earl's expression. "We are facing an enemy behind the enemy, my lord."

De Vere knelt, listening gravely.

She said, "We are facing something that doesn't care what happens, so long as Burgundy is taken—I don't think they care about the Visigoth Empire at all."

The Earl of Oxford continued to regard her, with a contained deliberation.

"You hold an ancient title," Ash said, "and whether in exile or not, you are one of the foremost soldiers of the age. My lord Oxford, I go back to Dijon, but you should not. You should go elsewhere."

Over protests, John de Vere said, "Explain, madam."

"Something demonic is our enemy . . ." And, when his expression changed, and he crossed himself, Ash leaned forward and said, "If you'll listen to me, this is what you should do. Christendom is subject, now. The Visigoth Empire either has treaties, or it has conquered, almost everything except Burgundy—and England, but England is in little danger."

"You think not?"

Ash took a breath. "There is an enemy behind the

enemy . . . The Stone Golem processes military problems, it tells Leofric and through him the King-Caliph how they should attack—and for the last twenty years it's said *attack Christendom*. But what speaks through the Stone Golem, that doesn't care about Christendom. Just Burgundy."

John de Vere repeated, "An enemy behind our enemy."

"Who wants Burgundy, not England; it's all Burgundy. The Visigoths will take every other city, and then they'll take Dijon, and the Faris will lay the countryside waste—I don't know why the Wild Machines hate Burgundy, but they do." The echo of voices shivering her spine. "They do . . ."

Oxford said briskly, "And you think that one mercenary company, reunited in Dijon, will prevent this?"

"Stranger things have happened in war, but I don't much care about the destruction of Burgundy." Ash caught Floria's eyes fixed on her. She ignored the woman's gaze. "I plan to go to Dijon—and then break out, take ship for England, be four hundred miles away, and see what happens to the crusade when the Burgundian Dukes are defeated and dead. The further away I am, the better . . ."

Voices in her mind: faint still.

". . . But if they don't stop at Burgundy, my lord of Oxford, then I can thing of only one thing that might stop the conquest."

De Vere's faded blue eyes blinked, in the pungent lantern light. "Which is?"

"We should part company here," Ash said. "You should sail east."

*"East?"*

"Sail to Constantinople—and ask the Turks for help against the Visigoths."

"The Turks?"

John de Vere began to laugh. It was a resonant deep bark that turned heads. He rested his arm across Dickon de Vere's shoulders—avoiding his young brother's bandaged head—and guffawed.

"Go to the Turks, for help? Madam captain!"

"Maybe they're *not* allied with the King-Caliph. I didn't see them at the crowning. My lord, there's what's left of the Burgundian army, and that's *it*. The Turks are going to try and take Christendom from the Visigoths anyway, you could persuade them to do it now—"

"Madam, I would sooner try to go back and take Carthage!"

Dark shapes occluded the waves. Ash stood, peering into the darkness. She did not need Rochester's runner, bare moments later, to tell her that these were the fabled galleys.

"Given the state their harbor's in . . ." Ash shrugged. "And we have two ships: maybe we should go back, and try and blast House Leofric off the cliff-face! Get the Stone Golem that way. My lord, we could go back—"

"BACK!"

Faint, now, but piercing as distant horns: the voices of the Wild Machines yammer in her mind:

"YOU WILL NOT TOUCH THE STONE GOLEM!—"

"—NOT HARM—"

"—NOT DESTROY—"

"—YOU AND YOUR PEOPLE WILL LEAVE!"

"YOU WILL ORDER THEM!"

"IT IS NOT TO BE TOUCHED!"

"IT IS PROTECTED!"

"YOU WILL NOT HARM THE *MACHINA REI MILITARIS*!"

Ash, hands rammed tight over her ears in a useless attempt to block the voices in her head, looked up with her eyes brimming over with tears.

"Oh, Christ—"

"What is it?" Floria's brusque voice, at odds with the gentle hands.

"The same place." Ash's eyes screwed up in pain. "The same place in my soul. I said, I said to you, de Vere, they use it as a channel. *It's how they talk*—"

Now she sees it, plain.

"They're *stone*. Deaf, blind, and dumb. Until they had the machine they couldn't talk to us . . . couldn't communicate with anything, couldn't do a thing!"

Floria stared down at her. Over the noise of oars from the galley, and the breaking waves of the sea, she said, "It's the *only* way they talk. Isn't it? It's their only channel to the outside world."

"It has to be . . ." Ash took her hands down and sat up.

Men are boarding the galleys. The headland of Carthage is a black blob, ten leagues to the east.

"You're not thinking of going back!"

"And be killed? No. I've seen their fleet. No."

She rested her chin on her fist, staring at the black waves.

"We turned Carthage upside down, but we failed. Two hundred men to strike at the capital of an empire, and we did it, and we failed. What we did wasn't enough."

There is no confusion on their faces: Antonio Angelotti, unaccustomedly dirty, black-powder burns pitting his padded jack; and Geraint kneeling and scratching at his cod. Only a grim, weary, anxious despair. John de Vere's embrace around his brother's shoulders tightened.

"I don't understand," Floria said, her husky voice thinning and lightening. "How could all this not be enough!"

"We failed," Ash said crisply. "We could have broken the link. If we'd taken the Stone Golem, destroyed it— we could have broken the only link between the Wild Machines and the world."

Ash looked at Floria; at the Earl of Oxford.

She said, "What we've done isn't enough—and it's worse than that. All we've done now is alert the enemy to what we know. We're worse off than when we started."

## WHY I LOVE WAR

(Q&A with Mary Gentle)

**Q:** In the ASH books, the reader feels as if he is there—
the battles, the armor, the Court-councils, even the
mud—everything feels extremely real. How did you
do that?

**A:** By doing it! In medieval combat groups I found out
what it's like to wear 15th century armor and clothes,
use replica swords and axes, "fight" in the heat, and
camp in the mud. And what it's like to command
large, unscripted battles, and short-notice skirmishes,
and deal with back-stabbing politics . . .

**Q:** You also have Masters degrees in Seventeenth Century Studies and in War Studies, correct? Why those
areas? And what exactly do you study in War Studies?

**A:** I wanted to get ASH right—the tactics, the strategy,
the medieval (and modern) military mind, the suffer-
ing. I don't really love war, but I remain fascinated
by the motives, methods and mechanics of war, and
its ethical and human costs.

**Q:** Why did you decide to focus on a mercenary captain
rather than the more traditional knights and nobility?

**A:** Medieval knights and nobles are extremely alien to
us; Ash, as a contract soldier, has much more in common with how we think and feel. She can act as a
bridge between us and them.

**Q:** You're also a practicing sword-fighter—can you tell

423

us more about that? Is it any different being a female
fighter?

**A:** I use museum-quality replica 15th century swords and
armor in a combat-sport. I haven't found any differences, actually, and as information about how many
women really took part in medieval combat becomes
widely known, even the novelty-value no longer ex-
ists!